The Golden Calf
A Novel

by

M. E. Braddon

The Golden Calf
A Novel
by M. E. Braddon

Copyright © 2024

All Rights reserved.

ISBN: 978-93-61420-82-5

Published by

DOUBLE 9 BOOKS

2/13-B, Ansari Road
Daryaganj, New Delhi – 110002
info@double9books.com
www.double9books.com
Tel. 011-40042856

This book is under public domain

ABOUT THE AUTHOR

Victorian-era English popular novelist Mary Elizabeth Braddon. Her best-known work is the sensational novel she wrote in 1862, Lady Audley's Secret, which has been many times dramatized and staged. Mary Elizabeth Braddon, who was raised in Soho, London, attended private schools. When Mary was five years old in 1840, her mother Fanny filed for divorce from her father Henry due to his adultery. Edward Braddon, Mary's brother, departed for India at the age of twelve and then moved to Australia, where he rose to the position of Premier of Tasmania. After three years of working as an actress, Adelaide Biddle and Clara became her friends. Braddon was able to provide for her mother and herself despite their little responsibilities. In 1861, Mary moved in with publisher John Maxwell after they first met in April. But Maxwell had already tied the knot with Mary Ann Crowley, with whom he shared five kids. Crowley was living with her family, while Braddon and Maxwell were living together as husband and wife. When Braddon's "wife" status was revealed as a façade, Maxwell attempted to justify their relationship in 1864 by telling the newspapers that they were lawfully married. However, Richard Brinsley Knowles wrote to these papers, letting them know that his sister-in-law and Maxwell's real wife was still alive. Up until Maxwell's wife passed away in 1874, Mary raised his children as a stepmother. After that, they were able to tie the knot at St. Bride's Church on Fleet Street.

CONTENTS

CHAPTER I
THE ARTICLED PUPIL

'Where is Miss Palliser?' inquired Miss Pew, in that awful voice of hers, at which the class-room trembled, as at unexpected thunder. A murmur ran along the desks, from girl to girl, and then some one, near that end of the long room which was sacred to Miss Pew and her lieutenants, said that Miss Palliser was not in the class-room.

'I think she is taking her music lesson, ma'am,' faltered the girl who had ventured diffidently to impart this information to the schoolmistress.

'Think?' exclaimed Miss Pew, in her stentorian voice. 'How can you think about an absolute fact? Either she is taking her lesson, or she is not taking her lesson. There is no room for thought. Let Miss Palliser be sent for this moment.'

At this command, as at the behest of the Homeric Jove himself, half a dozen Irises started up to carry the ruler's message; but again Miss Pew's mighty tones resounded in the echoing class-room.

'I don't want twenty girls to carry one message. Let Miss Rylance go.'

There was a grim smile on the principal's coarsely-featured countenance as she gave this order. Miss Rylance was not one of the six who had started up to do the schoolmistress's bidding. She was a young lady who considered her mission in life anything rather than to carry a message—a young lady who thought herself quite the most refined and elegant thing at Mauleverer Manor, and so entirely superior to her surroundings as to be absolved from the necessity of being obliging. But Miss Pew's voice, when fortified by anger, was too much even for Miss Rylance's calm sense of her own merits, and she rose at the lady's bidding, laid down her ivory penholder on the neatly written exercise, and walked out of the room quietly, with the slow and stately deportment imparted by a long course of instruction from Madame Rigolette, the fashionable dancing-mistress.

'Rylance won't much like being sent on a message,' whispered Miss Cobb, the Kentish brewer's daughter, to Miss Mullins, the Northampton carriage-builder's heiress.

'And old Pew delights in taking her down a peg,' said Miss Cobb, who was short, plump, and ruddy, a picture of rude health and unrefined good looks—a girl who bore 'beer' written in unmistakable characters across her forehead, Miss Rylance had observed to her own particular circle. 'I will say that for the old lady,' added Miss Cobb, 'she never cottons to stuckupishness.'

Vulgarity of speech is the peculiar delight of a schoolgirl off duty. She spends so much of her life under the all-pervading eye of authority, she is so drilled, and lectured, and ruled and regulated, that, when the eye of authority is off her, she seems naturally to degenerate into licence. No speech so interwoven with slang as the speech of a schoolgirl—except that of a schoolboy.

There came a sudden hush upon the class-room after Miss Rylance had departed on her errand. It was a sultry afternoon in late June, and the four rows of girls seated at the two long desks in the long bare room, with its four tall windows facing a hot blue sky, felt almost as exhausted by the heat as if they had been placed under an air-pump. Miss Pew had a horror of draughts, so the upper sashes were only lowered a couple of inches, to let out the used atmosphere. There was no chance of a gentle west wind blowing in to ruffle the loose hair upon the foreheads of those weary students.

Thursday afternoons were devoted to the study of German. The sandy-haired young woman at the end of the room furthest from Miss Pew's throne was Fräulein Wolf, from Frankfort, and it was Fräulein Wolf's mission to go on eternally explaining the difficulties of her native language to the pupils at Mauleverer Manor, and to correct those interesting exercises of Ollendorff's which ascend from the primitive simplicity of golden candlesticks and bakers' dogs, to the loftiest themes in romantic literature.

For five minutes there was no sound save the scratching of pens, and the placid voice of the Fräulein demonstrating to Miss Mullins that in an exercise of twenty lines, ten words out of every twenty were wrong, and then the door was opened suddenly—not at all in the manner so carefully instilled by the teacher of deportment. It was flung back, rather, as if with an angry hand, and a young woman, taller than the generality of her sex, walked quickly up the room to Miss Pew's desk, and stood before that bar of justice, with head erect, and dark flashing eyes, the incarnation of defiance.

'Was für ein Mädchen.' muttered the Fräulein, blinking at that distant figure, with her pale gray-green eyes.

Miss Pew pretended not to see the challenge in the girl's angry eyes. She turned to her subordinate, Miss Pillby, the useful drudge who did a little indifferent teaching in English grammar and geography, looked after the younger girls' wardrobes, and toadied the mistress of the house.

'Miss Pillby, will you be kind enough to show Ida Palliser the state of her desk?' asked Miss Pew, with awe-inspiring politeness.

'She needn't do anything of the kind,' said Ida coolly. 'I know the state of my desk quite as well as she does. I daresay it's untidy. I haven't had time to put things straight.'

'Untidy!' exclaimed Miss Pew, in her appalling baritone; 'untidy is not the word. It's degrading. Miss Pillby, be good enough to call over the various articles which you have found in Ida Palliser's desk.'

Miss Pillby rose to do her employer's bidding. She was a dull piece of human machinery to which the idea of resistance to authority was impossible. There was no dirty work she would not have done meekly, willingly even, at Miss Pew's bidding. The girls were never tired of expatiating upon Miss Pillby's meanness; but the lady herself did not even know that she was mean. She had been born so.

She went to the locker, lifted the wooden lid, and proceeded in a flat, drawling voice to call over the items which she found in that receptacle.

'A novel, "The Children of the Abbey," without a cover.'

'Ah!' sighed Miss Pew.

'One stocking with a rusty darning-needle sticking in it. Five apples, two mouldy. A square of hardbake. An old neck-ribbon. An odd cuff. Seven letters. A knife, with the blade broken. A bundle of pen-and-ink—well, I suppose they are meant for sketches.'

'Hand them over to me,' commanded Miss Pew.

She had seen some of Ida Palliser's pen-and-ink sketches before to-day—had seen herself represented in every ridiculous guise and attitude by that young person's facile pen. Her large cheeks reddened in anticipation of her pupil's insolence. She took the sheaf of crumpled paper and thrust it hastily into her pocket.

A ripple of laughter swept over Miss Palliser's resolute face; but she said not a word.

'Half a New Testament—the margins shamefully scribbled over,' pursued Miss Pillby, with implacable monotony. 'Three Brazil nuts. A piece of slate-pencil. The photograph of a little boy—'

'My brother,' cried Ida hastily. 'I hope you are not going to confiscate that, Miss Pew, as you have confiscated my sketches.'

'It would be no more than you deserve if I were to burn everything in your locker, Miss Palliser,' said the schoolmistress.

'Burn everything except my brother's portrait. I might never get another. Papa is so thoughtless. Oh, please, Miss Pillby, give me back the photo.'

'Give her the photograph,' said Miss Pew, who was not all inhuman, although she kept a school, a hardening process which is supposed to deaden the instincts of womanhood. 'And now, pray, Miss Palliser, what excuse have you to offer for your untidiness?'

'None,' said Ida, 'except that I have no time to be tidy. You can't expect tidiness from a drudge like me.'

And with this cool retort Miss Palliser turned her back upon her mistress and left the room.

'Did you ever see such cheek?' murmured the irrepressible Miss Cobb to her neighbour.

'She can afford to be cheeky,' retorted the neighbour. 'She has nothing to lose. Old Pew couldn't possibly treat her any worse than she does. If she did, it would be a police case.'

When Ida Palliser was in the little lobby outside the class room, she took the little boy's photograph from her pocket, and kissed it passionately. Then she ran upstairs to a small room on the landing, where there was nothing but emptiness and a worn-out old square piano, and sat down for her hour's practice. She was always told off to the worst pianos in the house. She took out a book of five-finger exercises, by a Leipsic professor, placed it on the desk, and then, just as she was beginning to play, her whole frame was shaken like a bulrush in a sudden gust of wind; she let her head fall forward on the desk, and burst into tears, hot, passionate tears, that came like a flood, in spite of her determination not to cry.

What was the matter with Ida Palliser? Not much, perhaps. Only poverty, and poverty's natural corollary, a lack of friends. She was the handsomest girl in the school, and one of the cleverest—clever in an exceptional way, which claimed admiration even from the coldest. She occupied the anomalous position of a pupil teacher, or an articled pupil. Her father, a military man, living abroad on his half pay, with a young second wife, and a five-year old son, had paid Miss Pew a lump sum of fifty pounds, and for those fifty pounds Miss Pew had agreed to maintain and educate Ida Palliser during the space of three years, to give her the benefit of instruction from the masters who attended the school, and to befit her for the brilliant and lucrative career of governess in a gentleman's family. As a set-off against these advantages, Miss Pew had full liberty to exact what services she pleased from Miss Palliser, stopping short, as Miss Green had suggested, of a police case.

Miss Pew had not shown herself narrow in her ideas of the articled pupil's capacity. It was her theory that no amount of intellectual labour, including some manual duties in the way of assisting in the lavatory on tub-nights, washing hair-brushes, and mending clothes, could be too much for a healthy young woman of nineteen. She always talked of Ida as a young woman. The other pupils of the same age she called girls; but of Ida she spoke uncompromisingly as a 'young woman.'

'Oh, how I hate them all!' said Ida, in the midst of her sobs. 'I hate everybody, myself most of all!'

Then she pulled herself together with an effort, dried her tears hurriedly, and began her five-finger exercises, *tum, tum, tum,* with the little finger, all the other fingers pinned resolutely down upon the keys.

'I wonder whether, if I had been ugly and stupid, they would have been a little more merciful to me?' she said to herself.

Miss Palliser's ability had been a disadvantage to her at Mauleverer Manor. When Miss Pew discovered that the girl had a knack of teaching she enlarged her sphere of tuition, and from taking the lowest class only, as former articled pupils had done, Miss Palliser was allowed to preside over the second and third classes, and thereby saved her employers forty pounds a year.

To teach two classes, each consisting of from fifteen to twenty girls, was in itself no trifling labour. But besides this Ida had to give music lessons to that lowest class which she had ceased to instruct in English and French, and whose studies were now conducted by Miss Pillby. She had her own studies, and she was eager to improve herself, for that career of governess in a gentleman's family was the only future open to her. She used to read the advertisements in the governess column of the *Times* supplement, and it comforted her to see that an all-accomplished teacher demanded from eighty to a hundred a year for her services. A hundred a year was Ida's idea of illimitable wealth. How much she might do with such a sum! She could dress herself handsomely, she could save enough money for a summer holiday in Normandy with her neglectful father and her weak little vulgar step-mother, and the half-brother, whom she loved better than anyone else in the world.

The thought of this avenue to fortune gave her fortitude. She braced herself up, and set herself valourously to unriddle the perplexities of a nocturne by Chopin.

'After all I have only to work on steadily,' she told herself; 'there will come an end to my slavery.'

Presently she began to laugh to herself softly:

'I wonder whether old Pew has looked at my caricatures,' she thought, 'and whether she'll treat me any worse on account of them?'

She finished her hour's practice, put her music back into her portfolio, which lived in an ancient canterbury under the ancient piano, and went to the room where she slept, in company with seven other spirits, as mischievous and altogether evilly disposed as her own. Mauleverer Manor had not been built for a school, or it would hardly have been called a manor. There were none of those bleak, bare dormitories, specially planned for the accommodation of thirty sleepers — none of those barrack-like rooms which strike desolation to the soul. With the exception of the large classroom which had been added at one end of the house, the manor was very much as it had been in the days of the Mauleverers, a race now as extinct as the Dodo. It was a roomy, rambling old house of the time of the Stuarts, and bore the date of its erection in many unmistakable peculiarities. There were fine rooms on the ground floor, with handsome chimney-pieces and oak panelling. There were small low rooms above, curious old passages, turns and twists, a short flight of steps here, and another flight there, various levels, irregularities of all kinds, and, in the opinion of every servant who had ever lived in the house, an unimpeachable ghost. All Miss Pew's young ladies believed firmly in that ghost; and there was a legend of a frizzy-haired girl from Barbados who had seen the ghost, and had incontinently gone out of one epileptic fit into another, until her father had come in a fly — presumably from Barbados — and carried her away for ever, epileptic to the last.

Nobody at present located at Mauleverer Manor remembered that young lady from Barbados, nor had any of the existing pupils ever seen the ghost. But the general faith in him was unshaken. He was described as an elderly man in a snuff-coloured, square-cut coat, knee-breeches, and silk stockings rolled up over his knees. He was supposed to be one of the extinct Mauleverers; harmless and even benevolently disposed; given to plucking flowers in the garden at dusk; and to gliding along passages, and loitering on the stairs in a somewhat inane manner. The bolder-spirited among the girls would have given a twelve-month's pocket money to see him. Miss Pillby declared that the sight of that snuff-coloured stranger would be her death.

'I've a weak 'art, you know,' said Miss Pillby, who was not mistress of her aspirates, — she managed them sometimes, but they often evaded her, — 'the doctor said so when I was quite a little thing.'

'Were you ever a little thing, Pillby?' asked Miss Rylance with superb disdain, the present Pillby being long and gaunt.

And the group of listeners laughed, with that frank laughter of school girls keenly alive to the ridiculous in other people.

There was as much difference in the standing of the various bedrooms at Mauleverer Manor as in that of the London squares, but in this case it was the inhabitants who gave character to the locality. The five-bedded room off the front landing was occupied by the stiffest and best behaved of the first division, and might be ranked with Grosvenor Square or Lancaster Gate. There were rooms on the second floor where girls of the second and third division herded in inelegant obscurity, the Bloomsbury and Camden Town of the mansion. On this story, too, slept the rabble of girls under twelve— creatures utterly despicable in the minds of girls in their teens, and the rooms they inhabited ranked as low as St. Giles's.

Ida Palliser was fortunate enough to have a bed in the butterfly-room, so called on account of a gaudy wall paper, whereon Camberwell Beauties disported themselves among roses and lilies in a strictly conventional style of art. The butterfly-room was the most fashionable and altogether popular dormitory at the Manor. It was the May Fair—a district not without a shade of Bohemianism, a certain fastness of tone. The wildest girls in the school were to be found in the butterfly-room.

It was a pleasant enough room in itself, even apart from its association with pleasant people. The bow window looked out upon the garden and across the garden to the Thames, which at this point took a wide curve between banks shaded by old pollard willows. The landscape was purely pastoral. Beyond the level meadows came an undulating line of low hill and woodland, with here and there a village spire dark against the blue.

Mauleverer Manor lay midway between Hampton and Chertsey, in a land of meadows and gardens which the speculating builder had not yet invaded.

The butterfly-room was furnished a little better than the common run of boarding-school bedchambers. Miss Pew had taken a good deal of the Mauleverer furniture at a valuation when she bought the old house; and the Mauleverer furniture being of a *rococo* and exploded style, the valuation had been ridiculously low. Thus it happened that a big wainscot wardrobe, with doors substantial enough for a church, projected its enormous bulk upon one side of the butterfly-room, while a tall narrow cheval glass stood in front of a window. That cheval was the glory of the butterfly-room. The girls could see how their skirts hung, and if the backs of their dresses fitted.

On Sunday mornings there used to be an incursion of outsiders, eager to test the effect of their Sabbath bonnets, and the sets of their jackets, by the cheval.

And now Ida Palliser came into the butterfly-room, yawning wearily, to brush herself up a little before tea, knowing that Miss Pew and her younger sister, Miss Dulcibella—who devoted herself to dress and the amenities of life generally—would scrutinize her with eyes only too ready to see anything amiss.

The butterfly-room was not empty. Miss Rylance was plaiting her long flaxen hair in front of the toilet table, and another girl, a plump little sixteen-year-old, with nut-brown hair, and a fresh complexion, was advancing and retiring before the cheval, studying the effect of a cherry-coloured neck-ribbon with a gray gown.

'Cherry's a lovely colour in the abstract,' said this damsel, 'but it reminds one too dreadfully of barmaids.'

'Did you ever see a barmaid?' asked Miss Rylance, languidly, slowly winding the long flaxen plait into a shining knob at the back of her head, and contemplating her reflection placidly with large calm blue eyes which saw no fault in the face they belonged to.

With features so correctly modelled, and a complexion so delicately tinted, Miss Rylance ought to have been lovely. But she had escaped loveliness by a long way. There was something wanting, and that something was very big.

'Good gracious, yes; I've seen dozens of barmaids,' answered Bessie Wendover, with her frank voice. 'Do you suppose I've never been into an hotel, or even into a tavern? When I go for a long drive with papa he generally wants brandy and soda, and that's how I get taken into the bar and introduced to the barmaid.'

'When you say introduced, of course you don't mean it,' said Miss Rylance, fastening her brooch. 'Calling things by their wrong names is your idea of wit.'

'I would rather have a mistaken idea of wit than none at all,' retorted Miss Wendover, and then she pirouetted on the tips of her toes, and surveyed her image in the glass from head to foot, with an aggravated air. 'I hope I'm not vulgar-looking, but I'm rather afraid I am,' she said. 'What's the good of belonging to an old Saxon family if one has a thick waist and large hands?'

'What's the good of anything at Mauleverer Manor?' asked Ida, coming into the room, and seating herself on the ground with a dejected air.

Bessie Wendover ran across the room and sat down beside her.

'So you were in for it again this afternoon, you poor dear thing,' she murmured, in a cooing voice. 'I wish I had been there. It would have been "Up, guards, and at 'em!" if I had. I'm sure I should have said something cheeky to old Pew. The idea of overhauling your locker! I should just like her to see the inside of mine. It would make her blood run cold.'

'Ah!' sighed Ida, 'she can't afford to make an example of you. You mean a hundred and fifty pounds a year. I am of no more account in her eyes than an artist's lay figure, which is put away in a dark closet when it isn't in use. She wanted to give you girls a lesson in tidiness, so she put me into her pillory. Fortunately I'm used to the pillory.'

'But you are looking white and worried, you dear lovely thing,' exclaimed Bessie, who was Ida Palliser's bosom friend. 'It's too bad the way they use you. Have this neck-ribbon,' suddenly untying the bow so carefully elaborated five minutes ago. 'You must, you shall; I don't want it; I hate it. Do, dear.'

And for consolation Miss Wendover tied the cherry-coloured ribbon under her friend's collar, patted Ida's pale cheeks, and kissed and hugged her.

'Be happy, darling, do,' she said, in her loving half-childish way, while Miss Rylance looked on with ineffable contempt. 'You are so clever and so beautiful; you were born to be happy.'

'Do you think so, pet?' asked Ida, with cold scorn; 'then I ought to have been born with a little more money.'

'What does money matter?' cried Bessie.

'Not very much to a girl like you, who has never known the want of it.'

'That's not true, darling. I never go home for the holidays that I don't hear father grumble about his poverty. The rents are so slow to come in; the tenants are always wanting drain-pipes and barns and things. Last Christmas his howls were awful. We are positive paupers. Mother has to wait ages for a cheque.'

'Ah, my pet, that's a very different kind of poverty from mine. You have never known what it is to have only three pairs of wearable stockings.'

Bessie looked as if she were going to cry.

'If you were not so disgustingly proud, you horrid thing, you need never feel the want of stockings,' she said discontentedly.

'If it were not for what you call my disgusting pride, I should degenerate into that loathsome animal a sponge,' said Ida, rising suddenly from her dejected attitude, and standing up before her admiring little friend,

'A daughter of the gods, divinely tall And most divinely fair.'

That fatal dower of beauty had been given to Ida Palliser in fullest measure. She had the form of a goddess, a head proudly set upon shoulders that were sloping but not narrow, the walk of a Moorish girl, accustomed to carrying a water-jug on her head, eyes dark as night, hair of a deep warm brown rippling naturally across her broad forehead, a complexion of creamiest white and richest carnation. These were but the sensual parts of beauty which can be catalogued. But it was in the glorious light and variety of expression that Ida shone above all compeers. It was by the intellectual part of her beauty that she commanded the admiration—enthusiastic in some cases, in others grudging and unwilling—of her schoolfellows, and reigned by right divine, despite her shabby gowns and her cheap ready-made boots, the belle of the school.

CHAPTER II
'I AM GOING TO MARRY FOR MONEY'

When a schoolgirl of sixteen falls in love with one of her schoolfellows there are no limits to her devotion. Bessie Wendover's adoration of Miss Palliser was boundless. Ida's seniority of three years, her beauty, her talent, placed her, as it were, upon a pinnacle in the eyes of the younger girl. Her poverty, her inferior position in the school, only made her more interesting to the warm-hearted Bessie, who passionately resented any slight offered to her friend. It was in vain that Miss Rylance took Bessie to task, and demonstrated the absurdity of this childish fancy for a young person whose future sphere of life must be necessarily remote from that of a Hampshire squire's daughter. Bessie despised this worldly wisdom.

'What is the use of attaching yourself to a girl whom you are never likely to see after you leave school?' argued Miss Rylance.

'I shall see her. I shall ask her home,' said Bessie, sturdily.

'Do you think your people will let you?'

'Mother will do anything I ask her, and father will do anything mother asks him. I am going to have Ida home with me all the summer holidays.'

'How do you know that she will come?'

'I shall make her come. It is very nasty of you to insinuate that she won't.'

'Palliser has a good deal of pride—pride and poverty generally go together, don't you know. I don't think she'll care about showing herself at the Grange in her old clothes and her three pairs of stockings, one on, one off, and one at the laundress's,' said Miss Rylance, winding up with a viperish little laugh as if she had said something witty.

She had a certain influence with Bessie, whom she had known all her life. It was she who had inspired Bessie with the desire to come to Mauleverer Manor, to be finished, after having endured eight years of jog-trot education from a homely little governess at home—who grounded the boys in Latin and mathematics before they went to Winchester, and made herself generally useful. Miss Rylance was the daughter of a fashionable physician, whose head-quarters were in Cavendish Square, but who spent his leisure at a something which he called 'a place' at Kingthorpe, a lovely little village between Winchester and Romsey, where the Wendovers were indigenous to the soil, whence they seemed to have sprung, like the armed men in the story; for remotest tradition bore no record of their having come there from anywhere else, nor was there record of a time when the land round Kingthorpe belonged to any other family.

Dr. Rylance, whose dainty verandah-shaded cottage stood in gardens of three and a half acres, and who rented a paddock for his cow, was always lamenting that he could not buy more land.

'The Wendovers have everything,' he said. 'It is impossible for a new man to establish himself.'

It was to be observed, however, that when land within a reasonable distance of Kingthorpe came into the market, Dr. Rylance did not put himself forward as a buyer. His craving for more territory always ended in words.

Urania Rylance had spent much of her girlhood at Kingthorpe, and had always been made welcome at The Knoll; but although she saw the Wendovers established upon their native soil, the rulers of the land, and revered by all the parish, she had grown up with the firm conviction that Dr. Rylance, of Cavendish Square, and Dr. Rylance's daughter were altogether superior to these country bumpkins, with their narrow range of ideas and their strictly local importance.

The summer days wore on at Mauleverer Manor, not altogether unpleasantly for the majority of the girls, who contrived to enjoy their lives in spite of Miss Pew's tyranny, which was considered vile enough to rank that middle-aged, loud-voiced lady with the Domitians and Attilas of history. There was a softening influence, happily, in the person of Miss Dulcibella, who was slim and sentimental, talked about sweetness and light, loved modern poetry, spent all her available funds upon dress, and was wonderfully girlish in her tastes and habits at nine-and-thirty years of age.

It was a splendid summer, a time of roses and sunshine, and the girls were allowed to carry on their studies in the noble old garden, in the summer-houses and pleasure domes which the extinct Mauleverers had made for themselves in their day of power. Grinding at history, grammar, and geography did not seem so oppressive a burden when it could be done under the shade of spreading cedars, amid the scent of roses, in an atmosphere of colour and light. Even Ida's labours seemed a little easier when she and her pupils sat in a fast-decaying old summer-house in the rose-garden, with a glimpse of sunlit river flashing athwart the roses.

So the time wore on until the last week in July, and then all the school was alive with excitement, and every one was looking forward to the great event of the term, 'breaking up.' 'Old Pew,' had sent out her invitations for a garden party, an actual garden party—not a mere namby-pamby entertainment among the girls themselves, in which a liberal supply of blanc-mange and jam tarts was expected to atone for the absence of the outside world. Miss Pew had taken it into her head that Mauleverer Manor ought to be better known, and that a garden party would be a good advertisement. With this idea, she had ordered a hundred invitation cards, and had disseminated them among the most eligible of her old pupils, and the parents and guardians of those damsels now at the Manor. The good old gardens, where velvet greensward and cedars of Lebanon cost little labour to maintain in perfect order, were worthy to be exhibited. The roses, Miss Dulcibella's peculiar care, were, in that lady's opinion, equal to anything outside Chatsworth or Trentham. A garden party, by all means, said Miss Dulcibella, and she gave the young ladies to understand that the whole thing was her doing.

'I waited till Sarah was in a good temper,' she told her satellites, half a dozen or so of the elder girls who worshipped her, and who, in the slang phraseology of the school, were known as Miss Dulcie's 'cracks,' 'and then I proposed a garden party. It required a great deal of talking to bring her even to think about such a thing. You see the expense will be enormous! Ices, tea and coffee, cakes, sandwiches, claret-cup. Thank goodness it's too late in the year for people to expect strawberries. Yes, my dears, you may thank me for your garden party.'

'Dear Miss Dulcibella,' exclaimed one.

'You too delicious darling,' cried another.

'What will you wear?' asked a third, knowing that Miss Dulcie was weak about dress, and had a morbid craving for originality.

'Well, dears,' began Miss Dulcie, growing radiant at the thrilling question, 'I have been thinking of making up my art needlework tunic— the pale green, you know, with garlands of passion flowers, worked in crewels—over a petticoat of the faintest primrose.'

'That will be quite too lovely,' exclaimed four enthusiasts in a chorus.

'You know how fond I am of those delicate tints in that soft Indian cashmere, that falls in such artistic folds.'

'Heavenly,' sighed the chorus, and Miss Dulcie went on talking for half-an-hour by Chertsey clock, in fact till the tea-bell broke up the little conclave.

What was Ida Palliser going to wear at the garden party? The question was far more serious for her than for Miss Dulcibella, who had plenty of money to spend upon her adornment. In Ida the necessity for a new gown meant difficulty, perhaps mortification.

'Why should I not spend the day in one of the garrets, darning stockings and packing boxes?' she said bitterly, when a grand discussion about the garden party was being held in the butterfly-room; 'nobody will want me. I have no relations coming to admire me.'

'You know you don't mean what you say,' said Miss Rylance. 'You expect to have half-a-dozen prizes, and to lord it over all of us.'

'I have worked hard enough for the prizes,' answered Ida. 'I don't think you need grudge me them.'

'I do not,' said Miss Rylance, with languid scorn. 'You know I never go in for prizes. My father looks upon school as only a preliminary kind of education. When I am at home with him in the season I shall have lessons from better masters than any we are favoured with here.'

'What a comfort it is for us to know that!' retorted Ida, her eyes dancing mischievously.

It was now within a week of the garden party. Miss Pew was grimmer of aspect and louder of voice than usual, and it was felt that, at the slightest provocation, she might send forth an edict revoking all her invitations, and the party might be relegated to the limbo of unrealized hopes. Never had the conduct of Miss Pew's pupils been so irreproachable, never had lessons been learned, and exercises prepared, so diligently.

Ida had received a kind little note from Mrs. Wendover, asking her to spend her summer holidays at Kingthorpe, and at Bessie's earnest desire had accepted the cordial invitation.

'You don't know what a foolish thing you are doing, Bess,' said Miss Palliser, when—reluctant to the last—she had written her acceptance, Bessie looking over her shoulder all the while. 'Foolish for you, foolish for me. It is a mistake to associate yourself with paupers. You will feel ashamed of me half-a-dozen times a day at Kingthorpe.'

'No, no, no!' cried the energetic Bessie; 'I shall never feel anything but pride in you. I shall be proud to show my people what a beautiful, brilliant, wonderful friend I have chosen for myself.'

'Ardent child!' exclaimed Ida, with a touch of sadness even in her mockery. 'What a pity you have not a bachelor brother to fall in love with me!'

'Never mind the brother. I have two bachelor cousins.'

'Of course! The rich Brian, and the poor Brian, whose histories I have heard almost as often as I heard the story of "Little Red Ridinghood" in my nursery days. Both good-looking, both clever, both young. One a man of landed estate. All Kingthorpe parish belongs to him, does it not?'

'All except the little bit that belongs to papa.'

'And Dr. Rylance's garden and paddock; don't forget that.'

'Could I forget the Rylances? Urania says that although her father has no land at Kingthorpe, he has influence.'

'The other cousin dependent on his talents, and fighting his way at the Bar. Is not that how the story goes, Bess?'

'Yes, darling. I am afraid poor Brian has hardly begun fighting yet. He is only eating his terms. I have no idea what that means, but it sounds rather low.'

'Well, Bess, if I am to marry either of your cousins, it must be the rich one,' said Ida, decisively.

'Oh, Ida, how can you say so? You can't know which you will like best.'

'My likes and dislikes have nothing to do with it. I am going to marry for money.'

Miss Rylance had brought her desk to that end of the table where the two girls were sitting, during the latter part of the conversation. It was evening, the hour or so of leisure allowed for the preparation of studies and the writing of home letters. Miss Rylance unlocked her desk, and took out her paper and pens; but, having got so far as this, she seemed rather inclined to join in the conversation than to begin her letter.

'Isn't that rather a worldly idea for your time of life?' she asked, looking at Ida with her usual unfriendly expression.

'No doubt. I should be disgusted if you or Bessie entertained such a notion. But in me it is only natural. I have drained the cup of poverty to the dregs. I thirst for the nectar of wealth. I would marry a soap-boiler, a linseed-crusher, a self-educated navvy who had developed into a great contractor—any plebian creature, always provided that he was an honest man.'

'How condescending!' said Miss Rylance. 'I suppose, Bessie, you know that Miss Pew has especially forbidden us all to indulge in idle talk about courtship and marriage?'

'Quite so,' said Bessie; 'but as old Pew knows that we are human, I've no doubt she is quite aware that this is one of her numerous rules which we diligently set at nought.'

Urania began her letter, but although her pen moved swiftly over her paper in that elegant Italian hand which was, as it were, a badge of honour at Mauleverer Manor, her ears were not the less open to the conversation going on close beside her.

'Marry a soap-boiler, indeed!' exclaimed Bessie, indignantly; 'you ought to be a duchess!'

'No doubt, dear, if dukes went about the world, like King Cophetua, on the look out for beggar-maids '

'I am so happy to think you are coming to Kingthorpe! It is the dearest old place. We shall be so happy!'

'It will not be your fault if we are not, darling,' said Ida, looking tenderly at the loving face, uplifted to hers. 'Well, I have written to my father to ask him for five pounds, and if he sends the five pounds I will go to Kingthorpe. If not, I must invent an excuse—mumps, or measles, or something—for staying away. Or I must behave so badly for the last week of the term that old Pew will revoke her sanction of the intended visit. I cannot come to Kingthorpe quite out at elbows.'

'You look lovely even in the gown you have on,' said Bessie.

'I don't know anything about my loveliness, but I know that this gown is absolutely threadbare.'

Bessie sighed despondently. She knew her friend's resolute temper, and that any offer of clothes or money from her would be worse than useless. It would make Ida angry.

'What kind of man is your father, darling?' she asked, thoughtfully.

'Very good-natured.'

'Ah! Then he will send the five pounds.'

'Very weak.'

'Ah! Then he may change his mind about it.'

'Very poor.'

'Then he may not have the money.'

'The lot is in the urn of fate, Bess, We must take our chance. I think, somehow, that the money will come. I have asked for it urgently, for I do want to come to Kingthorpe.' Bessie kissed her. 'Yes, dear, I wish with all my heart to accept your kind mother's invitation; though I know, in my secret soul, that it is foolishness for me to see the inside of a happy home, to sit beside a hospitable hearth, when it is my mission in life to be a dependent in the house of a stranger. If you had half a dozen small sisters, now, and your people would engage me as a nursery governess—'

'You a nursery governess!' cried Bessie, 'you who are at the top of every class, and who do everything better than the masters who teach you?'

'Well, if my perfection prove worth seventy pounds a-year when I go out into the world, I shall be satisfied,' said Ida.

'What will you buy with your five pounds?' asked Bessie.

'A black cashmere gown, as plain as a nun's, a straw hat, and as many collars, cuffs, and stockings as I can get for the rest of the money.'

Miss Rylance listened, smiling quietly to herself as she bent over her desk. To the mind of an only daughter, who had been brought up in a supremely correct manner, who had had her winter clothes and summer clothes at exactly the right season, and of the best that money could buy, there was a piteous depth of poverty and degradation in Ida Palliser's position. The girl's beauty and talents were as nothing when weighed against such sordid surroundings.

The prize-day came, a glorious day at the beginning of August, and the gardens of Mauleverer Manor, the wide reach of blue river, the meadows, the willows, the distant woods, all looked their loveliest, as if Nature was playing into the hands of Miss Pew.

'I am sure you girls ought to be very happy to live in such a place!' said one of the mothers, as she strolled about the velvet lawn with her daughters, 'instead of being mewed up in a dingy London square.'

'You wouldn't say that if you saw the bread and scrape and the sloppy tea we have for breakfast,' answered one of the girls.

'It's all very well for you, who see this wretched hole in the sunshine, and old Pew in her best gown and her company manners. The place is a whited sepulchre. I should like you to have a glimpse behind the scenes, ma.'

'Ma' smiled placidly, and turned a deaf ear to these aspersions of the schoolmistress. Her girls looked well fed and healthy. Bread and scrape evidently agreed with them much better than that reckless consumption of butter and marmalade which swelled the housekeeping bills during the holidays.

It was a great day. Miss Pew the elder was splendid in apple-green moiré antique; Miss Pew the younger was elegant in pale and flabby raiment of cashmere and crewel-work. The girls were in that simple white muslin of the *jeune Meess Anglaise*, to which they were languishing to bid an eternal adieu. There were a great many pretty girls at Mauleverer Manor, and on this day, when the white-robed girlish forms were flitting to and fro upon the green lawns, in the sweet summer air and sunshine, it seemed as if the old manorial mansion were a bower of beauty. Among the parents of existing pupils who had accepted the Misses Pew's invitation was Dr. Rylance, the fashionable physician, whose presence there conferred distinction upon the school. It was Miss Rylance's last term, and the doctor wished to assist at those honours which she would doubtless reap as the reward of meritorious studies. He was not blindly devoted to his daughter, but he was convinced that, like every thing else belonging to him, she was of the best quality; and he expected to see her appreciated by the people who had been privileged to educate her.

The distribution of prizes was the great feature of the day. It was to take place at four o'clock, in the ball room, a fine old panelled saloon, in which the only furniture was a pair of grand pianos, somewhat the worse for wear, a table at the end of the room on which the prizes were arranged, and benches covered with crimson cloth for the accommodation of the company.

There was to be a concert before the distribution. Four of the best pianoforte players in the school were to hammer out an intensely noisy version of the overture to *Zampa*, arranged for eight hands on two pianos. The crack singer was to sing 'Una voce,' and Ida Palliser was to play the 'Moonlight Sonata.'

Dr. Rylance had come early, on purpose to be present at this ceremonial. He was the most important guest who had yet arrived, and Miss Pew devoted herself to his entertainment, and went rustling up and down the terrace in front of the ballroom windows in her armour of apple-green moiré, listening deferentially to the physician's remarks.

Dr. Rylance was a large fair-complexioned man, who had been handsome in his youth, and who at seven-and-forty was still remarkably good-looking. He had fine teeth, good hair, full blue eyes, capable of the hardest, coldest stare that ever looked out of a human countenance. Mr. Darwin has told us that the eyes do not smile, that the radiance we fancy we see in the eye itself is only produced by certain contractions of the muscles surrounding it. Assuredly there was no smile in the eyes of Dr. Rylance. His smile, which was bland and frequent, gave only a vague impression of white teeth and brown whiskers. He had a fine figure, and was proud of his erect carriage. He dressed carefully and well, and was as particular as Brummel about his laundress. His manners were considered pleasing by the people who liked him; while those who disliked him accused him of an undue estimate of his own merits, and a tendency to depreciate the rest of humanity. His practice was rather select than extensive, for Dr. Rylance was a specialist. He had won his reputation as an adviser in cases of mental disease; and as, happily, mental diseases are less common than bodily ailments, Dr. Rylance had not the continuous work of a Gull or a Jenner. His speciality paid him remarkably well. His cases hung long on hand, and when he had a patient of wealth and standing Dr. Rylance knew how to keep him. His treatment was soothing and palliative, as befitted an enlightened age. In an age of scepticism no one could expect Dr. Rylance to work miraculous cures. It is in no wise to his discredit to say that he was more successful in sustaining and comforting the patient's friends than in curing the patient.

This was Laurence Rylance, a man who had begun life in a very humble way, had raised himself by his own efforts, if not to the top of the medical tree, certainly to a very comfortable and remunerative perch among its upper branches; a man thoroughly satisfied with himself and with what destiny had done for him; a man who, to be a new Caesar, would hardly have foregone the privilege of being Laurence Rylance.

'My daughter has done well during this last term, I hope, Miss Pew?' he said, interrogatively, but rather as if the question were needless, as he walked beside the rustling moiré.

'She has earned my entire approval,' replied Miss Pew, in her oiliest accents. 'She has application.' Dr. Rylance nodded assentingly. 'She has a charming deportment. I know of no girl in the school more thoroughly ladylike. I have never seen her with a collar put on crookedly, or with rough hair. She is a pattern to many of my girls.'

'That is all gratifying to my pride as a father; but I hope she has made progress in her studies.'

Miss Pew coughed gently behind a mittened hand.

'She has not made quite so great an advance as I should have wished. She has talent, no doubt; but it is hardly of a kind that comes into play among other girls. In after-life, perhaps, there may be development. I am sorry to say she is not in our roll-call of honour to-day. She has won no prize.'

'Perhaps she may have hardly thought it worth her while to compete,' said Dr. Rylance, hurt in his own individual pride by the idea that his daughter had missed distinction, just as he would have been hurt if anybody had called one of his pictures a copy, or made light of his blue china. 'With the Rylances it has always been Caesar or nothing.'

'I regret to say that my three most important prizes have been won by a young woman whom I cannot esteem,' said Miss Pew, bristling in her panoply of apple-green, at the thought of Ida Palliser's insolence. 'I hope I shall ever be just, at whatever sacrifice of personal feeling. I shall to-day bestow the first prize for modern languages, for music, and for English history and literature, upon a young person of whose moral character I have a very low opinion.'

'And pray who is this young lady?' asked Dr. Rylance.

'Miss Palliser, the daughter of a half-pay officer residing in the neighbourhood of Dieppe—for very good reasons, no doubt.

'Palliser; yes, I have heard my daughter talk of her. An insolent, ill-bred girl. I have been taught to consider her somewhat a disgrace to your excellent and well-managed school.'

'Her deportment is certainly deplorable,' admitted Miss Pew; 'but the girl has remarkable talents.'

More visitors were arriving from this time forward, until everyone was seated in the ball-room. Miss Pew was engaged in receiving people, and ushering them to their seats, always assisted by Miss Dulcibella—an image of limp gracefulness—and the three governesses—all as stiff as perambulating black-boards. Dr. Rylance strolled by himself for a little while, sniffed at the great ivory cup of a magnolia, gazed dreamily at the river—shining yonder across intervening gardens and meadows—and ultimately found his daughter.

'I am sorry to find you are not to be honoured with a prize, Ranie,' he said, smiling at her gently.

In no relation of life had he been so nearly perfect as in his conduct as a father. Were he ever so disappointed in his daughter, he could not bring himself to be angry with her.

'I have not tried for prizes, papa. Why should I compete with such a girl as Ida Palliser, who is to get her living as a governess, and who knows that success at school is a matter of life and death with her?'

'Do you not think it might have been worth your while to work as hard as Miss Palliser, for the mere honour and glory of being first in your school?'

'Did you ever work for mere honour and glory, papa?' asked Urania, with her unpleasant little air of cynicism.

'Well, my love, I confess there has been generally a promise of solid pudding in the background. Pray, who is this Miss Palliser, whom I hear of at every turn, and whom nobody seems to like?'

'There you are mistaken, papa. Miss Palliser has her worshippers, though she is the most disagreeable girl in the school. That silly little Bessie raves about her, and has actually induced Mrs. Wendover to invite her to The Knoll!'

'That is a pity, if the girl is ill-bred and unpleasant,' said Dr.Rylance.

'She's a horror,' exclaimed Urania, vindictively.

Five minutes later Dr. Rylance and his daughter made their entrance into the ball-room, which was full of people, and whence came the opening crash of an eight-handed 'Zampa.' Father and daughter went in softly, and with a hushed air, as if they had been going into church; yet the firing of a cannon or two more or less would hardly have disturbed the performers at the two pianos, so tremendous was their own uproar. They were taking the overture in what they called orchestral time; though it is doubtful whether even their playing could have kept pace with the hurrying of excited fiddles in a presto passage, or the roll of the big drum, simulating distant thunder. Be that as it may, the four performers were pounding along at a breathless pace; and if their pianissimo passages failed in delicacy, there was no mistake about their fortissimo.

'What an abominable row!' whispered Dr. Rylance. 'Is this what they call music?'

Urania smiled, and felt meritorious in that, after being chosen as one of the four for this very 'Zampa,' she had failed ignominiously as a timist, and had been compelled to cede her place to another pupil.

'I might have toiled for six weeks at the horrid thing,' she thought, 'and papa would have only called it a row.'

'Zampa' ended amidst polite applause, the delighted parents of the four players feeling that they had not lived in vain. And now the music mistress took her place at one of the pianos, the top of the instrument was lowered, and Miss Fane, a little fair girl with a round face and frizzy auburn hair, came simpering forward to sing 'Una voce,' in a reedy soprano, which had been attenuated by half-guinea lessons from an Italian master, and which frequently threatened a snap.

Happily on this occasion the thin little voice got through its work without disaster; there was a pervading sense of relief when the crisis was over, and Miss Fane had simpered her acknowledgments of the applause which rewarded a severely conscientious performance.

'Any more singing?' inquired Dr. Rylance of his daughter, not with the air of a man who pants for vocal melody.

'No, the next is the "Moonlight Sonata."'

Dr. Rylance had a dim idea that he had heard of this piece before. He waited dumbly, admiring the fine old room, with its lofty ceiling, and florid cornice, and the sunny garden beyond the five tall windows.

Presently Ida Palliser came slowly towards the piano, carrying herself like an empress. Dr. Rylance could hardly believe the evidence of his eyes. Was this the girl whose deportment had been called abominable, whom Urania had denounced as a horror? Was this the articled pupil, the girl doomed to life-long drudgery as a governess, this superb creature, with her noble form and noble face, looking grave defiance at the world which hitherto had not used her too kindly?

She was dressed in black, a sombre figure amidst the white muslins and rainbow sashes of her comrades. Her cashmere gown was of the simplest fashion, but it became the tall full figure to admiration. Below her linen collar she wore a scarlet ribbon, from which hung a silver locket, the only ornament she possessed. It was Bessie Wendover who had insisted on the scarlet ribbon, as a relief to that funereal gown.

'I was never so surprised in my life,' whispered Dr. Rylance to his daughter. 'She is the handsomest girl I ever saw.'

'Yes, she is an acknowledged beauty, said Urania, with a contraction of her thin lips; 'nobody disputes her good looks. It is a pity her manners are so abominable.'

'She moves like a lady.'

'She has been thoroughly drilled,' sneered Urania. 'The original savage in her has been tamed as much as possible.'

'I should like to know more of that girl,' said Dr. Rylance, 'for she looks as if she has force of character. I'm sorry you and she are not better friends.'

Ida seated herself at the piano and began to play, without honouring the assembly with one glance from her dark eyes. She sat looking straight before her, like one whose thoughts are far away. She played by memory, and at first her hands faltered a little as they touched the keys, as if she hardly knew what she was going to play. Then she recollected herself in a flash, and began the firm, slow, legato movement with the touch of a master hand, the melody rising and falling in solemn waves of sound, like the long, slow roll of a calm sea.

The 'Moonlight Sonata' is a composition of some length. Badly, or even indifferently performed, the 'Moonlight Sonata' is a trial; but no one grew weary of it to-day, though the strong young hands which gave emphasis to the profound beauties of that wonderful work were only the hands of a girl. Those among the listeners who knew least about music, knew that this was good playing; those who cared not at all for the playing were pleased to sit and watch the mobile face of the player as she wove her web of melody, her expression changing with every change in the music, but unmoved by a thought of the spectators.

Presently, just as the sonata drew to its close, an auburn head was thrust between Dr. Rylance and his daughter, and a girl's voice whispered,

'Is she not splendid? Is she not the grandest creature you ever saw?'

The doctor turned and recognized Bessie Wendover.

'She is, Bessie,' he said, shaking hands with her. 'I never was so struck by anyone in my life.'

Urania grew white with anger. Was it not enough that Ida Palliser should have outshone her in every accomplishment upon which school-girls pride themselves? Was it not enough that she should have taken complete possession of that foolish little Bessie, and thus ingratiated herself into the Wendover set, and contrived to get invited to Kingthorpe? No. Here was Urania's own father, her especial property, going over to the enemy.

'I am glad you admire her so much, papa,' she said, outwardly calm and sweet, but inwardly consumed with anger; 'for it will be so pleasant for you to see more of her at Kingthorpe.'

'Yes,' he said heartily, 'I am glad she is coming to Kingthorpe. That was a good idea of yours, Bessie.'

'Wasn't it? I am so pleased to find you like her. I wish you could get Ranie to think better of her.'

Now came the distribution of prizes and accessits. Miss Pew took her seat before the table on which the gaudily-bound books were arranged, and began to read out the names. It was a hard thing for her to have to award the three first prizes to a girl she detested; but Miss Pew knew the little world she ruled well enough to know that palpable injustice would weaken her rule. Ninety-nine girls who had failed to win the prize would have resented her favouritism if she had given the reward to a hundredth girl who had not fairly won it. The eyes of her little world were upon her, and she was obliged to give the palm to the real victor. So, in her dull, hard voice, looking straight before her, with cold, unfriendly eyes, she read out—

'The prize for modern languages has been obtained by Miss Palliser!' and Ida came slowly up to the table and received a bulky crimson volume, containing the poetical works of Sir Walter Scott.

'The prize for proficiency in instrumental music is awarded to Miss Palliser!'

Another bulky volume was handed to Ida. For variety the binding was green, and the inside of the book was by William Cowper.

'The greatest number of marks for English history and literature have been obtained by Miss Palliser.'

Miss Palliser was now the happy possessor of a third volume bound in blue, containing a selection from the works of Robert Southey.

With not one word of praise nor one smile of approval did Miss Pew sweeten the gifts which she bestowed upon the articled pupil. She gave that which justice, or rather policy, compelled her to give. No more. Kindliness was not in the bond.

Ida came slowly away from the table, laden with her prizes, her head held high, but not with pride in the trophies she carried. Her keenest feeling at this moment was a sense of humiliation. The prizes had been given her as a bone might be flung to a strange dog, by one whose heart held no love for the canine species. An indignant flush clouded the creamy whiteness of her forehead, angry tears glittered in her proud eyes. She made her way to the nearest door, and went away without a word to the crowd of younger girls, her own pupils, who had crowded round to congratulate and caress her. She was adored by these small people, and it was her personal influence as much as her talent which made her so successful a teacher.

Dr. Rylance followed her to the door with his eyes. He was not capable of wide sympathies, or of projecting himself into the lives of other people; but he did sympathize with this girl, so lonely in the splendour of her beauty, so joyless in her triumph.

'God help her, poor child, in the days to come!' he said to himself.

CHAPTER III
AT THE KNOLL

Between Winchester and Romsey there lies a region of gentle hills and grassy slopes shadowed by fine old yew trees, a land of verdure, lonely and exceeding fair; and in a hollow of this undulating district nestles the village of Kingthorpe, with its half-dozen handsome old houses, its richly cultivated gardens, and quaint old square-towered church. It is a prosperous, well-to-do little settlement, where squalor and want are unknown. Its humbler dwellings belong chiefly to the labourers on the Wendover estate, and those are liberally paid and well cared for. An agricultural labourer's wages at Kingthorpe might seem infinitely small to a London mechanic; but when it is taken into account that the tiller of the fields has a roomy cottage and an acre of garden for sixpence a-week, his daily dole of milk from the home farm, as much wood as he can burn, blankets and coals at Christmas, and wine and brandy, soup and bread from the great house, in all emergencies, he is perhaps not so very much worse off than his metropolitan brother.

There was an air of comfort and repose at Kingthorpe which made the place delightful to the eye of a passing wanderer—a spot where one would gladly have lain down the burden of life and rested for awhile in one of those white cottages that lay a little way back from the high road, shadowed by a screen of tall elms. There was a duck-pond in front of a low red-brick inn which reminded one of Birkett Foster, and made the central feature of the village; a spot of busy life where all else was stillness. There were accommodation roads leading off to distant farms, above which the tree-tops interlaced, and where the hedges were rich in blackberry and sloe, dog-roses and honeysuckle, and the banks in spring-time dappled with violet and primrose, purple orchids and wild crocus, and all the flowers that grow for the delight of village children.

Ida Palliser sat silent in her corner of the large landau which was taking Miss Wendover and her schoolfellows from Winchester station to Kingthorpe. Miss Rylance had accepted a seat in the Wendover landau at her father's desire; but she would have preferred to have had her own smart little pony-carriage to meet her at the station. To drive her own carriage, were it ever so small, was more agreeable to Urania's temper than to sit behind the over-fed horses from The Knoll, and to be thus, in some small measure, indebted to Bessie Wendover.

Ida Palliser's presence made the thing still more odious. Bessie was radiant with delight at taking her friend home with her. She watched Ida's eyes as they roamed over the landscape. She understood the girl's silent admiration.

'They are darling old hills, aren't they, dear?' she asked, squeezing Ida's hand, as the summer shadows and summer lights went dancing over the sward like living things.

'Yes, dear, they are lovely,' answered Ida, quietly.

She was devouring the beauty of the scene with her eyes. She had seen nothing like it in her narrow wanderings over the earth—nothing so simple, so beautiful, and so lonely. She was sorry when they left that open hill country and came into a more fertile scene, a high road, which was like an avenue in a gentleman's park, and then the village duck-pond and red homestead, the old gray church, with its gilded sun-dial, marking the hour of six, the gardens brimming over with roses, and as full of sweet odours as those spicy islands which send their perfumed breath to greet the seaman as he sails to the land of the Sun.

The carriage stopped at the iron gate of an exquisitely kept garden, surrounding a small Gothic cottage of the fanciful order of architecture,—a cottage with plate-glass windows, shaded by Spanish blinds, a glazed verandah sheltering a tesselated walk, sloping banks and terraces, on a very small scale, stone vases full of flowers, a tiny fountain sparkling in the afternoon sun.

This was Dr. Rylance's country retreat. It had been a yeoman's cottage, plain, substantial and homely as the yeoman and his household. The doctor had added a Gothic front, increased the number of rooms, but not the general convenience of the dwelling. He had been his own architect, and the result was a variety of levels and a breakneck arrangement of stairs at all manner of odd corners, so ingenious in their peril to life and limb that they might be supposed to have been designed as traps for the ignorant stranger.

'Don't say good-bye, Ranie,' said Bessie, when Miss Rylance had alighted, and was making her adieux at the carriage door; 'you'll come over to dinner, won't you, dear? Your father won't be down till Saturday. You'll be dreadfully dull at home.'

'Thanks, dear, no; I'd rather spend my first evening at home. I'm never dull,' answered Urania, with her air of superiority.

'What a queer girl you are!' exclaimed Bessie, frankly. 'I should be wretched if I found myself alone in a house. Do run over in the evening, at any rate. We are going to have lots of fun.'

Miss Rylance shuddered. She knew what was meant by lots of fun at The Knoll; a romping game at croquet, or the newly-established lawn-tennis, with girls in short petticoats and boys in Eton jackets; a raid upon the plum-trees on the crumbling red brick walls of the fine old kitchen-garden; winding up with a boisterous bout at hide-and-seek in the twilight; and finally a banquet of sandwiches, jam tarts, and syllabub in the shabby old dining-room.

'I'll come over to see Mrs. Wendover, if I am not too tired,' she said, with languid politeness, and then she closed the gate, and the carriage drove on to The Knoll.

Colonel Wendover's house was a substantial dwelling of the Queen Anne period, built of unmixed red brick, with a fine pediment, a stone shell over the entrance, four long narrow windows on each side of the tall door, and nine in each upper story, a house that looked all eyes, and was a blaze of splendour when the western sun shone upon its many windows. The house stood on a bit of rising ground at the end of the village, and dominated all meaner habitations. It was the typical squire's house, and Colonel Wendover was no bad representative of the typical squire.

A fine old iron gate opened upon a broad gravel drive, which made the circuit of a well-kept *parterre*, where the flowers grew as they only grow for those who love them dearly. This gate stood hospitably open at all times, and many were the vehicles which drove up to the tall door of The Knoll, and friendly the welcome which greeted all comers.

The door, like the gate, stood open all day long—indeed, open doors were the rule at Kingthorpe. Ida saw a roomy old hall, paved with black and white marble, a few family portraits, considerably the worse for wear, against panelled walls painted white, a concatenation of guns, fishing-rods, whips, canes, cricket-bats, croquet-mallets, and all things appertaining to the out-door amusements of a numerous family. A large tiger skin stretched before the drawing-room door was one memorial of Colonel Wendover's Indian life; a tiger's skull gleaming on the wall, between a pair of elephant's ears, was another. One side of the wall was adorned with a collection of Indian arms, showing all those various curves with which oriental ingenuity has improved upon the straight simplicity of the western sword.

It was not a neatly kept hall. There had been no careful study of colour in the arrangement of things—hats and caps were flung carelessly on the old oak chairs—there was a licentious mixture of styles in the furniture—half Old English, half Indian, and all the worse for wear: but Ida Palliser thought the house had a friendly look, which made it better than any house she had ever seen before.

Through an open door at the back of the hall she saw a broad gravel walk, long and straight, leading to a temple or summer-house built of red brick, like the mansion itself. On each side of the broad walk there was a strip of grass, just about wide enough for a bowling-green, and on the grass were orange-trees in big wooden tubs, painted green. Slowly advancing along the broad walk there came a large lady.

'Is that you mother?' asked Ida.

'No, it's Aunt Betsy. You ought to have known Aunt Betsy at a glance. I'm sure I've described her often enough. How good of her to be here to welcome us!' and Bessie flew across the hall and rushed down the broad walk to greet her aunt.

Ida followed at a more sober pace. Yes, she had heard of Aunt Betsy—a maiden aunt, who lived in her own house a little way from The Knoll. A lady who had plenty of money and decidedly masculine tastes, which she indulged freely; a very lovable person withal, if Bessie might be believed. Ida wondered if she too would be able to like Aunt Betsy.

Miss Wendover's appearance was not repulsive. She was a woman of heroic mould, considerably above the average height of womankind, with a large head nobly set upon large well-shaped shoulders. Bulky Miss Wendover decidedly was, but she carried her bulkiness well. She still maintained a waist, firmly braced above her expansive hips. She walked well, and was more active than many smaller women. Indeed, her life was full of activity, spent for the most part in the open air, driving, walking, gardening, looking after her cows and poultry, and visiting the labouring-classes round Kingthorpe, among whom she was esteemed an oracle.

Bessie hung herself round her large aunt like ivy on an oak, and the two thus united came up the broad walk to meet Ida, Bessie chattering all the way.

'So this is Miss Palliser,' said Aunt Betsy heartily, and in a deep masculine voice, which accorded well with her large figure. 'I have heard a great deal about you from this enthusiastic child,—so much that I was prepared to be disappointed in you. It is the highest compliment I can pay you to say I am not.'

'Where's mother?' asked Bessie.

'Your father drove her to Romsey to call on the new vicar. There's the phaeton driving in at the gate.'

It was so. Before Ida had had breathing time to get over the introduction to Aunt Betsy, she was hurried off to see her host and hostess.

They were very pleasant people, who did not consider themselves called on to present an icy aspect to a new acquaintance.

The Colonel was the image of his sister, tall and broad of figure, with an aquiline nose and a commanding eye, thoroughly good-natured withal, and a man whom everybody loved. Mrs. Wendover was a dumpy little woman, who had brought dumpiness and a handsome fortune into the family. She had been very pretty in girlhood, and was pretty still, with a round-faced innocent prettiness which made her look almost as young as her eldest daughter. Her husband loved her with a fondly protecting and almost paternal affection, which was very pleasant to behold; and she held him in devoted reverence, as the beginning and end of all that was worth loving and knowing in the Universe. She was not an accomplished woman, and had made the smallest possible use of those opportunities which civilization affords to every young lady whose parents have plenty of money; but she was a lady to the marrow of her bones—benevolent, kindly. thinking no evil, rejoicing in the truth—an embodiment of domestic love.

Such a host and hostess made Ida feel at home in their house in less than five minutes. If there had been a shade of coldness in their greeting her pride would have risen in arms against them, and she would have made herself eminently disagreeable. But at their hearty welcome she expanded like a beautiful flower which opens its lovely heart to the sunshine.

'It is so good of you to ask me here,' she said, when Mrs. Wendover had kissed her, 'knowing so little of me.'

'I know that my daughter loves you,' answered the mother, 'and it is not in Bessie's nature to love anyone who isn't worthy of love.'

Ida smiled at the mother's simple answer.

'Don't you think that in a heart so full of love some may run over and get wasted on worthless objects?' she asked.

'That's very true,' cried a boy in an Eton jacket, one of a troop that had congregated round the Colonel and his wife since their entrance. 'You know there was that half-bred terrier you doted upon, Bess, though I showed you that the roof of his mouth was as red as sealing-wax.'

'I hope you are not going to compare me to a half-bred terrier,' said Ida, laughing.

'If you were a terrier, the roof of your mouth would be as black as my hat,' said the boy decisively. It was his way of expressing his conviction that Ida was thoroughbred.

The ice being thus easily broken, Ida found herself received into the bosom of the family, and at once established as a favourite with all. There were two boys in Eton jackets, answering to the names of Reginald and Horatio, but oftener to the friendly abbreviations Reg and Horry. Both had chubby faces, liberally freckled, warts on their hands, and rumpled hair; and it was not easy for a new comer to distinguish Horatio from Reginald, or Reginald from Horatio. There was a girl of fourteen with flowing hair, who looked very tall because her petticoats were very short, and who always required some one to hug and hang upon. If she found herself deprived of human support she lolled against a wall.

This young person at once pounced upon Ida, as a being sent into the world to sustain her.

'Do you think you shall like me?' she asked, when they had all swarmed up to the long corridor, out of which numerous bedrooms opened.

'I like you already,' answered Ida.

'Do thoo like pigs?' asked a smaller girl, round and rosy, in a holland pinafore, putting the question as if it were relevant to her sister's inquiry.

'I don't quite know,' said Ida doubtfully.

''Cos there are nine black oneths, tho pwutty. Will thoo come and thee them?'

Ida said she would think about it: and then she received various pressing invitations to go and see lop-eared rabbits, guinea-pigs, a tame water-rat in the rushes of the duck-pond, a collection of eggs in the schoolroom, and the new lawn-tennis ground which father had made in the paddock.

'Now all you small children run away!' cried Bessie, loftily. 'Ida and I are going to dress for dinner.'

The crowd dispersed reluctantly, with low mutterings about rabbits, pigs, and water-rats, like the murmurs of a stage mob; and then Bessie led her friend into a large sunny room fronting westward, a room with three windows, cushioned window-seats, two pretty white-curtained beds, and a good deal of old-fashioned and heterogeneous furniture, half English, half Indian.

'You said you wouldn't mind sleeping in my room,' said Bessie, as she showed her friend an exclusive dressing-table, daintily draperied, and enlivened with blue satin bows, for the refreshment of the visitor's eye.

While the girls were contemplating this work of art the door was suddenly opened and Blanche's head was thrust in.

'I did the dressing-table, Miss Palliser, every bit, on purpose for you.'

And the door then slammed to, and Bessie rushed across the room and drew the bolt.

'We shall have them all one after another,' she said.

'Don't shut them out on my account.'

'Oh, but I must. You would have no peace. I can see they are going to be appallingly fond of you.'

'Let them like me as much as they can. Do you know, Bessie, this is my first glimpse into the inside of a home!'

'Oh, Ida, dear, but your father,' remonstrated Bessie.

'My father has never been unkind to me, but I have had no home with him. When my mother brought me home from India—she died very soon after we got home, you know'—Ida strangled a sob at this point—'I was placed with strangers, two elderly maiden ladies, who reared me very well, no doubt, in their stiff business-like way, and who really gave me a very good education. That went on for nine years,—a long time to spend with two old maids in a dull little house at Turnham Green,—and then I had a letter from my father to say he had come home for good. He had sold his commission and meant to settle down in some quiet spot abroad. His first duty would be to make arrangements for placing me in a high-class school, where I could finish my education; and he told me, quite at the end of his letter, that he had married a very sweet young lady, who was ready to give me all a mother's affection, and who would be able to receive me in my holidays, when the expense of the journey to France and back was manageable.'

'Poor darling!' sighed Bessie. 'Did your heart warm to the sweet young lady?'

'No, Bess; I'm afraid it must be an unregenerate heart, for I took a furious dislike to her. Very unjust and unreasonable, wasn't it? Afterwards, when my father took me over to his cottage, near Dieppe, to spend my holidays, I found that my stepmother was a kind-hearted, pretty little thing, whom I might look down upon for her want of education, but whom I could not dislike. She was very kind to me; and she had a baby boy. I have told you about him, and how he and I fell in love with each other at first sight.'

'I am horribly jealous of that baby boy,' protested Bessie. 'How old is he now?'

'Nearly five. He was two years and a half old when I was at Les Fontaines, and that was before I went to Mauleverer Manor.'

'And you have been at Mauleverer Manor more than two years without once going home for the holidays,' said Bessie. 'That seems hard.'

'My dear, poverty is hard. It is all of a piece. It means deprivation, humiliation, degradation, the severance of friends. My father would have had me home if he could have afforded it; but he couldn't. He has only just enough to keep himself and his wife and boy. If you were to see the little box of a house they inhabit in that tiny French village, you would wonder that anybody bigger than a pigeon could live in so small a place. They have a narrow garden, and there is an orchard on the slope of a hill behind the cottage, and a long white road leading to nowhere in front. It is all very nice in the summer, when one can live half one's life out of doors, but I am sure I don't know how they manage to exist through the winter.'

'Poor things!' sighed Bessie, who had a large stock of compassion always on hand.

And then she tied a bright ribbon at the back of Ida's collar, by way of finishing touch to the girl's simple toilet, which had been going on while they talked, and then, Bessie in white and Ida in black, like sunlight and shadow, they went downstairs to the drawing-room, where Colonel Wendover was stretched on his favourite sofa, reading a county paper. Since his retirement from active service into domestic idleness the Colonel had required a great deal of rest, and was to be found at all hours of the day extended at ease on his own particular sofa. During his intervals of activity he exhibited a large amount of energy. When he was indoors his stentorian voice penetrated from garret to cellar; when he was out of doors the same deep-toned thunder could be heard across a couple of paddocks. He pervaded the gardens and stables, supervised the home farm, and had a finger in every pie.

Mrs. Wendover was sitting in her own particular arm-chair, close to her husband's sofa—they were seldom seen far apart—with a large basket of crewel-work beside her, containing sundry squares of kitchen towelling and a chaos of many-coloured wools, which never seemed to arrive at any result.

The impression which Mrs. Wendover's drawing-room conveyed to a stranger was a general idea of homeliness and comfort. It was not fine, it was not aesthetic, it was not even elegant. A great bay window opened upon the garden, a large old-fashioned fireplace, with carved wooden chimney-piece faced the bay. The floor was polished oak, with only an island of faded Persian carpet in the centre, and Indian prayer rugs lying about here and there. There were chairs and tables of richly carved Bombay blackwood, Japanese cabinets in the recesses beside the fire-place, a five-leaved Indian screen between the fire-place and the door. There was just enough Oriental china to give colour to the room, and to relieve by glowing reds and vivid purples the faded dead-leaf tint of curtains and chair covers.

The gong began to boom as the two girls came into the room, and the rest of the family dropped in through the open windows at the same moment, Aunt Betsy bringing up the rear. There was no nursery dinner at The Knoll. Colonel Wendover allowed his children to dine with him from the day they were able to manage their knives and forks. Save on state occasions, the whole brood sat down with their father and mother to the seven o'clock dinner; as the young sprigs of the House of Orleans used to sit round good King Louis Philippe in his tranquil retirement at Claremont. Even the lisping girl who loved pigs had her place at the board, and knew how to behave herself. There was a subdued struggle for the seat next Ida, whom the Colonel had placed on his right, but Reginald, the elder of the Winchester boys, asserted his claim with a quiet firmness that proved irresistible. Grace was said with solemn brevity by the Colonel, whose sum total of orthodoxy was comprised in that brief grace, and in regular attendance at church on Sunday mornings; and then there came a period of chatter and laughter which might have been a little distracting to a stranger. Each of the boys and girls had some wonderful fact, usually about his or her favourite animal, to communicate to the father. Aunt Betsy broke in with her fine manly voice at every turn in the conversation. Ripples of laughter made a running accompaniment to everything. It was a new thing to Ida Palliser to find herself in the midst of so much happiness.

After dinner they all rushed off to play lawn tennis, carrying Ida along with them.

'It's a shame,' protested Bessie. 'I know you're tired, darling. Come and rest in a shady corner of the drawing-room.'

This sounded tempting, but it was not to be.

'No she's not,' asserted Blanche, boldly. 'You're not tired, are you, Miss Palliser?'

'Not too tired for just one game,' replied Ida. 'But you are never to call me Miss Palliser.'

'May I really call you Ida? That's too lovely.'

'May we all call you Ida?' asked Horatio. 'Don't begin by making distinctions. Blanche is no better than the rest of us.'

'Don't be jealous,' said Miss Palliser, laughing. 'I am going to be everybody's Ida.'

On this she was borne off to the garden as in a whirlwind.

There were some bamboo chairs and sofas on the grass in front of the bay window, and here the elder members of the family established themselves.

'I like that schoolfellow of Bessie's,' said Aunt Betsy, with her decided air, whereupon the Colonel and his wife assented, as they always did to any proposition of Miss Wendover's.

'She is remarkably handsome,' said the Colonel.

'She is good and thorough, and that's of much more consequence,' said his sister.

'She takes to the children, and that is so truly nice in her,' murmured Mrs. Wendover.

CHAPTER IV
WENDOVER ABBEY

The next day was fine. The children had all been praying for fine weather, that they might entertain Miss Palliser with an exploration of the surrounding neighbourhood. Loud whoops of triumph and sundry breakdown dances were heard in the top story soon after five o'clock, for the juvenile Wendovers were early risers, and when in high spirits made themselves distinctly audible.

The eight o'clock breakfast in the old painted dining-room—all oak panelling, but painted stone colour by generations of Goths and Vandals—was even more animated than the seven o'clock dinner.

Such a breakfast, after the thick bread and butter and thin coffee at Mauleverer. Relays of hot buttered cakes, and eggs and bacon, fish, honey, fresh fruit from the garden, a picturesque confusion of form and colour on the lavishly-furnished table, and youthful appetites ready to do justice to the good cheer.

'What are you going to do with Miss Palliser?' asked the Colonel. 'Am I to take her for a drive?'

'No, father, you can't have Miss Palliser to-day. She's going in the jaunting-car,' said Reginald, talking of the lady as if she were a horse. 'We're going to take her over to the Abbey.'

The Abbey was the ancestral home of the Wendovers, now in possession of Brian Wendover, only son of the Colonel's eldest brother, and head of the house.

'Well, don't upset her oftener than you can help,' replied the father. 'I suppose you don't much mind being spilt off an outside car, Miss Palliser? I believe young ladies of your age rather relish the excitement.'

'She needn't be afraid,' said Reginald; 'I am going to drive.'

'Then we are very likely to find ourselves reposing in a ditch before the day is over,' retorted Bessie. 'I hope you—or the pony—will choose a dry one.'

'I'll risk it, ditches and all,' said Ida, good-naturedly. 'I am longing to see the Abbey.'

'The rich Brian's Abbey,' said Bessie, laughing. 'What a pity he is not at home for you to see him too! Do you think Brian will be back before Ida's holidays are over, father?'

'I never know what that young man is going to do,' answered the Colonel. 'When last I heard from him he was fishing in Norway. He doesn't care much about the sport, he tells me; indeed, he was never a very enthusiastic angler; but he likes the country and the people. He ought to stay at home, and stand for the county at the next election. A young man in his position has no business to be idle.'

'Is he clever?' asked Ida.

'Too clever for my money,' answered the Colonel. 'He has too much book-learning, and too little knowledge of men and things. What is the good of a man being a fine Greek scholar if he knows nothing about the land he owns, or the cattle that graze upon it, and has not enough tact to make himself popular in his own neighbourhood? Brian is a man who would starve if his bread depended on his own exertions.'

'He's a jolly kind of cousin for a fellow to have,' suggested Horry, looking up from his eggs and bacon. 'He lets us do what we like at the Abbey. By the way, Blanche, have you packed the picnic basket?'

'Yes.'

'What have you put in?'

'That's my secret,' answered Blanche. 'Do you think I am going to tell you what you are to have for lunch? That would spoil all the fun.'

'Blanche isn't half a bad caterer,' said Reg. 'I place myself in her hands unreservedly; I will only venture to hint that I hope she hasn't forgotten the chutnee, Tirhoot, and plenty of it. What's the good of having a father who was shoulder to shoulder with Gough in the Punjab, if we are to run short of Indian condiments?'

At nine o'clock the young people were all ready to start. The jaunting-car held five, including the driver; Bessie and her friend were to occupy one side, Eva, the round child who loved pigs, was to have a seat, and a place was to be kept for Miss Rylance, who was to be invited to join the exploration party, much to the disgust of the Winchester lads, who denounced her as a stuck-up minx, and distinguished her with various other epithets of an abusive character selected from a vocabulary known only to Wyckhamists. Blanche and Horatio and a smaller boy, called Ernest, who was dressed like a gillie, and had all the wildness of a young Highlander, were to walk, with the occasional charity of a lift.

The jaunting-car was drawn by a large white pony, fat and pampered, overfed with dainties from the children's tables, and petted and played with until he had become almost human in his intelligence, and a match for his youthful masters in cunning and mischief. This impish animal had been christened Robin Goodfellow, a name that was shortened for convenience to Robin. Robin's eagerness to depart was now made known to the family by an incessant rattling of his bit.

Reginald took the reins, and got into his seat with the quiet grandeur of a celebrity in the four-in-hand club. Ida and Bessie were handed to their places by Horatio, the chubby Eva scrambled into her seat, with a liberal display of Oxford blue stocking, under the shortest of striped petticoats; and off they drove to the cottage, Dr. Rylance's miniature dwelling, where the plate-glass windows were shining in the morning sun, and the colours of the flower-beds were almost too bright to be looked at.

Bessie found Miss Rylance in the dainty little drawing-room, all ebonized wood and blue china, as neat as an interior by Mieris. The fair Urania was yawning over a book of travels—trying to improve a mind which was not naturally fertile—and she was not sorry to be interrupted by an irruption of noisy Wendovers, even though they left impressions of their boots on the delicate tones of the carpet, and made havoc of the cretonne chair-covers.

Miss Rylance had no passion for country life. Fields and trees, hills and winding streams, even when enlivened by the society of the lower animals, were not all-sufficient for her happiness. It was all very well for her father to oscillate between Cavendish Square and Kingthorpe, avoiding the expense and trouble of autumn touring, and taking his rest and his pleasure in this rustic retreat. But her summer holidays for the last three years had been all Kingthorpe, and Miss Rylance detested the picturesque village, the busy duck-pond, the insignificant hills, which nobody had ever heard of, and the monotonous sequence of events.

'We are going to the Abbey for a nice long day, taking our dinner with us, and coming round to Aunt Betsy's to tea on our way home,' said Bessie, as if she were proposing an entirely novel excursion; 'and we want you to come with us, Ranie.'

Miss Rylance stifled a yawn. She had been trying to pin her thoughts to a particular tribe of Abyssinians, who fought all the surrounding tribes, and always welcomed the confiding stranger with a shower of poisoned arrows. She did not care for the Wendover children, but they were better than those wearisome Abyssinians.

'You are very kind, but I know the Abbey so well,' she said, determined to yield her consent as a favour.

'Never mind that. Ida has never seen it. We are going to show her everything. We want her to feel one of us.'

'We shall have a jolly lunch,' interjected Blanche. 'There are some lemon cheesecakes that I made myself yesterday afternoon. Cook was in a good temper, and let me do it.'

'I hope you washed your hands first,' said Horatio. 'I'd sooner cook had made the cheesecakes.'

'Of course I washed my hands, you too suggestive pig. But I should hope that in a general way my hands are cleaner than cook's. It is only schoolboys who luxuriate in dirt.'

'You'll come, Ranie?' pleaded Bess.

'If you really wish it.'

'I do, or I shouldn't be here. But I hope you wish it too. You ought to be longing to get out of doors on such a lovely morning. Houses were never intended for such weather as this. Come and join the birds and butterflies, and all the happiest things in creation.'

'I must go for my hat and sunshade. I wasn't born full-dressed, like the birds and butterflies,' replied Urania.

She ran away, leaving Bessie and Ida in the drawing-room. The younger children having rushed in and left their mark upon the room, had now rushed out again to the jaunting-car.

'A pretty drawing-room, isn't it?' asked Bess. 'It looks so neat and fresh and bright after ours.'

'It doesn't look half so much like home,' said Ida.

'Perhaps not. But I believe it is just the exact thing a drawing-room ought to be in this latter part of the nineteenth century; or, at least, so Dr. Rylance says. How do you like the blue china? Dr. Rylance is an amateur of blue china. He will have no other. Dresden and Sevres have no existence for him. He recognizes nothing beyond his own particular breed of ginger-jars.'

Miss Rylance came back, dressed as carefully as if she had been going for a morning lounge in Hyde Park, hat and feather, pongee sunshade, mousquetaire gloves. The Wendovers all wore their gloves in their pockets, and cultivated blisters on the palms of their hands, as a mark of distinction, which implied great feats in rowing, or the pulling in of desperate horses.

Now they were all mounted on the car, just as the church clock struck ten. Reginald gave the reins a shake, cracked his whip, and Robin, who always knew where his young friends wanted to go, twisted the vehicle sharply round a corner and started at an agreeable canter, expressive of good spirits.

Robin carried them joltingly along a lovely lane till they came to a gentle acclivity, by which time, having given vent to his exuberance, the pony settled down into a crawl. Vainly did Reginald crack his whip—vain even stinging switches on Robin's fat sides. Out of that crawl nothing could move him. The sun was gaining power with every moment, and blazing down upon the occupants of the car; but Robin cared not at all. He was an animal of tropical origin, and had no apprehension of sunshine; his eyes were so constructed as to accommodate themselves to a superfluity of light.

'I think we shall be tolerably well roasted by the time we get to the Abbey,' said Bessie. 'Don't you think if we were all to get down and push the back of the car, Robin might go a little faster?'

'He'll go fast enough when he has blown a bit,' said Reg. 'Can't you admire the landscape?'

'We could, if we were not being baked,' replied Ida.

Miss Rylance sat silent under her pongee umbrella, and wished herself in Cavendish Square; even though western London were as empty and barren as the great wilderness.

They were on the ridge of a hill, overlooking undulating pastures and quiet sheep-walks, fair hills on which the yew-trees cast their dark shadows, a broad stretch of pastoral country with sunny gleams of water shining low in the distance.

Suddenly the road dipped, and Robin was going downhill with alarming speed.

'This means that we shall all be in the ditch presently,' said Bessie. 'Never mind. It's only a dry bed of dock and used-up stinging nettles. We shan't be much hurt.'

After two or three miraculous escapes they landed at the bottom of the hill, and Ida beheld the good old gates of Kingthorpe Abbey, low iron gates that stood open, between tall stone pillars supporting the sculptured escutcheon of the Wendovers. There was a stone lodge on each side of the gate, past which the car drove in triumph into an avenue of ancient yew-trees, low and wide-spreading, with a solemn gloom that would better have become a churchyard than a gentleman's park.

It was a noble old park, richly timbered with oaks as old as those immemorial trees that make the glory of Stoneleigh. There was a lake in a wooded hollow in front of the Abbey, a long low pile of stone, the newest part of which was as old as the days of the last Tudor. Nor had much money been spent on the restoration or decorative repair of that fine old house. It had been kept wind and weather proof. It had been protected against the injuries of time; and that was all. There it stood, a brave and solid monument of the remote past, grand in its stern simplicity and its historic associations.

'Oh, what a dear old house!' cried Ida, clasping her hands, as the car came out of the yew-tree avenue into the open space in front of the Abbey; a wide lawn, where four mighty cedars of Lebanon spread their dense shadows grave old trees—which were in somewise impostors, as they looked older than the house, and yet had been saplings in the days of Queen Anne. 'What a sweet old place!' repeated Ida; 'and how I envy the rich Brian!'

'Don't you think the rich Brian's wife will be still more enviable?' sneered Miss Rylance.

'That depends. She may be a Vere-de-Vereish kind of person, and pine amongst her halls and towers,' said Ida.

'Not if she had been brought up in poverty. She would revel in the advantages of her position as Mrs. Wendover of the Abbey,' asserted Miss Rylance.

'Would she? The Earl of Burleigh's wife had been poor, and yet did not enjoy being rich and great,' said Bessie. 'It killed her, poor thing. And yet she had married for love, and had no remorse of conscience to weigh her down.'

'She was a sensitive little fool,' said Ida; 'I have no patience with her.'

'Modern young ladies are not easily crushed,' remarked Miss Rylance; 'they make marrying for money a profession.'

'Is that your idea of life?' asked Ida.

'No; but I understand it is yours. I heard you say you meant to marry for money.'

'Then you must have been listening to a conversation in which you had no concern,' Ida answered coolly. 'I never said as much to you.'

The three girls, and the chubby Eva, had alighted from the car, which was being conveyed to the stables at a hand-gallop, and this conversation was continued on the broad gravel sweep in front of the Abbey. Just as the discussion was intensifying in unpleasantness, the arrival of the pedestrians made an agreeable diversion. Blanche and her two brothers had come by a short cut, across fields and common, had given chase to butterflies, experimented with tadpoles, and looked for hedge-birds' eggs in the course of their journey, and were altogether in a state of dilapidation—perspiration running down their sunburnt faces—their hats anyhow—their hands embellished with recent scratches—their boots coated with clay.

'Did ever anyone see such objects?' exclaimed Bessie, who had imbibed certain conventional ideas of decency at Mauleverer Manor: 'you ought to be ashamed of yourselves.'

'I daresay we ought, but we aren't,' retorted Horatio. 'I found a tadpole in an advanced stage of transmutation, Miss Palliser, and it has almost converted me to Darwinism. Given a single step and you may accept the whole ladder. If from tadpoles frogs, why not from monkeys man?'

'Go and be a Darwinian, and don't prose,' said Blanche, impatiently. 'We are going to show Ida the Abbey. How do you like the outside, darling?' asked the too-affectionate girl, favouring Miss Palliser with the full weight of her seven stone and three-quarters.

'I adore it. It is like a page out of an old chronicle.'

'Isn't it?' gasped Blanche; 'and you can fancy the fat old monks sitting on those stone benches, nodding in the sunshine. The house is hardly altered a bit since it was an actual abbey, except that half a dozen cells have been knocked into one comfortable bedroom. The long dark passages are just the same as they were when those sly old monks went gliding up and down them—such dear old passages, smelling palpably of ghosts.'

'Mice,' said Horatio.

'No, sir, ghosts. Do you suppose my sense of smell is of such inferior quality that I can't distinguish a ghost from a mouse?'

'Now, how about luncheon?' demanded Horatio. 'I propose that we all go and sit under that prime old cedar and discuss the contents of the picnic basket before we discuss the Abbey.'

'Why, it isn't half-past eleven,' said Bessie.

'Ah,' sighed Blanche, 'I'm afraid it's too early for lunch. We should have nothing left to look forward to all the rest of the day.'

'There'd be afternoon tea at Aunt Betsy's to build upon, said Horry. 'I gave her to understand we were to have something good: blue gages from the south wall, cream to a reckless extent.'

'Strawberry jam and pound-cake,' suggested Eva.

'If you go on like that you'll make me distracted with hunger,' said Blanche, a young person who at the seaside wanted twopence to buy buns directly after she had swallowed her dinner.

Bessie and Miss Rylance had been walking up and down the velvet sward beside the beds of dwarf roses and geraniums, with a ladylike stateliness which did credit to their training at Mauleverer. Ida was the centre of the juvenile group.

'Come and see the Abbey,' exclaimed Horry, putting his arm through Miss Palliser's, 'and at the stroke of one we will sit down to lunch under the biggest of the cedars—the tree which according to tradition was planted by John Evelyn himself, when he came on a visit to Sir Tristram Wendover.'

They all trooped into the Abbey, the hall door standing open, as in a fairy tale. Bessie and Urania followed at a more sober pace; but Ida had given herself over to the children, and they did what they liked with her, Blanche hanging on her bodily all the time.

They were now joined by Reginald, who appeared mysteriously from the back premises, where he had been seeing Robin eat his corn, having a fixed idea that it was in the nature of all grooms and stablemen to cheat horses.

The Abbey was furnished with a sober grandeur, in perfect tone with its architecture. Everything was solid and ponderous, save here and there, where in some lady's bower there appeared the spindle-legged tables and inlaid cabinets of the Chippendale period, which had an air of newness where all else was so old. The upper rooms were low and somewhat dark, the heavily mullioned windows being designed to exclude rather than to admit light. There was much tapestry, subdued in hue, but in good condition, and as frankly uninteresting in subject as the generality of old English needlework.

Below, the rooms were large and lofty, rich in carved chimney pieces, well preserved panelling, and old oak furniture. There were some fine pictures, from Holbein downwards, and the usual array of family portraits, which the boys and girls explained and commented upon copiously.

'There's my favourite ancestor, Sir Tristram,' cried Blanche pointing to a dark-eyed cavalier, with strongly-marked brow and bronzed visage. 'He was middle-aged when that picture was painted, but I know he was handsome in his youth. The face is still in the family.'

'Of course it is,' said Horatio—'on my shoulders.'

'Your shoulders!' ejaculated Blanche, contemptuously. 'As if my Sir Tristram ever resembled you. He fought in all the great battles, from Edgehill to Worcester,' continued the girl; 'and he was wounded seven times; and he was true to his master through every trial; and he had all the Wendover plate melted down; and he followed Charles the Second into exile; he mortgaged his estate to raise money for the king; and he married a very lovely French woman, who introduced turned-up noses into the family,' concluded Blanche, giving her tip-tilted nose a complacent toss.

'I thought it was a mercy that we were spared the old housekeeper,' said Urania, 'but really Blanche is worse.'

'Ida doesn't know all about our family, if you do,' protested Blanche. 'It is all new to her.'

'Yes, dear, it is all new and interesting to me,' said Ida.

'How much more deeply you would have been interested if Mr. Wendover had been here to expatiate upon his family tree,' said Urania.

'That might have made it still more interesting,' admitted Ida, with a frankness which took the sting out of Miss Rylance's remark.

The young Wendovers had shown Ida everything. They had opened cabinets, peered into secret drawers, sniffed at the stale *pot-pourri* in old crackle vases; they had dragged their willing victim through all the long slippery passages, by all the mysterious stairs and by-ways; they had obliged her to look at the interior of ghostly closets, where the ladies of old had stored their house linen or hung their mantuas and farthingales; they had made her look out of numerous windows to admire the prospect; they had introduced her to the state bedroom in which the heads of the Wendover race made a point of being born; they made her peep shuddering into the death-chamber where the family were laid in their last slumber. The time thus pleasantly occupied slipped away unawares; and the chapel clock was striking one as they all went trooping down the broad oak staircase for about the fifteenth time.

A gentleman was entering the hall as they came down. They could only see the top of his hat.

'It's father,' cried Eva.

'You little idiot; did you ever see my father in a stove-pipe hat on a week-day?' cried Reg, with infinite scorn.

'Then it's Brian.'

'Brian is in Norway.'

The gentleman looked up and greeted them all with a comprehensive smile. It was Dr. Rylance.

'So glad I have found you, young people,' he said blandly.

'Papa,' exclaimed Urania, in a tone which did not express unmitigated pleasure, 'this is a surprise. You told me you would not be down till late in the evening.'

'Yes, my dear: but the fine morning tempted me. I found my engagements would stand over till Monday or Tuesday, so I put myself into the eight o'clock train, and arrived at The Cottage just an hour after you and your friends had left for your picnic. So I walked over to join you. I hope I am not in the way.'

'Of course not,' said Bessie. 'I'm afraid you'll find us hardly the kind of company you are accustomed to; but if you will put up with our roughness and noise we shall feel honoured.'

'We are going to get lunch ready,' said Blanche. 'You grown-ups will find us under Evelyn's tree when you're hungry, and you'd better accommodate yourselves to be hungry soon.'

'Or you may find a dearth of provisions,' interjected Reg. 'I feel in a demolishing humour.'

The troop rushed off, leaving the three elder girls and Dr. Rylance standing in the hall, listlessly contemplative of Sir Tristram's dinted breast-plate, hacked by Roundhead pikes at Marston Moor.

CHAPTER V
DR. RYLANCE ASSERTS HIMSELF

The luncheon under Evelyn's tree took a cooler shade from Dr. Rylance's presence than from the far-reaching branches of the cedar. His politeness made the whole business different from what it would have been without him.

Blanche and the boys, accustomed to abandon themselves to frantic joviality at any outdoor feast of their own contriving, now withdrew into the background, and established themselves behind the trunk of the tree, in which retirement they kept up an insane giggling, varied by low and secret discourse, and from which shelter they issued forth stealthily, one by one, to pounce with crafty hands upon the provisions. These unmannerly proceedings were ignored by the elders, but they exercised a harassing influence upon poor little Eva, who had been told to sit quietly by Bessie, and who watched her brothers' raids with round-eyed wonder, and listened with envious ears to that distracting laughter behind the tree.

'Did you see Horry take quite half the cake, just now?' she whispered to Bessie, in the midst of a polite conversation about nothing particular.

And anon she murmured in horrified wonder, after a stolen peep behind the tree, 'Reg is taking off Dr. Rylance.'

The grown-up luncheon party was not lively. Tongue and chicken, pigeon-pie, cheese-cakes, tarts, cake, fruit—all had been neatly spread upon a tablecloth laid on the soft turf. Nothing had been forgotten. There were plates and knives and forks enough for everybody—picnicking being a business thoroughly well understood at The Knoll; but there was a good deal wanting in the guests.

Ida was thoughtful, Urania obviously sullen, Bessie amiably stupid; but Dr. Rylance appeared to think that they were all enjoying themselves intensely.

'Now this is what I call really delightful,' he said, as he poured out the sparkling Devonshire cider with as stately a turn of his wrist as if the liquor had been Cliquot or Roederer. 'An open-air luncheon on such a day as this is positively inspiring, and to a man who has breakfasted at seven o'clock on a cup of tea and a morsel of dry toast—thanks, yes, I prefer the wing if no one else will have it—such an unceremonious meal is doubly welcome. I'm so glad I found you. Lucky, wasn't it, Ranie?'

He smiled at his daughter, as if deprecating that stolid expression of hers, which would have been eminently appropriate to the funeral of an indifferent acquaintance,—a total absence of all feeling, a grave nullity.

'I don't see anything lucky in so simple a fact,' answered Urania. 'You were told we had come here, and you came here after us.'

'You might have changed your minds at the last moment and gone somewhere else. Might you not, now, Miss Palliser?'

'Yes, if we had been very frivolous people; but as to-day's exploration of the Abbey was planned last night, it would have indicated great weakness of mind if we had been tempted into any other direction,' answered Ida, feeling somewhat sorry for Dr. Rylance.

The coldest heart might compassionate a man cursed in such a disagreeable daughter.

'I am very glad you were not weak-minded, and that I was so fortunate as to find you,' said the doctor, addressing himself henceforward exclusively to Ida and her friend.

Bessie took care of his creature-comforts with a matronly hospitality which sat well upon her. She cut thin slices of tongue, she fished out savouriest bits of pigeon and egg, when he passed, by a natural transition, from chicken to pie. She was quite distressed because he did not care for tarts or cake. But the doctor's appetite, unlike that of the young people on the other side of the cedar, had its limits. He had satisfied his hunger long before they had, and was ready to show Miss Palliser the gardens.

'They are fine old gardens,' he said, approvingly. 'Perhaps their chief beauty is that they have not a single modern improvement. They are as old-fashioned as the gardens of Sion Abbey, before the good queen Bess ousted the nuns to make room for the Percies.'

They all rose and walked slowly away from the cedar, leaving the fragments of the feast to Blanche and her three brothers. Eva stayed behind, to make one of that exuberant group, and to see Reg 'take off' Urania and her father. His mimicry was cordially admired, though it was not always clear to his audience which was the doctor and which was his daughter. A stare, a strut, a toss, an affected drawl were the leading features of each characterization.

'I had no opportunity of congratulating you on your triumphs the other day, Miss Palliser,' said Dr. Rylance, who had somehow managed that Ida and he should be side by side, and a little in advance of the other two. 'But, believe me, I most heartily sympathized with you in the delight of your success.'

'Delight?' echoed Ida. 'Do you think there was any real pleasure for me in receiving a gift from the hands of Miss Pew, who has done all she could do to make me feel the disadvantages of my position, from the day I first entered her house to the day I last left it? The prizes gave me no pleasure. They have no value in my mind, except as an evidence that I have made the most of my opportunities at Mauleverer, in spite of my contempt for my schoolmistress.'

'You dislike her intensely, I see.'

'She has made me dislike her. I never knew unkindness till I knew her. I never felt the sting of poverty till she made me feel all its sharpness. I never knew that I was steeped in sinful pride until she humiliated me.'

'Your days of honour and happiness will come, said the doctor, 'days when you will think no more of Miss Pew than of an insect which once stung you.'

'Thank you for the comforting forecast,' answered Ida, lightly. 'But it is easy to prophesy good fortune.'

'Easy, and safe, in such a case as yours. I can sympathize with you better than you may suppose, Miss Palliser. I have had to fight my battle. I was not always Dr. Rylance, of Cavendish Square; and I did not enter a world in which there was a fine estate waiting for me, like the owner of this place.'

'But you have conquered fortune, and by your own talents,' said Ida. 'That must be a proud thought.'

Dr. Rylance, who was not utterly without knowledge of himself, smiled at the compliment. He knew it was by tact and address, smooth speech and clean linen, that he had conquered fortune, rather than by shining abilities. Yet he valued himself not the less on that account. In his mind tact ranked higher than genius, since it was his own peculiar gift: just as blue ginger-jars were better than Sevres, because he, Dr. Rylance, was a collector of ginger-jars. He approved of himself so completely that even his littlenesses were great in his own eyes.

'I have worked hard,' he said, complacently, 'and I have been patient. But now, when my work is done, and my place in the world fixed, I begin to find life somewhat barren. A man ought to reap some reward—something fairer and sweeter than pounds, shillings, and pence, for a life of labour and care.'

'No doubt,' assented Ida, receiving this remark as abstract philosophy, rather than as having a personal meaning. 'But I think I should consider pounds, shillings, and pence a very fair reward, if I only had enough of them.'

'Yes, now, when you are smarting under the insolence of a purse-proud schoolmistress, but years hence, when you have won independence, you will feel disappointed if you have won nothing better.'

'What could be better?'

'Sympathetic companionship—a love worthy to influence your life.'

Ida looked up at the doctor with naïve surprise. Good heavens, was this middle-aged gentleman going to drop into sentiment, as Silas Wegg dropped into poetry? She glanced back at the other two. Happily they were close at hand.

'What have you done with the children, Bessie?' asked Ida, as if she were suddenly distracted with anxiety about their fate.

'Left them to their own devices. I hope they will not quite kill themselves. We are all to meet in the stable yard at four, so that we may be with Aunt Betsy at five.'

'Don't you think papa and I had better walk gently home?' suggested Urania; 'I am sure it would be cruel to inflict such an immense party upon Miss Wendover.'

'Nonsense,' exclaimed Bessie. 'Why, if all old Pew's school was to march in upon her, without a moment's notice Aunt Betsy would not be put out of the way one little bit. If Queen Victoria were to drop in unexpectedly to luncheon, my aunt would be as cool as one of her own early cucumbers, and would insist on showing the Queen her stables, and possibly her pigs.'

'How do you know that?' asked Ida.

'Because she never had a visitor yet whom she did not drag into her stables, from archbishops downwards; and I don't suppose she'd draw the line at a queen,' answered Bessie, with conviction.

'I am going to drink tea with Miss Wendover, whatever Urania may do,' said Dr. Rylance, who felt that the time had come when he must assert himself. 'I am out for a day's pleasure, and I mean to drink the cup to the dregs.'

Urania looked at her father with absolute consternation. He was transformed; he had become a new person; he was forgetting himself in a ridiculous manner; letting down his dignity to an alarming extent. Dr. Rylance, the fashionable physician, the man whose nice touch adjusted the nerves of the aristocracy, to disport himself with unkempt, bare-handed young Wendovers! It was an upheaval of things which struck horror to Urania's soul. Easy, after beholding such a moral convulsion, to believe that the Wight had once been part of the mainland; or even that Ireland had originally been joined to Spain.

They all roamed into the rose-garden, where there were alleys of standard rose-trees, planted upon grass that was soft and springy under the foot. They went into the old vineries, where the big bunches of grapes were purpling in the gentle heat. Dr. Rylance went everywhere, and he contrived always to be near Ida Palliser.

He did not again lapse into sentiment, and he made himself fairly agreeable, in his somewhat stilted fashion. Ida accepted his attention with a charming unconsciousness; but she was perfectly conscious of Urania's vexation, and that gave a zest to the whole thing.

'Well, Ida, what do you think of Kingthorpe Abbey?' asked Bessie, when they had seen everything, even to the stoats and weasels, and various vermin nailed flat against the stable wall, and were waiting for Robin to be harnessed.

'It is a noble old place. It is simply perfect. I wonder your cousin can live away from it.'

'Oh, Brian's chief delight is in roaming about the world. The Abbey is thrown away upon him. He ought to have been an explorer or a missionary. However, he is expected home in a month, and you will be able to judge for yourself whether he deserves to be master of this old place. I only wish it belonged to the other Brian.'

'The other Brian is your favourite.'

'He is ever so much nicer than his cousin—at least, the children and I like him best. My father swears by the head of the house.'

'I think I would rather accept the Colonel's judgment than yours, Bess,' said Ida. 'You are so impulsive in your likings.'

'Don't say that I am wanting in judgment,' urged Bessie, coaxingly, 'for you know how dearly I love you. You will see the two Brians, I hope, before your holidays are over; and then you can make your own selection. Brian Walford will be with us for my birthday picnic, I daresay, wherever he may be now. I believe he is mooning away his time in Herefordshire, with his mother's people.'

'Is his father dead?'

'Yes, mother and father both, ages ago, in the days when I was a hard-hearted little wretch, and thought it a treat to go into mourning, and rather nice to be able to tell everybody, "Uncle Walford's dead. He had a fit, and he never speaked any more." It was news, you know, and in a village that goes for something.'

After a lengthy discussion, and some squabbling, it was decided that the children were to have the benefit of the jaunting-car for the homeward journey, and that Dr. Rylance and the three young ladies were to walk, attended by Reginald, who insisted upon attaching himself to their service, volunteering to show them the very nearest way through a wood, and across a field, and over a common, and down a lane, which led straight to the gate of Aunt Betsy's orchard.

Urania wore fashionable boots, and considered walking exercise a superstition of medical men and old-fashioned people; yet she stoutly refused a seat in the car.

'No, thanks, Horatio; I know your pony too well. I'd rather trust myself upon my own feet.'

'There's more danger in your high heels than in my pony, retorted Horatio. 'I shouldn't wonder if you dropped in for a sprained ankle before you got home.'

Urania risked the sprained ankle. She began to limp before she had emerged from the wood. She hobbled painfully along the rugged footpath between the yellow wheat. She was obliged to sit down and rest upon a furzy hillock on the common, good-natured Bess keeping her company, while Ida and Reginald were half a mile ahead with Dr. Rylance. Her delicate complexion was unbecomingly flushed by the time she and Bessie arrived wearily at the little gate opening into Miss Wendover's orchard.

There were only some iron hurdles between Aunt Betsy's orchard and the lawn before Aunt Betsy's drawing-room. The house was characteristic of the lady. It was a long red-brick cottage, solid, substantial, roomy, eschewing ornament, but beautified in the eyes of most people by an air of supreme comfort, cleanliness, and general well-being. In all Kingthorpe there were no rooms so cool as Aunt Betsy's in summer—none so warm in winter. The cottage had originally been the homestead of a small grass-farm, which had been bequeathed to Betsy Wendover by her father, familiarly known as the Old Squire, the chief landowner in that part of the country. With this farm of about two hundred and fifty acres of the most fertile pasture land in Hampshire and an income of seven hundred a year from consols, Miss Wendover found herself passing rich. She built a drawing-room with wide windows opening on to the lawn, and a bed-room with a covered balcony over the drawing-room. These additional rooms made the homestead all-sufficient for a lady of Aunt Betsy's simple habits. She was hospitality itself, receiving her friends in a large-hearted, gentleman-like style, keeping open house for man and beast, proud of her wine, still prouder of her garden and greenhouses, proudest of her stables; fond of this life, and of her many comforts, yet without a particle of selfishness; ready to leave her cosy fireside at a moment's notice on the bitterest winter night, to go and nurse a sick child, or comfort a dying woman; religious without ostentation, charitable without weakness, stern to resent an injury, implacable against an insult.

A refreshing sight, yet not altogether a pleasant one for Miss Rylance, met the eyes of the two young ladies as they neared the little iron gate opening from the orchard to the lawn. A couple of tea-tables had been brought out upon the grass before the drawing-room window. The youngsters were busily engaged at one table, Blanche pouring out tea, while her brothers and small sister made havoc with cake and fruit, home-made bread and butter, and jams of various hues. At the other table, less lavishly but more elegantly furnished, sat Miss Wendover and Ida Palliser, with Dr. Rylance comfortably established in a Buckinghamshire wickerwork chair between them.

'Does not that look a picture of comfort?' exclaimed Bessie.

'My father seems to be making himself very comfortable,' said Urania.

She hobbled across the lawn, and sank exhausted into a low chair, near her parent.

'My poor child, how dilapidated you look after your walk,' said Dr. Rylance; 'Miss Palliser and I enjoyed it immensely.'

'I cannot boast of Miss Palliser's robust health,' retorted Urania contemptuously, as if good health were a sign of vulgarity. 'I had my neuralgia all last night.'

Whenever the course of events proved objectionable, Miss Rylance took refuge in a complaint which she called her neuralgia, indicating that it was a species of disorder peculiar to herself, and of a superior quality to everybody else's neuralgia.

'You should live in the open air, like my sunburnt young friends yonder,' said the doctor, with a glance at the table where the young Wendovers were stuffing themselves; 'I am sure they never complain of neuralgia.'

Urania looked daggers but spoke none.

It was a wearisome afternoon for that injured young lady. Dr. Rylance dawdled over his tea, handed teacups and bread and butter, was assiduous with the sugar basin, devoted with the cream jug, talked and laughed with Miss Palliser, as if they had a world of ideas in common, and made himself altogether objectionable to his only child.

By-and-by, when there was a general adjournment to the greenhouses and stables, Urania contrived to slip her arm through her father's.

'I thought I told you that Miss Palliser was my favourite aversion, papa,' she said, tremulous with angry feeling.

'I have some faint idea that you did express yourself unfavourably about her,' answered the doctor, with his consulting-room urbanity, 'but I am at a loss to understand your antipathy. The girl is positively charming, as frank as the sunshine, and full of brains.'

'I know her. You do not,' said Urania tersely.

'My dear, it is the speciality of men in my profession to make rapid judgments.'

'Yes, and very often to make them wrong. I was never so much annoyed in my life. I consider your attention to that girl a deliberate insult to me; a girl with whom I never could get on—who has said the rudest things to me.'

'Can I be uncivil to a friend of your friend Bessie?'

'There is a wide distance between being uncivil and being obsequiously, ridiculously attentive.'

'Urania,' said the doctor in his gravest voice, 'I have allowed you to have your own way in most things, and I believe your life has been a pleasant one.'

'Of course, papa. I never said otherwise.'

'Very well, my dear, then you must be good enough to let me take my own way of making life pleasant to myself, and you must not take upon yourself to dictate what degree of civility I am to show to Miss Palliser, or to any other lady.'

Urania held her peace after this. It was the first deliberate snub she had ever received from her father, and she added it to her lengthy score against Ida.

CHAPTER VI
A BIRTHDAY FEAST

Ida Palliser's holidays were coming to an end, like a tale that is told. There was only one day more left, but that day was to be especially glorious; for it was Bessie Wendover's birthday, a day which from time immemorial — or, at all events, ever since Bessie was ten years old — had been sacred to certain games or festivities — a modernized worship of the great god Pan.

Sad was it for Bessie and all the junior Wendovers when the seventh of September dawned with gray skies, or east winds, rain, or hail. It was usually a brilliant day. The clerk of the weather appeared favourably disposed to the warm-hearted Bessie.

On this particular occasion the preparations for the festival were on a grander scale than usual, in honour of Ida, who was on the eve of departure. A cruel, cruel car was to carry her off to Winchester at six o'clock in the morning after the birthday; the railway station was to swallow her up alive; the train was to rush off with her, like a fiery dragon carrying off the princess of fairy tale; and the youthful Wendovers were to be left lamenting.

In six happy weeks their enthusiasm for their young guest had known no abatement. She had realized their fondest anticipations. She had entered into their young lives and made herself a part of them. She had given herself up, heart and soul, to childish things and foolish things, to please these devoted admirers; and the long summer holiday had been very sweet to her. The open-air life — the balmy noontides in woods and meadows, beside wandering trout streams — on the breezy hill-tops — the afternoon tea-drinking in gardens and orchards — the novels read aloud, seated in the heart of some fine old tree, with her auditors perched on the branches round about her, like gigantic birds — the boating excursions on a river with more weeds than water in it — the jaunts to Winchester, and dreamy afternoons in the cathedral — all had been delicious. She had lived in an atmosphere of homely domestic love, among people who valued her for herself, and did not calculate the cost of her gowns, or despise her because she had so few. The old church was lovely in her eyes; the old vicar and his wife had taken a fancy to her. Everything at Kingthorpe was delightful, except Urania. She certainly was a drawback; but she had been tolerably civil since the first day at the Abbey.

Ida had spent many an hour at the Abbey since that first inspection. She knew every room in the house—the sunniest windows—the books in the long library, with its jutting wings between the windows, and cosy nooks for study. She knew almost every tree in the park, and the mild faces of the deer looking gravely reproachful, as if asking what business she had there. She had lain asleep on the sloping bank above the lake on drowsy afternoons, tired by wandering far a-field with her young esquires. She knew the Abbey by heart—better than even Urania knew it; though she had used that phrase to express utter satiety. Ida Palliser had a deeper love of natural beauty, a stronger appreciation of all that made the old place interesting. She had a curious feeling, too, about the absent master of that grave, gray old house—a fond, romantic dream, which she would not for the wealth of India have revealed to mortal ear, that in the days to come Brian's life would be in somewise linked with hers. Perhaps this foolish thought was engendered of the blankness of her own life, a stage on which the players had been so few that this figure of an unknown young man assumed undue proportions.

Then, again, the fact that she could hear very little about Mr. Wendover from his cousins, stimulated her curiosity about him, and intensified her interest in him. Brian's merits were a subject which the Wendover children always shirked, or passed over so lightly that Ida was no wiser for her questioning; and maidenly reserve forbade her too eager inquiry.

About Brian Walford, the son of Parson Wendover, youngest of the three brothers, for seven years vicar of a parish near Hereford, and for the last twelve years at rest in the village churchyard, the young Wendovers had plenty to say. He was good-looking, they assured Ida. She would inevitably fall in love with him when they met. He was the cleverest young man in England, and was certain to finish his career as Lord Chancellor, despite the humility of his present stage of being.

'He has no fortune, I suppose?' hazarded Ida, in a conversation with Horatio.

She did not ask the question from any interest in the subject. Brian Walford was a being whose image never presented itself to her mind. She only made the remark for the sake of saying something.

'Not a denarius,' said Horry, who liked occasionally to be classical. 'But what of that? If I were as clever as Brian I shouldn't mind how poor I was. With his talents he is sure to get to the top of the tree.'

'What can he do?' asked Ida.

'Ride a bicycle better than any man I know.'

'What else?'

'Sing a first-rate comic song.'

'What else?'

'Get longer breaks at billiards than any fellow I ever played with.'

'What else?'

'Pick the winner out of a score of race-horses in the preliminary canter.'

'Those are great gifts, I have no doubt,' said Ida. 'But do eminent lawyers, in a general way, win their advancement by riding bicycles and singing comic songs?'

'Don't sneer, Ida. When a fellow is clever in one thing he is clever in other things. Genius is many-sided, universal. Carlyle says as much. If Napoleon Bonaparte had not been a great general, he would have been a great writer like Voltaire—or a great lawyer like Thurlow.'

From this time forward Ida had an image of Brian Walford in her mind. It was the picture of a vapid youth, fair-haired, with thin moustache elaborately trained, and thinner whiskers—a fribble that gave half its little mind to its collar, and the other half to its boots. Such images are photographed in a flash of lightning on the sensitive brain of youth, and are naturally more often false guesses than true ones.

There was delightful riot in the house of the Wendovers on the night before the picnic. The Colonel had developed a cold and cough within the last week, so he and his wife had jogged off to Bournemouth, in the T-cart, with one portmanteau and one servant, leaving Bessie mistress of all things. It was a grief to Mrs. Wendover to be separated from home and children at any time, and she was especially regretful at being absent on her eldest daughter's birthday; but the Colonel was paramount. If his cough could be cured by sea air, to the sea he must go, with his faithful wife in attendance upon him.

'Don't let the children turn the house quite out of windows, darling,' said Mrs. Wendover, at the moment of parting.

'No, mother dear, we are all going to be goodness itself.'

'I know, dears, you always are. And I hope you will all enjoy yourselves.'

'We're sure to do that, mother,' answered Reginald, with a cheerfulness that seemed almost heartless.

The departing parent would not have liked them to be unhappy, but a few natural tears would have been a pleasing tribute. Not a tear was shed. Even the little Eva skipped joyously on the doorstep as the phaeton drove away. The idea of the picnic was all-absorbing.

The Colonel and his wife were to spend a week at Bournemouth. Ida would see them no more this year.

'You must come again next summer, Mrs. Wendover said heartily, as she kissed her daughter's friend.

'Of course she must,' cried Horry. 'She is coming every summer. She is one of the institutions of Kingthorpe. I only wonder how we ever managed to get on so long without her.'

All that evening was devoted to the packing of hampers, and to general skirmishing. The picnic was to be held on the highest hill-top between Kingthorpe and Winchester, one of those little Lebanons, fair and green, on which the yew-trees flourished like the cedars of the East, but with a sturdy British air that was all their own.

The birthday dawned with the soft pearly gray and tender opal tints which presage a fair noontide. Before six o'clock the children had all besieged Bessie's door, with noisy tappings and louder congratulations. At seven, they were all seated at breakfast, the table strewn with birthday gifts, mostly of that useless and semi-idiotic character peculiar to such tributes—ormolu inkstands, holding a thimbleful of ink—penholders warranted to break before they have been used three times—purses with impossible snaps—photograph frames and pomatum-pots.

Bessie pretended to be enraptured with everything. The purse Horry gave her was 'too lovely.' Reginald's penholder was the very thing she had been wanting for an age. Dear little Eva's pomatum-pot was perfection. The point-lace handkerchief Ida had worked in secret was exquisite. Blanche's crochet slippers were so lovely that their not being big enough was hardly a fault. They were much too pretty to be worn. Urania contributed a more costly gift, in the shape of a perfume cabinet, all cut-glass, walnut-wood, and ormolu.

'Urania's presents are always meant to crush one,' said Blanche disrespectfully; 'they are like the shields and bracelets those rude soldiers flung at poor Tarpeia.'

Urania was to be one of the picnic party. She was to be the only stranger present. There had been a disappointment about the two cousins. Neither Brian had accepted the annual summons. One was supposed to be still in

Norway, the other had neglected to answer the letter which had been sent more than a week ago to his address in Herefordshire.

'I'm afraid you'll find it dreadfully like our every-day picnics,' Bessie said to Ida, as they were starting.

'I shall be satisfied if it be half as pleasant.'

'Ah, it would have been nice enough if the two Brians had been with us. Brian Walford is so amusing.'

'He would have sung comic songs, I suppose?' said Ida rather contemptuously.

'Oh, no; you must not suppose that he is always singing comic songs. He is one of those versatile people who can do anything.'

'I don't want to be rude about your own flesh and blood Bess, but in a general way I detest versatile people,' said Ida.

'What a queer girl you are, Ida! I'm afraid you have taken a dislike to Brian Walford,' complained Bessie.

'No,' said Ida, deep in thought,—the two girls were standing at the hall-door, waiting for the carriage,—'it is not that.'

'You like the idea of the other Brian better?'

Ida's wild-rose bloom deepened to a rich carnation.

'Oh, Ida,' cried Bessie; 'do you remember what you said about marrying for money?'

'It was a revolting sentiment; but it was wrung from me by the infinite vexations of poverty.'

'Wouldn't it be too lovely if Brian the Great were to fall in love with you, and ask you to be mistress of that dear old Abbey which you admire so much?

'Don't be ecstatic, Bessie. I shall never be the mistress of the Abbey. I was not born under a propitious star. There must have been a very ugly concatenation of planets ruling the heavens at the hour of my birth. You see, Brian the Great does not even put himself in the way of falling captive to my charms.'

This was said half in sport, half in bitterness; indeed, there was a bitter flavour in much of Ida Palliser's mirth. She was thinking of the stories she had read in which a woman had but to be young and lovely, and all creation bowed down to her. Yet her beauty had been for the most part a cause of vexation, and had made people hate her. She had been infinitely happy during the last six weeks; but embodied hatred had been close at hand in the presence of Miss Rylance; and if anyone had fallen in love with her during that time, it was the wrong person.

The young ladies were to go in the landau, leaving the exclusive enjoyment of Robin's variable humours to Horatio and the juveniles. There was a general idea that Robin, in conjunction with a hilly country, might be sooner or later fatal to the young Wendovers; but they went on driving him, nevertheless, as everybody knew that if he did ultimately prove disastrous to them it would be with the best intentions and without loss of temper.

Bessie and Ida took their seats in the roomy carriage, Reginald mounted to the perch beside the coachman, and they drove triumphantly through the village to the gate of Dr. Rylance's cottage, where Urania stood waiting for them.

'I hope we haven't kept you long?' said Bessie.

'Not more than a quarter of an hour,' answered Urania, meekly; 'but that seems rather long in a broiling sun. You always have such insufferably hot weather on your birthdays, Bessie.'

'It will be cool enough on the hills by-and-by,' said Bess, apologetically.

'I daresay there will be a cold wind,' returned Urania, who wore an unmistakable air of discontent. 'There generally is on these unnatural September days.'

'One would think you bore a grudge against the month of September because I was born in it,' retorted Bessie. And then, remembering her obligations, she hastened to add, 'How can I thank you sufficiently for that exquisite scent-case? It is far too lovely.'

'I am very glad you like it. One hardly knows what to choose.'

Miss Rylance had taken her seat in the landau by this time, and they were bowling along the smooth high road at that gentle jog-trot pace affected by a country gentleman's coachman.

The day was heavenly; the wind due south; a day on which life—mere sensual existence—is a delight. The landscape still wore its richest summer beauty—not a leaf had fallen. They were going upward, to the hilly region between Kingthorpe and Winchester, to a spot where there was a table-shaped edifice of stones, supposed to be of Druidic origin.

The young Wendovers were profoundly indifferent to the Druids, and to that hypothetical race who lived ages before the Druids, and have broken out all over the earth in stony excrescences, as yet vaguely classified. That three-legged granite table, whose origin was lost in the remoteness of past time, seemed to the young Wendovers a thing that had been created expressly for their amusement, to be climbed upon or crawled under as the fancy moved them. It was a capital rallying-point for a picnic or a gipsy tea-drinking.

'We are to have no grown-ups to-day,' said Reginald, looking down from his place beside the coachman. 'The pater and mater are away, and Aunt Betsy has a headache; so we can have things all our own way.'

'You are mistaken, Reginald,' said Urania; 'my father is going to join us by-and-by. I hope he won't be considered an interloper. I told him that it was to be a young party, and that I was sure he would be in the way; but he wouldn't take my advice. He is going to ride over in the broiling sun. Very foolish, I think.'

'I thought Dr. Rylance was in London?'

'He was till last night. He came down on purpose to be at your picnic.'

'I am sure I feel honoured,' said Bessie.

'Do you? I don't think *you* are the attraction,' answered Urania, with a cantankerous glance at Miss Palliser.

Ida's dark eyes were looking far away across the hills. It seemed as if she neither heard Miss Rylance's speech nor saw the sneer which emphasized it.

Dr. Rylance's substantial hunter came plodding over the turfy ridge behind them five minutes afterwards, and presently he was riding at a measured trot beside the carriage door, congratulating Bessie on the beauty of the day, and saying civil things to every one.

'I could not resist the temptation to give myself a day's idleness in the Hampshire air,' he said.

Reginald felt unutterably savage. What a trouble-feast the man was. They would have to adapt the proceedings of the day to his middle-aged good manners. There could be no wild revelry, no freedom. Dr. Rylance was an embodiment of propriety.

Half-an-hour after dinner they were all scattered upon the hills.

Reginald, who cherished a secret passion for Ida, which was considerably in advance of his years, and who had calculated upon being her guide, philosopher, and friend all through the day, found himself ousted by the West End physician, who took complete possession of Miss Palliser, under the pretence of explaining the history—altogether speculative—of the spot. He discoursed eloquently about the Druids, expatiated upon the City of Winchester, dozing in the sunshine yonder, among its fat water meadows.

He talked of the Saxons and the Normans, of William of Wykeham, and his successors, until poor Ida felt sick and faint from very weariness. It was all very delightful talk, no doubt—the polished utterance of a man who read his *Saturday Review* and *Athenaeum* diligently, saw an occasional number of *Fors Clavigera*, and even skimmed the more aesthetic papers in the *Architect*; but to Ida this expression of modern culture was all weariness. She would rather have been racing those wild young Wendovers down the slippery hill-side, on which they were perilling their necks; she would rather have been lying beside the lake in Kingthorpe Park, reading her well-thumbed Tennyson, or her shabby little Keats.

Her thoughts had wandered ever so far away when she was called back to the work-a-day world by finding that Dr. Rylance's conversation had suddenly slipped from archaeology into a more personal tone.

'Are you really going away to-morrow?' he asked.

'Yes,' answered Ida, sadly, looking at one of the last of the butterflies, whose brief summertide of existence was wearing to its close, like her own.

'You are going back to Maulevcrer Manor?'

'Yes. I have another half-year of bondage, I am going back to drudgery and self-contempt, to be brow-beaten by Miss Pew, and looked down upon by most of her pupils. The girls in my own class are very fond of me, but I'm afraid their fondness is half pity. The grown-up girls with happy homes and rich fathers despise me. I hardly wonder at it. Genteel poverty certainly is contemptible. There is nothing debasing in a smock-frock or a fustian jacket. The labourers I see about Kingthorpe have a glorious air of independence, and I daresay are as proud, in their way, as if they were dukes. But shabby finery—genteel gowns worn threadbare: there is a deep degradation in those.'

'Not for you,' answered Dr. Rylance, earnestly, with an admiring look in his blue-gray eyes. They were somewhat handsome eyes when they did not put on their cruel expression. 'Not for you. Nothing could degrade, nothing could exalt you. You are superior to the accident of your surroundings.'

'It's very kind of you to say that; but it's a fallacy, all the same,' said Ida. 'Do you think Napoleon at St. Helena, squabbling with Sir Hudson Lowe, is as dignified a figure as Napoleon at the Tuileries, in the zenith of his power? But I ought not to be grumbling at fate. I have been happy for six sunshiny weeks. If I were to live to be a century old, I could never forget how good people at Kingthorpe have been to me. I will go back to my old slavery, and live upon the memory of that happiness.'

'Why should you go back to slavery?' asked Dr. Rylance, taking her hand in his and holding it with so strong a grasp that she could hardly have withdrawn it without violence. 'There is a home at Kingthorpe ready to receive you. If you have been happy there in the last few weeks, why not try if you can be happy there always? There is a house in Cavendish Square whose master would be proud to make you its mistress. Ida, we have seen very little of each other, and I may be precipitate in hazarding this offer; but I am as fond of you as if I had known you half a lifetime, and I believe that I could make your life happy.'

Ida Palliser's heart thrilled with a chill sense of horror and aversion. She had talked recklessly enough of her willingness to marry for money, and, lo! here was a prosperous man laying two handsomely furnished houses at her feet—a man of gentlemanlike bearing, good-looking, well-informed, well-spoken, with no signs of age in his well-preserved face and figure; a man whom any woman, friendless, portionless, a mere waif upon earth's surface, at the mercy of all the winds that blow, ought proudly and gladly to accept for her husband.

No, too bold had been her challenge to fate. She had said that she would marry any honest man who would lift her out of the quagmire of poverty: but she was not prepared to accept Dr. Rylance's offer, generous as it sounded. She would rather go back to the old treadmill, and her old fights with Miss Pew, than reign supreme over the dainty cottage at Kingthorpe and the house in Cavendish Square. Her time had not come.

Dr. Rylance had not risen to eloquence in making his offer; and Ida's reply was in plainest words.

'I am very sorry,' she faltered. 'I feel that it is very good of you to make such a proposal; but I cannot accept it.'

'There is some one else,' said the doctor. 'Your heart is given away already.'

'No,' she answered sadly; 'my heart is like an empty sepulchre.'

'Then why should I not hope to win you? I have been hasty, no doubt: but I want if possible to prevent your return to that odious school. If you would but make me happy by saying yes, you could stay with your kind friends at The Knoll till the day that makes you mistress of my house. We might be married in time to spend November in Italy. It is the nicest month for Rome. You have never seen Italy, perhaps?'

'No. I have seen very little that is worth seeing.'

'Ida, why will you not say yes? Do you doubt that I should try my uttermost to make you happy?'

'No,' she answered gravely, 'but I doubt my own capacity for that kind of happiness.'

Dr. Rylance was deeply wounded. He had been petted and admired by women during the ten years of his widowhood, favoured and a favourite everywhere. He had made up his mind deliberately to marry this penniless girl. Looked at from a worldling's point of view, it would seem, at the first glance, an utterly disadvantageous alliance: but Dr. Rylance had an eye that could sweep over horizons other than are revealed to the average gaze, and he told himself that so lovely a woman as Ida Palliser must inevitably become the fashion in that particular society which Dr. Rylance most affected: and a wife famed for her beauty and elegance would assuredly be of more advantage to a fashionable physician than a common-place wife with a fortune. Dr. Rylance liked money; but he liked it only for what it could buy. He had no sons, and he was much too fond of himself to lead laborious days in order to leave a large fortune to his daughter. He had bought a lease of his London house, which would last his time; he had bought the freehold of the Kingthorpe cottage; and he was living up to his income. When he died there would be two houses of furniture, plate, pictures, horses and carriages, and the Kingthorpe cottage, to be realized for Urania. He estimated these roughly as worth between six and seven thousand pounds, and he considered seven thousand pounds an ample fortune for his only daughter. Urania was in happy ignorance of the modesty of his views. She imagined herself an heiress on a much larger scale.

To offer himself to a penniless girl of whose belongings he knew absolutely nothing, and to be peremptorily refused! Dr. Rylance could hardly believe such a thing possible. The girl must be trifling with him, playing her fish, with the fixed intention of landing him presently. It was in the nature of girls to do that kind of thing. 'Why do you reject me?' he asked seriously; 'is it because I am old enough to be your father?'

'No, I would marry a man old enough to be my grandfather if I loved him,' answered Ida, with cruel candour.

'And I am to understand that your refusal is irrevocable? he urged.

'Quite irrevocable. But I hope you believe that I am grateful for the honour you have done me.'

'That is the correct thing to say upon such occasions, answered Dr. Rylance, coldly; 'I wonder the sentence is not written in your copy books, among those moral aphorisms which are of so little use in after life.'

'The phrase may seem conventional, but in my case it means much more than usual,' said Ida; 'a girl who has neither money nor friends has good reason to be grateful when a gentleman asks her to be his wife.'

'I wish I could be grateful for your gratitude,' said Dr. Rylance, 'but I can't. I want your love, and nothing else. Is it on Urania's account that you reject me?' he urged. 'If you think that she would be a hindrance to your happiness, pray dismiss the thought. If she did not accommodate herself pleasantly to my choice her life would have to be spent apart from us. I would brook no rebellion.'

The cruel look had come into Dr. Rylance's eyes. He was desperately angry. He was surprised, humiliated, indignant. Never had the possibility of rejection occurred to him. It had been for him to decide whether he would or would not take this girl for his wife; and after due consideration of her merits and all surrounding circumstances, he had decided that he would take her.

'Is my daughter the stumbling-block?' he urged.

'No,' she answered, 'there is no stumbling-block. I would marry you to-morrow, if I felt that I could love you as a wife ought to love her husband. I said once—only a little while ago—that I would marry for money. I find that I am not so base as I thought myself.'

'Perhaps the temptation is not large enough,' said Dr. Rylance. 'If I had been Brian Wendover, and the owner of Kingthorpe Abbey, you would hardly have rejected me so lightly.'

Ida crimsoned to the roots of her hair. The shaft went home. It was as if Dr. Rylance had been inside her mind and knew all the foolish day-dreams she had dreamed in the idle summer afternoons, under the spreading cedar branches, or beside the lake in the Abbey grounds. Before she had time to express her resentment a cluster of young Wendovers came sweeping down the greensward at her side, and in the next minute Blanche was hanging upon her bodily, like a lusty parasite strangling a slim young tree.

'Darling,' cried Blanche gaspingly, 'such news. Brian has come—cousin Brian—after all, though he thought he couldn't. But he made a great effort, and he has come all the way as fast as he could tear to be here on Bessie's birthday. Isn't it too jolly?'

'All the way from Norway?' asked Ida.

'Yes,' said Urania, who had been carried down the hill with the torrent of Wendovers, 'all the way from Norway. Isn't it nice of him?'

Blanche's frank face was brimming over with smiles. The boys were all laughing. How happy Brian's coming had made them!

Ida looked at them wonderingly.

'How pleased you all seem!' she said. 'I did not know you were so fond of your cousin. I thought it was the other you liked.'

'Oh, we like them both,' said Blanche, 'and it is so nice of Brian to come on purpose for Bessie's birthday. Do come and see him. He is on the top of the hill talking to Bess; and the kettle boils, and we are just going to have tea. We are all starving.'

'After such a dinner!' exclaimed Ida.

'Such a dinner, indeed!—two or three legs of fowls and a plate or so of pie!' ejaculated Reginald, contemptuously. 'I began to be hungry a quarter of an hour afterwards. Come and see Brian.'

Ida looked round her wonderingly, feeling as if she was in a dream.

Dr. Rylance had disappeared. Urania was smiling at her sweetly, more sweetly than it was her wont to smile at Ida Palliser.

'One would think she knew that I had refused her father,' mused Ida.

They all climbed the hill, the children talking perpetually, Ida unusually silent. The smoke of a gipsy fire was going up from a hollow near the Druid altar, and two figures were standing beside the altar; one, a young man, with his arm resting on the granite slab, and his head bent as he talked, with seeming earnestness, to Bessie Wendover. He turned as the crowd approached, and Bessie introduced him to Miss Palliser. 'My cousin Brian—my dearest friend Ida,' she said.

'She is desperately fond of the Abbey,' said Blanche; 'so I hope she will like you. "Love me, love my dog," says the proverb, so I suppose one might say, "Love my house, love me."'

Ida stood silent amidst her loquacious friends, looking at the stranger with a touch of wonder. No, this was not the image which she had pictured to herself. Mr. Wendover was very good-looking—interesting even; he had the kind of face which women call nice—a pale complexion, dreamy gray eyes, thin lips, a well-shaped nose, a fairly intellectual forehead. But the Brian of her fancies was a man of firmer mould, larger features, a more resolute air, an eye with more fire, a brow marked by stronger lines. For some unknown reason she had fancied the master of the Abbey like that Sir Tristram Wendover who had been so loyal a subject and so brave a soldier, and before whose portrait she had so often lingered in dreamy contemplation.

'And you have really come all the way from Norway to be at Bessie's picnic?' she faltered at last, feeling that she was expected to say something.

'I would have come a longer distance for the sake of such a pleasant meeting,' he answered, smiling at her.

'Bessie,' cried Blanche, who had been grovelling on her knees before the gipsy fire, 'the kettle will go off the boil if you don't make tea instantly. If it were not your birthday I should make it myself.'

'You may,' said Bessie, 'although it is my birthday.'

She had walked a little way apart with Urania, and they two were talking somewhat earnestly.

'Those girls seem to be plotting something,' said Reginald, 'a charade for to-night, perhaps. It's sure to be stupid if Urania's in it.'

'You mean that it will be too clever,' said Horatio.

'Yes, that kind of cleverness which is the essence of stupidity.'

While Bessie and Miss Rylance conversed apart, and all the younger Wendovers devoted their energies to the preparation of a tremendous meal, Ida and Brian Wendover stood face to face upon the breezy hill-top, the girl sorely embarrassed, the young man gazing at her as if he had never seen anything so lovely in his life.

'I have heard so much about you from Bessie,' he said after a silence which seemed long to both. 'Her letters for the last twelve months have been a perpetual paean—like one of the Homeric hymns, with you for the heroine. I had quite a dread of meeting you, feeling that, after having my expectations strung up to such a pitch, I must be disappointed. Nothing human could justify Bessie's enthusiasm.'

'Please don't talk about it. Bessie's one weak point is her affection for me. I am very grateful. I love her dearly, but she does her best to make me ridiculous.'

'I am beginning to think Bessie a very sensible girl,' said Brian, longing to say much more, so deeply was he impressed by this goddess in a holland gown, with glorious eyes shining upon him under the shadow of a coarse straw hat.

'Have you come back to Hampshire for good?' asked Ida, as they strolled towards Bessie and Urania.

'For good! No, I never stay long.'

'What a pity that lovely old Abbey should be deserted!'

'Yes, it is rather a shame, is it not? But then no one could expect a young man to live there except in the hunting season—or for the sake of the shooting.'

'Could anyone ever grow tired of such a place?' asked Ida.

She was wondering at the young man's indifferent air, as if that solemn abbey, those romantic gardens, were of no account to him. She supposed that this was in the nature of things. A man born lord of such an elysium would set little value upon his paradise. Was it not Eve's weariness of Eden which inclined her ear to the serpent?

And now the banquet was spread upon the short smooth turf, and everybody was ordered to sit down. They made a merry circle, with the tea-kettle in the centre, piles of cake, and bread and butter, and jam-pots surrounding it. Blanche and Horatio were the chief officiators, and were tremendously busy ministering to the wants of others, while they satisfied their own hunger and thirst hurriedly between whiles. The damsel sat on the grass with a big crockery teapot in her lap, while her brother watched and managed the kettle, and ran to and fro with cups and saucers. Bessie, as the guest of honour, was commanded to sit still and look on.

'Dreadfully babyish, isn't it?' said Urania, smiling with her superior air at Brian, who had helped himself to a crust of home-made bread, and a liberal supply of gooseberry jam.

'Uncommonly jolly,' he answered gaily. 'I confess to a weakness for bread and jam. I wish people always gave it at afternoon teas.'

'Has it not a slight flavour of the nursery?'

'Of course it has. But a nursery picnic is ever so much better than a swell garden-party, and bread and jam is a great deal more wholesome than salmon-mayonaise and Strasbourg pie. You may despise me as much as you like, Miss Rylance. I came here determined to enjoy myself.'

'That is the right spirit for a picnic,' said Ida, 'People with grand ideas are not wanted.'

'And I suppose in the evening you will join in the dumb charades, and play hide-and-seek in the garden, all among spiders and cockchafers.'

'I will do anything I am told to do,' answered Brian, cheerily. 'But I think the season of the cockchafer is over.'

'What has become of Dr. Rylance?' asked Bessie, looking about her as if she had only that moment missed him.

'I think he went back to the farm for his horse,' said Urania. 'I suppose he found our juvenile sports rather depressing.'

'Well, he paid us a compliment in coming at all,' answered Bessie, 'so we must forgive him for getting tired of us.'

The drive home was very merry, albeit Bessie and her friend were to part next morning—Ida to go back to slavery. They were both young enough to be able to enjoy the present hour, even on the edge of darkness.

Bessie clasped her friend's hand as they sat side by side in the landau.

'You must come to us at Christmas,' she whispered: 'I shall ask mother to invite you.'

Brian was full of talk and gaiety as they drove home through the dusk. He was very different from that ideal Brian of Ida's girlish fancy—the Brian who embodied all her favourite attributes, and had all the finest qualities of the hero of romance. But he was an agreeable, well-bred young man, bringing with him that knowledge of life and the active world which made his talk seem new and enlightening after the strictly local and domestic intellects of the good people with whom she had been living.

With the family at The Knoll conversation had been bounded by Winchester on one side, and Romsey on the other. There was an agreeable freshness in the society of a young man who could talk of all that was newest in European art and literature, and who knew how the world was being governed.

But this fund of information was hinted at rather than expressed. To-night Mr. Wendover seemed most inclined to mere nonsense talk—the lively nothings that please children. Of himself and his Norwegian adventures he said hardly anything.

'I suppose when a man has travelled so much he gets to look upon strange countries as a matter of course,' speculated Ida. 'If I had just come from Norway, I should talk of nothing else.'

The dumb-charades and hide-and-seek were played, but only by the lower orders, as Bessie called her younger brothers and sisters.

Ida strolled in the moonlit garden with Mr. Wendover, Bessie, Urania, and Mr. Ratcliffe, a very juvenile curate, who was Bessie's admirer and slave. Urania had no particular admirer. She felt that every one at Kingthorpe must needs behold her with mute worship; but there was no one so audacious as to give expression to the feeling; no one of sufficient importance to be favoured with her smiles. She looked forward to her first season in London next year, and then she would be called upon to make her selection.

'She is worldly to the tips of her fingers,' said Ida, as she and Bessie talked apart from the others for a few minutes: 'I wonder she does not try to captivate your cousin.'

'What—Brian? Oh, he is not at all in her line. He would not suit her a bit.'

'But don't you think it would suit her to be mistress of the Abbey?'

Bessie gave a little start, as if the idea were new.

'I don't think she has ever thought of him in that light,' she said.

'Don't you? If she hasn't she is not the girl I think her.'

'Oh, I know she is very worldly; but I don't think she's so bad as that.'

'Not so bad as to be capable of marrying for money—no, I suppose not,' said Ida, thoughtfully.

'I'm sure you would not, darling, said Bessie. 'You talked about it once, when you were feeling bitter; but I know that in your heart of hearts you never meant it. You are much too high-minded.'

'I am not a bit high-minded. All my high-mindedness, if I ever had any, has been squeezed out of me by poverty. My only idea is to escape from subjection and humiliation—a degrading bondage to vulgar-minded people.'

'But would the escape be worth having at the cost of your own degradation?' urged Bessie, who felt particularly heroic this evening, exalted by the moonlight, the loveliness of the garden, the thought of parting with her dearest friend. 'Marry for love, dearest. Sacrifice everything in this world rather than be false to yourself.'

'You dear little enthusiast, I may never be asked to make any such sacrifice. I have not much chance of suitors at Mauleverer, as you know— and as for falling in love—'

'Oh, you never know when the fatal moment may come. How do you like Brian?'

'He is very gentlemanlike; he seems very well informed.'

'He is immensely clever,' answered Bessie, almost offended at this languid praise; 'he is a man who might succeed in any line he chose for himself. Do you think him handsome?'

'He is certainly nice looking.'

'How cool you are! I had set my heart upon your liking him.'

'What could come of my liking?' asked Ida with a touch of bitterness. 'Is there a portionless girl in all England who would not like the master of Wendover Abbey?'

'But for his own sake,' urged Bessie, with a vexed air; 'surely he is worthy of being liked for his own sake, without a thought of the Abbey.'

'I cannot dissociate him from that lovely old house and gardens. Indeed, to my mind he rather belongs to the Abbey than the Abbey belongs to him. You see I knew the Abbey first.'

Here they were interrupted by Brian and Urania, and presently Ida found herself walking in the moonlight in a broad avenue of standard roses, at the end of the garden, with Mr. Wendover by her side, and the voices of the other three sounding ever so far away. On the other side of a low quickset hedge stretched a wide expanse of level meadow land, while in the farther distance rose the Wiltshire hills, and nearer the heathy highlands of the New Forest. The lamp-lit windows of Miss Wendover's cottage glimmered a little way off, across gardens and meadows.

'And so you are really going to leave us to-morrow morning?' said Brian, regretfully.

'By the eight o'clock train from Winchester. To-morrow evening I shall be sitting on a form in a big bare class-room, listening to the babble of a lot of girls pretending to learn their lessons.'

'Are you fond of teaching?'

'Just imagine to yourself the one occupation which is most odious to you, and then you may know how fond I am of teaching; and of school-girls; and of school-life altogether.'

'It is very hard that you should have to pursue such an uncongenial career.'

'It seems so to me; but, perhaps, that is my selfishness. I suppose half the people in this world have to live by work they hate.'

'Allowing for the number of people to whom all kind of work is hateful, I dare say you are right. But I think, in a general way, congenial work means successful work. No man hates the profession that brings him fame and money; but the doctor without patients, the briefless barrister, can hardly love law or medicine.'

He beguiled Ida into talking of her own life, with all its bitterness. There was something in his voice and manner which tempted her to confide in him. He seemed thoroughly sympathetic.

'I keep forgetting what strangers we are,' she said, apologizing for her unreserve.

'We are not strangers. I have heard of you from Bessie so much that I seem to have known you for years. I hope you will never think of me as a stranger.'

'I don't think I ever can, after this conversation. I am afraid you will think me horribly egotistical.'

She had been talking of her father and stepmother, the little brother she loved so fondly, dwelling with delight upon his perfections.

'I think you all that is good and noble. How I wish this were not your last evening at the Knoll!'

'Do you think I do not wish it? Hark, there's Bessie calling us.'

They went back to the house, and to the drawing-room, which wore quite a festive appearance, in honour of Bessie's birthday; ever so many extra candles dotted about, and a table laid with fruit and sandwiches, cake and claret-cup, the children evidently considering a superfluity of meals indispensable to a happy birthday. Blanche and her juniors were sitting about the room, in the last stage of exhaustion after hide-and-seek.

'This has been a capital birthday,' said Horatio, wiping the perspiration from his brow, and then filling for himself a bumper of claret-cup; 'and now we are going to dance. Blanche, give us the Faust Waltz, and go on playing till we tell you to leave off.'

Blanche, considerably blown, and with her hair like a mop, sat down and began to touch the piano with resolute fingers and forcible rhythm. ONE, two, three, ONE, two, three. The boys pushed the furniture into the corners. Brian offered himself to Ida; Bessie insisted upon surrendering the curate to Urania, and took one of her brothers for a partner; and the three couples went gliding round the pretty old room, the cool night breezes blowing in upon them from wide-open windows.

They danced and played, and sang and talked, till midnight chimed from the old eight-day clock in the hall,—a sound which struck almost as much consternation to Bessie's soul as if she had been Cinderella at the royal ball.

'TWELVE O'CLOCK! and the little ones all up!' she exclaimed, looking round the circle of towzled heads with remorseful eyes. 'What would mother say? And she told me she relied on my discretion! Go to bed, every one of you, this instant!'

'Oh, come, now,' remonstrated Blanche, 'there's no use in hustling us off like that, after letting us sit up hours after our proper time. I'm going to have another sandwich; and there's not a bit of good in leaving all those raspberry tarts. The servants won't thank us. *They* have as many jam tarts as they like.'

'You greedy little wretches; you have been doing nothing but eat all day,' said Ida. 'When I am back at Mauleverer I shall remember you only as machines for the consumption of pudding and jam. Obey your grown-up sister, and go to bed directly.'

'Grown up, indeed! How long has she been grown up, I should like to know!' exclaimed Blanche vindictively. 'She's only an inch and a quarter taller than me, and she's a mere dumpling compared with Horry.'

The lower orders were got rid of somehow — driven to their quarters, as it were, at the point of the bayonet, and then the grown-ups bade each other good-night; the curate escorting Miss Rylance to her home, and Brian going up to the top floor to a bachelor's room.

'Who is going to drive Miss Palliser to the station?' he asked, as they stood, candlestick in hand, at the foot of the stairs.

'I am, of course,' answered Reginald. 'Robin will spin us over the hills in no time. I've ordered the car for seven sharp.'

There was very little sleep for either Bessie or her guest that night. Both girls were excited by memories of the day that was past, and by thoughts of the day that was coming. Ida was brooding a little upon her disappointment in Brian Wendover. He had very pleasant manners, he seemed soft-hearted and sympathetic, he was very good-looking — but he was not the Brian of her dreams. That ideal personage had never existed outside her imagination. It was a shock to her girlish fancy. There was a sense of loss in her mind.

'I must be very silly,' she told herself, 'to make a fancy picture of a person, and to be vexed with him because he does not resemble my portrait.'

She was disappointed, and yet she was interested in this new acquaintance. He was the first really interesting young man she had ever met, and he was evidently interested in her. And then she pictured him at the Abbey, in the splendid solitude of those fine old rooms, leading the calm, studious life which Bessie had talked of — an altogether enviable life, Ida thought.

Mr. Wendover was in the dining-room at half-past six when the two girls went down to breakfast. All the others came trooping down a few minutes afterwards, Reginald got up to the last degree of four-in-handishness which the resources of his wardrobe allowed, and with a flower in his buttonhole. There was a loud cry for eggs and bacon, kippered herrings, marmalade, Yorkshire cakes; but neither Ida nor Bessie could eat.

'Do have a good breakfast,' pleaded Blanche affectionately; 'you will be having bread and scrape to-morrow. We have got a nice hamper for you, with a cake and a lot of jam puffs and things; but those will only last a short time.'

'You dear child, I wouldn't mind the bread and scrape, if there were only a little love to flavour it,' answered Ida softly.

The jaunting-car came to the door as the clock struck seven. Ida's luggage was securely bestowed, then, after a perfect convulsion of kissing, she was handed to her place, Reginald jumped into his seat and took the reins, and Brian seated himself beside Ida.

'You are not going with them?' exclaimed Bessie.

'Yes I am, to see that Miss Palliser is not spilt on the hills.'

'What rot!' cried Reginald. 'I should be rather sorry for myself if I were not able to manage Robin.'

'This is a new development in you, who are generally the laziest of living creatures,' said Bessie to Brian, and before he could reply, Robin was bounding cheerily through the village, making very little account of the jaunting-car and its occupants. Urania was at her garden gate, fresh and elegant-looking in pale blue cambric. She smiled at Ida, and waved her a most gracious farewell.

'I don't think I ever saw Miss Rylance look so amiable,' said Ida. 'She does not often favour me with her smiles.'

'Are you enemies?' asked Brian.

'Not open foes; we have always maintained an armed neutrality. I don't like her, and she doesn't like me, and we both know it. But perhaps I ought not to be so candid. She may be a favourite of yours.'

'She might be, but she is not. She is very elegant, very lady-like— according to her own lights—very viperish.'

It was a lovely drive in the crisp clear air, across the breezy hills. Ida could not help enjoying the freshness of morning, the beauty of earth, albeit she was going from comfort to discomfort, from love to cold indifference or open enmity.

'How I delight in this landscape!' she exclaimed. 'Is it not ever so much better than Norway?' appealing to Brian.

'It is a milder, smaller kind of beauty,' he answered. 'Would you not like to see Norway?'

'I would like to see all that is lovely on earth; yet I think I could be content to spend a life-time here. This must seem strange to you, who grow weary of that beautiful Abbey.'

'It is not of his house, but of himself, that a man grows weary,' answered Brian.

Robin was in a vivacious humour, and rattled the car across the hills at a good pace. They had a quarter of an hour to wait at the busy little station. Brian and Ida walked up and down the platform talking, while Reginald looked after the pony and the luggage. They found so much to say to each other, that the train seemed to come too soon.

They bade each other good-bye with a tender look on Brian's part, a blush on Ida's. Reginald had to push his cousin away from the carriage window, in order to get a word with the departing guest.

'We shall all miss you awfully,' he said; 'but mind, you must come back at Christmas.'

'I shall be only too glad, if Mrs. Wendover will have me. Good-bye.'

The train moved slowly forward, and she was gone.

'Isn't she a stunner?' asked Reginald of his cousin, as they stood on the platform looking at each other blankly.

'She is the handsomest girl I ever saw, and out and away the nicest,' answered Brian.

CHAPTER VII
IN THE RIVER-MEADOW

The old hackneyed round of daily life at Mauleverer Manor seemed just a little worse to Ida Palliser after that happy break of six weeks' pure and perfect enjoyment. Miss Pew was no less exacting than of old. Miss Pillby, for whose orphaned and friendless existence there had been no such thing as a holiday, and who had spent the vacation at Mauleverer diligently employed in mending the house-linen, resented Ida's visit to The Knoll as if it were a personal injury, and vented her envy in sneers and innuendoes of the coarsest character.

'If *I* were to spoon upon one of the rich pupils, I dare say I could get invited out for the holidays,' she said, *à propos* to nothing particular; 'but I am thankful to say I am above such meanness.'

'I never laid myself under an obligation I didn't feel myself able to return,' said Miss Motley, the English governess, who had spent her holidays amidst the rank and fashion of Margate. 'When I go to the sea-side with my sister and her family, I pay my own expenses, and I feel I've a right to be made comfortable.'

Miss Pillby, who had flattered and toadied every well-to-do pupil, and laboured desperately to wind herself into the affections of Bessie Wendover, that warm-hearted young person seeming particularly accessible to flattery, felt herself absolutely injured by the kindness that had been lavished upon Ida. She drank in with greedy ears Miss Palliser's description of The Knoll and its occupants—the picnics, carpet-dances, afternoon teas; and the thought that all these enjoyments and festivities, the good things to eat and drink, the pleasant society, ought to have been hers instead of Ida's, was wormwood.

'When I think of my kindness to Bessie Wendover,' she said to Miss Motley, in the confidence of that one quiet hour which belonged to the mistresses after the pupils' curfew-bell had rung youth and hope and gaiety into retirement, 'when I think of the mustard poultices I have put upon her chest, and the bronchial troches I have given her when she had the slightest touch of cold or cough, I am positively appalled at the ingratitude of the human race.'

'I don't think she likes bronchial troches,' said Miss Motley, a very matter-of-fact young person who saved money, wore thick boots, and was never unprovided with an umbrella: 'I have seen her throw them away directly after you gave them to her.'

'She ought to have liked them,' exclaimed Miss Pillby, sternly. 'They are very expensive.'

'No doubt she appreciated your kindness,' said Miss Motley, absently, being just then absorbed in an abstruse calculation as to how many yards of merino would be required for her winter gown.

'No, she did not,' said Miss Pillby. 'If she had been grateful she would have invited me to her home. I should not have gone, but the act would have given me a higher idea of her character.'

'Well, she is gone, and we needn't trouble ourselves any more about her,' retorted Miss Motley, who hated to be plagued about abstract questions, being a young woman of an essentially concrete nature, born to consume and digest three meals a day, and having no views that go beyond that function.

Miss Pillby sighed at finding herself in communion with so coarse a nature.

'I don't easily get over a blow of that sort,' she said; 'I am too tender-hearted.'

'So you are,' acquiesced Miss Motley. 'It doesn't pay in a big boarding-school, however it may answer in private families.'

Ida, having lost her chief friend and companion, Bessie Wendover, found life at Mauleverer Manor passing lonely. She even missed the excitement of her little skirmishes, her passages-at-arms, with Urania Rylance, in which she had generally got the best of the argument. There had been life and emotion in these touch-and-go speeches, covert sneers, quick retorts, innuendoes met and flung back in the very face of the sneerer. Now there was nothing but dull, dead monotony. Many of the old pupils had departed, and many new pupils had come, daughters of well-to-do parents, prosperous, well-dressed, talking largely of the gaieties enjoyed by their elder sisters, of the wonderful things done by their brothers at Oxford or Cambridge, and of the grand things which were to happen two or three years hence, when they themselves should be 'out.' Ida took no interest in their prattle. It was so apt to sting her with the reminder of her own poverty, the life of drudgery and dependence that was to be her portion till the end of her days. She did not, in the Mauleverer phraseology, 'take to' the new girls. She left them to be courted by Miss Pillby, and petted by Miss Dulcibella. She felt as lonely as one who has outlived her generation.

Happily the younger girls in the class which she taught were fond of her, and when she wanted company she let these juveniles cluster round her in her garden rambles; but in a general way she preferred loneliness, and to work at the cracked old piano in the room where she slept. Beethoven and Chopin, Mozart and Mendelssohn were companions of whom she never grew weary.

So the slow days wore on till nearly the end of the month, and on one cool, misty, afternoon, when the river flowed sluggishly under a dull grey sky she walked alone along that allotted extent of the river-side path which the mistresses and pupil-teachers were allowed to promenade without *surveillance*. This river walk skirted a meadow which was in Miss Pew's occupation, and ranked as a part of the Mauleverer grounds, although it was divided by the high road from the garden proper.

A green paling, and a little green gate, always padlocked, secured this meadow from intrusion on the road-side, but it was open to the river. To be entrusted with the key of this pastoral retreat was a privilege only accorded to governesses and pupil-teachers.

It was supposed by Miss Pew that no young person in her employment would be capable of walking quite alone, where it was within the range of possibility that her solitude might be intruded upon by an unknown member of the opposite sex. She trusted, as she said afterwards, in the refined feeling of any person brought into association with her, and, until rudely awakened by facts, she never would have stooped from the lofty pinnacle of her own purity to suspect the evil consequences which arose from the liberty too generously accorded to her dependents.

Ida detested Miss Pillby and despised Miss Motley; and the greatest relief she knew to the dismal monotony of her days was a lonely walk by the river, with a shabby Wordsworth or a battered little volume of Shelley's minor poems for her companions. She possessed so few books that it was only natural for her to read those she had until love ripened with familiarity.

On this autumnal afternoon she walked with slow steps, while the river went murmuring by, and now and then a boat drifted lazily down the stream. The boating season was over for the most part—the season of picnics and beanfeasts, and Cockney holiday-making, and noisy revelry, smart young women, young men in white flannels, with bare arms and sunburnt noses. It was the dull blank time when everybody who could afford to wander far from this suburban paradise, was away upon his and her travels. Only parsons, doctors, schoolmistresses, and poverty stayed at home. Yet now and then a youth in boating costume glided by, his shoulders bending slowly to the lazy dip of his oars, his keel now and then making a rushing sound among long trailing weeds.

Such a youth presently came creeping along the bank, almost at Ida's feet, but passed her unseen. Her heavy lids were drooping, her eyes intent upon the familiar page. The young man looked up at her with keen gray eyes, recognised her, and pushed his boat in among the rushes by the bank, moored it to a pollard willow, and with light footstep leaped on shore.

He landed a few yards in the rear of Ida's slowly moving figure, followed softly, came close behind her, and read aloud across her shoulder:

'There was a Power in this sweet place,
An Eve in this garden; a ruling grace
Which to the flowers, did they waken or dream,
Was as God is to the starry scheme.'

Ida looked round, first indignant, then laughing.

'How you startled me!' she exclaimed; 'I thought you were some horrid, impertinent stranger; and yet the voice had a familiar sound. How are they all at The Knoll? It is nearly a fortnight since Bessie wrote to me. If she only knew how I hunger for her letters.'

'Very sweet of you,' answered Mr. Wendover, holding the girl's hand with a lingering pressure, releasing it reluctantly when her rising colour told him it would be insolent to keep it longer.

How those large dark eyes beamed with pleasure at seeing him! Was it for his own sake, or for love of her friends at Kingthorpe? The smile was perhaps too frank to be flattering.

'Very sweet of you to care so much for Bessie's girlish epistles,' he said lazily; 'they are full of affection, but the style of composition always recalls our dear Mrs. Nickleby. "Aunt Betsy was asking after you the other day: and that reminds me that the last litter of black Hampshires was sixteen— the largest number father ever remembers having. The vicar and his wife are coming to dinner on Tuesday, and do tell me if this new picture that everybody is talking about is really better than the Derby Day," and that sort of thing. Not a very consecutive style, don't you know.'

'Every word is interesting to me,' said Ida, with a look that told him she was not one of those young ladies who enjoy a little good-natured ridicule of their nearest and dearest. 'Is it long since you left Kingthorpe?'

'Not four-and-twenty hours. I promised Bessie that my very first occupation on coming to London should be to make my way down here to see you, in order that I may tell her faithfully and truly whether you are well and happy. She has a lurking conviction that you are unable to live without her, that you will incontinently go into a galloping consumption, and keep the fact concealed from all your friends until they receive a telegram summoning them to your death-bed. I know that is the picture Bessie's sentimental fancies have depicted.'

'I did not think Bessie was so morbid,' said Ida, laughing. 'No, I am not one of those whom the gods love. I am made of very tough material, or I should hardly have lived till now. I see before me a perspective of lonely, loveless old age—finishing in a governess' almshouse. I hope there are almshouses for governesses.'

'Nobody will pity your loneliness or lovelessness,' retorted Brian, 'for they will both be your own fault.'

She blushed, looking dreamily across the dark-gray river to the level shores beyond—the low meadows—gentle hills in the back-ground—the wooded slopes of Weybridge and Chertsey. If this speaker, whose voice dropped to so tender a tone, had been like the Brian of her imaginings—if he had looked at her with the dark eyes of Sir Tristram's picture, how differently his speech would have affected her! As it was, she listened with airy indifference, only blushing girlishly at his compliment, and wondering a little if he really admired her—he the owner of that glorious old Abbey—the wealthy head of the house of Wendover—the golden fish for whom so many pretty fishers must have angled in days gone by.

'Did you stay at The Knoll all the time,' she inquired, her thoughts having flown back to Kingthorpe; 'or at the Abbey?'

'At The Knoll. It is ever so much livelier, and my cousins like to have me with them.'

'Naturally. But I wonder you did not prefer living in that lovely old house of yours. To occupy it must seem like living in the Middle Ages.'

'Uncommonly. One is twelve miles from a station, and four from post-office, butcher, and baker. Very like the Middle Ages. There is no gas even in the offices, and there are as many rats behind the wainscot as there were Israelites in Egypt. All the rooms are draughty and some are damp. No servant who has not been born and bred on the estate will stay more than six months. There is a deficient water supply in dry summers, and there are three distinct ghosts all the year round. Extremely like the Middle Ages.'

'I would not mind ghosts, rats, anything, if it were my house' exclaimed Ida, enthusiastically. 'The house is a poem.'

'Perhaps; but it is not a house; in the modern sense of the word, that is to say, which implies comfort and convenience.'

Ida sighed, deeply disgusted at this want of appreciation of the romantic spot where she had dreamed away more than one happy summer noontide, while the Wendover children played hide-and-seek in the overgrown old shrubberies.

No doubt life was always thus. The people to whom blind fortune gave such blessings were unable to appreciate them, and only the hungry outsiders could imagine the delight of possession.

'Are you living in London now?' she asked, as Mr. Wendover lingered at her side, and seemed to expect the conversation to be continued indefinitely.

His boat was safe enough, moving gently up and down among the rushes, with the gentle flow of the tide. Ida looked at it longingly, thinking how sweet it would be to step into it and let it carry her—any whither, so long as it was away from Mauleverer Manor.

'Yes, I am in London for the present.'

'But not for long, I suppose.'

'I hardly know. I have no plans. I won't say with Romeo that I am fortune's fool—but I am fortune's shuttlecock; and I suppose that means pretty much the same.'

'It was very kind of you to come to see me,' said Ida.

'Kind to myself, for in coming I indulged the dearest wish of my soul,' said the young man, looking at her with eyes whose meaning even her inexperience could not misread.

'Please don't pay me compliments,' she said, hastily, 'or I shall feel very sorry you came. And now I must hurry back to the house—the tea-bell will ring in a few minutes. Please tell Bessie I am very well, and only longing for one of her dear letters. Good-bye.'

She made him a little curtsey, and would have gone without shaking hands, but he caught her hand and detained her in spite of herself.

'Don't be angry,' he pleaded; 'don't look at me with such cold, proud eyes. Is it an offence to admire, to love you too quickly? If it is, I have sinned deeply, and am past hope of pardon. Must one serve an apprenticeship to mere formal acquaintance first, then rise step by step to privileged friendship, before one dares to utter the sweet word love? Remember, at least, that I am your dearest friend's first cousin, and ought not to appear to you as a stranger.'

'I can remember nothing when you talk so wildly,' said Ida, crimson to the roots of her hair. Never before had a young lover talked to her of love. 'Pray let me go. Miss Pew will be angry if I am not at tea.'

'To think that such a creature as you should be under the control of any such harpy,' exclaimed Brian. 'Well, if I must go, at least tell me I am forgiven, and that I may exist upon the hope of seeing you again. I suppose if I were to come to the hall-door, and send in my card, I should not be allowed to see you?'

'Certainly not. Not if you were my own cousin instead of Bessie's. Good-bye.'

'Then I shall happen to be going by in my boat every afternoon for the next month or so. There is a dear good soul at the lock who lets lodgings. I shall take up my abode there.'

'Please never land on this pathway again,' said Ida earnestly 'Miss Pew would be horribly angry if she heard I had spoken to you. And now I must go.'

She withdrew her hand from his grasp, and ran off across the meadow, light-footed as Atalanta. Her heart was beating wildly, beating furiously, when she flew up to her room to take off her hat and jacket and smooth her disordered hair. Never before had any man, except middle-aged Dr. Rylance, talked to her of love: and that this man of all others, this man, sole master of the old mansion she so intensely admired, her friend's kinsman, owner of a good old Saxon name; this man, who could lift her in a moment from poverty to wealth, from obscurity to place and station; that this man should look at her with admiring eyes, and breathe impassioned words into her ear, was enough to set her heart beating tumultuously, to bring hot blushes to her cheeks. It was too wild a dream.

True, that for the man himself, considered apart from his belongings, his name and race, she cared not at all. But just now, in this tumult of excited feeling, she was disposed to confuse the man with his surroundings—to think of him, not as that young man with gray eyes and thin lips, who had walked with her at The Knoll, who had stood beside her just now by the river, but as the living embodiment of fortune, pride, delight.

Perhaps the vision really dominant in her mind was the thought of herself as mistress of the Abbey, herself as living for ever among the people she loved, amidst those breezy Hampshire hills, in the odour of pine-woods—rich, important, honoured, and beloved, doing good to all who came within the limit of her life. Yes, that was a glorious vision, and its reflected light shone upon Brian Wendover, and in somewise glorified him.

She went down to tea with such a triumphant light in her eyes that the smaller pupils who sat at her end of the table, so as to be under her *surveillance* during the meal, exclaimed at her beauty.

'What a colour you've got, Miss Palliser!' said Lucy Dobbs, 'and how your eyes sparkle! You look as if you'd just had a hamper.'

'I'm not quite so greedy as you, Lucy,' retorted Ida; 'I don't think a hamper would make my eyes sparkle, even if there were anybody to send me one.'

'But there is somebody to send you one,' argued Lucy, with her mouth full of bread and butter; 'your father isn't dead?'

'No.'

'Then he might send you a hamper.'

'He might, if he lived within easy reach of Mauleverer Manor,' replied Ida; 'but as he lives in France—'

'He could send a post-office order to a confectioner in London, and the confectioner would send you a big box of cakes, and marmalade, and jam, and mixed biscuits, and preserved ginger,' said Lucy, her cheeks glowing with the rapture of her theme. 'That is what my mamma and papa did, when they were in Switzerland, on my birthday. I never had such a hamper as that one. I was ill for a week afterwards.'

'And I suppose you were very glad your mother and father were away,' said Ida, while the other children laughed in chorus.

'It was a splendid hamper,' said Lucy, stolidly. 'I shall never forget it. So you see your father might send you a hamper,' she went on, for the sake of argument, 'though he is in France.'

'Certainly,' said Ida, 'if I were not too old to care about cakes and jam.'

'*We* are not too old,' persisted Lucy; 'you might share them among us.'

Ida's heart had not stilled its stormy vehemence yet. She talked lightly to her young companions, and tried to eat a little bread and butter, but that insipid fare almost choked her. Her mind was overcharged with thought and wonder.

Could he have meant all or half he said just now?—this young man with the delicate features, pale complexion, and thin lips. He had seemed intensely earnest. Those gray eyes of his, somewhat too pale of hue for absolutely beauty, had glowed with a fire which even Ida's inexperience recognised as something above and beyond common feeling. His hand had trembled as it clasped hers. Could there be such a thing as love at first sight?

and was she destined to be the object of that romantic passion? She had read of the triumphs of beauty, and she knew that she was handsome. She had been told the fact in too many ways—by praise sometimes, but much more often by envy—to remain unconscious of her charms. She was scornful of her beauty, inclined to undervalue the gift as compared with the blessings of other girls—a prosperous home, the world's respect, the means to gratify the natural yearnings of youth—but she knew that she was beautiful. And now it seemed to her all at once that beauty was a much more valuable gift than she had supposed hitherto—indeed, a kind of talisman or Aladdin's lamp, which could win for her all she wanted in this world—Wendover Abbey and the position of a country squire's wife. It was not a dazzling or giddy height to which to aspire; but to Ida just now it seemed the topmost pinnacle of social success.

'Oh, what a wretch I am!' she said to herself presently; 'what a despicable, mercenary creature! I don't care a straw for this man; and yet I am already thinking of myself as his wife.'

And then, remembering how she had once openly declared her intention of marrying for money, she shrugged her shoulders disdainfully.

'Ought I to hesitate when the chance comes to me?' she thought. 'I always meant to marry for money, if ever such wonderful fortune as a rich husband fell in my way.'

And yet she had refused Dr. Rylance's offer, without a moment's hesitation. Was it really as he had said, in the bitterness of his wrath, because the offer was not good enough, the temptation not large enough? No, she told herself, she had rejected the smug physician, with his West End mansion and dainty Hampshire villa, his courtly manners, his perfect dress, because the man himself was obnoxious to her. Now, she did not dislike Brian Wendover—indeed, she was rather inclined to like him. She was only just a little disappointed that he was not the ideal Brian of her dreams. The dark-browed cavalier, with grave forehead and eagle eyes. She had a vague recollection of having once heard Blanche say that her cousin Brian of the Abbey was like Sir Tristram's portrait; but this must have been a misapprehension upon her part, since no two faces could have differed more than the pale delicate-featured countenance of the living man and the dark rugged face in the picture.

She quieted the trouble of her thoughts as well as she could before tea was over and the evening task of preparation,—the gulfs and straits, the predicates and noun sentences, rule of three, common denominators, and all the dry-as-dust machinery was set in motion again.

Helping her pupils through their difficulties, battling with their stupidities, employed her too closely for any day-dreams of her own. But when prayers had been read, and the school had dispersed, and the butterfly-room was hushed into the silence of midnight, Ida Palliser lay broad awake, wondering at what Fate was doing for her.

'To think that perhaps I am going to be rich after all—honoured, looked up to, able to help those I love,' she thought, thrilling at the splendour of her visions.

Ah! if this thing were verily to come to pass, how kind, how good she would be to others! She would have them all at the Abbey,—the shabby old half-pay father, shabby no longer in those glorious days; the vulgar little stepmother, improved into elegance, the five year old brother, that loveliest and dearest of created beings. How lovely to see him rioting in the luxuriance of those dear old gardens, rolling on that velvet sward, racing his favourite dogs round and round the grand old cedars! What a pony he should ride! His daily raiment should be Genoa velvet and old point lace. He should be the admiration and delight of half the county. And Bessie—how kind she could be to Bessie, repaying in some small measure that which never could be fully repaid—the kindness shown by the prosperous girl to the poor dependent. And above all,—vision sweeter even than the thought of doing good,—how she would trample on Urania Rylance—how the serpentine coils of that damsel's malice and pride could be trodden under foot! Not a ball, not a dinner, not a garden-party given at the Abbey that would not be a thorn in Urania's side, a nail in Urania's coffin.

So ran her fancies—in a very fever—all through the troubled night; but when the first streak of the autumn dawn glimmered coldly in the east, dismal presage of the discordant dressing-bell, then she turned upon her pillow with a weary sigh, and muttered to herself:—

'After all I daresay Mr. Wendover is only fooling me. Perhaps it is his habit to make love to every decent-looking girl he meets.'

The next day Ida walked on the same riverside path, but this time not alone. Her natural modesty shrank from the possibility of a second *tête-à-tête* with her admirer, and she stooped from her solitary state to ask Fräulein Wolf to accompany her in her afternoon walk.

Fräulein was delighted, honoured even, by the request. She was a wishy-washy person, sentimental, vapourish, altogether feeble, and she intensely admired Ida Palliser's vigorous young beauty.

The day was bright and sunny, the air deliciously mild, the river simply divine. The two young women paced the path slowly, talking of German poetry. The Fräulein knew her Schiller by heart, having expounded him daily for the last four years, and she fondly believed that after Shakespeare Schiller was the greatest poet who had ever trodden this globe.

'And if God had spared him for twenty more years, who knows if he would not have been greater than Shakespeare? inquired the Fräulein, blandly.

She talked of Schiller's idea of friendship, as represented by the Marquis of Posa.

'Ah,' sighed Ida, 'I doubt if there is any such friendship as that out of a book.'

'I could be like the marquis,' said the Fräulein, smiling tenderly.' Oh, Ida, you don't know what I would do for anyone I loved—for a dear and valued friend, like you for instance, if you would only let me love you; but you have always held me at arm's length.'

'I did not mean to do so,' answered Ida, frankly; 'but perhaps I am not particularly warm-hearted. It is not in my nature to have many friends. I was very fond of Bessie Wendover, but then she is such a dear clinging thing, like a chubby child that puts its fat arms round your neck—an irresistible creature. She made me love her in spite of myself.'

'Why cannot I make you love me?' asked the fair Gertrude, with a languishing look.

Ida could have alleged several reasons, but they would have been unflattering, so she only said feebly,—

'Oh, I really like you very much, and I enjoy talking about German literature with you. Tell me more about Schiller—you know his poetry so well—and Jean Paul. I never can quite understand the German idolatry of him. He is too much in the clouds for me.'

'Too philosophic, you mean,' said Fräulein. 'I love philosophy.'

'"Unless philosophy can make a Juliet, it helps not, it avails not,"' said a manly voice from the river close by, and Brian Wendover shot his boat in against the bank and leapt up from among the rushes like a river-god.

Miss Palliser blushed crimson, but it hardly needed her blushes to convince Fräulein Wolf that this young stranger was a lover. Her sentimental soul thrilled at the idea of having plunged into the very midst of an intrigue.

Ida's heart throbbed heavily, not so much with emotion at beholding her admirer as at the recollection of her visions last night. She tried to look calm and indifferent.

'How do you do?' she said, shaking hands with him. 'Mr. Wendover—Miss Wolf, our German mistress.'

The Fräulein blushed, sniggered, and curtseyed.

'This gentleman is Bessie Wendover's first cousin, Fräulein,' said Ida, with an explanatory air. 'He was staying at The Knoll during the last part of my visit.'

'Yes, and you saw much of each other, and you became heart-friends,' gushed Miss Wolf, beaming benevolently at Brian with her pale green orbs.

Brian answered in very fair German, sinking his voice a little so as only to be heard by the Fräulein, who was in raptures with this young stranger. So good looking, so elegant, and speaking Hanoverian German. He told her that he had seen only too little of Ida at The Knoll, but enough to know that she was his 'Schicksal'; and then he took the Fräulein's hand and pressed it gently.

'I know you are our friend,' he said.

'Bis den Tod,' gasped Gertrude.

After this no one felt any more restraint. The Fräulein dropped into her place of confidante as easily as possible.

'What brings you here again this afternoon, Mr. Wendover?' asked Ida, trying to sustain the idea of being unconcerned in the matter.

'My load-star; the same that drew me here yesterday, and will draw me here to-morrow.'

'You had better not come here any more; you have no idea what a terrible person Miss Pew is. These river-side fields are her own particular property. Didn't you see the board, "Trespassers will be prosecuted"?'

'Let her prosecute. If her wrath were deadly, I would risk it. You know what Romeo says—

"Wert thou as far
As that vast shore washed with the farthest sea,
I would adventure for such merchandize"

And shall I be afraid of Miss Pew, when the path to my paradise lies so near?'

'Please don't talk such nonsense,' pleaded Ida; 'Fräulein will think you a very absurd person.'

But Miss Wolf protested that she would think nothing of the sort. Sentiment of that kind was her idea of common sense.

'I am established at Penton Hook,' said Brian. 'I live on the water, and my only thought in life is to be near you. I shall know every stump of willow—every bulrush before I am a month older.'

'But surely you are not going to stay at Penton Hook for a month!' exclaimed Ida, 'buried alive in that little lock-house?'

'I shall have my daily resurrection when I see you.'

'But you cannot imagine that I shall walk upon this path every afternoon, in order that you may land and talk nonsense?' protested Ida.

'I only imagine that this path is your daily walk, and that you would not be so heartless as to change your habits in order to deprive me of the sunshine of your presence,' replied Brian, gazing at her tenderly, as if Miss Wolf counted for nothing, and they two were standing alone among the reeds and willows.

'You will simply make this walk impossible for me. It is quite out of the question that I should come here again so long as you are likely to be lying in wait for me. Is it not so, Fräulein? You know Miss Pew's way of thinking, and how she would regard such conduct.'

Fräulein shook her head dolefully, and admitted that in Miss Pew's social code such a derogation from maiden dignity would be, in a manner, death—an offence beyond all hope of pardon.

'Hang Miss Pew!' exclaimed Brian. 'If Miss Pew were Minerva, with all the weight and influence of her father, the Thunderer, to back her up, I would defy her. Confess now, dear Fräulein—liebste Fräulein'—how tender his accents sounded in German!—'*you* do not think it wrong for me to see the lady of my love for a few all-too-happy moments once a day?'

The Fräulein declared that it was the most natural thing in the world for them thus to meet, and that she for her part would be enchanted to play propriety, and to be her dearest Ida's companion on all such occasions, nor would thumbscrew or rack extort from her the secret of their loves.

'Nonsense!' exclaimed Ida, 'in future I shall always walk in the kitchen garden; the walls are ten feet high, and unless you had a horse that could fly, like Perseus, you would never be able to get at me.'

'I will get a flying horse,' answered Brian. 'Don't defy me. Remember there are things that have been heard of before now in love-stories, called ladders.'

After this their conversation became as light and airy as that dandelion seed which every breath of summer blows across the land. They were all three young, happy in health and hope despite of fortune. Ida began to think that Brian Wendover, if in nowise resembling her ideal, was a very agreeable young man. He was full of life and spirits; he spoke German admirably. He had the Fräulein's idolized Schiller on the tip of his tongue. He quoted Heine's tenderest love songs. Altogether his society was much more intellectual and more agreeable than any to be had at Mauleverer Manor. Miss Wolf parted from him reluctantly, and thought that Ida was unreasonably urgent when she insisted on leaving him at the end of half an hour's dawdling walk up and down the river path.

'Ach, how he is handsome! how he is clever! What for a man!' exclaimed Miss Wolf, as they went back to the Manor grounds, across the dusty highroad, the mere passage over which had a faint flavour of excitement, as a momentary escape into the outside world. 'How proud you must be of his devotion to you!'

'Indeed I am not,' answered Ida, frankly. 'I only wonder at it. We have seen so little of each other; we have known each other so short a time.'

'I don't think time counts for lovers,' argued the romantic Gertrude. 'One sees a face which is one's fate, and only wonders how one can have lived until that moment, since life must have been so empty without *him*.'

'Have you done that sort of thing often?' asked Ida, with rather a cynical air. 'You talk as if it were a common experience of yours.'

Fräulein Wolf blushed and simpered.

'There was one,' she murmured, 'when I was very young. He was to me as a bright particular star. His father kept a shop, but, oh, his soul would have harmonized with the loftiest rank in the land. He was in the Landwehr. If you had seen him in his uniform—ach, Himmel! He went away to the Franco-Prussian war. I wept for him; I thought of him as Leonora of her Wilhelm. He came back. Ach!'

'Was he a ghost? Did he carry you off to the churchyard?'

'Neither to churchyard nor church,' sighed Gertrude. 'He was false! He married his father's cook—a fat, rosy-cheeked Swabian. All that was delicate and refined in his nature, every poetical yearning of his soul, had been trampled out of him in that hellish war!'

'I dare say he was hungry after a prolonged existence upon wurst,' said Ida, 'and that instinct drew him to the cook-maid.'

After this there came many afternoons on which the Fräulein and Ida walked in the meadow path by the river, and walk there when they would, the light wherry always came glancing along the tide, and shot in among the reeds, and Miss Palliser's faithful swain was in attendance upon her. On doubtful afternoons, when Ida was inclined to stay indoors, the sentimental Fräulein was always at her side to urge her to take the accustomed walk. Not only was Mr. Wendover's society agreeable to her poetic soul, but he occasionally brought some tender offering in the shape of hothouse grapes or Jersey pears, which were still more welcome to the fair German.

The governesses, Miss Motley, Miss Pillby, and Mademoiselle were always on duty on fine afternoons, in attendance upon the pupils' regulation walks—long dusty perambulations of dull high roads; and thus it happened that Ida and the Fräulein had the meadow path to themselves.

Nothing occurred during the space of a fortnight to disturb their sense of security. The river-side seemed a kind of Paradise, without the possibility of a serpent. Ida's lover had not yet made her any categorical and formal offer of marriage. Indeed, he had never been one minute alone with her since their first meeting; but he talked as if it was a settled thing that they two were to be man and wife in the days to come. He did not speak as if their marriage were an event in the near future; and at this Ida wondered a little, seeing that the owner of Wendover Abbey could have no need to wait for a wife—to consider ways and means—and to be prudently patient, as struggling professional youth must be. This was curious; for that he loved her passionately there could be little doubt. Every look, every tone told her as much a hundred times in an hour. Nor did she make any protest when he spoke of her as one pledged to him, though no formal covenant had been entered upon. She allowed him to talk as he pleased about their future; and her only wonder was, that in all his conversation he spoke so little of the house in which he was born, and indeed of his belongings generally.

Once she expatiated to Fräulein Wolf in Brian's presence upon the picturesque beauties of the Abbey.

'It is the dearest, noblest old house you can conceive,' she said; 'and the old, old gardens and park are something too lovely: but I believe Mr. Wendover does not care a straw about the place.'

'You know what comes of familiarity,' answered Brian, carelessly. 'I have seen too much of the Abbey to be moved to rapture by its Gothic charms every time I see it after the agony of separation.'

'But you would like to live there?'

'I would infinitely prefer living anywhere else. The place is too remote from civilization. A spot one might enjoy, perhaps, on the downhill side of sixty; but in youth or active middle age every sensible man should shun seclusion. A man has to fight against an inherent tendency to lapse into a vegetable.'

'Fox did not become a vegetable,' said Ida; 'yet how he adored St. Ann's Hill!'

'Fox was a hard drinker and a fast liver,' answered Brian. 'If he had not let the clock run down now and then, the works would have worn out sooner than they did.'

'But do you never feel the need of rest?' asked Ida.

Brian stifled a yawn.

'No; I'm afraid I have never worked hard enough for that. The need will come, perhaps, later—when the work comes.'

On more than one occasion when Ida talked of the Abbey, Mr. Wendover replied in the same tone. It was evident that he was indifferent to the family seat, or that he even disliked it. He had no pride in surroundings which might have inspired another man.

'One would think you had been frightened by the family ghost,' Ida said laughingly, 'you so studiously avoid talking about the Abbey.'

'I have not been frightened by the ghost—I am too modern to believe in ghosts.'

'Oh, but it is modern to believe in everything impossible—spirit-rapping, thought-reading.'

'Perhaps; but I am not of that temper.' And then, with a graver look than Ida had ever seen in his face, he said, 'You are full of enthusiasm about that old place among the hills, Ida. I hope you do not care more for the Abbey than for me.'

She crimsoned and looked down. The question touched her weakness too nearly.

'Oh, no,' she faltered; 'what are cedars and limestone as compared with humanity?'

'And if I were without the Abbey—if the Abbey and I were nothing to each other—should I be nobody in your sight?'

'It is difficult to dissociate a man from his surroundings,' she answered; 'but I suppose you would be just the same person?'

'I hope so,' said Brian. '"The rank is but the guinea stamp, the man's a man for a' that." But the guinea stamp is an uncommonly good thing in its way, I admit.'

These afternoon promenades between four and five o'clock, while the rest of the school was out walking, had been going on for a fortnight, and no harm to Ida had come of her indiscretion. Perhaps she hardly considered how wrong a thing she was doing in violating Miss Pew's confidence by conduct so entirely averse from Miss Pew's ideas of good behaviour. The confidence had been so grudgingly given, Miss Pew had been so systematically unkind, that the girl may be forgiven for detesting her, nay, even for glorying in the notion of acting in a manner which would shock all Miss Pew's dearest prejudices. Her meeting with her lover could scarcely be called clandestine, for she took very little pains to conceal the fact. If the affair had gone on secretly for so long, it was because of no artifice on her part.

But that any act of any member of the Mauleverer household could remain long unknown was almost an impossibility. If there had been but one pair of eyes in the establishment, and those the eyes of Miss Pillby, the thing would have been discovered; for those pale unlovely orbs were as the eyes of Argus himself in their manifold power to spy out the proceedings of other people—more especially of any person whom their owner disliked.

Now Miss Pillby had never loved Ida Palliser, objecting to her on broad grounds as a person whose beauty and talents were an indirect injury to mediocre people. Since Ida's visit to The Knoll her angry feeling had intensified with every mention of the pleasures and comforts of that abode. Miss Pillby, who never opened a book for her own pleasure, who cared nothing for music, and whose highest notion of art was all blacklead pencil and bread-crumbs, had plenty of vacant space in her mind for other people's business. She was a sharp observer of the fiddle-faddle of daily life; she had a keen scent for evil motives underlying simple actions. Thus when she perceived the intimacy which had newly arisen between the Fräulein and Miss Palliser, she told herself that there must be some occult reason for the fact. Why did those two always walk together? What hidden charm had they discovered in the river-meadow?

For this question, looked at from Miss Pillby's point of view, there could be only one answer. The attraction was masculine. One or other of the damsels must have an admirer whom she contrived to see somehow, or to correspond with somehow, during her meadow walk. That the thing had gone so far as it really had gone, that any young lady at Mauleverer could dare to walk and talk with an unlicensed man in the broad light of day, was more than Miss Pillby's imagination could conceive. But she speculated upon some transient glimpse of a man on the opposite bank, or in the middle distance of the river—a handkerchief waved, a signal given, perhaps a love-letter hidden in a hollow tree. This was about the culminating point to which any intrigue at Mauleverer had ever reached hitherto. Beyond this Miss Pillby's fancy ventured not.

It was on the second Sunday in October, when the Mauleverer pupils were beginning to look forward, almost hopefully, to the Christmas vacation, that a flood of light streamed suddenly upon Miss Pillby's troubled mind. The revelation happened in this wise. Evening service at a smart little newly-built church, where the function was Anglican to the verge of Ritualism, was a privilege reserved for the elder and more favoured of the Mauleverer flock. All the girls liked this evening service at St. Dunstan's. It had a flavour of dissipation. The lamps, the music, the gaily decorated altar, the Saint's-day banners and processional hymn, were faintly suggestive of the opera. The change from the darkness of the country road to the glow and glitter of the tabernacle was thrilling. Evening service at St. Dunstan's was the most exciting event of the week. There was a curate who intoned exquisitely, with that melodious snuffle so dear to modern congregations, and whose voice had a dying fall when he gave out a hymn which almost moved girl-worshippers to tears. He was thought to be in a consumption—had a little dry hacking cough, actually caused by relaxed tonsils, but painfully recalling her of the camelias. The Mauleverer girls called him interesting, and hoped that he would never marry, but live and die like St. Francis de Sales. On this particular Sunday, Miss Pew—vulgarly Old Pew—happened to be unusually amiable. That morning's post had brought her the promise of three new pupils, daughters of a mighty sheep farmer lately returned from Australia, and supposed to be a millionaire. He was a widower, and wanted motherly care for his orphans. They were to be clothed as well as fed at Mauleverer; they were to have all those tender cares and indulgences which a loving mother could give them. This kind of transaction was eminently profitable to the Miss Pews. Maternal care meant a tremendous list of extra charges—treats, medical attendance, little comforts of all kinds, from old port to lamb's-wool sleeping-socks. Orphans of this kind were the pigeons whose tender breasts furnished the down with which that experienced crow, Miss Pew, feathered her nest. She had read the Australian's letter over three times before evening service, and she was inclined to think kindly of the human race; so when Miss Palliser asked if she too—she, the Pariah, might go to St. Dunstan's—she, whose general duty of a Sunday evening was to hear the little ones their catechism, or keep them quiet by reading aloud to them 'Pilgrim's Progress' or 'Agathos,' perhaps—Miss Pew said, loftily, 'I do not see any objection.'

There was no kindness, no indulgence in her tone, but she said she saw no objection, and Ida flew off to put on her bonnet,—that poor little black lace bonnet with yellow rosebuds which had done duty for so many services.

It was a relief to get a way from school, and its dull monotony, even for a couple of hours; and then there was the music. Ida loved music too passionately to be indifferent to the harmony of village voices, carefully trained to sing her favourite hymns to the sound of a small but excellent organ.

The little church was somewhat poorly attended on this fine autumn evening, when the hunter's moon hung like a big golden shield above the river, glorifying the dipping willows, the narrow eyots, haunts of swan and cygnet, and the distant woodlands of Surrey. It was a night which tempted the free to wander in the cool shadowy river-side paths, rather than to worship in the warm little temple.

The Mauleverer girls made a solid block of humanity on one side of the nave, but on the other side the congregation was scattered thinly in the open oaken seats.

Miss Pillby, perusing those figures within her view, as she stood in the back row of the school seats, perceived a stranger—a stranger of elegant and pleasing appearance, who was evidently casting stolen glances at the lambs of the Mauleverer fold. Nor was Miss Pillby's keen eye slow to discover for which lamb those ardent looks were intended. The object of the stranger's admiration was evidently Ida Palliser.

'I thought as much,' mused Miss Pillby, as she listened, or seemed to listen, to the trials and triumphs of the children of Israel, chanted by fresh young voices with a decidedly rural twang; 'this explains everything.'

When they left the church, Miss Pillby was perfectly aware of the stranger following the Mauleverer flock, evidently in the hope of getting speech with Miss Palliser. He hung on the pathway near them, he shot ahead of them, and then turned and strolled slowly back. All in vain. Ida was too closely hemmed in and guarded for him to get speech of her; and the maiden procession passed on without any violation of the proprieties.

'Did you see that underbred young man following us as we came home?' asked Miss Pillby, with a disgusted air, as she shared an invigorating repast of bread and butter and toast and water with the pupils who had been to church. 'Some London shopman, no doubt, by his bad manners.' She stole a look at Ida, who flushed ever so slightly at hearing Brian Wendover thus maligned.

Fräulein Wolf slept in the room occupied by Miss Pillby and Miss Motley—three narrow iron bedsteads in a particularly inconvenient room, always devoted to governesses, and supposed to be a temple of learning.

While Miss Motley was saying her prayers, Miss Pillby wriggled up to the Fräulein, who was calmly brushing her flaxen tresses, and whispered impetuously, 'I have seen him! I know all about it!'

'Ach, Himmel,' cried the Fräulein. 'Thou wouldst not betray?'

'Not for the world.'

'Is he not handsome, godlike?' demanded the Fräulein, still in German.

'Yes, he is very nice-looking. Don't tell Palliser that I know anything about him. She mightn't like it.'

The Fräulein shook her head, and put her finger to her lips, just as Miss Motley rose from her knees, remarking that it was impossible for anybody to pray in a proper business-like manner with such whispering and chattering going on.

Next day Miss Pillby contrived to get a walk in the garden before the early dinner. Here among the asparagus beds she had a brief conversation with a small boy employed in the kitchen-garden, a youth whose mother washed for the school, and had frequent encounters with Miss Pillby, that lady having charge of the linen, and being, in the laundress's eye, a power in the establishment. Miss Pillby had furthermore been what she called 'kind' to the laundress's hope. She had insisted upon his learning his catechism, and attending church twice every Sunday, and she had knitted him a comforter, the material being that harsh and scrubby worsted which makes the word comforter a sound of derision.

Strong in the sense of these favours, Miss Pillby put it upon the boy as a duty which he owed to her and to society to watch Ida Palliser's proceedings in the river-meadow. She also promised him sixpence if he found out anything bad.

The influence of the Church Catechism, learned by rote, parrot fashion, had not awakened in the laundress's boy any keen sense of honour. He had a dim feeling that it was a shabby service which he was called upon to perform; but then of course Miss Pillby, who taught the young ladies, and who was no doubt a wise and discreet personage, knew best; and a possible sixpence was a great temptation.

'Them rushes and weeds down by the bank wants cutting. Gar'ner told me about it last week,' said the astute youth. 'I'll do 'em this very afternoon.'

'Do, Sam. Be there between four and five. Keep out of sight as much as you can, but be well within hearing. I want you to tell me all that goes on.'

'And when shall I see you agen, miss?'

'Let me see. That's rather difficult. I'm afraid it can't be managed till to-morrow. You are in the house at six every morning to clean the boots?'

'Yes, miss.'

'Then I'll come down to the boot-room at half-past six to-morrow morning and hear what you've got to tell me.'

'Lor, miss, it's such a mucky place—all among the coal-cellars.'

'I don't mind,' said Miss Pillby; which was quite true. There was no amount of muckiness Miss Pillby would not have endured in order to injure a person she disliked.

'I have never shrunk from my duty, however painful it might be, Sam!' she said, and left the youth impressed by the idea of her virtues.

In the duskiness of the October dawn Miss Pillby stole stealthily down by back stairs and obscure passages to the boot-room, where she found Sam hard at work with brushes and blacking, by the light of a tallow candle, in an atmosphere flavoured with coals.

'Well, Sam?' asked the vestal, eagerly.

'Well, miss, I seed 'em and I heerd 'em,' answered the boy; 'such goin's on. Orful!'

'What kind of thing, Sam?'

'Love-makin',' miss; keepin' company. The young ladies hadn't been there five minutes when a boat dashes up to the bank, and a young gent jumps ashore. My, how he went on! I was down among the rushes, right under his feet, as you may say, most of the time, and I heerd him beautiful. How he did talk; like a poetry book!'

'Did he kiss her?'

'Yes, miss, just one as they parted company. She was very stand-offish with him, but he catched hold of her just as she was wishing of him good-bye. He gave her a squeedge like, and took her unawares. It was only one kiss, yer know, miss, but he made it last as long as he could. The foreigner looked the other way.'

'Shameful creatures, both of them!' exclaimed Miss Pillby. 'There's your sixpence, Sam, and don't say a word to anybody about what you've seen, till I tell you. I may want you to repeat it all to Miss Pew. If I do, I'll give you another sixpence.'

'Lawks, miss, that would be cheap at a shilling,' said the boy. 'It would freeze my blood to have to stand up to talk before Miss Pew.'

'Nonsense, Sam, you will be only telling the truth, and there can be nothing to frighten you. However, I dare say she will be satisfied with my statement. She won't want confirmation from you.'

'Confirmation from me,' muttered Sam, as Miss Pillby left his den. 'No, I should think not. Why, that's what the bishops do. Fancy old Pew being confirmed too—old Pew in a white frock and a veil. That is a good'un,' and Sam exploded over his blacking-brush at the preposterous idea.

It was Miss Pew's habit to take a cup of tea and a square of buttered toast every morning at seven, before she left her pillow; in order to fortify herself for the effort of getting up and dressing, so as to be in her place, at the head of the chief table in the school dining room, when eight o'clock struck. Had Miss Pew consulted her own inclination she would have reposed until a much later hour; but the maintenance of discipline compelled that she should be the head and front of all virtuous movements at Mauleverer Manor. How could she inveigh with due force against the sin of sloth if she were herself a slug-a-bed? Therefore did Miss Pew vanquish the weakness of the flesh, and rise at a quarter past seven, summer and winter. But this struggle between duty and inclination made the lady's temper somewhat critical in the morning hours.

Now it was the custom for one of the mistresses to carry Miss Pew's tea-tray, and to attend at her bedside while she sipped her bohea and munched her toast. It was a delicate attention, a recognition of her dignity, which Miss Pew liked. It was the *lever du roi* upon a small scale. And this afforded an opportunity for the mistress on duty to inform her principal of any small fact in connection with the school or household which it was well for Miss Pew to know. Not for worlds would Sarah Pew have encouraged a spy, according to her own view of her own character; but she liked people with keen eyes, who could tell her everything that was going on under her roof.

'Good morning, Pillby,' said Miss Pew, sitting up against a massive background of pillows, like a female Jove upon a bank of clouds, an awful figure in frilled white raiment, with an eye able to command, but hardly to flatter; 'what kind of a day is it?'

'Dull and heavy,' answered Miss Pillby; 'I shouldn't wonder if there was a thunderstorm.'

'Don't talk nonsense, child; it's too late in the year for thunder. We shall have the equinoctial gales soon, I dare say.'

'No doubt,' replied Miss Pillby, who had heard about the equinox and its carryings on all her life without having arrived at any clear idea of its nature and properties. 'We shall have it very equinoctial before the end of the month, I've no doubt.'

'Well, is there anything going on? Any of the girls bilious? One of my black draughts wanted anywhere?'

Miss Pew was not highly intellectual, but she was a great hand at finance, household economies, and domestic medicine. She compounded most of the doses taken at Mauleverer with her own fair hands, and her black draughts were a feature in the school. The pupils never forgot them. However faint became the memory of youthful joys in after years, the flavour of Miss Pew's jalap and senna was never obliterated.

'No; there's nobody ill this morning,' answered Miss Pillby, with a faint groan.

'Ah, you may well sigh,' retorted her principal; 'the way those girls ate veal and ham yesterday was enough to have turned the school into a hospital—and with raspberry jam tart after, too.'

Veal with ham was the Sunday dinner at Mauleverer, a banquet upon which Miss Pew prided herself, as an instance of luxurious living rarely to be met with in boarding-schools. If the girls were ill after it, that was their look out.

'There's something wrong, I can see by your face, said Miss Pew, after she had sipped half her tea and enjoyed the whole of her toast; 'is it the servants or the pupils?'

Strange to say, Miss Pew did not look grateful to the bearer of evil tidings. This was one of her idiosyncrasies. She insisted upon being kept informed of all that went wrong in her establishment, but she was apt to be out of temper with the informant.

'Neither,' answered Miss Pillby, with an awful shake of her sandy locks; 'I don't believe there is a servant in this house who would so far forget herself. And as to the pupils—'

'We know what they are,' snapped Miss Pew; 'I never heard of anything bad enough to be beyond their reach. Who is it?'

'Your clever pupil teacher, Ida Palliser.'

'Ah,' grunted Miss Pew, setting down her cup; 'I can believe anything of her. That girl was born to be troublesome. What has she done now?'

Miss Pillby related the circumstances of Miss Palliser's crime setting forth her own cleverness in the course of her narrative—how her misgivings had been excited by the unwonted familiarity between Ida and the Fräulein—a young person always open to suspicion as a stranger in the land—how her fears had been confirmed by the conduct of an unknown man in the church; and how, urged by her keen sense of duty, she had employed Mrs. Jones's boy to watch the delinquents.

'I'll make an example of her,' said Miss Pew, flinging back the bed-clothes with a tragic air as she rose from her couch. 'That will do, Pillby. I want no further details. I'll wring the rest out of that bold-faced minx in the face of all the school. You can go.'

And without any word of praise or thanks from her principal, Miss Pillby retired: yet she knew in her heart that for this piece of ill news Miss Pew was not ungrateful.

Never had Sarah Pew looked more awful than she appeared that morning at the breakfast table, clad in sombre robes of olive green merino, and a cap bristling with olive-green berries and brambly twigs—a cap which to the more advanced of the pupils suggested the head-gear of Medusa.

Miss Dulcibella, gentle, limp, sea-greeny, looked at her stronger-minded sister, and was so disturbed by the gloom upon that imperial brow as to be unable to eat her customary rasher. Not a word did Miss Pew speak to sister or mistresses during that brief but awful meal; but when the delft breakfast cups were empty, and the stacks of thick bread and butter had diminished to nothingness, and the girls were about to rise and disperse for their morning studies, Miss Pew's voice arose suddenly amidst them like the sound of thunder.

'Keep your seats, if you please, young ladies. I am about to make an example; and I hope what I have to say and do may be for the general good. Miss Palliser, stand up.'

Ida rose in her place, at that end of the table where she was supposed to exercise a corrective influence upon the younger pupils. She stood up where all the rest were seated, a tall and perfect figure, a beautiful statuesque head, supported by a neck like a marble column. She stood up among all those other girls the handsomest of them all, pale, with flashing eyes, feeling very sure that she was going to be ill-treated.

'Pray, Miss Palliser, who is the person whom it is your daily habit to meet and converse with in my grounds? Who is the man who has dared to trespass on my meadow at your invitation?'

'Not at my invitation,' answered Ida, as calm as marble 'The gentleman came of his own accord. His name is Brian Wendover, and he and I are engaged to be married.'

Miss Pew laughed a loud ironical laugh, a laugh which froze the blood of all the seventeen-year-old pupils who were not without fear or reproach upon the subject of clandestine glances, little notes, or girlish carryings-on in the flirtation line.

'Engaged?' she exclaimed, in her stentorian voice, 'That is really too good a joke. Engaged? Pray, which Mr. Brian Wendover is it?

'Mr. Wendover of the Abbey.'

'Mr. Wendover of the Abbey, the head of the Wendover family?' cried Miss Pew. 'And you would wish us to believe that Mr. Wendover, of Wendover Abbey—a gentleman with an estate worth something like seven thousand a year, young ladies—has engaged himself to the youngest of my pupil-teachers, whose acquaintance he has cultivated while trespassing on my meadow? Miss Palliser, when a gentleman of Mr. Wendover's means and social status wishes to marry a young person in your position—a concatenation which occurs very rarely in the history of the human race— he comes to the hall door. Mr. Wendover no more means to marry you than he means to marry the moon. His views are of quite a different kind, and you know it.'

Ida cast a withering look at her tyrant, and moved quickly from her place.

'You are a wretch to say such a thing to me,' she cried passionately; 'I will not stay another hour under your roof to be so insulted.'

'No, you will not stay under my roof, Miss Palliser,' retorted Miss Pew. 'My mind was made up more than an hour ago on that point. You will not be allowed to stay in this house one minute longer than is needed for the packing up of your clothes, and that, I take it,' added the schoolmistress, with an insolent laugh, 'will not be a lengthy operation. You are expelled, Miss Palliser—expelled from this establishment for grossly improper conduct; and I am only sorry for your poor father's sake that you will have to begin your career as a governess with disgrace attached to your name.'

'There is no disgrace, except in your own foul mind,' said Ida. 'I can imagine that as nobody ever admired you or made love to you when you were young, you may have mistaken ideas as to the nature of lovers and love-making'—despite the universal awe, this provoked a faint, irrepressible titter—'but it is hard that you should revenge your ignorance upon me. Mr. Wendover has never said a word to me which a gentleman should not say. Fräulein Wolf, who has heard his every word, knows that this is true.'

'Fräulein will leave this house to-morrow, if she is not careful,' said Miss Pew, who had, however, no intention of parting with so useful and cheap a teacher.

She could afford to revenge herself upon Ida, whose period of tutelage was nearly over.

'Fräulein knows that Mr. Wendover speaks of our future as the future of man and wife.'

'Ja wohl,' murmured the Fräulein, 'that is true; ganz und gan.'

'I will not hear another word!' cried Miss Pew, swelling with rage, while every thorn and berry on her autumnal cap quivered. 'Ungrateful, impudent young woman! Leave my house instantly. I will not have these innocent girls perverted by your vile example. In speech and in conduct you are alike detestable.'

'Good-bye, girls,' cried Ida, lightly: 'you all know how much harm my speech and my example have done you. Good-bye, Fräulein; don't you be afraid of dismissal, — you are too well worth your salt.'

Polly Cobb, the brewer's daughter, sat near the door by which Ida had to make her exit. She was quite the richest, and perhaps the best-natured girl in the school. She caught hold of Ida's gown and thrust a little Russia-leather purse into her hand, with a tender squeeze.

'Take it, dear,' she whispered; 'I don't want it, I can get plenty more. Yes, yes, you must; you shall. I'll make a row, and get myself into disgrace, if you refuse. You can't go to France without money.'

'God bless you, dear. I'll send it you back,' answered Ida.

'Don't; I shall hate you if you do.'

'Is that young woman gone?' demanded Miss Pew's awful voice.

'Going, going, gone!' cried Miss Cobb, forgetting herself in her excitement, as the door closed behind Ida.

'Who was that?' roared Miss Pew.

Half a dozen informants pronounced Miss Cobb's name.

Now Miss Cobb's people were wealthy, and Miss Cobb had younger sisters, all coming on under a homely governess to that critical stage in which they would require the polishing processes of Mauleverer Manor: so Sarah Pew bridled her wrath, and said quietly —

'Kindly reserve your jocosity for a more appropriate season, Miss Cobb. Young ladies, you may proceed with your matutinal duties.'

CHAPTER VIII
AT THE LOCK-HOUSE

Miss Pew had argued rightly that the process of packing would not be a long one with Ida Palliser. The girl had come to Mauleverer with the smallest number of garments compatible with decency; and her stock had been but tardily and scantily replenished during her residence in that manorial abode. It was to her credit that she had contrived still to be clean, still to be neat, under such adverse conditions; it was Nature's royal gift that she had looked grandly beautiful in the shabbiest gowns and mantles ever seen at Mauleverer.

She huddled her poor possessions into her solitary trunk—a battered hair trunk which had done duty ever since she came as a child from India. She put a few necessaries into a convenient morocco bag, which the girls in her class had clubbed their pocket-money to present to her on her last birthday; and then she washed the traces of angry tears from her face, put on her hat and jacket, and went downstairs, carrying her bag and umbrella.

One of the housemaids met her in the hall, a buxom, good-natured country girl.

'Is it true that you are going to leave us, miss?' she asked.

'What! you all know it already?' exclaimed Ida.

'Everybody is talking about it, miss. The young ladies are all on your side; but they dare not speak up before Miss Pew.'

'I suppose not. Yes, it is quite true; I am expelled, Eliza; sent out into the world without a character, because I allowed Mr. Wendover to walk and talk with the Fräulein and me for half an hour or so in the river-meadow! Mr. Wendover, my best, my only friend's first cousin. Rather hard, isn't it?'

Hard? it's shameful,' cried the girl. 'I should like to see old Pew turning me off for keeping company with my young man. But she daren't do it. Good servants are hard to get nowadays; or any servants, indeed, for the paltry wages she gives.'

'And governesses are a drug in the market,' said Ida, bitterly. 'Good-bye, Eliza.'

'Where are you going, miss? Home?'

'Yes; I suppose so.'

The reckless tone, the careless words alarmed the good-hearted housemaid.

'Oh, miss, pray go home, straight home—wherever your home is. You are too handsome to be going about alone among strangers. It's a wicked world, miss—wickeder than you know of, perhaps. Have you got money enough to get you home comfortable?'

'I'll see,' answered Ida, taking out Miss Cobb's fat little purse and looking into it.

There were two sovereigns and a good deal of silver—a tremendous fortune for a schoolgirl; but then it was said that Cobb Brothers coined money by the useful art of brewing.

'Yes; I have plenty of money for my journey,' said Ida.

'Are you certain sure, now, miss?' pleaded the housemaid; 'for if you ain't, I've got a pound laid by in my drawer ready to put in the Post Office Savings Bank, and you're as welcome to it as flowers in May, if you'll take it off me.'

'God bless you, Eliza. If I were in any want of money, I'd gladly borrow your sovereign; but Miss Cobb has lent me more than I want. Good-bye.'

Ida held out her hand, which the housemaid, after wiping her own paw upon her apron, clasped affectionately.

'God bless you, Miss Palliser,' she said fervently; 'I shall miss the sight of your handsome face when I waits at table.'

A minute more and Ida stood in the broad carriage sweep, with her back to the stately old mansion which had sheltered her so long, and in which, despite her dependency and her poverty, she had known some light-hearted hours. Now, where was she to go? and what was she to do with her life? She stood with the autumn wind blowing about her—the fallen chestnut leaves drifting to her feet—pondering that question.

Was she or was she not Brian Wendover's affianced wife? How far was she to trust in him, to lean upon him, in this crucial hour of her life? There had been so much playfulness in their love-making, his tone had been for the most part so light and sportive, that now, when she stood, as it were, face to face with destiny, she hardly knew how to think of him, whether as a rock that she might lean upon, or as a reed that would give way at her touch. Rock or reed, womanly instinct told her that it was not to this fervent admirer she must apply for aid or counsel yet awhile. Her duty was to go home at once—to get across the Channel, if possible, as quickly as Miss Pew's letter to her father.

Intent on doing this, she walked along the dusty high road by the river, in the direction of the railway station. This station was more than two miles distant, a long, straight walk by the river, and then a mile or so across fields and by narrow lanes to an arid spot, where some newly-built houses were arising round a hopeless-looking little loop-line station in a desert of agricultural land.

She had walked about three-quarters of a mile, when she heard the rapid dip of oars, as if in pursuit of her, and a familiar voice calling to her.

It was Brian, who almost lived in his boat, and who had caught sight of her in the distance, and followed at racing speed.

'What are you doing?' he asked, coming up close to the bank, and standing up in his boat. 'Where are you going at such a pace? I don't think I ever saw a woman walk so fast.'

'Was I walking fast?' she asked, unconscious of the impetus which excitement had given to her movements.

She knew in her heart of hearts that she did not love him—that love—the passion which she had read of in prose and poetry was still a stranger to her soul: but just at this moment, galled and stung by Miss Pew's unkindness, heart-sick at her own absolute desolation, the sound of his voice was sweet in her ears, the look of the tall slim figure, the friendly face turned towards her, was pleasant to her eyes. No, he was not a reed, he was a rock. She felt protected and comforted by his presence.

'Were you walking fast! Galloping like a three-year-old—*quæ velut latis equa trima campis*,' quoted Brian. 'Are you running away from Mauleverer Manor?'

'I am going away,' she answered calmly. 'I have been expelled.'

'Ex—what?' roared Brian.

'I have been expelled—sent away at a minute's notice—for the impropriety of my conduct in allowing you to talk to me in the river-meadow.'

Brian had been fastening his boat to a pollard willow as he talked. He leapt on to the bank, and came close to Ida's side.

'My darling, my dearest love, what a burning shame! What a villainous old hag that Pew woman must be! Bessie told me she was a Tartar, but this beats everything. Expelled! Your conduct impeached because you let me talk to you—I, Bessie's cousin, a man who at the worst has some claim to be considered a gentleman, while you have the highest claim to be considered a lady. It is beyond all measure infamous.'

'It was rather hard, was it not?' said Ida quietly.

'Abominable, insufferable! I—well. I'll call upon the lady this afternoon, and make her acquainted with my sentiments upon the subject. The wicked old harridan.'

'Please don't,' urged Ida, smiling at his wrath; 'it doesn't give me any consolation to hear you call her horrid names.'

'Did you tell her that I had asked you to be my wife?'

'I said something to that effect—in self-defence—not from any wish to commit you: and she told me that a man in your position, who intended to marry a girl in my position, would act in a very different manner from the way in which you have acted.'

'Did she? She is a wise judge of human nature—and of a lover's nature, above all. Well, Ida, dearest, we have only one course open to us, and that is to give her the lie at once—by our conduct. Deeds, not words, shall be our argument. You do care for me—just a little—don't you, pet? just well enough to marry me? All the rest will come after?'

'Whom else have I to care for?' faltered Ida, with downcast eyes and passionately throbbing heart. 'Who else has ever cared for me?'

'I am answered. So long as I am the only one I will confide all the rest to Fate. We will be married to-morrow.'

'To-morrow! No, no, no.'

'Yes, yes, yes. What is there to hinder our immediate marriage? And what can be such a crushing answer to that old Jezebel! We will be married at the little church where I saw you last Sunday night, looking like St. Cecilia when you joined in the Psalms. We have been both living in the same parish for the last fortnight. I will run up to Doctors' Commons this afternoon, bring back the licence, interview the parson, and have everything arranged for our being married at ten o'clock to-morrow morning.'

'No, no, not for the world.'

For some time the girl was firm in her refusal of such a hasty union. She would not marry her lover except in the face of the world, with the full consent of his friends and her own. Her duty was to go by the first train and boat that would convey her to Dieppe, and to place herself in her father's care.

'Do you think your father would object to our marriage?' asked Brian.

'No, I am sure he would not object,' she answered, smiling within herself at the question.

As if Captain Palliser, living upon his half-pay, and the occasional benefactions of a rich kinsman, could by any possibility object to a match that would make his daughter mistress of Wendover Abbey!

'Then why delay our marriage, in order to formally obtain a consent which you are sure of beforehand! As for my friends, Bessie's people are the nearest and dearest, and you know what their feelings are on your behalf.'

'Bessie likes me as her friend. I don't know how she might like me as her cousin's wife,' said Ida.

'Then I will settle your doubts by telling you a little secret. Bessie sent me here to try and win you for my wife. It was her desire as well as mine.'

More arguments followed, and against the lover's ardent pleading there was only a vague idea of duty in the girl's mind, somewhat weakened by an instinctive notion that her father would think her an arrant fool for delaying so grand a triumph as her marriage with a man of fortune and position. Had he not often spoken to her wistfully of her beauty, and the dim hope that her handsome face might some day win her a rich husband?

'It's a poor chance at the best,' he told her. 'The days of the Miss Gunnings have gone by. The world has grown commercial. Nowadays money marries money.'

And this chance, which her father had speculated upon despondently as a remote contingency, was now at her feet. Was she to spurn it, and then go back to the shabby little villa near Dieppe, and expect to be praised for her filial duty?

While she wavered, Brian urged every argument which a lover could bring to aid his suit. To-morrow they might be married, and in the meanwhile Ida could be safely and comfortably housed with the good woman at the lock-house. Brian would give up his lodgings to her, and would stay at the hotel at Chertsey. Ida listened, and hesitated: before her lay the dry, dusty road, the solitary journey by land and sea, the doubtful welcome at home. And here by her side stood the wealthy lover, the very embodiment of protecting power—is not every girl's first lover in her eyes as Olympian Jove?—eager to take upon himself the burden of her life, to make her footsteps easy.

'Step into the boat, dearest,' he said; 'I know your heart has decided for me. You are not afraid to trust me, Ida?'

'Afraid? no,' she answered, frankly, looking at him with heavenly confidence in her large dark eyes; 'I am only afraid of doing wrong.'

'You can do no wrong with me by your side, your husband to-morrow, responsible for all the rest of your existence.'

'True, after to-morrow I shall be accountable to no one but you,' she said, thoughtfully. 'How strange it seems!'

'At the worst, I hope you will find me better than old Pew,' answered Brian, lightly.

'You are too good—too generous,' she said; 'but I am afraid you are acting too much from impulse. Have you considered what you are going to do? have you thought what it is to marry a penniless girl, who can give you none of the things which the world cares for in exchange for your devotion?'

'I have thought what it is to marry the woman I fondly love, the loveliest girl these eyes ever looked upon. Step into my boat, Ida; I must row you up to the lock, and then start for London by the first train I can catch. I don't know how early the licence-shop closes.'

She obeyed him, and sank into a seat in the stern of the cockle-shell craft, exhausted, mentally and physically, by the agitation of the last two hours, She felt an unspeakable relief in sitting quietly in the boat, the water rippling gently past, like a lullaby, the rushes and willows waving in the mild western breeze. Henceforth she had little to do in life but to be cared for and cherished by an all-powerful lord and master. Wealth to her mind meant power; and this devoted lover was rich. Fate had been infinitely kind to her.

It was a lovely October morning, warm and bright as August. The river banks still seemed to wear their summer green, the blue bright water reflected the cloudless blue above. The bells were ringing for a saint's-day service as Brian's boat shot past the water-side village, with its old square-towered church. All the world had a happy look, as if it smiled at Ida and her choice.

They moved with an easy motion past the pastoral banks, here and there a villa garden, here and there a rustic inn, and so beneath Chertsey's wooded heights to the level fields beyond, and to a spot where the Thames and the Abbey River made a loop round a verdant little marshy island; and here was the silvery weir, brawling noisily in its ceaseless fall, and the lockhouse, where Mr. Wendover had lodgings.

The proprietress of that neat abode had just been letting a boat through the lock, and stood leaning lazily against the woodwork, tasting the morning air. She was a comfortable, well-to-do person, who rented a paddock or two by the towing-path, and owned cows. Her little garden was gay with late geraniums and many-coloured asters.

'Mrs. Topman, I have brought you a young lady to take care of for the next twenty-four hours,' said Brian, coolly, as he handed Ida out of the boat. 'Miss Palliser and I are going to be married to-morrow morning; and, as her friends all live abroad, I want you to take care of her, in a nice, motherly way, till she and I are one. You can give her my rooms, and I can put up at the inn.'

Mrs. Topman curtseyed, and gazed admiringly at Ida.

'I shall be proud to wait upon such a sweet young lady,' she said. 'But isn't it rather sudden? You told me there was a young lady in the case, but I never knowed you was going to be married off-hand like this.'

'I never knew it myself till an hour ago, Mrs. Topman, answered Brian, gaily. 'I knew that I was to be one of the happiest of men some day; but I did not know bliss was so near me. And now I am off to catch the next train from Chertsey. Be sure you give Miss Palliser some breakfast; I don't think she has had a very comfortable one.'

He dashed into the cottage, and came out again five minutes afterwards, having changed his boating clothes for a costume more appropriate to the streets of London. He clasped Ida's hand, murmured a loving good-bye, and then ran with light footsteps along the towing-path, while Ida stood leaning against the lock door looking dreamily down at the water.

How light-hearted he was! and how easily he took life! This marriage, which was to her an awful thing, signifying fate and the unknown future, seemed to him as a mere whim of the hour, a caprice, a fancy. And yet there could be no doubt of his affection for her. Even if his nature was somewhat shallow, as she feared it must be, he was at least capable of a warm and generous attachment. To her in her poverty and her disgrace he had proved himself nobly loyal.

'I ought to be very grateful to him,' she said to herself; and then in her schoolgirl phrase she added, 'and he is very nice.'

Mrs. Topman was in the house, tidying and smartening that rustic sitting-room, which had not been kept too neatly during Mr. Wendover's occupation. Presently came the clinking of cups and saucers, and anon Mrs. Topman appeared on the doorstep, and announced that breakfast was ready.

What a luxurious breakfast it seemed to the schoolgirl after a month of the Mauleverer bread and scrape! Frizzled bacon, new laid eggs, cream, marmalade, and a dainty little cottage loaf, all served with exquisite cleanliness. Ida was too highly strung to do justice to the excellent fare, but she enjoyed a cup of strong tea, and ate one of the eggs, to oblige Mrs. Topman, who waited upon her assiduously, palpably panting with friendly curiosity.

'Do take off your hat, miss,' she urged; 'you must be very tired after your journey—a long journey, I daresay. Perhaps you would like me to send a boy with a barrow for your luggage directly after breakfast. I suppose your trunks are at the station?'

'No; Mr. Wendover will arrange about my trunk by-and-by,' faltered Ida; and then looking down at her well-worn gray cashmere gown, she thought that it was hardly a costume in which to be married. Yet how was she to get her box from Mauleverer Manor without provoking dangerous inquiries? And even if she had the box its contents would hardly solve the question of a wedding gown. Her one white gown would be too cold for the season; her best gown was black. Would Brian feel very much ashamed of her, she wondered, if she must needs be married in that shabby gray cashmere?

And then it occurred to her that possibly Brian, while procuring the licence, might have a happy thought about a wedding gown, and buy her one ready made at a London draper's. He, to whom money was no object, could so easily get an appropriate costume. It would be only for him to go into a shop and say, 'I want a neat, pretty travelling dress for a tall, slim young lady,' and the thing would be packed in a box and put into his cab in a trice. Everything in life is made so easy for people with ample means.

It was some time before Mrs. Topman would consent to leave her new lodger. She was so anxious to be of use to the sweet young lady, and threw out as many feelers as an octopus in the way of artfully-devised conjectures and suppositions calculated to extract information. But Miss Palliser was not communicative.

'You *must* be tired after your journey. Those railways are so hot and so dusty,' said Mrs. Topman, with a despairing effort to discover whence her unexpected guest had come that morning.

'I am rather tired,' admitted Ida; 'I think, if you don't mind, I'll take a book and lie down on that comfortable sofa for an hour or two.'

'Do miss. You'll find some books of Mr. Wendover's on the cheffonier. But perhaps you'll be glad to take a little nap. Shall I draw down the blind and darken the room for you?'

'No, thanks; I like the sunshine.'

Mrs. Topman unwillingly withdrew, and Ida was alone in the sitting-room which her lover had occupied for the last fortnight.

Much individuality can hardly be expected in a temporary lodging — a mere caravansary in life's journey; and yet, even in the brief space of a fortnight, a room takes some colour from the habits and ideas of the being who has lived in it.

Ida looked round curiously, wondering whether she would discover any indications of her lover's character in Mrs. Topman's parlour. The room, despite its open casements, smelt strongly of tobacco. That was a small thing, for Ida knew that her lover smoked. She had seen him several times throw away the end of his cigar as he sprang from his boat by the river meadow. But that array of various pipes and cigar-holders — that cedar cigar box — that brass tobacco jar on the mantelpiece, hinted at an ardent devotion to the nymph Nicotina such as is rarely pleasing to woman.

'I am sorry he is so wedded to his pipes,' thought Ida with a faint sigh.

And then she turned to the cheffonier to inspect her lover's stock of literature.

A man who loves his books never travels without a few old favourites — Horace or Montaigne, Elia, an odd volume of De Quincey, a battered Don Juan, a worn-out Faust, a shabby Shelley, or a ponderous Burton in his threadbare cloth raiment.

But there was not one such book among Mr. Wendover's possessions. His supply of mental food consisted of a half a dozen shilling magazines, the two last numbers of *Punch*, and three or four sporting papers. Ida turned from them with bitter disappointment. She seemed to take the measure of Brian Wendover's mind in that frivolous collection, and she was deeply pained at the idea of his shallowness.

'What has he done with himself in the long evenings?' she asked herself. 'Has he done nothing but smoke and read those magazines?'

She took up the *Cornhill*, and found its graver essays uncut. It was the same with the other magazines. Only the most frivolous articles had been looked at. Mr. Wendover was evidently anything but a reading man.

'No wonder he does not like the Abbey,' she thought. 'The country must always seem dull to a man who does not care for books.'

And then she reminded herself remorsefully of his generous affection, his single-minded devotion to her, and how much gratitude she owed him.

She read all that was worth reading in the magazines, she laughed at all that was laughable in *Punch,* and the long, slow day wore on somehow. Mrs. Topman brought her lunch, and consulted her about dinner.

'You will not dine until Mr. Wendover comes back, I suppose, miss? You and he can have a nice little dinner together at seven.'

Ida blushed at the mere notion of hobnobbing alone with a gentleman in that water-side lodging.

'No thanks; this will be my dinner,' she answered quietly. 'Please don't get anything more for me. No doubt Mr. Wendover will dine at the hotel, if he has not dined in London I shall want nothing more except a cup of tea.'

After luncheon Ida went out and strolled by the river, that river of which no one ever seems to grow weary. She wandered about the level meadows, where the last of the wild-flowers were blooming, or she sat on the bank, watching the ripple of the water, the slow smooth passage of pleasure-boat or barge, and the day was long but not dreary. It was so new to her to be idle, to be able to fold her hands and watch the stream, and not to fear reproof because she had ceased from toil. At Mauleverer, at this tranquil afternoon hour, while those rooks were sailing so calmly high above her head—yonder belated butterfly fluttering so happily over the feathery grasses—all nature so full of rest—they were grinding away in the hot schoolroom, grinding at the weekly geography lesson, addling their brains with feeble efforts to repeat by rote dry-as-dust explanations about the equator and the torrid zone, latitude, longitude, winds and tides, the height of mountains, the population of towns, manufactures, creeds; not trying in the least to understand, or caring to remember; only intent on getting over to-day's trouble and preparing in some wise to meet the debts of to-morrow.

'Oh, thank God, to have got away from that treadmill,' said Ida, looking up at the bright blue sky; 'can I ever be sufficiently grateful to Providence, and to the man whose love has rescued me?'

Her deliverer came strolling across the fields in quest of her presently, tired and dusty, but delighted to be with her again. He sat down by her side, and put his arm round her waist for the first time in his life.

'Don't,' he said, as she instinctively recoiled from him; 'you are almost my own now. I have got the licence, I have seen the parson, and he is quite charmed at the idea of marrying us to-morrow morning. He had heard of your little escapade, it seems, and he thinks we are doing quite the wisest thing possible.'

'He had heard—already!' exclaimed Ida, deeply mortified. 'Has Miss Pew been calling out my delinquencies from the house-top? Oh, no,—I understand. Tuesday is Mr. Daly's afternoon for Bible class, and he has been at the school.'

'Exactly; and Miss Pew unburdened her mind to him.'

'Did he think me a dreadful creature?'

'He thinks you charming, but that I ought to have gone to the hall-door when I courted you; as I should have done, dearest, only I wanted to be sure of you first. He was all kindness, and will marry us quietly at nine o'clock to-morrow, just after Matins, when there will be nobody about to stare at us; and he has promised to say nothing about our marriage until we give him leave to make the fact public.'

'I am glad of that,' said Ida, looking at her shabby gown. 'Do you think it will matter much—will you be very much ashamed of me, if I am married in this threadbare old cashmere?'

She had a faint hope that he would exclaim, 'My love, I have brought you a wedding dress from Regent Street; come and see it.' But he only smiled at her tenderly, and said—

'The gown does not matter a jot; you are lovelier in your shabby frock than any other bride in satin and pearls. And some of these days you shall have smart frocks.'

He said it hopefully, but as if it were a remote contingency.

He spoke very much as her impecunious father might have spoken. He, the master of Wendover Abbey, to whom the possession of things that money could buy must needs be a dead certainty. But it was evidently a part of his character to make light of his wealth; assuredly a pleasant idiosyncrasy.

They dawdled about on the bank for half an hour or so, talking somewhat listlessly, for Ida was depressed and frightened by the idea of that fateful event, giving a new colour to all her life to come, which was so soon to happen. Brian was very kind, very good to her; she wished with all her heart that she had loved him better; yet it seemed to her that she did love him—a little. Surely this feeling was love, this keen sense of obligation, this warm admiration for his generous and loyal conduct. Yes, this must be love. And why, loving him, should she feel this profound melancholy at the idea of a marriage which satisfied her loftiest ambition?

Perhaps the cause of her depression lay in the strangeness of this sudden union, its semi-clandestine character, her loneliness at a crisis in life when most girls are surrounded by friends. Often in her reckless talk with Bessie Wendover she had imagined her marriage. She would marry for money. Yes, the soap-boiler, the candlestick maker—anybody. It should be a splendid wedding—a dozen of the prettiest girls at Mauleverer for her bridesmaids, bells ringing, flowers strewn upon her pathway, carriage and four, postilions in blue jackets and white favours, all the world and his wife looking on and wondering at her high fortune. This is how fancy had painted the picture when Ida discoursed of her future in the butterfly-room at Mauleverer; Miss Rylance listening and making sarcastic comments; Bessie in fits of smothered laughter at all the comic touches in the description; for did not true-hearted Bessie know that the thing was a joke, and that her noble Ida would never so degrade herself as to marry for money? And now Ida was going to do this thing, scarcely knowing why she did it, not at all secure in her own mind of future happiness; not with unalloyed pride in her conquest, but yielding to her lover because he was the first who had ever asked her; because he was warm and true when all else in life seemed cold and false; and because the alternative—return to the poor home—was so dreary.

The conversation flagged as the lovers walked in the twilight. The sun was sinking behind the low hedge of yonder level meadow. Far away in mountainous regions the same orb was setting in rocky amphitheatres, distant, unapproachable. Here in this level land he seemed to be going down into a grave behind that furthest hedge.

It was a lovely evening—orange and rosy lights reflected on the glassy river, willows stirred with a murmurous movement by faintest zephyrs—a wind no louder than a sigh. Brian proposed that they should go on the river; his boat was there ready, it was only to step into the light skiff, and drift lazily with the stream.

They got into the Abbey river, among water-lilies whose flowers had all died long ago, face downwards. The season of golden flowers, buttercup, marsh-mallow, was over. The fields were grayish-green, with ruddy tinges here and there. The year was fading.

Ida sat in dead silence watching the declining light, one listless hand dipping in the river.

Brian was thoughtful, more thoughtful than she had known him in any period of their acquaintance.

'Where shall we go for our honeymoon? he asked abruptly, jingling some loose coins in his pocket.

'Oh, that is for you to decide. I—I know what I should like best,' faltered Ida.

'What is that?'

'I should like you to take me to Dieppe, where we could see my father, and explain everything to him.'

'Did you write to him to-day?'

'No; I thought I would tell him nothing till after our marriage. You might change your mind at the last.'

'Cautious young party,' said Brian, laughing. 'There is no fear of that. I am too far gone in love for that. For good or ill I am your faithful slave. Yes, we will go to Dieppe if you like. It is late in the year for a place of that kind; but what do we care for seasons? Do you think your father and I will be able to get on?'

'My father is the soul of good nature. He would get on with anyone who is a gentleman, and I am sure he will like you very much. My stepmother is—well, she is rather vulgar. But I hope you won't mind that. She is very warm-hearted.'

'Vulgarians generally are, I believe,' answered Brian lightly. 'At least, one is always told as much. It is hard that the educated classes should monopolize all the cold hearts. Vulgar but warm-hearted—misplaces her aspirates—but affectionate! That is the kind of thing one is told when Achilles marries a housemaid. Never mind, Ida, dearest, I feel sure I shall like your father; and for his sake I will try to make myself agreeable to his wife. And your little brother is perfection. I have heard enough about him from those dear lips of yours.'

'He is a darling little fellow, and I long to see him again. How I wish they could all be with me to-morrow!'

'It would make our wedding more domestic, but don't you think it would vulgarize it a little?' said Brian. 'There is something so sweet to me in the idea of you and me alone in that little church, with no witnesses but the clerk and the pew-opener.'

'And God!' said Ida, looking upward.

'Did you ever read the discourses of Colonel Bob Ingersoll?' asked Brian, smiling at her.

'No; what has that to do with it?'

'He has curious ideas of omnipotence; and I fancy he would say that the Infinite Being who made every shining star is hardly likely to be on the look-out for our wedding.'

'He cares for the lilies and the sparrows.'

'That's a gospel notion. Colonel Bob is not exactly a gospel teacher,'

'Then don't you learn of him, Brian,' said Ida, earnestly.

CHAPTER IX
A SOLEMN LEAGUE AND COVENANT

The sun shone upon Ida's wedding morn. She was dressed and down before seven—her shabby cashmere gown carefully brushed, her splendid hair neatly arranged, her linen collar and cuffs spotlessly clean. This was all she could do in the way of costume in honour of this solemn day. She had not even a new pair of gloves. Mrs. Topman, who was to go to church with her in a fly from Chertsey, was gorgeous in purple silk and a summer bonnet—a grand institution, worn only on Sundays. Breakfast was ready in the neat little parlour, but Ida would only take a cup of tea. She wandered out to the river-side, and looked at the weir and the little green island round which the shining blue water twined itself like a caress. All things looked lovely in the pure freshness of morning.

'What a sweet spot it is!' said Ida to Mrs. Topman, who stood at her gate, watching for the fly, which was not due for half an hour; 'I should almost like to spend my life here.'

'Almost, but not quite,' answered the matron. 'Young folks like you wants change. But I hope you and Mr. Wendover will come here sometimes in the boating season, in memory of old times.'

'We'll come often,' said Ida; 'I hope I shall always remember how kind you have been to me.'

A distant church clock struck the half hour.

'Only half-past seven,' exclaimed Mrs. Topman, 'and Simmons's fly is not to be here till eight. Well, we *are* early.'

Ida strolled a little way along the bank, glad to be alone. It was an awful business, this marriage, when she came to the very threshold of Hymen's temple. Yesterday it had seemed to her that she and Brian Wendover were familiar friends; to-day she thought of him almost as a stranger.

'How little we know of each other, and yet we are going to take the most solemn vow that ever was vowed,' she thought, as she read the marriage service in a Prayer-book which Mrs. Topman had lent her for that purpose.

'It's as well to read it over and understand what you're going to bind yourself to,' said the matron; 'I did before I married Topman. It made me feel more comfortable in my mind to know what I was doing. But I must say it's high time there was a change made in the service. It never can have been intended by Providence for all the obedience to be on the wife's side, or God Almighty wouldn't have made husbands such fools. If Topman hadn't obeyed me he'd have died in a workhouse; and if I'd obeyed him I shouldn't have a stick of furniture belonging to me.'

Ida was not deeply interested in the late Mr. Topman's idiosyncrasies, but she was interested in the marriage bond, which seemed to her a very solemn league and covenant, as she read the service beside the quietly flowing river.

'For better for worse, for richer or poorer, in sickness and in health, to love and to cherish, till death us do part.'

Yes, those were awful words—words to be pronounced by her presently, binding her for the rest of her life. She who was marrying a rich man for the sake of his wealth was to swear to be true to him in poverty. She who was marrying youth and good spirits was to swear to be true to sickness and feeble age. A terrible covenant! And of this man for whom she was to undertake so much she knew so little.

The fly drove along the towing-path, and drew up in front of Mrs. Topman's garden gate as the Chertsey clocks struck the hour, and Mrs. Topman and her charge took their places in that vehicle, and were jolted off at a jog-trot pace towards the town, and then on by a dusty high road towards that new church in the fields at which the Mauleverer girls deemed it such a privilege to worship.

It was about forty minutes' drive from the lock to the church, and Matins were only just over when the fly drew up at the Gothic door.

The incumbent was hovering near in his surplice, and the pew-opener was all in a fluster at the idea of a runaway marriage. Brian came out of the dusky background—the daylight being tempered by small painted windows in heavy stone mullions—as Ida entered the church. Everything was ready. Before she knew how it came to pass, she was standing before the altar, and the fatal words were being spoken.

'Brian Walford, wilt thou have this woman to be thy wedded wife?'

'Brian Walford!' she heard the words as in a dream. Surely Walford was the second name of Bessie's other cousin, the poor cousin! Ida had heard Bessie so distinguish him from the master of the Abbey. But no doubt Walford was some old family name borne by both cousins.

Brian Walford! She had not much time to think about this, when the same solemn question was asked of her.

And then in a low and quiet voice the priest read the rest of the time-hallowed ceremonial, and Brian and Ida, glorified by a broad ray of morning sunshine streaming through an open window, stood up side by side man and wife.

Then came the signing of the register in the snug little vestry, Mrs. Topman figuring largely as witness.

'I did not know your name was Walford,' said Ida, looking over her husband's shoulder as he wrote.

'Didn't you? Second names are of so little use to a man, unless he has the misfortune to be Smith or Jones, and wants to borrow dignity from a prefix. Wendover is good enough for me.'

The young couple bade Mrs. Topman good-bye at the churchdoor. The fly was to take them straight to the station, on the first stage of their honeymoon trip.

'You know where to send my luggage,' Brian said to his landlady at parting.

'Yes, sir, I've got the address all right;' and the fly drove along another dusty high road, still within sight of the river, till it turned at right angles into a bye road leading to the station.

At that uncongenial place they had to wait a quarter of an hour, walking up and down the windy platform, where the porter abandoned himself to the contemplation of occasional looks, and was sometimes surprised by the arrival of a train for which he had waited so long as to have become sceptical as to the existence of such things as trains in the scheme of the universe. The station was a terminus, and the line was a loop, for which very few people appeared to have any necessity.

'Would you mind telling me where we are going, Brian?' Ida asked her husband presently, when they had discussed the characteristics of the station, and Brian had been mildly facetious about the porter.

She had grown curiously shy since the ceremonial. Her lover seemed to her transformed into another person by those fateful words. He was now the custodian of her life, the master of her destiny.

'Would I mind telling you, my dearest? What a question! You proposed Dieppe for our honeymoon, and we are going to Dieppe.'

'Does this train go to Newhaven?'

'Not exactly. Nothing in this life is so convenient as that. This train will deposit us at Waterloo Station. The train for Newhaven leaves London Bridge at seven, in time for the midnight boat. We will go to my chambers and have some lunch.'

'Chambers!' exclaimed Ida, wonderingly. 'Have you really chambers in London?'

'Yes.'

'What a strange man you are!'

'That hardly indicates strangeness. But here at last is our train.'

A train had come slowly in and deposited its handful of passengers about ten minutes ago, and the same train was now ready to start in the opposite direction.

Ida and her husband got into an empty first-class compartment and the train moved slowly off. And now that they were alone, as it were within four walls, she summoned up courage to say something that had been on her mind for the last quarter of an hour—a very hard thing for a bride of an hour old to say, yet which must be said somehow.

'Would you mind giving me a little money, while we are in London, to buy some clothes?' she began hesitatingly. 'It is a dreadful thing to have to ask you, when, if I were not like the beggar girl in the ballad, I should have a trousseau. But I don't know when I may get my box from Mauleverer, and when I do most of the things in it are too shabby for your wife; and in the meantime I have nothing, and I should not like to disgrace you, to make you feel ashamed of me while we are on our honeymoon tour.'

She sat with downcast eyes and flaming cheeks, deeply humiliated by her position, hating her poverty more than she had ever hated it in her life before. She felt that this rich husband of hers had not been altogether kind to her—that he might by a little forethought have spared her this shame. He must have known that she had neither clothes nor money. He who had such large means had done nothing to sweeten her poverty. On this her wedding morning he had brought her no gift save the ring which the law prescribed. He had not brought her so much as a flower by way of greeting; yet she knew by the gossip of her schoolfellows that it was the custom for a lover to ratify his engagement by some splendid ring, which was ever afterwards his betrothed's choicest jewel. The girls had talked of their elder sisters' engagement-rings: how one had diamonds, another rubies, another catseyes, more distinguished and artistic than either.

And now she sat with drooping eyelids, expecting her lover-husband to break into an outburst of self-reproach, then pour a shower of gold into her lap. But he did neither. He rattled some loose coins in his pocket, just as he had done yesterday when he talked of the honeymoon; and he answered hesitatingly, with evident embarrassment.

'Yes, you'll want some new clothes, I daresay. All girls do when they marry, don't they? It's a kind of unwritten law—new husband, new gowns. But I'm sure you can't look better than you do in that gray gown, and it looks to me just the right thing for travelling. And for any other little things you may want for the moment, if a couple of sovereigns will do'—producing those coins—'you can get anything you like as we drive to my chambers. We could stop at a draper's on our way.'

Ida was stricken dumb by this reply. Her cheeks changed from crimson to pale. Her wealthy husband—the man whose fortune was to give her all those good things she had ever pictured to herself in the airy visions of a splendid future—offered her, with a half-reluctant air, as if offering his life's blood, two sovereigns with which to purchase a travelling outfit. What could she buy for two sovereigns? Not all the economy of her girlhood could screw half the things she wanted out of that pitiful sum.

She thought of all those descriptions of weddings which were so eagerly devoured at Mauleverer, whenever a fashionable newspaper fell in the way of those eager neophytes. She recalled the wonderful gifts which the bridegroom and the bridegroom's friends showered on the bride—the glorious gown and bonnet in which the bride departed on her honeymoon journey. And she was offered two sovereigns, wherewith to supply herself with all things needful for comfort and respectability.

Pride gave her strength to refuse the sordid boon. She had the contents of her small travelling bag, and she was going to her father's house, where her step-mother would, perhaps, contrive to provide what was absolutely necessary. Anything was better than to be under an obligation to this rich husband who so little understood her needs.

Could she have married that most detestable of all monsters, a miser? No, she could hardly believe that. It was not in a Wendover to be mean. And all that she had observed hitherto of Brian's way of acting and thinking rather indicated a recklessness about money than an undue care of pounds, shillings, and pence.

'If you don't object to this gown and hat, I can manage very well till we get to my father's house,' she said quietly.

'I adore you in that hat and gown,' replied Brian, eagerly, dropping the sovereigns back into his pocket; and so the question was settled.

An elderly lady came into the carriage at the next station, and there was no renewal of confidences between bride and bridegroom till they came to Waterloo, nor even then, for there is not much opportunity for confidential utterances in a hansom, and it was that convenient vehicle which carried Brian and his bride to the Temple.

They alighted at a gate on the Embankment, and made their way by a garden to a row of grave old houses, with a fine view of the river. Brian led his wife into one of these houses and up the uncarpeted stair to the third floor, where he ushered her into a room with two old-fashioned windows looking out upon grass, and trees, and old-fashioned buildings, all grave and gray, and having an air of sober peacefulness, as of a collegiate or monastic seclusion, while beyond the broad green lawn shone the broad blue river.

'What a nice old place!' said Ida, looking down at the garden. 'How quiet, how grave, how learned-looking! I don't wonder you like this *pied-à-terre* in London, as a change from your grand old Abbey.'

Brian gave a little nervous cough, as if something were choking him. He came to the window, and put his arm round his wife's waist.

'Ida,' he began, somewhat huskily, 'I am going to tell you a secret.'

'What is that?' she asked, turning and looking at him.

'The Abbey does not belong to me!'

'What?' she cried, with wide-open eyes.

'You have been rather fond of talking about the Abbey; but I hope your heart is not too much set upon it. You told me the other day, you know, that you did not value me upon account of the Abbey or my position as its owner. I hope that was the truth, Ida; for Wendover Abbey belongs to my cousin. You have married the poor Brian and not the rich one!'

'What?' she cried. 'You have lied to me all this time—you have fooled and deluded me!'

She turned and faced him with eyes that flamed indignant fire, lips that quivered with unrestrained passion.

'It was not my doing,' he faltered, shrinking before her like the veriest craven; 'it was the girls—Urania and Bessie—who started the notion as a practical joke, just to see what you would think of me, believing me to be my cousin. And when you seemed to like me—a little—Bessie, who is fond of me and who adores you, urged me to follow up my advantage.'

'But not to cheat me into a marriage. No; it is not in Bessie to suggest such falsehood.'

'She hardly contemplated an immediate marriage. I was to win your heart, and when I was sure of that—'

'You were to tell me the truth,' said Ida, looking him straight in the eyes.

His head drooped upon his breast.

'And you did not tell me. You knew that I saw in you Brian Wendover, the head of the family, the owner of a great estate; that I was proud of being loved and sought by a man who stooped from such a high position to love me, who renounced the chance of a brilliant marriage to marry me, a penniless body! You knew that it was in that character I admired you and respected you, and was grateful to you! Not as the briefless barrister—the man without means or position!'

'You harped a good deal upon the Abbey. But I had some right to suppose you liked me for my own sake, and that you would forgive me for a stratagem which was prompted by my love for you. How could I know that you looked upon marriage as a matter of exchange and barter?'

'No,' said Ida, bitterly. 'You are right. You could not know how mean I am. I did not know it myself till now. And now,' she pursued, with flashing eyes, with a look in her splendid face that seemed to blight and wither him, with all her beauty, all her womanhood, up in arms against him, 'and now to punish you for having kept the truth from me, I will tell *you* the truth—plainly. I have never cared one straw for you. I thought I did while I still believed you Brian Wendover of the Abbey. I was dazzled by your position; I was grateful in advance for all the good things that your wealth was to bring me. I tried to delude myself into the belief that I really loved you; but the voice of my conscience told me that it was not so, that I was, in sober truth, the basest of creatures—a woman who marries for money. And now, standing here before you, I know what a wretch I seem—what a wretch I am.'

'You are my wife,' said Brian, trying to take her hand; 'and we must both make the best of a bad bargain.'

'Your wife?' she echoed, in a mocking voice.

'Yes, my very wife, Ida. The knot that was tied to-day can only be loosened by death—or dishonour.'

'You have married me under a false name.'

'No, I have not. You married Brian Walford Wendover. There is no other man of that name.'

'You have cheated me into a miserable marriage. I will never forgive that cheat. I will never acknowledge you as my husband. I will never bear your name, or be anything to you but a stranger, except that I shall hate you all the days of my life. That will be the only bond between us,' she added, with a bitter laugh.

'Come, Ida,' said Brian, soothingly, feeling himself quite able to face the situation now the first shock was over, 'I was prepared for you to be disappointed—to be angry, even; but you are carrying matters a little too far. Even your natural disappointment can hardly excuse such language as this. I am the same man I was yesterday morning when I asked you to marry me.'

'No, you are not. I saw you in a false light—glorified by attributes that never belonged to you.'

'In plain words, you thought me the owner of a big house and a fine income. I am neither; but I am the same Brian Wendover, for all that—a briefless barrister, but with some talent; not without friends; and with as fair a chance of success as most young men of my rank.'

'You are an idler—I have heard that from your uncle—self-indulgent, fond of trivial pleasures. Such men never succeed in life. But if you were certain to be Lord Chancellor—if you could this moment prove yourself possessed of a splendid fortune—my feelings would be unchanged. You have lied to me as no gentleman would have lied. I will own no husband who is not a gentleman.'

'You carry things with a high hand,' said Brian, with sullen wrath; and then love prevailed over anger, and he flung himself on his knees at her feet, clasping her reluctant hands, urging every impassioned argument which young lips could frame; but to all such prayers she was marble. 'You are my wife,' he pleaded; 'you are my snared bird; your wings are netted, darling. Do you think I will let you go? Yes, I was false, but it was love made me deceive you. I loved you so well that I dared not risk losing you.'

'You have lost me for ever,' she cried, breaking from him and moving towards the door; 'perhaps, had you been loyal and true, you might have taught me to love you for your own sake. Women are easier won by truth than falsehood.'

'It seems to me they are easier won by houses and lands,' answered Brian, with a sneer.

And then he followed her to the door, caught her in his arms, and held her against his passionately beating heart, covering her angry face with kisses.

'Let me go!' she cried, tearing herself from his arms, with a shriek of horror; 'your kisses are poison to me. I hate you—I hate you!'

He recoiled a few paces, and stood looking at her with a countenance in which the passionate love of a moment ago gave place to gloomy anger.

'So be it,' he said; 'if we cannot be friends we must be enemies. You reveal your character with an admirable candour. You did not mind marrying a man who was absolutely repulsive to you—whose kisses are poison—so long as you thought he was rich. But directly you are told he is poor you inform him of your real sentiments with a delightful frankness. Suppose this confession of mine were a hoax, and that I really were the wealthy Brian after all—playing off a practical joke to test your feelings— what a sorry figure you would cut!'

'Despicable,' said Ida, with her hand on the handle of the door. 'Yes, I know that. I despise and loathe myself as much as I despise and loathe you. I have drained the cup of poverty to the dregs, and I languished for the elixir of wealth. When you asked me to marry you, I thought Fate had thrown prosperity in my way—that it would be to lose the golden chance of a lifetime if I refused you.'

'Not much gold about it,' said Brian, lightly.

He had one of those shallow natures to which the tragedy of life is impossible. He was disappointed—angry at the turn which affairs had taken; but he was not reduced to despair. To take things easily had been his complete code of morals and philosophy from earliest boyhood. He was not going to break his heart for any woman, were she the loveliest, the cleverest, the noblest that ever the gods endowed with their choicest gifts. She might be ever so fair, but if she were not fair for him she was, in a manner, non-existent. Life, in his philosophy, was too short to be wasted in following phantoms.

'You must have thought me a mean cad this morning, when I offered you a couple of sovereigns,' he said; 'yet they constituted a third of my worldly possessions, and I was sorely puzzled how we were to get to Dieppe on less than four pounds. I have been living from hand to mouth ever since I left the university, picking up a few pounds now and then by literature, writing criticisms for a theatrical journal, and so on—by no means a brilliant living. Perhaps, after all, it is as well you take things so severely,' he added, with a sneer. 'If we had been well disposed towards each other, we must have starved.'

'I could have lived upon a crust with a husband whom I loved and respected; but not with a man who could act a lie, as you did,' said Ida.

She took her bag from the chair where Brian had thrown it as they entered the room, and went out on the landing.

'Good-bye, Mrs. Wendover,' he called after her; 'let me know if I can ever be of any use to you.'

She was going downstairs by this time, and he was looking down at her across the heavy old banister rail.

'I suppose you are going straight to your father's?'

'Yes.'

'Hadn't you better stop and have some lunch? The train doesn't go for hours.'

'No, thanks.'

The gray gown fluttered against the sombre brown panelling as his wife turned the corner of the lower landing and disappeared from his view— perhaps for ever.

Brian went back to his room, and stood in the middle of it, looking round him with a contemplative air. It was a pleasant room, arranged with rather a dandified air—pipes, walking-sticks, old engravings, *bric-à-brac*— the relics of his college life.

'Well, if she had been more agreeable, I should have had to get new rooms, and that would have been a bore,' he said to himself; and then he sank into a chair, gave a laugh that was half a sob, and wiped a mist of tears from his eyes.

'What fools we have both been!' he muttered to himself, 'I knew she was in love with the Abbey; but I don't believe a word she says about hating me!'

And yet—and yet—she had seemed very much in earnest when she tore herself from his arms with that agonized shriek.

CHAPTER X
A BAD PENNY

Ida made her way back to the Embankment somehow, hardly knowing where she was going or what she was going to do. The airy castle which she had built for herself had fallen about her ears, and she was left standing amidst the ruins. Wendover Abbey, wealth, position, independence, the world's respect, were all as far from her as they had been a month ago. Her sense of disappointment was keen, but not so keen as the sense of her self-abasement. Her own character stood revealed to herself in all its meanness—its sordid longing for worldly wealth—its willingness to stoop to falsehood in the pursuit of a woman's lowest aim, a good establishment. Seen in the light of abject failure, the scheme of her life seemed utterly detestable. Success would have gilded everything. As the wife of the rich Brian she would have done her duty in all wifely meekness and obedience, and would have gone down to the grave under the comforting delusion that she had in no wise forfeited honour or self-respect. Cheated, duped, degraded, she now felt all the infamy implied in her willingness to marry a man for whom she cared not a straw.

'Oh, it was cruel, iniquitous,' she said to herself, as she hurried along the dusty pavement, impelled by agitated thoughts, 'to trade upon my weakness—my misery—to see me steeped to the lips in odious poverty, and to tempt me with the glitter of wealth. I never pretended to love him— never—thank God for that! I let him tell me that he loved me, and I consented to be his wife; but I pretended no love on my side. Thank God for that! He cannot say that I lied to him.'

She hurried along, citywards, following the stream of people, and found herself presently in broad, busy Queen Victoria Street, with all the traffic hastening by her, staring helplessly at the cabs, and omnibuses, waggons, carriages streaming east and west under the murky London sky, vaguely wondering what she was to do next.

He—her husband—had asked her if she were going back to her father, and she had said 'Yes.' Indeed it was the only course open to her. She must go home and face the situation, and accept any paternal reproof that might be offered her. She had lost a day. No doubt Miss Pew's indictment would have arrived before her; and she would have to explain her conduct to father and step-mother. But the little white-walled house near Dieppe was the only shelter the universe held for her, and she must go there.

'Wendover Abbey!' she repeated to herself. I the mistress of Wendover Abbey! That was too good a joke, 'Why did I not see the folly of such a dream? But it was just like other dreams. When one dreams one is a queen, or that one can fly, there is no consciousness of the absurdity of the thing.'

She stood staring at the omnibuses till the conductor of one that was nearly empty murmured invitingly in her ear, 'London Bridge?'

It was the place to which she wanted to go. She nodded to the man, who opened his door and let her in.

She was at the station at a quarter to four, and the train for Newhaven did not leave till seven—a long dismal stretch of empty time to be lived through. But she could not improve her situation by going anywhere else. The station, with its dingy waiting-rooms and garish refreshment-room, was as good an hotel for her as any other. She was faint for want of food, having taken nothing since her apology for breakfast at seven o'clock.

'Can one get a cup of tea here?' she asked of the dry-as-dust matron in charge of the waiting-room; whereupon the matron good-naturedly offered to fetch her some tea.

'If you would be so kind,' she faltered, too exhausted to speak above a whisper; 'I don't like going into that crowded refreshment-room.'

'No, to be sure—not much used to travelling alone, I daresay. You will be better when you've had a cup of tea.'

The tea, with a roll and butter, revived exhausted nature. Ida paid for this temperate refreshment, went to the booking-office, made some inquiries about her ticket, and bought herself a book at the stall, wherewith to beguile the time and to distract her mind from brooding on its own miseries.

She felt it was a frightful extravagance as she paid away two of Miss Cobb's shillings for Bulwer's 'Caxtons;' but she felt also that to live through those three tedious hours without such aid would be a step on the road to a lunatic asylum.

Armed with her book, she went back to the waiting-room, settled herself in a corner of the sofa, and remained there absorbed, immovable; while travellers came and went, all alike fussy, flurried, and full of their own concerns—not one of them stopping to notice the pale, tired-looking girl reading in the remotest corner of the spacious room.

A somewhat stormy passage brought the boat which carried Ida and her fortunes to straggling, stony, smelly Dieppe, now abandoned to its native population, and deprived of that flavour of fashion which pervades its beach in the brighter months of August and September. The town looked gray, cold, and forbidding in the bleak October morning, when Ida found herself alone amidst its stoniness, the native population only just beginning to bestir itself in the street above the quay, and making believe, by an inordinate splashing and a frantic vehemence in the use of birch-brooms, to be the cleanest population under the sun; an assertion of superiority somewhat belied by an all-pervading odour of decomposed vegetable matter, a small heap of which refuse, including egg-shells and fishy offal— which the town in the matutinal cleansing process offered up to the sun-god as incense upon an altar—lay before every door, to be collected by the local scavenger at his leisure, or to be blown about and disseminated by the winds of heaven.

Alone upon the stony quay, in the freshness and chilliness of early morning, Ida took temporary refuge in the humblest *café* she could find, where a feeble old woman was feebly brooming the floor, and where there was no appearance of any masculine element. Here she expended another of Miss Cobb's shillings upon a cup of coffee and a roll. She had spent five and twenty shillings for her second-class ticket. The debt to Miss Cobb now amounted to a sovereign and a half; and Ida Palliser thought of it with an aching sense of her own helplessness to refund so large a sum. Yesterday morning, believing herself about to become the wife of a rich man, she had thought what fun it would be to send 'Cobby' a five-pound note in the prettiest of ivory purses from one of those shops in the street yonder.

She drank her coffee slowly, not anxious to hasten the hour of a home-coming which could not be altogether pleasant. She was as fond of her father as adverse circumstances had allowed her to be; she adored her half-brother, and was not unkindly disposed towards her step-mother. But to go back to them penniless, threadbare, disgraced—go back to be a burden upon their genteel poverty. That was bitter.

She had made up her mind to walk to Les Fontaines rather than make any further inroad upon Miss Cobb's purse for coach-hire. What was she that she should be idle or luxurious, or spare the labour of her young limbs? She went along the narrow stony street where the shops were only now being opened, past the wide market where the women were setting out their stalls in front of the fine old church, and where Duguesclin, heroic and gigantic, defied the stormy winds that had ruffled his sculptured hair.

Two years and a half ago it had been a treat to her to walk in that market-place, hanging on her father's arm, to stand in the sombre stillness of that solemn cathedral, while the organ rolled its magnificent music along the dusky aisles. They two had chaffered for fruit at those stalls, laughing gaily with the good-tempered countrywomen. They had strolled on the beach and amused themselves economically, from the outside, with the diversions of the *établissement*. An afternoon in Dieppe had meant fun and holiday-making. Now she looked at the town with weary eyes, and thought how dull and shabby it had grown.

The walk to Les Fontaines, along a white dusty road, seemed interminable. If she had not been told again and again that it was only four miles from the town to the village, she would have taken the distance for eight—so long, so weary, seemed the way. There were hills in the background, hills right and left of her, orchards, glimpses of woodland—here and there a peep of sea—a pretty enough road to be whirled along in a comfortable carriage with a fast horse, but passing flat, stale, and unprofitable to the heavy-hearted pedestrian.

At last the little straggling village, the half-dozen new houses—square white boxes, which seemed to have been dropped accidentally in square enclosures of ragged garden—white-walled penitentiaries on a small scale, deriving an air of forced liveliness from emerald-green shutters, here a tree, and there a patch of rough grass, but never a flower—for the scarlet geraniums in the plaster vases on the wall of the grandest of the mansions had done blooming, and beyond scarlet geraniums on the wall the horticultural taste of Les Fontaines had never risen. The old cottages, with heavy thatched roofs and curious attic windows, with fruit trees sprawling over the walls, and orchards in the rear, were better than the new villas; but even these lacked the neatness and picturesque beauty of an English cottage in a pastoral landscape. There was a shabby dustiness, a barren, comfortless look about everything; and the height of ugliness was attained in the new church, a plastered barn, with a gaudily painted figure of our Blessed Lady in a niche above the door, all red and blue and gold, against the white-washed wall.

Ida thought of Kingthorpe,—the rustic inn with its queer old gables, shining lattices, quaint dovecots, the green, the pond, with its willowy island, the lovely old Gothic church—solid, and grave, and gray—calm amidst the shade of immemorial yews. The country about Les Fontaines was almost as pretty as that hilly region between Winchester and Romsey; but the English village was like a gem set in the English landscape, while the French village was a wart on the face of a smiling land.

'Why call it Les Fontaines?' Ida wondered, in her parched and dusty weariness. 'It is the dryest village I ever saw; and I don't believe there is anything like a fountain within a mile.'

Her father's house was one of the white boxes with green shutters. It enjoyed a dignified seclusion behind a plaster wall, which looked as if anyone might knock it down in very wantonness. The baby-boy had varied the monotony of his solitary sports by picking little bits out of it. There was a green door opening into this walled forecourt or garden, but the door was not fastened, so Ida pushed it open and went in. The baby-boy, now a sturdy vagabond of five years old, was digging an empty flower-bed. He caught sight of his sister, and galloped off into the house before she could take him in her arms, shouting, 'Maman, une dame—une dame! lady, lady, lady!' exercising his lungs upon both those languages which were familiar to his dawning intelligence.

His mother came out at his summons, a pretty, blue-eyed woman with an untidy gown and towzley hair, aged and faded a little since Ida had seen her.

'Oh, Ida,' she said, kissing her step-daughter heartily enough, despite her reproachful tone, 'how could you go on so! We have had such a letter from Miss Pew. Your father is awfully cut up. And we were expecting you all yesterday. He went to Dieppe to meet the afternoon boat. Where have you been since Tuesday?'

'I slept at the lock-house with a nice civil woman, who gave me a night's lodging,' said Ida, somewhat embarrassed by this question.

'But why not have come home at once, dear?' asked the step-mother mildly. She always felt herself a poor creature before her Juno-like daughter.

'I was flurried and worried—hardly knew what I was doing for the first few hours after I left Mauleverer; and I let the time slip by till it was too late to think of travelling yesterday,' answered Ida. 'Old Pew is a demon.'

'She seems to be a nasty, unkind old thing,' said Mrs. Palliser; 'for, after all, the worst she can bring against you is flirting with your friend's cousin. I hope you are engaged to him, dear; for that will silence everybody.'

'No, I am not engaged to him—he is nothing to me,' answered Ida, crimsoning; 'I never saw him, except in Fräulein's company. Neither you nor my father would like me to marry a man without sixpence.'

'But in Miss Pew's letter she said you declared you were engaged to Mr. Wendover of the Abbey, a gentleman of wealth and position. She was wicked enough to say she did not believe a word you said; but still, Ida, I do hope you were not telling falsehoods.'

'I hardly knew what I said,' replied Ida, feeling the difficulties of her position rising up on every side and hemming her in. She had never contemplated this kind of thing when she repudiated her marriage and turned her face homewards. 'She maddened me by her shameful attack, talking to me as if I were dirt, degrading me before the whole school. If you had been treated as I was you would have been beside yourself.'

'I might have gone into hysterics,' said Mrs. Palliser, 'but I don't think I should have told deliberate falsehoods: and to say that you were engaged to a rich man when you were not engaged, and the man hasn't a sixpence, was going a little too far. But don't fret, dear,' added the step-mother, soothingly, as the tears of shame and anger—anger against fate, life, all things—welled into Ida's lovely eyes. 'Never mind. We'll say no more about it. Come upstairs to your own room—it's Vernie's day-nursery now, but you won't mind that, I know—and take off your hat. Poor thing, how tired and ill you look!'

'I feel as if I was going to be ill and die, and I hope I am,' said Ida, petulantly.

'Don't, dear; it's wicked to say such a thing as that. You needn't be afraid of your poor pa; he takes everything easily.'

'Yes, he is always good. Where is he?'

'Not up yet. He comes down in time for his little *déjeûner à la fourchette*. Poor fellow, he had to get up so early in India.'

Captain Palliser had for the last seven years been trying to recover those arrears of sleep incurred during his Eastern career. He had been active enough under a tropical sky, when his mind was kept alive by a modicum of hard work and a very wide margin of sport—pig-sticking, peacock-shooting, paper-chases, all the delights of an Indian life. But now, vegetating on a slender pittance in the semi-slumberous idleness of Les Fontaines, he had nothing to do and nothing to think about; and he was glad to shorten his days by dozing away the fresher hours of the morning, while his wife toiled at the preparation of that elaborate meal which he loved to talk about as tiffin.

Poor little Mrs. Palliser made strenuous efforts to keep the sparsely furnished dusty house as clean and trim as it could be kept; but her life was a perpetual conflict with other people's untidiness.

The house was let furnished, and everything was in the third-rate French style—inferior mahogany and cheap gilding, bare floors with gaudy little rugs lying about here and there, tables with flaming tapestry covers, chairs cushioned with red velvet of the commonest kind, sham tortoiseshell clock and candelabra on the dining-room chimney-piece, alabaster clock and candelabra in the drawing-room. There was nothing home-like or comfortable in the house to atone for the smallness of the rooms, which seemed mere cells to Ida after the spaciousness of Mauleverer Manor and The Knoll. She wondered how her father and mother could breathe in such rooms.

That bed-chamber to which Mrs. Palliser introduced her step-daughter was even a shade shabbier than the rest of the house. The boy had run riot here, had built his bricks in one corner, had stabled a headless wooden horse and cart in another, and had scattered traces of his existence everywhere. There were his little Windsor chair, the nurse-girl's rocking chair, a battered old table, a heap of old illustrated newspapers, and torn toy-books.

'You won't mind Vernon's using the room in the day, dear, will you?' said Mrs. Palliser, apologetically. 'It shall be tidied for you at night.'

This meant that in the daytime Ida would have no place for retreat, no nook or corner of the house which she might call her own. She submitted meekly even to this deprivation, feeling that she was an intruder who had no right to be there.

'I should like to see my father soon,' she said, with a trembling lip, stooping down to caress Vernon, who had followed them upstairs.

He was a lovely, fair-haired boy, with big candid blue eyes, a lovable, confiding child, full of life and spirits and friendly feeling towards all mankind and the whole animal creation, down to its very lowest forms.

'You shall have your breakfast with him,' said Mrs. Palliser, feeling that she was conferring a great favour, for the Captain's breakfast was a meal apart. 'I don't say but what he'll be a little cross to you at first; but you must put up with that. He'll come round afterwards.'

'He has not seen me for two years and a half,' said Ida, thinking that fatherly affection ought to count for something under such circumstances.

'Yes, it's only two years and a half,' sighed Mrs. Palliser, 'and you were to have stayed at Mauleverer Manor three years. Miss Pew is a wicked old woman to cheat your father out of six months' board and tuition. He paid her fifty pounds in one lump when he articled you—fifty pounds—a heap of money for people in our position; and here you are, come back to us like a bad penny.'

'I am very sorry,' faltered Ida, reddening at that unflattering comparison. 'But I worked very hard at Mauleverer, and am tolerably experienced in tuition. I must try to get a governess's situation directly, and then I shall be paid a salary, and shall be able to give you back the fifty pounds by degrees.'

'Ah, that's the dreadful part of it all,' sighed Mrs. Palliser, who was very seldom in the open air, and had that despondent view of life common to people who live within four narrow walls. 'Goodness knows how you are ever to get a situation without references. Miss Pew says you are not to refer to her; and who else is there who knows anything of you or your capacity?'

'Yes, there is some one else. Bessie Wendover and her family.'

'The people you went to visit in Hampshire. Ah! there went another five pounds in a lump. You have been a heavy expense to us, Ida. I don't know whether anyone wanting to employ you as a governess would take such a reference as that. People are so particular. But we must hope for the best, and in the meantime you can make yourself useful at home in taking care of Vernon and teaching him his letters. He is dreadfully backward.'

'He is an angel,' said Ida, lifting the cherub in her arms, and letting the fair, curly head nestle upon her shoulder. 'I will wait upon him like a slave. You do love me, don't you, pet?'

'Ess, I love 'oo, but I don't know who 'oo is. *Connais pas*,' said Vernon, shaking his head vehemently.

'I am your sister, darling, your only sister.'

'My half-sister,' said Vernon. 'Maman said I had a half-sister, and she was naughty. *Dites donc*, would a whole sister be twice as big as you?'

Thus in his baby language, which may be easier imagined than described, gravely questioned the boy.

'I am your sister, dearest, heart and soul. There is no such thing as half-love or half-sisterhood between us. You should not have talked to him like that, mother,' said Ida, turning her reproachful gaze upon her step-mother, who was melted to tears.

'Your father was so upset by Miss Pew's letter,' she murmured apologetically. 'To pay fifty pounds for you, and for it to end in such humiliation as that. You must own that it was hard for us.'

'It was harder for me,' said Ida; 'I had to stand up and face that wicked woman, who knew that I had done no wrong, and who wreaked her malignity upon me because I am cleverer and better-looking than ever she was in her life.'

'I must go and make your father's omelette,' said the stepmother, 'while you tidy yourself for breakfast. I think there's some water on the washstand, and Vernon shall bring you a clean towel.'

The little fellow trotted out after his mother, and trotted back presently with the towel—one towel, which was about in proportion to the water-jug and basin. Ida shuddered, remembering the plentitude of water and towels at The Knoll. She made her toilet as well as she could, with the scantiest materials, as she might have done on board ship; shook and brushed the shabby gray cashmere—her wedding gown, she thought, with a bitter smile—before she put it on again, and then went down the bare narrow deal staircase, superb in all the freshness of her youth and beauty, which neither care nor poverty could spoil.

Captain Palliser was pacing up and down his little dining parlour, looking flurried and anxious. He turned suddenly as Ida entered, and stood staring at her.

'By Jove, how handsome you have grown!' he said, and then he look her in his arms and kissed her. 'But you know, my dear, this is really too bad,' he went on in a fretful tone,' to come back upon us like a bad penny.'

'That is what my step-mother said just now.'

'My dear, how can one help saying it, when it's the truth? After my paying fifty pounds, don't you know, and thinking that you were comfortably disposed of for the next three years, and that at the expiry of the term Miss Pew would place you in a gentleman's family, where you would receive from sixty to a hundred per annum, according to your acquirements—those were her very words—to have you sent back to us like this, in disgrace, and to be told that you had been carrying on in an absurd way with a young man on the bank of a river. It is most humiliating. And now my wife tells me the young man has not a sixpence which makes the whole thing so very culpable.'

'Please let me tell you the extent of my iniquity, father, and then you can judge what right Miss Pew had to expel me.'

Whereupon Ida quietly described her afternoon promenades upon the river-path, with the Fräulein always in her company, and how her friend's cousin had been permitted to walk up and down with them.

'Nobody supposes there was any actual harm,' replied Captain Palliser, 'but you must have been perfectly aware that you were acting foolishly— that this kind of thing was a violation of the school etiquette. Come, now, you knew Miss Pew would disapprove of such goings on, did you not?'

'Well, yes, no doubt I knew old Pew would be horrified. Perhaps it was the idea of that which gave a zest to the thing.'

'Precisely! and you never thought of my fifty pounds, and you ran this risk for the sake of a young man without a penny, who never could be your husband.'

Ida grew scarlet and then deadly pale.

'There, don't look so distressed, child. I must try to forget my fifty pounds, and to think of your future career. It is a deuced awkward business—here come the omelette and the coffee—an escapade of this kind is always cropping up against a girl in after life—sit down and make yourself comfortable—capital dish of kidneys—the world is so small; and of course every pupil at Mauleverer Manor will gabble about this business. No mushrooms!—what is the little woman thinking about?'

Captain Palliser seated himself, and arranged his napkin under his chin, French fashion. His features were of that aqulllile type which seems to have been invented on purpose for army men. His eyes were light blue, like his boy's—Ida's dark eyes were a maternal inheritance—his hair was auburn, sprinkled with gray, his moustache straw-colour and with a carefully trained cavalry droop. His clothes and boots were perfect of their kind, albeit they had seen good wear. He had been heard to declare that he had rather wear feathers and war-paint, like a red Indian, than a coat made by a third-rate tailor. He was tall and inclining to stoutness, broad-shouldered, and with an easy carriage and a nonchalant air, which were not without their charm. He had what most people called a patrician look—that is to say the air of never having done anything useful in the whole course of his existence—not such a patrician as a Palmerston, a Russell, a Derby, or a Salisbury, but the ideal lotus-eating aristocrat, who dresses, drives, and dines and gossips through a languid existence.

The Captain's career in the East had not been particularly brilliant. His lines had not lain in great battles or stirring campaigns. Except during the awful episode of the Mutiny, when he was still a young man, he had seen little active service. His life, since his return from India, had been a blank.

His mind, never vigorous, had rusted slowly in the slow monotony of his days. He had come to accept the rhythmical ebb and flow of life's river as all-sufficient for content. Breakfast and dinner were the chief events of his life—if it was well with these it was well with him.

There was a rustic tavern where in summer a good many people came to dine, either in the house or the garden, and in a room adjoining the kitchen there was a small French billiard-table with very big balls. Here the Captain played of an evening with the *habitués* of the place, and was much looked up to for his superior skill. An occasional drive into Dieppe on the *banquette* of the diligence, and a saunter by the sea, was his only other amusement.

His daughter poured out his coffee, and ministered to his various wants as he breakfasted, eating with but little appetite herself, albeit the fare was excellent.

Captain Palliser talked in a desultory way as he ate, not often looking up from his plate, but meandering on. Happily for Ida, who had been reduced to the lowest stage of self-abasement by her welcome, he said no more about Miss Pew or his daughter's gloomy prospects. It was not without a considerable mental effort that he was able to bring his thoughts to bear upon other people's business. He had strained his mind a good deal during the last twenty-four hours, and he was very glad to relax the tension of the bow.

'Rather a dull kind of life for a man who has been used to society—eh, Ida?' he murmured, as he ate his omelette; 'but we contrive to rub on somehow. Your step-mother likes it, and the boy likes it—wonderful healthy air, don't you know—no smoke—no fogs—only three miles from the sea, as the crow flies. It suits them, and it's cheap—a paramount consideration with a poor devil on half-pay; and in the season there are some of the best people in Europe to be seen at the *établissement*.'

'I suppose you go to Dieppe often in the season, father?' said Ida, pleased to find he had dropped Miss Pew and the governess question.

'Well, yes; I wander in almost every fine day.'

'You don't walk?' exclaimed Ida, surprised at such activity in a man of his languid temper.

'Oh, no; I never walk. I just wander in—on the diligence—or in, a return fly. I wander in and look about me a little, and perhaps take a cup of coffee with a friend at the Hôtel des Bains. There is generally some one I know at the Bains or the Royal. Ah, by-the-bye whom, do you think I saw there a fortnight ago?'

'I haven't the least idea,' answered Ida; 'I know so few of your friends.'

'No, of course not. You never saw Sir Vernon Palliser, but you've heard me talk about him.'

'Your rich brother, the wicked old baronet in Sussex, who never did you a kindness in his life?'

'My dear, old Sir Vernon has been dead two years.'

'I never heard of his death.'

'No, by-the-bye. It wasn't worth while worrying you about it, especially as we could not afford to go into mourning. Your step-mother fretted about that dreadfully, poor little woman; as if it could matter to her, when she had never seen the man in her life. She said if one had a baronet in one's family one ought to go into mourning for him. I can't understand the passion some women have for mourning. They are eager to smother themselves in crape at the slightest provocation, and for a mean old beggar like Vernon, who never gave me a sixpence. But as I was saying, these two young fellows turned up the other day in front of the Hôtel des Bains.'

'Which two young fellows, my dear father? I haven't the faintest idea of whom you are talking,' protested Ida, who found her father's conversation very difficult to follow.

'Why, Sir Vernon, of course—the present Sir Vernon and his brother Peter: ugly name, isn't it, Ida? but there has always been a Peter in the family; and as a rule,' added Captain Palliser, growing slower and dreamier of speech as he fell into reminiscences of the past—'as a rule the Peter Pallisers have gone to the dogs. There was Major Palliser—fought in the Peninsula—knew George the Fourth—married a very pretty woman and beat her—died in the Bench.'

'Tell me about the present Sir Vernon,' asked Ida, more interested in the moving, breathing life of to-day than in memories of the unknown dead. 'Is he nice?'

'He is a fine, broad-shouldered young fellow—seven or eight and twenty. No, not handsome—my brother Vernon was never distinguished for beauty, though he had all the markings of race. There is nothing like race, Ida; you see it in a man's walk; you hear it in every tone of a man's voice.'

'Dear father, I was asking about this particular Sir Vernon,' urged Ida, with a touch of impatience, unaccustomed to this slow meandering talk.

'And I was telling you about him,' answered the Captain, slightly offended. His little low-born wife never hurried and hustled his thoughts in this way. She was content to sit at his feet, and let him meander on for hours. True that she did not often listen, but she was always respectful. 'I was remarking that Sir Vernon is a fine young fellow, and likely to live to see himself a great-grandfather. His brother, too, is nearly as big and healthy— healthy to a degree. The breakfast I saw those two young men devour at the hotel would have made your hair stand on end. But, thank heaven, I have never been the kind of man to wait for dead men's shoes.'

'I see,' said Ida. 'If these boys had been sickly and had died young, you would have succeeded to the baronetcy.'

'To the baronetcy and to the estate in Sussex, which is a very fine estate, worth eight thousand a year.'

'Then, of course, they are strong, and likely to live to the age of Methuselah!' exclaimed Ida, with a laugh of passing bitterness. 'Who ever heard of luck coming our way? It is not in our race to be fortunate.'

The shame and agony of her own failure to win fortune were still strong upon her.

'Who knows what might happen?' said the Captain, with amiable listlessness. 'I have never allowed my thoughts to dwell upon the possibilities of the future; yet it is a fact that, so long as those young men remain unmarried, there are only two lives between me and wealth. They feel the position themselves; for when Sir Vernon came over here to lunch, he patted my boy on the head and said, in his joking way, "If Peter and I had fallen down a crevasse the other day in the Oberland, this little chap would have been heir to Wimperfield."'

'No doubt Sir Vernon and his brother will marry and set up nurseries of their own within the next two or three years,' said Ida, carelessly. Eager as she had been to be rich during those two and a half bitter years in which she had so keenly felt the sting of poverty, she was not capable of seeing her way to fortune through the dark gate of death.

'Yes, I daresay they will both marry,' replied Captain Palliser, gravely, folding his napkin and whisking an accidental crumb off his waistcoat. 'Young men always get drifted into matrimony. If they are rich all the women are after them, If they are poor—well, there is generally some woman weak enough to prefer dual starvation to bread and cheese and solitude. Vernon told me he had no idea of marriage. He and his brother are both rovers—fond of mountain-climbing, yachting, every open-air amusement.'

'Did you see much of them while they were at Dieppe?'

'They only stayed three days. They walked over here to lunch, put the poor little woman in a fluster—although they were very pleasant and easy about everything—invited me to dinner, tipped the boy munificently, and went off by the night-boat, bound straight for Wimperfield and the partridges. Very fine partridge shooting at Wimperfield! Vernon asked me to go across with him and stay at the old place for a week or two; but my sporting days are over. I can't get up early; and I can't walk in shooting-boots. Besides, the little woman would have fretted if I had left her alone so long.'

'But the change would have done you good, father.'

'No, my dear; any change of habits would worry me. I have dropped into my groove and I must stay in it. What a pity you were not here when your cousins called! Who knows what might have happened? Vernon might have fallen over head and ears in love with you.'

'Don't, father!' cried Ida, with absolute pain in her voice. 'Don't talk about marrying for money. There is nothing in life so revolting, so degrading. Be sure, it is a sin which always brings its own punishment.'

'My dear,' said the Captain, gravely, 'there are so many love-matches which bring their own punishment, that I am inclined to believe that marrying for money is a virtue which ought to ensure its own reward. You may depend, if we could get statistics upon the subject, one would find that after ten years' marriage the couples who were drawn together by prudential motives are just as fond of each other as those more romantic pairs who wedded for love. A decade of matrimony rounds a good many sharp angles, and dispels a good many illusions.'

CHAPTER XI
ACCOMPLISHMENTS AT A DISCOUNT

Now began for Ida a life of supreme dullness—an empty, almost hopeless, life, waiting upon fortune. Her father was kind to her in his easy-going, lymphatic way, liking well enough to have her about him, pleased with her affection for his boy, proud of her beauty and her talents, but with no earnest care for her welfare in the present or the future. What was to become of wife, son and daughter when he was dead and gone, was a question which Captain Palliser dared not ask himself. For the widow there would be a pittance, for son and daughter nothing. It was therefore vital that Ida should either marry well or become a money-earning personage. Of marriage at Les Fontaines there seemed not the faintest probability, since the experiences of the past afford so few instances of wandering swains caught and won by a face at a window, or the casual appearance of a beautiful girl on a country road.

Of friends or acquaintance, in his present abode, Captain Palliser had none. The only people he had ever cared for were the men and women he had known in India; and he had lost sight of those since his marriage. They were scattered; and he was too proud to expose his fallen fortunes to those who had known him in his happier days, those days when the careless expenditure of his modest capital had given him a false air of easy circumstances.

His life at Les Fontaines suited him well enough, individually. It was a kind of hibernation. He slept a good deal, and ate a good deal, and smoked incessantly, and took very little exercise. For all that is best and noblest in life, Captain Palliser might just as well have been dead. He had outlived hope and ambition, thought, invention. He exercised no influence upon the lives of others, except upon the little homely wife, who was a slave to him. He was no possible good in the world. Yet his daughter was fond of him, and pleased to bear him company when he would have her; and under her influence his sluggish intellect brightened a little.

For the first few weeks of her residence at Les Fontaines, Ida was tortured by a continually recurring fear of Brian Wendover's pursuit. He had let her go coolly enough; but what if he were to change his mind and follow and claim her? She belonged to him. She was his goods, his chattels— to have and to hold till death did them part. Her life was no longer her own to dispose of as she pleased. Would he let her alone?—he who had held her in his arms with passionate force, who had entreated her to stay with him, and had surrendered her reluctantly in sullen anger.

What if anger, which had been stronger with him than love at that last moment, should urge him to denounce her—to tell the world how base a thing she was—a woman who had been eager to marry a rich man and had been trapped by a pauper! She glanced with a sickening dread at every letter which her father received, lest it should be from Brian, telling her shameful story. She counted the days as they went by, saying to herself, 'A fortnight since we were married; surely if he had meant to claim me he would have come before now.' 'Three weeks! now I must be safe!' And then came the dull November morning which completed the calendar month since her wedding-day, and her husband had made no sign. She began to feel easier, to believe that he repented his marriage as deeply as she did, and that he was very glad to be free from its bondage.

And now she was able to think more seriously of her future. She had answered a great many advertisements in the *Times*, wherein paragons were demanded for the tuition of youth or the companionship of age; but as she saw the papers only on the day after their publication, other paragons, on the spot, were beforehand with her. She did not receive a single answer to those carefully written letters, setting forth her qualifications and her willingness to work hard.

'I shall waste a small fortune in postage-stamps, father,' she said at last, 'and shall be no nearer the mark. My only chance is to advertise. Will you give me the money for an advertisement? I am sorry to ask you, but—'

'My dear, you are always asking me for money,' replied Captain Palliser, peevishly; which was hardly fair, as she had asked him nothing since her return, except the sum of thirty shillings, being the exact amount of which she stood indebted to kind-hearted Miss Cobb. 'However, I suppose you must have it.' He produced a half sovereign from his meagrely-furnished purse. 'It is only right you should do something; indeed, anything is better than wasting your life in such a hole as this. But what if you do get any answers to your advertisement? Who is to give you a character, since that old witch at Mauleverer Manor has chosen to put up her back against you?'

'That must be managed somehow,' answered Ida, moodily. 'Will it not be enough for the people to know who you are, and that I have never been in a situation before? Why should they apply to the schoolmistress who finished my education?'

'People are so suspicious,' said the Captain, 'and the handsomer a girl is the more questions they ask. They seem to think she has no right to be so handsome. However you must risk it.'

Ida wrote her advertisement, an unvarnished statement of her qualifications as a teacher, and of her willingness to be useful; not a word about references. The advertisement appeared a few days later, and the little family at Les Fontaines anxiously awaited the result, even little Vernon eagerly expressing himself on the subject, his youthful ears being open to every topic discussed in his presence, and his youthful mind quick to form opinions.

'You shan't go away!' he exclaimed. 'Ma, she shan't go, shall she? lady shan't have her; I want her always; you mustn't go, sissie,' all in baby language, with a curious perversion of consonants. He had climbed on her knee, and had his arms round her neck—energetic young arms which almost throttled her. She had been his chief companion and playfellow for the last five weeks, had read him all his favourite fairy-tales over and over again, had sat with him of an evening till he fell asleep, an invincible defence against bogies and vague fears of darkness. She had taken him for long rural rambles, over breezy downs towards the sea, had dug and delved with him on the lonely beach below the great white lighthouse, warmly coated and shawled, and working hard in the November wind; and now, just when he had grown fonder of her than anyone else in the world, she was going to leave him. He lifted up his head and howled, and refused all comfort from mother or father. Ida cried with him. 'My pet, I can't bear to leave you, but I must; my darling, I shall come back,' she protested, clasping him to her breast, kissing his fair tearful face, soft round cheeks, lovely blue eyes swimming in tears.

'To-morrow?' inquired Vernon, with a strangled sob.

'No, darling, not to-morrow; there would be no use in my going just for one day; but I am not going yet—I don't know when I am going—Vernon must not cry. See how unhappy he is making poor mamma.'

Mrs. Palliser put her hands before her face, and made a bohooing noise to keep up the illusion; whereupon the affectionate little fellow slipped off his sister's knee, and ran to his mother to administer comfort.

'I am not going away yet, Vernon; indeed, I hardly know whether I am ever going at all. I have come back like a bad penny, and I seem likely to be as difficult to get rid of as other bad pennies,' said Ida, despondingly, for three posts had gone by since the insertion of her advertisement, and had brought her nothing. The market was evidently overstocked with young ladies knowing French and German, able to play and sing, and willing to be useful.

After this Vernon would hardly let his sister out of his sight. He had a suspicion that she would leave him unawares—slip out of the door some day, and be gone without a moment's warning. That is how joy flees.

'My pet, be reasonable,' said Ida; 'I can't go away without my trunk.'

This comforted him a little, and he made a point of sitting upon one of Ida's trunks, when they two were alone in that barely furnished chamber which served for her bed-room and his day-nursery.

She contrived to tell him fairy-tales, and to keep him amused; albeit she was now busy at carefully overhauling, patching, and repairing her scanty wardrobe—trying to make neat mending do duty for new clothes, and getting ready against any sudden summons. She could not bring herself to ask her father for money, sadly as she wanted new garments. He had given her five pounds in August, and two sovereigns since her return, and the way he had doled out those sums indicated the low state of his funds. No, the gown that had been new at The Knoll must still be her best gown. Last winter's jacket, albeit threadbare in places, must do duty for this winter. Before the next summer she might be in the receipt of a salary and able to clothe herself decently, and to send presents to this beloved boy, who was not much better clad than herself.

But the days wore on, and brought no answer to her advertisement.

'I shouldn't wonder if it were the foreign address,' said Captain Palliser, when they were all speculating upon the cause of this dismal silence. 'People are suspicious of anyone living abroad. If you had been able to advertise from a rectory in Lincolnshire, or even an obscure street at the west end of London, they'd have thought better of you. But Boulogne, Calais, Dieppe, they all hint at impecuniosity and enforced exile. It's very unlucky.'

The postman stopped at the little green gate next morning, and Ida flew to receive his packet. It was a letter for her—a bulky letter—in a hand she knew well, and her heart seemed to stop beating as she looked at the address.

The hand was Bessie Wendover's. Who could tell what new trouble the letter might announce? Brian might have told his family the whole history of his marriage and her unworthy conduct. Oh, what shame, what agony, if this were so! And how was she to face her father when he asked her the contents of the letter? She ran out into the garden—the little bare, joyless garden—to read her letter alone, and to gain time.

This is how the dreaded epistle ran:—

'My dear darling, ill-used, cruel thing,—

'However could you treat me so badly? What is friendship worth, if you set no higher value upon it than this? I don't believe you know what friendship means, or you never could act so. How miserable you have made me! how wretched you must have been yourself! you proud, noble-minded darling—under the sting of such vile treatment.

'I wrote to you three times last month, and could not imagine why my letters were unanswered. Brian had told me that you were perfectly well, and looking splendid when he saw you in October, so I did not think it could be illness that kept you silent; and at last I began to feel angry, and to fancy you had forgotten me, and were ungrateful. No, I don't mean that, dearest. What reason had you for gratitude? The obligation was all on my side.

'Towards the end of October I wrote to Brian, telling him of your silence, and asking if he could find out if you were well. He answered with one of his short, unsatisfactory scrawls that he had reason to know you were quite well. After this I felt *really* offended; for I thought you must have deceived me all along, and that you had never cared a straw about me; so I coiled myself up in my dignity, and, although I felt very unhappy, I resolved never to write you another line till you wrote to me. I was very miserable, but still I felt that I owed a duty to my own self-respect, don't you know; and just at this time we all went to Bournemouth, where we were very gay. Father and mother knew no end of people there, and I began to feel what it really is to be out, which no girl ever could at Kingthorpe, where there are about three parties in a twelvemonth.

'Well, darling, so I went on leading a frivolous life among people I did not care twopence for, and hardening my heart against my dearest friend, when, on the day we came home, I happened to take up the *Times* in the railway carriage. I hate newspapers in a common way, but one reads such things when one is travelling, and out of mere idleness I amused myself skimming the advertisements, which I found ever so much more interesting than the leading articles. What should my eye light upon but an advertisement from a young lady wanting to go out as a governess— address I.P., Le Rosier, Les Fontaines, near Dieppe—and the whole murder was out. You must have left old Pew's and be living with your father. I was horribly indignant with you—as, indeed, I am still—for not having told me anything about it; but directly I got home I telegraphed to Polly Cobb, as the best-natured girl I knew at Mauleverer, asking where you were, and why you had left. I had such a letter from her next day—spelling bad, but full of kind feeling—giving me a full account of the row, and old Pew's detestable conduct. She told me that Fräulein vouched for your having behaved with the most perfect propriety, and never having seen Brian out of her presence; but Brian's meanness in not having told me about the trouble he had brought upon you is more than I can understand.

'Well, darling, I went off to Aunt Betsy, who is always my *confidante* in all delicate matters, because she's ever so much cleverer than dear warm-hearted mother, who never could keep a secret in her life, sweet soul, and is no better than a speaking-tube for conveying information to the Colonel. I told Aunt Betsy everything—how it was all Brian's fault, and how I adore you, and how miserable I felt about you, and how you were trying to get a situation as governess, in spite of that malignant old Pew—she must be a lineal descendant of the wicked fairy—having said she would give you no certificate of character or ability.

'Now, what do you think that sweetest and best of aunties said? "Let her come to me," she said; "I am getting old and dull, and I want something bright and clever about me, to cheer me and rouse me when I feel depressed. Let her come to me as a companion and amanuensis, help me to look after my cottagers, who are getting too much for me, and play to me of an evening. I like that girl, and I should like to have her in my house."

'I was enchanted at the thought of your being always near us, and I fancied you wouldn't altogether dislike it; although Kingthorpe certainly is the dullest, sleepiest old hole in the universe. So I begged Aunt Betsy to write to you *instanter*; said I knew you would be charmed to accept such a situation, and that she would secure a treasure; and, in all probability, you'll have a letter from her to-morrow.

'And now, dear, I must repeat that you have treated me shamefully. Why did you not write to me directly you left Mauleverer? Could you think that I could believe you had really done wrong—that I could possibly be influenced by the judgment of that old monster, Pew? If you could think so, you are not worthy to be loved as I love you. However, come to us, sweetest, directly you get auntie's letter, and all shall be forgiven and forgotten, as the advertisements say.'

Ida kissed the loving letter. So far, therefore, Brian had not betrayed her; and, having kept her secret so long, it might be supposed he would keep it for all time.

Poor little warm-hearted Bessie! Was not she by her foolish falsification—a piece of mild jocosity, no doubt—the prime author of all the evil that had followed? And yet Ida could not feel angry with her, any more than she could have been angry with Vernon for some piece of sportive mischief.

'Thank God, he has kept our wretched secret,' she thought, as she folded Bessie's long letter, and went back to the house. 'I am grateful to him for that.'

She went in radiant, gladdened at the thought of being able to relieve her father and step-mother of the burden of her maintenance; for the fact that she was a burden had not been hidden from her. They had been kind; they had given her to eat and to drink of their best, and had admired her talents and accomplishments; but they had let her know at the same time that she was a failure, and that her future was a dark problem still far from solution—a problem which troubled them in the silent watches of the night. Nor did they forget to remind her from time to time that by her imprudence—pardonable although that imprudence might be—she had forfeited six months' board and lodging, together with those educational advantages the Captain's fifty pounds had been intended to purchase for her. These facts had been reiterated, not altogether unkindly, but in a manner that made life intolerable; and she felt that were she to continue at Les Fontaines for the natural term of her existence, the same theme would still furnish the subject for parental harpings.

'Father,' she said, going behind Captain Palliser's chair, as he smoked his after-breakfast cigar, and read yesterday's *Times*, 'I want you to read this letter. It is a foolish schoolgirl letter, perhaps; but it will show you that my friends are not going to discard me on account of Miss Pew.'

The Captain laid down his paper, and slowly made his way through Bessie's lengthy epistle, which, although prettily written, with a good deal of grace in the slopes and curves of the penmanship, gave him considerable trouble to decipher. It was only when he had discovered that all the B's looked like H's, and that all the G's were K's, and all the L's S's, and had, as it were, made a system for himself, that he was able to get on comfortably.

'Bless my soul,' he murmured, 'why cannot girls write legibly?'

'It is the real Mauleverer hand, papa, and is generally thought very pretty,' said Ida.

'Pretty, yes; you might have a zigzag pattern over the paper that would be just as pretty. One wants to be able to read a letter. This is almost as bad as Arabic. However, the girl seems a good, warm-hearted creature, and very fond of you; and I should think you could not do better than accept her aunt's offer. It will be a beginning.'

'It is Hobson's choice, papa; but I am sure I shall be happy with Miss Wendover,' said Ida; and then she gave a faint sigh, and her heart sank at the thought of that Damoclesian sword always hanging over her head—the possibility of her husband claiming her.

Mrs. Palliser was much more rapturous when she heard the contents of the letter—much more interested in all details about Ida's future home. She wanted to know what Miss Wendover was like—how many servants she kept—whether carriage or no carriage—what kind of a house she lived in, and how it was furnished.

'You will be quite a grand lady,' she said, with a touch of envy, when Ida had described the cosy red-brick cottage, the verandahed drawing-room and conservatory added by Miss Wendover, the pair of cobs which that lady drove, the large well-kept gardens; 'you will look down upon us with our poor ways, and this house, in which all the rooms smell of whitewash.'

'No, indeed, mamma, I shall always think of you with affection; for you have been very kind to me, although I know I have been a burden.'

'Everything is a burden when one is poor,' sighed her stepmother; 'even one extra in the washing-bills makes a difference; and we shall feel it awfully when Vernon grows up. Boys are so extravagant; and one cannot talk to them as one can to girls.'

'But I hope you will be better off then, mamma.'

'My dear, you might as well hope we should be dukes and duchesses. What chance is there of any improvement? Your poor papa has no idea of earning money. I'm sure I have said to him, often and often, "Reginald, do *something*. Write for the magazines! Surely you can do *that*? Other men in your position do it." "Yes," he growled, "and that's why the magazines are so stupid." No, Ida, your father's circumstances will never improve; and when the time comes for giving Vernon a proper education we shall be paupers.'

'Poor papa!' sighed Ida; 'I am afraid he is not strong enough to make any great effort.'

'He has given way, my dear; that is the root of it all. We shall never be better off, unless those two healthy, broad-shouldered young men were to go and get themselves swallowed up by an earthquake; and that is rather too much for anyone to expect.'

'What young men?' asked Ida, absently.

'Your two cousins.'

'Oh, Sir Vernon and his brother. No, I don't suppose they will die to oblige us poor creatures.'

'They went up the what's-its-name Horn, in Switzerland,' said Mrs. Palliser, plaintively. 'It made my blood run cold to hear them talk about it. "By Jove, Peter, I thought it was all over with you," said Sir Vernon, when he told us how foolhardy his brother had been. But you see they got to the bottom all safe and sound, though ever so many people have been killed on that very mountain.'

'I'm glad they did, mamma. We may want their money very badly, but we are not murderers, even in thought.'

'God forbid!' sighed the little woman. 'They are fine-grown, gentlemanly young men, too. Sir Vernon gave my Vernie a sovereign, and promised him a pony next year; but, good gracious! how could we afford to keep a pony, even if we had a stable? "You had better make it the other kind of pony," says your father, and then they all burst out laughing.'

'So little makes a man laugh!' said Ida, somewhat contemptuously. That picture of her father making sport of his poverty irritated her. 'Well, dear mamma,' she said presently, moved by one of those generous impulses which were a part of her frank, unwise nature, 'if ever I can earn a hundred a year—and there are many governesses who get as much—you shall have fifty to help pay Vernon's schooling.'

'You are a dear generous 'arted girl,' exclaimed the stepmother, and the two women kissed again with tears, an operation which they usually performed in the hour of domestic trouble.

Miss Wendover's letter came next day, a hearty, frank, affectionate letter, offering a home that was really meant to be like home, and a salary of forty pounds a year, 'just to buy your gowns,' Miss Wendover said. 'I know it is not sufficient remuneration for such accomplishments as yours, but I want *you* rather than your accomplishments and I am not rich enough to give as much as you are worth. But you will, at least, stave off the drudgery of a governess's life till you are older, and better able to cope with domineering mothers and insolent pupils.'

Such a salary was a long way off that hundred per annum which Ida had set before her eyes as the golden goal to be gained by laborious pianoforte athletics and patient struggles with the profundities of German grammar; but, as Captain Palliser paid, it was a beginning; and Ida was very glad so to begin. She wrote to Miss Wendover gratefully accepting her offer, and in a very humble spirit.

'I fear it is pity that prompts your kind offer,' she wrote, 'and that you take me because you know I left Mauleverer Manor in disgrace, and that nobody else would have me. I am a bad penny. That is what my father called me when I came home to him. And now I am to go back to Kingthorpe as a bad penny. But, please God, I will try to prove to you that I am not altogether worthless; and, whatever may happen, I shall love you and be grateful to you till the end of my life.

'As you are so kind as to say I may come as soon as I like, I shall be with you on the day after you receive this letter.'

Ida's preparations for departure were not elaborate. Her scanty wardrobe had been put in the neatest possible order. A few hours sufficed for packing trunk and bonnet-box. On the last afternoon Mrs. Palliser came to her highly elated, and proposed a walk to Dieppe, and a drive home in the diligence which left the Market Place at five o'clock.

'I am going to give you a new hat,' she said, triumphantly. 'You must have a new hat.'

'But, dear mamma, I know you can't afford it.'

'I *will* afford it, Ida. You will have to go to church at Kingthorpe'—Mrs. Palliser regarded church-going as an oppressive condition of prosperous respectability. One of the few privileges of being hard up and quite out of society was that one need not go to church—'and I should like you to appear like a lady. You owe it to your pa and I. A hat you must 'ave. I can pay for it out of the housekeeping money, and your pa will never know the difference.'

'No, mamma, but you and Vernon will have to pinch for it,' said Ida, knowing that there was positively no margin to that household's narrow means of existence.

'A little pinching won't hurt us. Vernie is as bilious as he can be; he eats too many compots and little fours. I shall keep him to plain bread and butter for a bit, and it will do him a world of good. There's no use talking, Ida, I mean you to 'ave a 'at; and if you won't come and choose it I must choose it myself,' concluded the little woman, dropping more aspirates as she grew more excited.

So mother and daughter walked to Dieppe in the dull November afternoon, Vernon trudging sturdily by his sister's side. They bought the hat, a gray felt with partridge plumage, which became Ida's rich dark bloom to perfection; and then they went to the Cathedral, and knelt in the dusky aisle, and heard the solemn melody of the organ, and the subdued voices of the choir, in the plaintive music of Vesper Psalms, monotonous somewhat, but with a sweet soothing influence, music that inspired gentle thoughts.

Then they went back to the Market-Place, and were in time to get good places on the *banquette* of the diligence, before the big white Norman horses trotted and ambled noisily along the stony street.

Ida left Dieppe late on the following evening, by the same steamer that had brought her from Newhaven. The British stewardess recognised her.

'Why, you was only across the other day, miss!' she said; 'what a gad-about you must be!'

She arrived in London by ten o'clock next morning, and left Waterloo at a quarter-past eleven, reaching Winchester early in the day. How different were her feelings this time, as the train wound slowly over those chalky hills! how full of care was her soul! And yet she was no longer a visitor going among strangers—this time she went to an assured home, she was to be received among friends. But the knowledge that her liberty was forfeited for ever, that she was a free-agent only on sufferance, made her grave and depressed. Never again could she feel as glad and frank a creature as she had been in the golden prime of the summer that was gone, when she and Bessie and Urania Rylance came by this same railway, over those green English hill-sides, to the city that was once the chief seat of England's power and splendour.

A young man in a plain gray livery and irreproachable top-boots stood contemplatively regarding the train as it came into the station. He touched his hat at sight of Miss Palliser, and she remembered him as Miss Wendover's groom.

'Any luggage, ma'am?' he asked, as she alighted; as if it were as likely as not that she had come without any.

'There is one box, Needham. That is all besides these things.'

Her bonnet-box—frail ark of woman's pride—was in the carriage, with a wrap and an umbrella, and her dressing bag.

'All right, ma'am. If you'll show me which it is I'll tell the porter to bring it. I've got the cobs outside.'

'Oh, I am so sorry,—how good of Miss Wendover!'

'They wanted exercise, 'um. They was a bit above themselves, and the drive has done 'em good.'

Miss Wendover's cherished brown cobs, animals which in the eyes of Kingthorpe were almost as sacred as that Egyptian beast whose profane slaughter was more deeply felt than the nation's ruin—to think that these exalted brutes should have been sent to fetch that debased creature, a salaried companion. But then Aunt Betsy was never like anyone else.

Needham took the cobs across the hills at a pace which he would have highly disapproved in any other driver. Had Miss Wendover so driven them, he would have declared she was running them off their legs. But in his own hands, Brimstone and Treacle—so called to mark their difference of disposition—could come to no harm. 'They wanted it,' he told Miss Palliser, when she remarked upon their magnificent pace, 'they never got half work enough.'

The hills looked lovely, even in this wintry season—yew trees and grass gave no token of November's gloom. The sky was bright and blue, a faint mist hung like a veil over the city in the valley, the low Norman tower of the cathedral, the winding river, and flat fertile meadows—a vision very soon left far in the rear of Brimstone and Treacle.

'How handsome they look!' said Ida, admiring their strong, bold crests, like war-horses in a Ninevite picture, their shining black-brown coats. 'Is Brimstone such a very vicious horse?'

'Vicious, mum? no, not a bit of vice about him,' answered Needham promptly, 'but he's a rare difficult horse to groom. There ain't none but me as dares touch him. I let the boy try it once, and I found the poor lad half an hour afterwards standing in the middle of the big loose box like a statter, while Brimstone raced round him as hard as he could go, just like one of them circus horses. The boy dursn't stir. If he'd moved a limb, Brimstone 'ud have 'molished him.'

'What an awful horse! But isn't that viciousness?'

'Lor', no mum. That ain't vice,' answered the groom smiling amusedly at the lady's ignorance. Vice is crib-biting, or jibbing, or boring or summat o' that kind. Brimstone is a game hoss, and he's got a bit of a temper, but he ain't got no vice.'

Here was Kingthorpe, looking almost as pretty as it had looked when she gazed upon it with tearful eyes in her sad farewell at the close of summer. The big forest trees were bare, but there were flowers in all the cottage gardens, even late lingering roses on southern walls, and the clipped yew-tree abominations—dumb-waiters, peacocks, and other monstrosities—were in their pride of winter beauty. The ducks were swimming gaily in the village pond, and the village inn was still glorious with red geraniums, in redder pots. The Knoll stood out grandly above all other dwellings—the beds full of chrysanthemums, and a bank of big scarlet geraniums on each side of the hall door.

It seemed strange to be driven swiftly past the familiar carriage-drive, and round into the lane leading to Miss Wendover's cottage. It was only an accommodation lane—or a back-out lane, as the boys called it, since no two carriages could pass each other in that narrow channel—and in bad weather the approach to the Homestead was far from agreeable. A carriage and horses had been known to stick there, with wheels hopelessly embedded in the clay, while Miss Wendover's guests picked their footsteps through the mud.

But the Homestead, when attained, was such a delightful house that one forgot all impediments in the way thither. The red brick front—old red brick, be it noted, which has a brightness and purity of colour never retained for above a twelvemonth by the red brick of to-day—glowing, athwart its surrounding greenery, like the warm welcome of a friend; the exquisite neatness of the garden, where every flower that could be coaxed into growing in the open air bloomed in perfection; the spick-and-span brightness of the windows; the elegant order that prevailed within, from cellar to garret; the old, carefully-chosen furniture, which had for the most part been collected from other old-world homesteads; the artistic colouring of draperies and carpets—all combined to make Miss Wendover's house delightful.

'My house had need be orderly,' she said, when her friends waxed rapturous; 'I have so little else to think about.'

Yet the sick and poor, within a radius of ten miles, might have testified that Miss Wendover had thought and care for all who needed them, and that she devoted the larger half of her life to other people's interests.

It was a clear, balmy day, one of those lovely autumn days which hang upon the edge of winter, and Miss Wendover was pacing her garden walks bare-headed, armed with gardening scissors and formidable brown leather gauntlets, nipping a leaf here, or a withered rosebud there, with eyes whose eagle glance not so much as an aphis could escape. From the slope of her lawn Aunt Betsy saw the cobs turn into the lane, and she was standing at the gate to welcome the traveller when the carriage drew up.

There was no carriage-drive on this side of the house, only a lawn with a world of flower-beds. Those visitors who wanted to enter in a ceremonious manner had to drive round by shrubbery and orchard to the back, where there were an old oak door and an entrance-hall. On this garden front there were only glass doors and long French windows, verandahs, and sunny parlours, opening one out of another.

'How do you do, my dear?' said the spinster heartily, as Ida alighted; 'I am very glad to see you. Why, how bright and blooming you look—not a bit like a sea-sick traveller.'

'Dear Miss Wendover, I ought to look bright when I am so glad to come to you; and, as to the other thing, I am never sea-sick.'

'What a splendid girl! That unhappy little Bessie can't cross to the Wight without being a martyr. But, Ida, I am not going to be called Miss Wendover. Only bishops and county magnates, and people of that kind, call me by that name. To you I am to be Aunt Betsy, as I am to the children at The Knoll.'

'Is not that putting me too much on a level—'

'With my own flesh and blood? Nonsense! I mean you to be as my own flesh and blood. I could not bear to have anyone about me who was not.'

'You are too good,' faltered Ida. 'How can I ever repay you?'

'You have only to be happy. It is your nature to be frank and truthful, so I will say nothing about that.'

Ida blushed deepest scarlet. Frank and truthful—she—whose very name was a lie! And yet there could be no wrong done to Miss Wendover, she told herself, by her suppression of the truth. It was a suppression that concerned only Brian Walford and herself. No one else could have any interest in the matter.

Betsy Wendover herself led the way to the bed-chamber that had been prepared for the new inmate. It was a dear old room, not spacious, but provided with two most capacious closets, in each of which a small gang of burglars could have hidden—dear old closets, with odd little corner cupboards inside them, and a most elaborate system of shelves. One closet had a little swing window at the top for ventilation, and this, Miss Wendover told Ida, was generally taken for a haunted corner, as the ventilating window gave utterance to unearthly noises in the dead watches of the night, and sometimes gave entrance to a stray cat from adjacent tiles. A cat less agile than the rest of his species had been known to entangle himself in the little swing window, and to hang there all the night, sending forth unearthly caterwaulings, to the unspeakable terror of Miss Wendover's guest, unfamiliar with the mechanism of the room, and wondering what breed of Hampshire demon or afrit was thus making night hideous.

There was a painted wooden dado halfway up the wall, and a florid rose and butterfly paper above it. There was a neat little brass bedstead on one side of the room, a tall Chippendale chest of drawers, with writing-table and pigeon-holes on the other side; the dearest, oldest dressing-table and shield-shaped glass in front of the broad latticed window; while in another window there was a cushioned seat, such as Mariana of the Moated Grange sat upon when she looked across the fens and bewailed her dead-and-gone joys. There were old cups and saucers on the high, narrow chimney-piece, below which a cosy fire burned in a little old basket grate. Altogether the room was the picture of homely comfort.

'Oh, what a lovely room!' cried Ida, inwardly contrasting this cheery chamber with that white-washed den at Les Fontaines, with its tawdry mahogany and brass fittings, its florid six feet of carpet on a deal floor stained brown, its alabaster clock and tin candelabra—a cheap caricature of Parisian elegance.

'I'm glad you like it, my dear, 'answered Miss Wendover. 'Bessie said it would suit you; and all I ask you is to keep it tidy. I hope I am not a tyrant; but I am an old maid. Of course, I shall never pry into your room; but I warn you that I have an eye which takes in everything at a flash; and if I happen to go past when your door is open, and see a bonnet and shawl on your bed, or a gown sprawling on your sofa, my teeth will be set on edge for the next half-hour.'

'Dear Miss Wen—, dear Aunt Betsy,' said Ida, corrected by a frown, 'I hope you will come into my room every day, and give me a good scolding if it is not exactly as you like. Everything in this house looks lovely. I want to learn your nice neat ways.'

'Well, my love, you might learn something worse,' replied Miss Wendover, with innocent pride. 'And now come down to luncheon; I kept it back on purpose for you, and I am sure you must be starving.'

The luncheon was excellent, served with a tranquil perfection only to be attained by careful training; and yet Miss Wendover's youthful butler three years ago had been a bird boy; while her rosy-cheeked parlour-maid was only eighteen, and had escaped but two years from the primitive habits of cottage life. Aunt Betsy had a genius for training young servants.

'You had better unpack your boxes directly after luncheon, said Miss Wendover, when Ida had eaten with very good appetite, 'and arrange your things in your drawers. That will take you an hour or so, I suppose—say till five o'clock, when Bessie is coming over to afternoon tea.'

'Oh, I am so glad! I am longing to see Bessie. Is she as lovable and pretty as ever?'

'Well, yes,' replied Aunt Betsy, with a critical air; 'I think she has rather improved. She is plump enough still, in all conscience, but not quite so stumpy as she was last summer. Her figure is a little less like a barrel.'

'I hope she was very much admired at Bournemouth.'

'Yes, strange to say, she had a good many admirers,' answered Miss Wendover coolly. 'She made a point of never being enthusiastic about her relations. She had always partners at the dances, I am told, even when there was a paucity of dancing men; and she was considered rather remarkable at lawn tennis. No doubt she will tell you all about it this afternoon. I have some work to do in the village, and I shall leave you two girls together.'

This was a delicacy which touched Ida. She was very anxious to see Bessie, and to talk to her as they could only talk when they were alone. She wanted to know her faithful friend's motive for that cruel deception about Brian Walford. That the frank, tender-hearted Bessie could have so deceived her from any unworthy motive was impossible.

Five o'clock struck, and Ida was sitting alone in the drawing-room, waiting to receive her friend, just as if she were the daughter of the house, instead of a salaried dependent. The pretty carved Indian tea-table—a gem in Bombay blackwood—was wheeled in front of the fire-place, which was old, as regarded the high wooden mantel-piece and capacious breadth of the hearth, but essentially new in its glittering tiles and dainty brass fire-irons.

The clock had hardly finished striking when Bessie bounced into the room, rosy and smiling, in sealskin jacket and toque.

'Oh, you darling! isn't this lovely?' she exclaimed, hugging Ida. 'You are to live here for ever and ever, and never, never, never to leave us again, and never to marry, unless you marry one of the Brians. Don't shudder like that, pet, they are both nice! And I'm sure you like Brian Walford, though, perhaps, not quite so much as he liked you. You do like him now, don't you, darling?' urged Bess.

Ida had withdrawn from her embrace, and was seated before the low Bombay table, occupied with the tea pot. There was no light but the fire and one shaded lamp on a distant table. The curtains were not yet drawn, and white mists were rising in the garden outside, like a sea.

'Bessie,' Ida began, gravely, as her old schoolfellow sat on a low stool in front of the fire, 'how could you deceive me like that? What could put such a thing in your head—*you*, so frank, so open?'

'I am sure I hardly know,' answered Bess, innocently. 'It was my birthday, don't you know, and we were all wild. Perhaps the champagne had something to do with it, though I didn't take any. But that sort of excitement communicates itself; and running up and down hill gets into one's head. We all thought it would be such fun to pass off penniless B. W. for his wealthy cousin—and just to see how you liked him, with that extra advantage. But there was no harm in it, was there, dear? Of course, he told you afterwards, when you saw him at Mauleverer?'

'Yes, he told me—afterwards.'

'Naturally; and having begun to like him as the rich Brian, you didn't leave off liking him because of his poverty—did you, darling? The man himself was the same.'

Ida was silent, remembering how, with the revelation of the fraud that had been practised upon her, the very man himself had seemed to undergo a transformation—as if a disguise, altering his every characteristic, had been suddenly flung aside.

She did not answer Bessie's question, but, looking down at her with grave, searching eyes, she said,—'Dear Bessie, it was a very foolish jest. I know it is not in your nature to mean unkindly to anyone, least of all to me, to whom you have been an angel of light; but all practical jokes of that kind are liable to inflict pain and humiliation upon the victim—however innocently meant. Whose idea was it, Bess? Not yours, I think?'

'No; it was Urania who proposed it. She said it would be such fun.'

'Miss Rylance is not usually so—funny.'

'No; but she was particularly jolly that day, don't you remember? in positively boisterous spirits—for her.'

'And the outcome of her amiability was this suggestion?'

'Yes, darling. She had noticed that you had a kind of romantic fancy about Brian of the Abbey—that you had idealised his image, as it were—and set him up as a kind of demi-god. Not because of his wealth, darling—don't suppose that we supposed that—but on account of that dear old Abbey and its romantic associations, which gave a charm to the owner. And so she said what fun it would be to pass off Brian Walford as his cousin, and see if you fell in love with him. 'I know she is ready to lay her heart at the feet of the owner of the Abbey,' Urania said; and I thought it would be too delicious if you were to fall in love with Brian Walford, who could not help falling in love with you, for of course it would end in your marrying him, and his getting on splendidly at the Bar; for, with his talents, he must do well. He only wants a motive for industry. And then you would be our very own cousin! I hope it wasn't a very wicked idea, Ida, and that you will find it in your heart to forgive me,' pleaded Bess, kneeling by her friend's chair, with clasped bands upon Ida's knees, and sweet, half-tearful face looking up, 'My darling, I have never been angry with you,' answered Ida, clasping the girl to her heart, with a stifled sob. 'But I don't think Miss Rylance meant so kindly. Her idea sprang from a malevolent heart. She wanted to humiliate me—to drag my most sordid characteristics into the light of day—to make me more abject than poverty had made me already. That was the motive of her joke.'

'Never mind her motive, dear. All I am interested in is your opinion of Brian. I hope he behaved nicely at Mauleverer.'

'Very nicely.'

'Cobb says that Fräulein positively raves about him—declares he is quite the most gentlemanly young man she ever saw—a godly young man she called him, in her funny English. And, she says, that he was madly in love with you. Of course he made you an offer?'

'How could he do that when I was always with the Fräulein?'

'Oh, nonsense. Brian is not the kind of young man to be kept at bay by a mild nonentity like the Fräulein. He told me before he left that he was desperately in love with you, and that he meant to win you for his wife. I asked him how he intended to keep a wife, and he said he should write for the magazines, and do theatrical criticisms for the newspapers, till briefs began to drop in. He was determined to win you if you were to be won. So I feel sure that he made you an offer, unless, indeed, that horrid old Pew spoiled all by her venomous conduct.'

'That is it, dear. Miss Pew brought matters to an abrupt close.'

'And you are not engaged to Brian?' said Bess, dolefully.

'No.'

'And he didn't follow you to Dieppe?'

'No.'

'Then he is not half so fine a fellow as I thought him.'

'Suppose, Bessie, that after a little mild flirtation, with Fräulein Wolf for an audience, we both discovered that our liking for each other was of the very coolest order, and that it was wiser to let the acquaintance end?'

'You might feel that; but I would never believe it of Brian. Why, he raved about you; he was passionately in love. He told me there was no sacrifice he would not make to call you his wife.'

'He had so much to sacrifice,' said Ida, with a cynical air.

'Don't be unkind, Ida. Of course I know that he has his fortune to make; but he is so thoroughly nice—so full of fun.'

'Did you ever know him do anything good or great, anything worth being remembered—anything that proved the depth and nobility of his nature?' asked Ida, earnestly.

'Good gracious! no, not that I can remember. He is always nice, and amusing. He doesn't like carrying a basket, or skates, and things; but of course, where there are younger boys one couldn't expect him to do that; and he hates plain girls and old women; but I suppose that is natural, for even father does it, in his secret soul, though he is always so utterly sweet to the poor things. But I am sure Brian Walford has a tender heart, because he is so fond of kittens.'

'I didn't mean to insinuate that he was a modern Domitian,' answered Ida, smiling at Bessie's childish earnestness. 'What I mean is that there is no depth in his nature, no nobility in his character. He is shallow, and, I fear, selfish. But, Bessie, my pet, I am going to ask you a favour.'

'Ask away,' cried Bessie, cheerfully; 'I can't give you the moon, but anything which I really do possess is yours this instant.'

'Don't let us ever talk of Brian Walford. I can never get over the feeling of humiliation which Miss Rylance's practical joke caused me; and my only chance of forgetting it is to forget your cousin's existence.'

'Oh, but he will come to The Knoll, I hope, at Christmas, and then you will think better of him.'

'If he should come I—I hope I shall not see him.'

'Has he offended you so deeply?'

'Don't let us talk about him, Bess. Tell me all about your Bournemouth triumphs. I hear you were the belle of the place.'

'Then you have heard a most egregious fib. There were dozens of girls with nineteen-inch waists, before whom I felt myself a monster of dumpiness. But I got on pretty well. I don't pretend to be a good dancer, but I can generally adapt myself to the badness of other people's steps, and that goes for something.'

And now having got away from all painful subjects, Bessie rattled on at a tremendous pace, describing girls and gowns, and partners, and tennis tournaments, and yachting excursions, all in a breath, as she sat in front of the fire sipping her tea, and devouring a particular kind of buttered bun for which Miss Wendover's cook was famous.

'Aunt Betsy's tea is always nicer than any one else's; and so are her buns and her butter; in fact everything in this house is nicer than it is anywhere else,' said Bessie, pausing in her reminiscences. 'You are in clover here, Ida.'

'Thanks to your goodness, Bess.'

'To mine? But I have positively nothing to do with it.'

'Yes, you have. It is from the wish to please her warm-hearted little niece that Miss Wendover has been so good to me.'

'But if you had been plain or stupid she would have only been kind to you at a distance. Aunt Betsy has her idiosyncrasies, and one of them is a liking for beauty in individuals, as well as in chairs and tables and cups and saucers. You will see that all her servants are pretty. She picks them for their good looks, I believe, and trains them afterwards. She would not have so much as a bad-looking stable boy.'

'Hard upon ugliness to be shut out of this paradise,' said Ida.

'Oh, but she finds places for the ugly boys and girls, with people whose teeth are not so easily set on edge, she says herself. And now I must be off, to change my frock for dinner. You know the back way to The Knoll—across the fields to the little door in the kitchen-garden. You will always come that way, of course. When are you coming to see us? To-morrow?'

'You forget that my time is not my own. I will come whenever Miss Wendover can best spare me.'

'Oh, you will have plenty of spare time, I am sure.'

'I hope not too much, or I shall be too sharply reminded that Miss Wendover has taken me out of charity.'

'Charity fiddlestick! A prize-winner like you! And now good-bye, pet, or I shall be late for dinner, which offends the Colonel beyond measure.'

Bessie scampered off, Ida following her to the glass door, only in time to see her running across the lawn as fast as her feet could carry her. It was characteristic of Bessie to cut everything very fine in the way of time.

CHAPTER XII
THE SWORD OF DAMOCLES

And now began for Ida a life of exceeding peacefulness, comfort, happiness even; for how could a girl fail to be happy among people who were so friendly and kind, who so thoroughly respected her, and so warmly admired her for gifts altogether independent of fortune—who never, by word or look, reminded her that she was in anywise of less importance than themselves?

Nor had the girl any cause to fear that she was a useless member of Miss Wendover's household. That lady found plenty of occupation for her young companion—varied and pleasant duties, which made the days seem too short, and the leisure of the long winter evenings an agreeable relief from the busy hours of daylight.

That exquisite neatness which gave such a charm to Wendover's house was not attained without labour. The polished surface of the old Chippendale bureaus, the inlaid Sheraton chairs and tables, could only be maintained by daily care. A housemaid's perfunctory dusting was not sufficient here; and Miss Wendover, gloved and aproned, and armed with leathers and brushes, gave at least half an hour every morning to the care of her old furniture. Another half hour was devoted to china; and the floral arrangements indoors, even in this wintry season, occupied half an hour more. This was all active work, about which Aunt Betsy and Ida went merrily, talking tremendously as they polished and dusted, and upon all possible subjects, for Miss Wendover's lonely evenings had enabled her to read almost as much as Southey, and she delighted in telling Ida the curious out-of-the-way facts that were stored up in her memory.

Sometimes there was an hour or so given to culinary matters—new dishes, new kickshaws, *hors d'oeuvres,* savouries—to be taught the young, teachable cook-maid; for whenever Miss Wendover went to a great dinner, her eagle eye was on the alert to discover some modern improvement in the dishes or the table arrangements.

Then there was gardening, which absorbed a good deal of time in fine weather; for Aunt Betsy held that no gardener, however honestly inclined, would long feel interested in a garden to which its owner was indifferent. Miss Wendover knew every flower that grew—could bud, and graft, and pot, and prune, and do everything that her youthful gardeners could do, beside being ever so much more learned in the science of gardening.

Then there were inspections of piggery and poultry-yard, medicines and particular foods to be prepared for the poultry, hospitals to be established and looked after in odd corners of the orchard, and the propagation of species to be carried on by mechanical contrivances.

On wet days there was art needlework, for which Miss Wendover had what artists would call a great deal of feeling, without being very skilful as an executant. Under her direction, Ida began a mauresque border for a tawny plush curtain which was to be a triumph of art when completed, and which was full of interest in progress. She worked at this of an evening, while Miss Wendover, who had a fine full voice, and a perfect enunciation, read aloud to her. Then, when Miss Wendover was tired, Ida went to the piano and played for an hour or so, while the elder lady gave herself up to rare idleness and dreamy thought.

These were home duties only. The two ladies had occupations abroad of a more exacting nature. Miss Wendover until now had given two botany lessons, and one physical science lesson, every week in the village school. The botany lessons she now handed over to Ida, whom she coached for that purpose. Summer or winter these lessons were always given out of doors, in the course of an hour's ramble in field, lane, or wood. Then Miss Wendover had a weekly class for domestic economy, a class attended by all the most promising girls, from thirteen years old upwards, within five miles. This class was held in the kitchen or housekeeper's room at the Homestead; and many were the savoury messes of broth or soup, cheap stews and meat puddings, and the jellies and custards compounded at these lessons, to be sent off next day to the sick poor upon Miss Wendover's list.

Then there was house to house visiting all over the widely-scattered parish, much talk with gaffers and goodies, in all of which Ida assisted. She would have hated the work had Miss Wendover been a person of the Pardiggle stamp; but as love was the governing principle of all Aunt Betsy's work, her presence was welcome as sunshine or balmy air; so welcome that her sharpest lectures (and she could lecture when there was need) were received with meekness and even gratitude. In these visits Ida learned to know a great deal about the ways and manners of the agricultural poor, all the weakness and all the nobility of the rural nature.

Every Saturday or half-holiday at the village school—blessed respite which gave the hard-worked mistress time to mend her clothes, and make herself bright and trim for Sunday, and opened for the master brilliant possibilities in the way of a jaunt to Bomsey or Winchester—Miss Wendover gave a dinner to all the school children under twelve. She had taken up Victor Hugo's theory that a substantial meat dinner, even on one day out of seven, will do much to build up the youthful constitution and to prevent scrofulous diseases. Moved by these considerations, she had fitted up a disused barn as a rustic dining-hall, the walls plastered and whitewashed, or buff-washed, the massive cross timbers painted a dark red, a long deal table and a few forms the only furniture. Here every Saturday, at half-past one o'clock, she provided a savoury meat dinner; and very strong must be that temptation or that necessity which would induce Aunt Betsy to abandon her duties as hostess at this weekly feast. It was she who said grace before and after meat—save when some suckling parson was admitted to the meal; it was she who surveyed and improved the manners of her guests by sarcastic hints or friendly admonitions; and it was she who furnished intellectual entertainment in the shape of anecdote, historical story, or excruciating conundrum.

Ida was allowed to assist at these banquets, and there was nothing in her new life which she enjoyed more than the sight of all those glad young faces round the board, or the sound of that frank, rustic laughter. Some there were naturally of a bovine dullness, in whom even Miss Wendover could not awaken a ray of intelligence; but these were few. The generality of the children were far above the average rustic in brightness of intellect, and this superiority might fairly be ascribed to Aunt Betsy's influence.

A fortnight before Christmas, by which time Ida had been at the Homestead more than a month, Miss Wendover suggested a drive to Winchester, and before starting she handed Ida a ten-pound note. 'You may want some additional finery for Christmas,' she said kindly. 'Girls generally do. So you may as well buy it to-day.'

'But, dear Aunt Betsy, I have only been with you a month.'

'Never mind that, my dear. We will not be particular as to quarter-days. When I think you want money I shall give it to you, and we can make up our accounts at the end of the year.'

'You are ever so much too good to me,' said Ida, with a loving look that said a good deal more than words.

There was a light frost that whitened the hills, and the keen freshness of the air stimulated Brimstone to conduct of a somewhat riotous character, but Miss Wendover's firm hand held his spirits in check. Treacle was a sagacious beast, who never did more work than he was absolutely obliged to do, and who allowed Brimstone to drag the phaeton while he trotted complacently on the other side of the pole. But Miss Wendover would stand no nonsense, even from the amiable Treacle. She sent the pair across the hills at a splendid pace, and drove them under the old archway and down the stony street with a style which won the admiration of every experienced eye.

They drew up at the chief draper's of the town; and here Miss Wendover retired to hold a solemn conference with the head milliner, a judicious and accomplished person who made Aunt Betsy's gowns and bonnets—all of a solid and substantial architecture, as if modelled on the adjacent cathedral. Ida, left alone amidst all the fascinations of the chief shop in a smart county town, and feeling herself a Croesus, had much need of fortitude and coolness of temper. Happily she remembered what a little way that five-pound note had gone in preparing her for her summer visit to The Knoll, and this brought wisdom. Before spending sixpence upon herself she bought a gown—an olive merino gown, and velvet to trim it withal—for her stepmother.

'I don't think she gets a new gown much oftener than I do,' she thought; 'and even if this costs four or five shillings for carriage it will be worth the money, as a Christmas surprise.'

The gown left only trifling change out of two sovereigns, so that by the time Ida had bought herself a dark brown cloth jacket and a brown cashmere gown there were only four sovereigns left out of the ten. She spent one of these upon some pale pink cashmere for an evening dress, and half a sovereign on gloves, as she knew Miss Wendover liked to see people neatly gloved. Ten shillings more were spent upon calico, and another sovereign went by-and-by at the bootmaker's, leaving the damsel with just twenty shillings out of her quarter's wage; but as the need of pocket-money at Kingthorpe, except for the Sunday offertory, was nil, she felt herself passing rich in the possession of that last remaining sovereign. She would have liked to spend it all upon Christmas gifts for her young friends at The Knoll; but this fond wish she relinquished with a sigh. Paupers could not be givers of gifts. Whatever she gave must be the fruit of her own labour—some delicate piece of handiwork made out of cheap materials.

'They are all too good to think meanly of me because I can only show my gratitude in words,' she told herself.

As Christmas drew near Ida listened anxiously for any allusion to Brian Walford as a probable visitor; and to her infinite relief, just three days before the festival, she heard that he was not coming. He had been invited, and he had left his young cousins in suspense as to his intentions till the last moment, and then had written to say that he had accepted an invitation to Norfolk, where there would be shooting, and a probability of a stag-hunt on foot.

'Which I call horridly mean of him,' protested Horatio, who had come across the fields expressly to announce this fact to Ida. 'Why can't he come and shoot here? I don't mean to say that there is anything particular to shoot, but he and I could go out together and try our luck. Our hills are splendid for hares.'

'Do you mean that there are plenty of hares?' inquired Ida.

'No, not exactly that. But it would be capital ground for them, don't you know, if there were any.'

'And where is your other cousin Brian?' asked Ida, merely for the sake of conversation.

All interest, all idle dreaming about the unknown Brian was over with her since the fatal mistake which had marred her life. She could not conceive that anything save evil could ever arise to her henceforward out of that hated name.

'Oh, he is in Sweden, or Turkey, or Russia, or somewhere,' replied Horatio, with a disgusted air; 'always on the move, instead of keeping up the Abbey in proper style, and cultivating his cousins. A man with such an income is bound in duty to his fellow-creatures to keep a pack of foxhounds. What else was he sent into the world for, I should like to know?'

'Perhaps to cultivate the knowledge of his fellow-creatures in distant countries, and to improve his mind.'

'Rot!' exclaimed Horatio, who was not choice in his language. 'What does he want with mind? or to make a walking Murray or Baedeker of himself? Society requires him to lay out his money to the local advantage. Here we are, with no foxhounds nearer than the New Forest, when we ought to have a pack at our door!'

Ida could not enter into the keen sense of deprivation caused by a dearth of foxhounds, so she went on quietly with her work, shading the wing of the inevitable swallow flitting across the inevitable bulrushes which formed the design for a piano back.

Presently Bessie came bouncing in, her sealskin flung on anyhow, and the most disreputable thing in hats perched sideways on her bright brown curls.

'Mother is going to let us have a dance,' she burst forth breathlessly, 'on Twelfth Night! Won't that be too jolly? A regular party, don't you know, with a crumb-cloth, and a pianiste from Winchester, and perhaps a cornet. It's only another guinea, and if father's in a good temper he's sure to say yes. You must come over to The Knoll every evening to practise your waltzing. We shall have nothing but round dances in the programme. I'll take care of that!'

'But if there are any matrons who like to have a romp in the Lancers or the Caledonians, ain't it rather a shame to leave them out in the cold?' suggested Horatio. 'You're so blessed selfish, Bess.'

'We are not going to have any matrons. Mother will matronize the whole party. We are going to have the De Travers, and the Pococks, and the Ducies, and the Bullinghams over from Bournemouth.'

'And where the deuce are you going to put 'em?'

'Oh, we can put up at least twenty—on spare mattresses, don't you know, in the old nursery, and in the dressing-rooms and bath-room; and as for us, why, of course, *we* can sleep anywhere.'

'Thank you,' replied Horatio; 'I hope you don't suppose I am going to turn out of my den, or to allow a pack of girls to ransack my drawers and smoke my favourite pipe.'

'I don't suppose any decent-minded girl would consent to sleep in such a loathsome hole,' retorted Bessie. 'She would prefer a pillow and a rug on the landing.'

'My den is quite as tidy as that barrack of yours,' said the Wykhamiste, 'though I haven't yet risen to disfiguring my walls with kitchen plates and fourpenny fans. The cheap aesthetic is not my line.

'Don't pretend to be cantankerous, Horatio,' said Ida, looking at him with the loveliest eyes, twinkling a little at his expense; 'we all know that you are brimming over with good-humour. Perhaps Aunt Betsy will take in some of your visitors, Bess. I am sure they shall be welcome to my room, if I have to sleep in the poultry yard.'

'Happy thought,' cried Bessie; 'I'll sound the dear creature as to her views on the subject this very day.'

Aunt Betsy was all goodness, and offered to accommodate half a dozen young ladies of neat and cleanly habits. She protested that she would have no candle-grease droppers or door-mat despisers in her house.

'The Homestead is the only toy I have,' she said,' and I won't have it ill-used.'

So six irreproachable young women, the pride of careful mothers, were billeted on Miss Wendover, while the more Bohemian damsels were to revel in the improvised accommodation of The Knoll.

That particular Christmas-tide at Kingthorpe was a time of innocent mirth and youthful happiness which might have banished black care, for the nonce, from the oldest, weariest breast. For Ida, still young and fresh, loving and lovable, the contagion of that youthful mirth was irresistible.

She forgot by how fine a hair hung the sword that dangled over her guilty head—or began to think that the hair was tough enough to hold good for ever. And what mattered the existence of the sword provided it was never to fall? Sometimes it seemed to her in the pure and perfect happiness of this calm rural home, this useful, innocent life, as if that ill-advised act of hers had never been acted—as if that autumn morning, that one half-hour in the modern Gothic church, still smelling of mortar and pitch-pine, set in flat fields, from which October mists were rising ghostlike, was no more than a troubled dream—a dream that she had dreamed and done with for ever. Could it be that such an hour—so dim, so shadowy to look back upon from the substantial footing of her present existence—was to give colour to all the rest of her life? No, it was the dark dream of a troubled past, and she had nothing to do but to forget it as soon as possible.

Forgetfulness—or at least a temporary kind of forgetfulness—was tolerably easy while Brian Walford was civil enough to stay away from Kingthorpe; but the problem of life would be difficult were he to appear in the midst of that cordial circle—difficult to impossibility.

'It is evident that he doesn't mean to come while I am here,' she told herself, 'and that at least is kind. But in that case I must not stay here too long. It is not fair that I should shut him out of his uncle's house. It is I who am the interloper.'

She thought with bitterest grief of any change from this peaceful life among friends who loved her, to service in the house of a stranger; but her conscience recognised the necessity for such a change.

She had no right to squat upon the family of the man she had married—to exclude him from his rightful heritage, she who refused to acknowledge his right as her husband. He had done her a deep wrong; he had deceived her cruelly; and she deemed that she had a right to repudiate a bond tainted by fraud; but she knew that she had no right to banish him from his family circle—to dwell, under false pretences, by the hearth of his kindred.

'I did wrong in coming here,' she thought; 'it was a mean thing to do. Yet how could I resist the temptation, when no other place offered, and when I knew I was such a burden at home?'

In the very midst of her happiness, therefore, there was always this corroding care, this remorseful sense of wrong-doing. This present life of hers was all blissful, but it was bliss which could not, which must not, last. Yet what fortitude would be needed ere she could break this flowery bondage, loosen these dear fetters which love had laid upon her!

Once, during that jovial Christmas season, she hinted at a possible change in the future.

'What a happy day this has been!' she said as she walked across the wintry fields with Miss Wendover on the verge of midnight, after a Christmas dinner and a long evening of Christmas games at The Knoll, Needham marching in front of them with an unnecessary lantern, and all the stars of heaven shining in blue frosty brilliance above their heads, 'and what a happy home! I feel it is a privilege to have seen so much of it; and by-and-by, when I am among strangers—'

'What do you mean?' exclaimed Aunt Betsy, sharply; 'there is to be no such by-and-by; or, if there ever be such a time, it will be your making, not mine. You suit me capitally, and I mean to keep you as long as ever I can, without absolute selfishness. If an eligible husband should want to carry you off, I must let you go; but I will part with you to no one less than a husband—unless, indeed,' and here Betsy Wendover's voice took a colder and graver tone, 'unless you should want to better yourself, as the servants say, and get more money than I can afford to give you. I know your accomplishments are worth much more; but it is not everybody to whom you would be as their own flesh and blood.'

'Oh, Aunt Betsy, can you think that I should ever set money in the scale against your kindness—your infinite goodness to me?'

'When you talk of a change by-and-by, you set me thinking. Perhaps you are already beginning to tire of this rustic dullness.'

'No, no, no; I never was so happy in my life—never since I was a child playing about on board the ship that brought my mother and me to England. Everybody was kind to me, and made much of me. My mother and I adored each other; and I did not know that she was dying. Soon after we landed she grew dangerously ill, and lay for weeks in a darkened room, which I was not allowed to enter. It was a dreary, miserable time; a lonely, friendless child pining in a furnished lodging, with no one but a servant and a sick-nurse to speak to; and then, one dark November morning, the black hearse and coaches came to the door, and I stood peeping behind a corner of the parlour blind, and saw my mother's coffin carried out of the house. No; from the time we left the ship till I came to The Knoll I had never known what perfect happiness meant.'

'Surely you must have had some happy days with your father?' said Aunt Betsy.

'Very few. There was always a cloud. Papa is not the kind of man who can be cheerful under difficulties. Besides, I have seen so little of him, poor dear. He did not come home from India till I was thirteen, and then he fell in love with my stepmother, and married her, and took her to France, where he fancies it is cheaper to live than in England. Yet I cannot help thinking there are corners of dear old England where he might find a prettier home and live quite as cheaply.'

'Of course, if he were a sensible man; but I gather from all you have told me that there is a gentlemanlike helplessness about him—as of a person who ought to have inherited a handsome income, and is out of his element as a struggler.'

'That is quite true,' answered Ida; 'my father was not born to wrestle with Fate.'

They were at the glass door which opened into the morning-room by this time. The room was steeped in rosy light—such a pretty room, with chintz curtains and chintz-covered easy-chairs, low, luxurious, inviting; the only ponderous piece of furniture an old Japanese cabinet, rich in gold work upon black lacquer. On the dainty little octagon table there was a large shallow brown glass vase full of Christmas roses; and there was an odour of violets from the celadon china jars on the chimney-piece. Aunt Betsy's favourite Persian cat, a marvel of fluffy whiteness, rose from the hearth to welcome them. It was a delightful picture of home life.

Miss Wendover seemed in no hurry to go to bed. She seated herself in the low arm-chair by the fire, and allowed the Persian to rub its white head and arch its back against her dark brocade skirt. No one within twenty miles of Winchester wore such brocades or such velvets as Miss Wendover's. They were supposed to be woven on purpose for her. Her gowns were gowns of the old school, and lasted for years, smelling of the sandal or camphor wood chests in which they reposed for months at a stretch, yet, by virtue of some wonderful tact in the wearer, never looked dowdy or out of date.

'Now,' said Miss Wendover, with a resolute air, 'let us understand each other, my dear Ida. I don't quite like what you said just now; and I want to hear for certain that you are satisfied with your life here.'

'I am utterly happy here, dear Aunt Betsy. Is that a sufficient answer? Only, when I came here, I felt that it was charity—an impulse of kindness for a friendless girl—that prompted you to offer me a home; that, in accepting your kindness, I had no right to become an encumbrance; that, having enjoyed your genial hospitality for a space, I ought to move on upon my journey, to go where I could be of more use.'

'You too ridiculous girl, can you suppose that you are not useful to me?' exclaimed Aunt Betsy, impatiently. 'Is there a single hour of your day unoccupied? Granted that my original motive was a desire to give a comfortable home to a dear girl who seemed in need of new surroundings, but that idea would hardly have occurred to me unless I had begun to feel the want of some energetic helpmate to lighten the load of my daily duties. The experiment has answered admirably, so far as I am concerned. But it is just possible you feel otherwise. You may think that you could make better use of your powers—earn double my poor salary, win distinction by your fine playing, dress better, see more of the world. I daresay to a girl of your age Kingthorpe seems a kind of living death.'

'So far from that, I love Kingthorpe with all my heart, so much that I almost hate myself for not having been born here, for not being able to say these are my native fields, I was cradled among these hills.'

'So be it. If you love Kingthorpe and love me, you have nothing to do but to stay here till the hero of your life-story comes to carry you off.'

'There will be no such hero.'

'Oh, yes, there will! Every story, however humble, has its hero; but yours is going to be a very magnificent personage, I hope.'

The little clock on the chimney-piece chimed the half-hour after midnight, whereupon Aunt Betsy started up and called for her candle. She and Ida kissed as they wished each other good night on the threshold of the elder lady's room.

After this conversation, how could Ida ever again broach the subject of departure? and yet she felt that sooner or later she must depart. Honour, conscience, womanly feeling, forbade that she should remain at the cost of Brian Walford's banishment.

CHAPTER XIII
KINGTHORPE SOCIETY

On New Year's Eve Miss Wendover gave one of her famous dinner-parties; famous because it was always said that her dinners were, on their scale, better than anybody else's—yea, even that Dr. Rylance's, although that gentleman spared no expense, and had been known to induce the French cook from the Dolphin at Southampton to come over and prepare the feast for him.

Miss Wendover's dinner was an excuse for the bringing forth of rich stores of old china, old glass, and older silver—the accumulations of aunts and uncles for past generations, and in some part of the lady herself, who had the true spirit of a collector, that special gift which the French connoisseur calls *le flair*. Ida and the lady of the house worked diligently all the morning in papering and polishing these treasures; and the dinner table, with its antique silver, Derby china, heavy diamond-cut glass, and white and scarlet exotics, was a picture to gladden the eyes of Aunt Betsy's guests.

The party consisted of Colonel and Mrs. Wendover, with their daughter Bessie, admitted to this sacred function for the first time in her young life, and duly impressed with the solemnity of the occasion; the Vicar and his wife; the new curate, an Oxford M.A., and a sprig of a good old family tree, altogether something very superior in the way of curates; Mr. and Mrs. Hildrop Havenant, the great people of a neighbouring settlement, with their eldest son, also an Oxonion; and Dr. and Miss Rylance.

'Be sure you two girls look your best to-night,' said Miss Wendover, as she sat before the fire with Bessie and Ida, enjoying the free and easy luxury of a substantial afternoon tea, which would enable them all to be gracefully indifferent to the more solid features of dinner, and duly on the alert, to make conversation. 'We shall have three eligible men.'

'How do you make three, Aunt Betsy?' inquired her niece. 'Of course we all know that young Hildrop Havenant is heir to nearly all the land between Havenant and Romsey; but he is such a mass of affectation that I can't imagine anybody wanting to marry him. And as for Mr. Jardine—'

'Is he a mass of affectation, too, Bess?' inquired Aunt Betsy with intention, for Mr. Jardine, the curate, was supposed to have impressed the damsel's fancy more deeply than she would care to own. 'He is an Oxford man.'

'There is Oxford and Oxford,' said Bess. 'If all the Oxford men were like young Havenant, the only course open to the rest of the world would be to burn Oxford, just as Oxford burned the martyrs.'

'Well, we may count Mr. Jardine as an eligible, I suppose?'

'But that only makes two. Who is your third?' asked Bessie.

'Dr. Rylance.'

'Dr. Rylance an eligible?' cried Bessie, with girlhood's frank laughter at the absurd idea of middle age coming into the market to bid for youth. 'Why, auntie, the man must be fifty.'

'Five-and-forty at most, and very young-looking for his age; very polished, very well off. There are many girls who would be proud to win such a husband,' said Miss Wendover, glancing at Ida in the firelight.

She wanted to test the girl's temper—to find out, were it possible, whether this girl, whom she so inclined to love, tried in the fierce furnace of poverty, had acquired mercenary instincts. She had heard from Urania of that reckless speech about marrying for money, and she wanted to know how much or how little that speech had implied.

Ida was silent. She had never told anyone of Dr. Rylance's offer. She would have deemed it dishonourable to let anyone into the secret of his humiliation—to let his little world know that he, so superior a person, could offer himself and be rejected.

'What do you think now, Bess,' pursued Miss Wendover; 'would it not be rather a nice thing if Dr. Rylance were to marry Ida? We all know how much he admires her.'

'It would be a very horrid thing!' cried the impetuous Bess. 'I would ever so much rather Ida married poor Brian, although they had to pig in furnished lodgings for the first ten years of their life. Crabbed age and youth cannot dwell together.'

'But Dr. Rylance is not crabbed, and he is not old.'

'Let him marry a lady of the same doubtful age, which seems old to me, but young to you, and then no one will find fault with him,' said Bess, savagely. 'I feel an inward and spiritual conviction that Ida is doomed to marry Brian Walford. The poor fellow was so hopelessly in love with her when he left this place, that, if she had not a stone inside her instead of a heart, she would have accepted him; but *magno est amor et praevalebit!'* concluded Bess, with a mighty effort; 'I'm sure I hope that's right.'

'I think it must be time for you to go home and dress, if you really wish to look nice to-night,' said Ida, severely. 'You know you generally find yourself without frilling, or something wrong, at the last moment.'

'Heavens!' exclaimed Bessie, starting up and upsetting the petted Persian, which had been reposing in her lap, and which now skulked off resentfully, with a swollen tail, to hide its indignation under a chair, 'you are as bad as an oracle. I have yards and yards of frilling to sew on before I dress—my sleeves—my neck—my sweeper.'

'Shall I run over and sew the frills on for you?' asked Ida.

'You! when you are going to wear that lovely pink gown. You will want hours to dress. No: Blanche must make herself useful for once in her ridiculous life. *Au revoir*, auntie darling. Go, lovely rose'—to Ida—'and make yourself still lovelier in order to captivate Dr. Rylance.'

The dinner was over. It had passed without a hitch, and the gentlemen were now enjoying their claret and conversation in a comfortable semicircle in front of Miss Wendover's roomy hearth.

The conversation was for the most part strictly local, Colonel Wendover and Mr. Hildrop Havenant leading, and the Vicar a good second; but now and then there was a brief diversion from the parish to European politics, when Dr. Rylance—who secretly abhorred parochial talk—dashed to the fore and talked with an authority which it was hard for the others to keep under. He spoke of the impending declaration of war—there is generally some such thing—as if he had been at the War Office that morning in confidential converse with the chief officials; but this was more than Squire Havenant could endure, and he flatly contradicted the physician on the strength of his morning's correspondence. Mr. Havenant always talked of his letters as if they contained all the law and the prophets. His correspondents were high in office, unimpeachable authorities, men who had the ear of the House, or who pulled the strings of the Government.

'I am told on the best authority that there will be no war,' he said, swelling, or seeming to swell, as he spoke.

He was a large man, with a florid complexion and gray mutton-chop whiskers.

Dr. Rylance shrugged his shoulders and smiled blandly. It was the calm, incredulous smile with which he encountered any rival medico who was bold enough to question his treatment.

'That is not the opinion of the War Office,' he said quietly.

'But it is the opinion of men who dictate to the War Office,' replied Mr. Havenant.

'We couldn't have a better place for the working men's club than old Parker's cottage,' said the Vicar, addressing himself to Colonel Wendover.

'If Russia advances a foot farther, there must be war in Beloochistan,' said Dr. Rylance; 'and if England is blind to the exigencies of the situation, I should like to know how you are going to get your troops through the Bolan Pass.'

'A single line to Romsey would send up the value of land fifty per cent,' said the Colonel, who cared much more about Hampshire than Hindostan, although the best years of his life had been spent under Indian skies.

Hildrop Havenant pricked up his ears, and forgot all about the War Office.

'If the railway company had the pluck they ought to get that Bill through next Session,' he said, meaning a Bill for a loop between Winchester and Romsey.

While the elder gentlemen prosed over their wine the two younger men had found their way, first to the garden, for a cigar under the frosty moon, then back to Miss Wendover's pretty drawing room, where Ida was playing Schumann's 'Träumerei' at one end of the room with Bessie for her only audience, while Miss Rylance, Miss Wendover, and the three matrons made a stately group around and about the fire-place.

Urania was providing the greater part of the conversation. She had spent a delightful fortnight in Cavendish Square at the end of November, and had been everywhere and seen everything—winter exhibitions—new plays.

'I had no idea there could be so many nice people in town out of the season,' she said with a grand air. 'But then my father knows all the nicest people; he cultivates no Philistines.'

The Vicar's wife required to have this last remark explained to her. She only knew the Philistines of Scripture, an unfortunate people who seem always to have been in the wrong.

'And you saw some good pictures?' inquired Aunt Betsy.

'A few good ones and acres of daubs,' replied Urania. 'Why will so many people paint? There are pictures which are an affliction to the eye—an outrage upon common sense. Instead of a huge gallery lined from floor to ceiling with commonplace, why cannot we have a Temple with a single Watts, or Burne Jones, or Dante Bossetti, which one could go in and worship quietly in a subdued light?'

'That is a horridly expensive way of seeing pictures,' said the Vicar's wife; 'I hate paying a shilling for seeing a single picture. If it is ever so good one feels one has had so little for one's money. Now at the Academy there are always at least fifty pictures which delight me.'

'You must be very easy to please,' said Urania.

'I am,' replied the Vicar's wife, curtly, 'and that is one of the blessings for which I am thankful to God. I hate your *nil admiraris*,' added the lady, as if it were the name of a species.

After this Urania became suddenly interested in Schumann, and glided across the room to see what the music meant.

'That is very sweet,' she murmured, sinking into a seat by Bessie; 'classical, of course?'

'Schumann,' answered Ida, briefly.

'I thought so. It has that delicious vagueness one only finds in German music—a half-developed meaning—leaving wide horizons of melodious uncertainty.'

This was a conversational style which Miss Rylance had cultivated since her entrance into the small world of Kingthorpe, and the larger world of Cavendish Square, as a grown-up young woman. She had seen a good deal of a semi-artistic, quasi-literary circle, in which her father was the medical oracle, attending actresses and singers without any more substantial guerdon than free admittance to the best theatres on the best nights; prescribing for newspaper-men and literary lions, who sang his praises wherever they went.

Urania had fallen at once into all the tricks and manners of the new school. She had taken to short waists and broad sashes, and a style of drapery which accentuated the elegant slimness of her figure. She affected out-of-the-way colours, and quaint combinations—pale pinks and olive greens, tawny yellow and faded russet—and bought her gowns at a Japanese warehouse, where limp lengths of flimsy cashmere were mixed in artistic confusion with sixpenny teapots and paper umbrellas. In a word,

Miss Rylance had become a disciple of the peacock-feather school of art, and affected to despise every other development of intellect, or beauty.

This was the first time that she and Ida had met since the latter's return to Kingthorpe, except indeed for briefest greetings in the churchyard after morning service. Ida had not yet upbraided her for the trick of which she was the author and originator, but Urania was in no wise grateful for this forbearance. She had acted with deliberate maliciousness; and she wanted to know that her malice had given pain. The whole thing was a failure if it had not hurt the girl who had been audacious enough to outshine Miss Rylance, and to fascinate Miss Rylance's father. Urania had no idea that the physician had offered himself and his two houses to Ida Palliser, nay, had even pledged himself to sacrifice his daughter at the shrine of his new love. She knew that he admired Miss Palliser more than he had ever admired anyone else within her knowledge, and this was more than enough to make Ida hateful.

Ida was particularly obnoxious this evening, in that pale pink cashmere gown, with a falling collar of fine old Brussels point, a Christmas gift from Mrs. Wendover. The gown might not be the highest development of the Grosvenor Gallery school, but it was at once picturesque and becoming, and Ida was looking her loveliest.

'Why have you never come to see me since your return?' inquired Urania, with languid graciousness.

'I did not think you wanted me,' Ida answered, coolly.

'I am always glad to see my friends. I stop at home on Thursday afternoons on purpose; but perhaps you have not quite forgiven Bess and me for that little bit of fun we indulged in last September,' said Urania.

'I have quite forgiven Bess her share of the joke,' answered Ida, scanning Miss Rylance's smiling countenance with dark, scornful eyes, 'because I know she had no idea of giving me pain.'

'But won't you forgive me too? Are you going to leave me out in the cold?'

'I don't think you care a straw whether I forgive or do not forgive you. You wanted to wound me—to humiliate me—and you succeeded—to a certain degree. But you see I have survived the humiliation. You did not hurt me quite so much as you intended, perhaps.'

'What a too absurd view to take of the thing!' cried Urania, with an injured air. 'An innocent practical joke, not involving harm of any kind; a little girlish prank played on the spur of the moment. I thought you were more sensible than to be offended—much less seriously angry—at any such nonsense.'

Ida contemplated her enemy silently for a few moments, as her hands wandered softly through one of those Kinder-scenen which she knew by heart.

'If I am mistaken in your motives it is I who have to apologize,' she said, quietly. 'Perhaps I am inclined to make too much of what is really nothing. But I detest all practical jokes, and I should have thought you were the very last person to indulge in one, Miss Rylance. Sportiveness is hardly in your line.'

'Nobody is always wise,' murmured Urania, with her disagreeable simper.

'Not even Miss Rylance?' questioned Ida, without looking up from the keys.

'Please don't quarrel,' pleaded Bessie, piteously; 'such a bad use for the last night of the year. It was more my fault than anyone else's, though the suggestion did certainly come from Urania—but no harm has come of it—nor good either, I am sorry to say—and I have repented in sackcloth and ashes. Why should the dismal failure be raked up to-night?'

'I should not have spoken of it if Miss Rylance had been silent,' said Ida; and here, happily, the two young men came in, and made at once for the group of girls by the piano, whereupon Urania had an opportunity of parading her newest ideas, all second, third, or even fourth-hand, before the young Oxonians. One young Oxonian was chillingly indifferent to the later developments of modern thought, and had eyes for no one but Bessie, whose childish face beamed with smiles as he talked to her, although his homely theme was old Sam Jones's rheumatics, and the Providence which had preserved Martha Morris's boy from instant death when he tumbled into the fire. It was only parish talk, but Bessie felt as happy as if one of the saints of old had condescended to converse with her—proud and pleased, too, when Mr. Jardine told her how grateful old Jones was for her occasional visits, and how her goodness to Mrs. Morris had made a deep impression upon that personage, commonly reported to have 'a temper' and to be altogether a difficult subject.

The conversation drifted not unnaturally from parochial to more personal topics, and Mr. Jardine showed himself interested in Bessie's pursuits, studies, and amusements.

'I hear so much of you from those two brothers of yours,' said the Curate—'fine, frank fellows. They often join me in my walks.'

'I'm sure it is very good of you to have anything to say to them,' replied Bessie, feeling, like other girls of eighteen, that there could hardly be anything more despicable—from a Society point of view—than her two brothers.' They are laboriously idle all through the holidays.'

'Well, I daresay they might work a little more, with ultimate advantage,' said Mr. Jardine, smiling; 'but it is pleasant to see boys enjoy life so thoroughly. They are fond of all open air amusements, and they are keen observers, and I find that they think a good deal, which is a stage towards work.'

'They are not utterly idiotic,' sighed Bessie; 'but they never read, and they break things in a dreadful way. The legs of our chairs snap under those two boys as if old oak were touchwood; and Blanche and Eva, who ought to know better, devote all their energies to imitating them.'

The other gentlemen had come in by this time, and Dr. Rylance came gliding across the room with his gentlemanly but somewhat catlike tread, and planted himself behind Ida, bending down to question her about her music, and letting her see that he admired her as much as ever, and had even forgiven her for refusing him. But she rose as soon as she decently could, and left the piano.

'Miss Rylance will sing, I hope,' she said, politely. Miss Wendover came over to make the same request, and Urania sang the last fashionable ballad, 'Blind Man's Holiday,' in a hard chilly voice which was as unpleasant as a voice well could be without being actually out of tune.

After this Bessie sang 'Darby and Joan,' in a sweet contralto, but with a doleful slowness which hung heavily upon the spirits of the company, and a duly dismal effect having been produced, the young ladies were cordially thanked for—leaving off.

A pair of whist-tables were now started for the elders, while the three girls and the two Oxonians still clustered round the piano, and seemed to find plenty to talk about till sweetly and suddenly upon the still night air came the silver tones of the church bells.

Miss Wendover started up from the card-table with a solemn look, as the curate opened a window and let in a flood of sound. A silent hush fell upon everyone.

'The New Year is born,' said Aunt Betsy; 'may it spare us those we love, and end as peacefully for us as the year that is just dead.'

And then they all shook hands with each other and parted.

The dance at The Knoll was a success, and Ida danced with the best men in the room, and was as much courted and admired as if she had been the greatest heiress in that part of Hampshire. Urania Rylance went simpering about the room telling everybody, in the kindest way, who Miss Palliser was, and how she had been an ill-used drudge at a suburban finishing school, before that dear good Miss Wendover took her as a useful companion; but even that crushing phrase, 'useful companion,' did not degrade Ida in the eyes of her admirers.

'Palliser's a good name,' said one youth. 'There's a Sir Vernon Palliser—knew him and his brother at Cambridge—members of the Alpine Club—great athletes. Any relation?'

'Very distant, I should think, from what I know of Miss Palliser's circumstances;' answered Miss Rylance, with an incredulous sneer.

But Urania failed in making youth and beauty contemptible, and was fain to admit to herself that Ida Palliser was the belle of the room. Dr. Rylance, who had not been invited, but who looked so well and so young that no one could be angry with him for coming, hung upon Miss Palliser's steps, and tortured her with his politeness.

For Ida the festivity was not all happiness. She would have been happier at the Homestead, sitting by the fire reading aloud to Miss Wendover—happier almost anywhere—for she had not only to endure a kind of gentlemanly persecution from Dr. Rylance, but she was tormented by an ever-present dread of Brian Walford's appearance. Bessie had sent him a telegram only that morning, imploring him, as a personal favour, to be present at her ball, vowing that she would be deeply offended with him if he did not come; and more than once in the course of the evening Bessie had told Ida that there was still time, there was a train now just due at Winchester, and that might have brought him. Ida breathed more freely after midnight, when it was obviously too late for any one else to arrive.

'It is your fault,' said Bessie, pettishly. 'If you had not treated him very unkindly at Mauleverer he would be here to-night. He never failed me before.'

Ida reddened, and then grew very pale.

'I see,' she said, 'you think I deprive you of your cousin's society. I will ask Miss Wendover to let me go back to France.'

'No, no, no, you inhuman creature! how can you talk like that? You know that I love you ever so much better than Brian, though he is my own kith and kin. I would not lose you for worlds. I don't care a straw about his coming, for my own sake. Only I should so like you to marry him, and be one of us. Oh, here's that odious Dr. Rylance stealing after you. Aunt Betsy is quite right—the man would like to marry you—but you won't accept him, will you, darling?—not even to have your own house in Cavendish Square, a victoria and brougham, and all those blessings we hear so much about from Urania. Remember, you would have her for a stepdaughter into the bargain.'

'Be assured, dear Bess, I shall never be Urania's stepmother. And now, darling, put all thoughts of matrimony out of your head; for me, at least.'

That brief flash of Christmas and New Year's gaiety was soon over. The Knoll resumed its wonted domestic calm. Dr. Rylance went back to Cavendish Square, and only emerged occasionally from the London vortex to spend a peaceful day or two at Kingthorpe. His daughter was not installed as mistress of his town house, as she had fondly hoped would be the case. She was permitted to spend an occasional week, sometimes stretched to ten days or a fortnight, in Cavendish Square; but the cook-housekeeper and the clever German servant, half valet half butler, still reigned supreme in that well-ordered establishment; and Urania felt that she had no more authority than a visitor. She dared not find fault with servants who had lived ten years in her father's service, and who suited him perfectly—even had there been any legitimate reason for fault-finding, which there was not.

Dr. Rylance having got on so comfortably during the last twelve years of his life without a mistress for his town house, was disinclined to surrender his freedom to a daughter who had more than once ventured to question his actions, to hint that he was not all-wise. He considered it a duty to introduce his daughter into the pleasant circles where he was petted and made much of; and he fondly hoped she would speedily find a husband sufficiently eligible to be allowed the privilege of taking her off her father's hands. But in the meanwhile, Urania in London was somewhat of a bore; and Dr. Rylance was never more cheerful than when driving her to Waterloo Station.

Miss Rylance's life, therefore, during this period alternated between rural seclusion and London gaiety. She came back to the pastoral phase of her existence with the feelings and demeanour of a martyr; and her only consolation was found in those calm airs of superiority which seemed justified by her intimate acquaintance with society, and her free use of a kind of jargon which she called modern thought.

'How you can manage to exist here all the year round without going out of your mind is more than I can understand,' she told Bessie.

'Well, I know Kingthorpe is dull,' replied Bess, meekly, 'but it's a dear old hole, and I never find the days too long, especially when those odious boys are at home.'

'But really now, Bessie, don't you think it is time you should leave off playing with boys, and begin wearing gloves?' sneered Urania.

'I did wear gloves at Bournemouth, religiously—mousquetaires, up to my elbows; never went out without them. No, Ranie, I am never dull at old Kingthorpe; and then there is always a hope of Bournemouth.'

'Bournemouth is worse than this!' exclaimed Urania. 'There is nothing so laboriously dismal as a semi-fashionable watering-place.'

Talk as she might, Miss Rylance could not sour Bessie's happy disposition with the vinegar of discontent. Hers was a sweet, joyous soul; and just now, had she dared to speak the truth, she would have said that this pastoral village of Kingthorpe, this cluster of fine old houses and comfortable cottages, grouped around an ancient parish church, was to her the central point of the universe, to leave which would be as Eve's banishment from Eden. The pure and tender heart had found its shrine, and laid down its offering of reverent devotion. Mr. Jardine had said nothing as yet, but he had sedulously cultivated Bessie Wendover's society, and had made himself eminently agreeable to her parents, who could find no fault with a man who was at once a scholar and a gentleman, and who had an income which made him comfortably independent of immediate preferment.

He was enthusiastic, and he could afford to give his enthusiasm full scope. Kingthorpe suited him admirably. It was a parish rich in sweet associations. The present Vicar was a good, easy-going man, a High Churchman of the old school rather than the new, yet able to sympathize with men of more advanced opinions and fiercer energies.

Thus it was that while Miss Rylance found her bower at Kingthorpe a place of dullness and discontent, Bessie rose every morning to a new day of joy and gladness, which began, oh! so sweetly, in the early morning service, in which John Jardine's deep musical voice gave new force and meaning to the daily lessons, new melody to the Psalms. Ida was always present at this morning service, and the two girls used to walk home together through the dewy fields, sometimes one, sometimes the other going out of her way to accompany her friend. Bessie poured all her innocent secrets into Ida's ear, expatiating with sweet girlish folly upon every look and tone of Mr. Jardine's, asking Ida again and again if she thought that he cared, ever so little, for her.

'You never tell me any of your secrets, Ida,' she said, reproachfully, after one of these lengthy discussions. 'I am always prosing about my affairs, until I must seem a lump of egotism. Why don't you make me listen sometimes? I should be deeply interested in any dream of yours, if it were ever so wild.'

'My darling, I have no dreams, wild or tame,' said Ida. She could not say that she had no secret, having that one dreadful secret hanging over her and overshadowing her life.

'And have you never been in love?'

'Never. I once thought—almost thought—that I was in love. It was like drifting away in a frail, dancing little boat over an unknown sea—all very well while the sun shone and the boat went gaily—suddenly the boat fell to pieces, and I found myself in the cold, cruel water.'

'Horrid!' cried Bess, with a shudder. 'That could not have been real love.'

'No, dear, it was a will-o'-the-wisp, not the true light.'

'And you have got over it?'

'Quite. I am perfectly happy in the life I lead now.'

This was the truth. There are these calm pauses in most lives—blessed intervals of bliss without passion—a period in which heart and mind are both at rest, and yet growing and becoming nobler and purer in the time of repose, just as the body grows during sleep.

And thus Ida's life, full and useful, glided on, and the days went by only too swiftly; for it was never out of her mind that these days of tranquil happiness were numbered, that she was bound in honour to leave Kingthorpe before Brian Walford could feel the oppression of banishment from his kindred. At present Brian Walford was living in Paris, with an old college friend, both these youths being supposed to be studying the French language and literature, with a view to making themselves more valuable at the English bar. He had given up his chambers in the Temple, as too expensive for a man living from hand to mouth. He was understood to be contributing to the English magazines, and to be getting his living decently, which was better than languishing under the cognizance of the Lamb and Flag, with no immediate prospect of briefs.

CHAPTER XIV
THE TRUE KNIGHT

Kingthorpe, beautiful even in the winter, with its noble panorama of hills and woods, was now looking its loveliest in the leafy month of June. Ida had been living with Miss Wendover nearly eight months, and had become to her as a daughter, waiting upon her with faithful and loving service, always a bright and cheerful companion, joining with heart and hand in all good works. Her active life, her freedom from daily cares, had brightened her proud young beauty. She was lovelier than she had ever been as the belle of Mauleverer Manor, for that defiant look which had been the outcome of oppression had now given place to softness and smiles. The light of happiness beamed in her dark eyes. Between December and June this tranquil existence had scarcely been rippled by anything that could be called an event, save the one grand event of Bessie Wendover's life—her engagement to John Jardine, who had proposed quite unexpectedly, as Bessie declared, one evening in May, when the two had gone into a certain copse at the back of The Knoll gardens, famous as the immemorial resort of nightingales. Here, instead of listening to the nightingales, or silently awaiting a gush of melody from those pensive birds, Mr. Jardine had poured out his own melodious strain, which took the form of an ardent declaration. Bessie, who had been doing 'he loves me, loves me not,' with every flower in the garden—forgetting that from a botanical point of view the result was considerably influenced by the nature of the flower— pretended to be intensely surprised; made believe there was nothing further from her thoughts; and then, when her emboldened lover folded her to his breast, owned shyly, and with tears, that she had loved him desperately ever since Christmas, and that she would have been heartbroken had he married anyone else.

Colonel and Mrs. Wendover received the Curate's declaration with the coolness which is so aggravating in parents, who would hardly be elated if the sons of God came down once more to propose for the daughters of men.

They both considered that Bessie was ridiculously young—much too young to receive an offer of marriage. They consented, ultimately, to an engagement; but Bessie was not to be married till after her twenty-first birthday. This meant two years from next September, and Mr. Jardine pleaded hard for a milder sentence. Surely one year would be long enough to wait, when Bessie and he were so sure of their own minds.

'Bessie is too young to be sure of anything,' said the Colonel; 'and two years will only give you time to find a living and a nice cosy vicarage, or rectory, as the case may be.'

Mr. Jardine did not venture to remind Colonel Wendover that for him the cosiness of vicarage or rectory was a mere detail as compared with a worthy field for his labours. He meant to spend his life where it would be of most use to his fellow-creatures; even although the call of duty should come to him from the smokiest of manufacturing towns, or in the flat, dull fields of Lincolnshire, among pitmen and stockingers. He was not the kind of man to consider the snug rectory houses or fat glebes, but rather the kind of man to take upon himself some long-neglected parish, and ruin himself in building church and schools.

Fortunately for Bessie's hopes, however, Colonel Wendover did not know this.

The Curate complained to Aunt Betsy of her brother's hardness.

'Why cannot we be married at the end of this year?' he said. 'We have pledged ourselves to spend our lives together. Why should we not begin that bright new life—bright and new, at least to me—in a few months? That would be ample time for the Colonel and Mrs. Wendover to get accustomed to the idea of Bessie's marriage.'

'But a few months will not make her old enough or wise enough for a clergyman's wife,' said Miss Wendover.

'She has plenty of wisdom—the wisdom of a generous and tender heart—the best kind of wisdom. All her instincts, all her impulses, are pure, and true, and noble. What can age give her better than that? Girl as she is, my parish will be the better for her sweet influence. She will be the sunshine of my people's life as well as of mine. How will she grow wiser by living two years longer, and reading novels, and dancing at Bournemouth? I don't want her to be worldly-wise; and the better kind of wisdom comes from above. She will learn that in the quiet of her married home.'

'I see,' said Miss Wendover, smiling at him; 'you don't quite like the afternoon dances and tennis parties at Bournemouth.'

'Pray don't suppose I am jealous,' said the Curate. 'My trust in my darling's goodness and purity is the strongest part of my love. But I don't want to see the best years of her youth, her freshness, her girlish energy and enthusiasm, frittered away upon dances, and tennis, and dress, which has lately been elevated into an art. I want her help, I want her sympathy, I want her for my own—the better part of myself—going hand in hand with me in all my hopes and acts.'

'Two years sounds a long time,' said Miss Wendover, musingly, 'and I suppose, at your age and Bessie's, it is a long time; though at mine the years flow onward with such a gliding motion that it is only one's looking-glass, and the quarterly accounts, that tell one time is moving. However, I have seen a good many of these two-year engagements—'

'Yes.'

'And I have seldom seen one of them last a twelvemonth.'

'They have ended unhappily?'

'Quite the contrary. They have ended in a premature wedding. The young people have put their heads together, and have talked over the flinty-hearted parents; and some bright morning, when the father and mother have been in a good temper, the order for the trousseau has been given, the bridesmaids have received notice, and in six weeks the whole business was over, And the old people rather glad to have got rid of a love-sick damsel and her attendant swain. There is no greater nuisance in a house than engaged sweethearts. Who knows whether you and Bessie may not be equally fortunate?'

'I hope we may be so,' said the Curate; 'but I don't think we shall make ourselves obnoxious.'

'Oh, of course you think not. Every man believes himself superior to every form of silliness, but I never saw a lover yet who did not lapse sooner or later into mild idiocy.'

'*Amare et sapere vix deo conceditur.*'

'Of course. Indeed, with the gods of Olympus it was quite the other way. Nothing could be more absurd than their goings on.'

Ida was delighted at her friend's happiness, and was never tired of hearing about Mr. Jardine's virtues. Love had already begun to exercise a sobering influence upon Bessie. She no longer romped with the boys, and she wore gloves. She had become very studious of her appearance, but all those little coquettish arts of the toilet which she had learned last autumn at Bournemouth, the cluster of flowers pinned on her shoulder, the laces and frivolities, were eschewed; lest Mr. Jardine should be reminded of the wanton-eyed daughters of Zion, with their tinkling ornaments, and chains, and bracelets, and mufflers, and rings, and nose-jewels. She began to read with a view to improving her mind, and plodded laboriously through certain books of the advanced Anglican school which her lover had told her were good. But she learnt a great deal more from Mr. Jardine's oral instructions than from any books, and when the Winchester boys came home for an occasional Sunday they found her brimful of ecclesiastical knowledge, and at once nicknamed her the Perambulating Rubric, or by the name of any feminine saint which their limited learning suggested. Fortunately for Bessie, however, their jests were not unkindly meant, and they liked Mr. Jardine, whose knowledge of natural history, the ways and manners of every creature that flew, or walked, or crawled, or swam in that region of hill and valley, made him respectable in their eyes.

'He's not half a bad fellow—for a parson,' said Horatio, condescendingly.

'And wouldn't he make a jolly schoolmaster?' exclaimed Reginald. 'Boys would get on capitally with Jardine. They'd never try to bosh *him*.'

'Schoolmaster, indeed?' echoed Bessie, with an offended air.

'I suppose you think it wouldn't be good enough for him? You expect him to be made an archbishop off-hand, without being educated up to his work by the rising generation. No doubt you forget that there have been such men as Arnold, and Temple, and Moberly. Pray what higher office can a man hold in this world than to form the minds of the rising generation?'

'I wish your master would form your manners,' said Bessie, 'for they are simply detestable.'

It was nearly the end of June, and the song of the nightingales was growing rarer in the twilight woods.

Ida started early one heavenly midsummer morning, with her book and her luncheon in a little basket, to see the old lodge-keeper at Wendover Abbey, who had nursed the elder Wendovers when they were babies in the nurseries at the Abbey, and who had lived in a Gothic cottage at the gate— built on purpose for her by the last squire—ever since her retirement from active service. This walk to the Abbey was one of Ida's favourite rambles, and on this June morning the common, the wood, the corn-fields, and distant hills were glorious with that fleeting beauty of summer which gives a glamour to the most commonplace scenery.

She had a long idle morning before her, a thing which happened rarely. Miss Wendover had driven to Romsey with the Colonel and his wife, to lunch with some old friends in the neighbourhood of that quiet town, and was not likely to be home till afternoon tea. Bessie was left in charge of the younger members of the household, and was further deeply engaged in an elaborate piece of ecclesiastical embroidery, all crimson and gold, and peacock floss, which she hoped to finish before All Saints' Day.

Old Mrs. Rowse, the gatekeeper, was delighted to see Miss Palliser. The young lady was a frequent visitor, for the old woman was entitled to particular attention as a sufferer from chronic rheumatism, unable to do more than just crawl into her little patch of garden, or to the grass-plat before her door on a sunny afternoon. Her days were spent, for the most part, in an arm-chair in front of the neat little grate, where a handful of fire burnt, winter and summer, diffusing a turfy odour.

Ida liked to hear the old woman talk of the past. She had been a bright young girl, under-nurse when the old squire was born; and now the squire had been lying at rest in the family vault for nigh upon fifteen years, and here she was still, without kith or kin, or a friend in the world except the Wendovers.

She liked to hold forth upon the remarkable events of her life—from her birth in a labourer's cottage, about half a mile from the Abbey, to the last time she had been able to walk as far as the parish church, now five years ago. She was cheerful, yet made the most of her afflictions, and seemed to think that chronic rheumatism of her particular type was a social distinction. She was also proud of her advanced age, and had hopes of living into the nineties, and having her death recorded in the county papers.

That romantic feeling about the Abbey, which had taken possession of Ida's mind on her first visit, had hardly been lessened by familiarity with the place, or even by those painful associations which made the spot fatal to her. The time-old deserted mansion was still to her fancy a poem in stone; and although she could not think about its unknown master without a shudder, recalling her miserable delusion, she could not banish his image from her thoughts, when she roamed about the park, or explored the house, where the few old servants had grown fond of her and suffered her to wander at will.

When she had spent an hour with Mrs. Rowse, she walked on to the Abbey, and seated herself to eat her sandwiches and read her beloved Shelley under the cedar beneath which she and the Wendover party had picnicked so gaily on the day of her first visit. Shelley harmonized with her thoughtful moods, for with most of his longer poems there is interwoven that sense of wrong and sorrow, that idea of a life spoiled and blighted by the oppression of stern social laws, which could but remind Ida of her own entanglement. She had bound herself by a chain that could never be broken, and here she read of how all noblest and grandest impulses are above the law, and refuse to be so bound; and how, in such cases, it is noble to defy and trample upon the law. A kind of heroic lawlessness, spiritualized and diffused in a cloud of exquisite poetry, was what she found in her Shelley; and it comforted her to know that before her time there had been lofty souls caught in the web of their own folly.

When she was tired of reading she went into the Abbey. The great hall door stood open to admit the summer air and sunshine. Ida wandered from one room to another as freely as if she had been in her own house, knowing that any servant she met would be pleased to see her there. The old housekeeper was a devoted admirer of Miss Palliser; the two young housemaids were her pupils in a class which met every Sunday afternoon for study of the Scriptures. She had no fear of being considered an intruder. Many of the casements stood open, and there was the scent of flowers in the silent old rooms, where all was neat and prim, albeit a little faded and gray.

Ida loved to explore the library, where the books were for the most part quaint and old, original editions of seventeenth and eighteenth century books, in sober, substantial bindings. It was pleasant to take out a volume of one of the old poets, or the eighteenth century essayists, and to read a few stanzas, or a paper of Addison's or Steele's, standing by the open window in the air and sunlight.

The rooms in which she roamed at will were the public apartments of the Abbey, and, although beautiful in her eyes, they had the stiffness and solemnity of rooms which are not for the common uses of daily life.

But on one occasion Mrs. Mawley, the housekeeper, in a particularly communicative mood, showed her the suite of rooms in which Mr. Wendover lived when he was alone; and here, in the study where he read, and wrote, and smoked, and brooded in the long quiet days, she saw those personal belongings which gave at least some clue to the character of the man. Here, on shelves which lined the room from floor to ceiling, she saw the books which Brian Wendover had collected for his own especial pleasure, and the neatness of their arrangement and classification told her that the master of Wendover Abbey was a man of calm temper and orderly habits.

'You'll never see a book out of place when he leaves the room,' said Mrs. Mawley. 'I've seen him take down fifty volumes of a morning, when he's at his studies. I've seen the table covered with books, and books piled up on the carpet at each side of his chair, but they'd all be back on their shelves, as neat as a new pin, when I went to tidy up the room after him. I never allow no butter-fingered girls in this room, except to sweep or scrub, under my own eye. There's not many ornaments, but what there is is precious, and the apple of master's eye.'

It was a lovely room, with a panelled oak ceiling, and a fine old oak mantel-piece, on which were three or four pieces of Oriental crackle. The large oak writing-table was neatly arranged with crimson leather blotting-book, despatch-box, old silver inkstand, and a pair of exquisite bronze statuettes of Apollo and Mercury, which seemed the presiding geniuses of the place.

'I don't believe Mr. Wendover could get on with his studies if those two figures weren't there,' said Mrs. Mawley.

The rooms were kept always aired and ready—no one knew at what hour the master might return. He was a good master, honoured and beloved by the old servants, who had known him from his infancy; and his lightest whim was respected. The fact that he should have given the best part of his life since he left Oxford to roving about foreign countries was lamented; but this roving temper was regarded as only an eccentric manner of sowing those wild oats which youth must in some wise scatter; and it was hoped that with ripening years he would settle down and spend his days in the home of his ancestors. He might come home at any time, he had informed Mrs. Mawley in his last letter, received six weeks ago.

That glimpse of the room in which he lived gave Ida a vivid idea of the man—the calm, orderly student who had won high honours at the University, and was never happier than when absorbed in books that took him back to the past—to that very past which was presided over by the two pagan gods on the writing-table. She noted that the wide block of books nearest Mr. Wendover's chair were all Greek and Latin; and straying round the room she found Homers and Horaces, Greek playwrights and historians, repeating themselves many times, in various quaint costly editions. A scholar evidently—perhaps pragmatical and priggish. Bessie's coolness about her cousin implied that he was not altogether agreeable.

'Perhaps I should have liked him no better than the false Brian,' she said to herself to-day, as she stood musing before the old brown books in the library, thinking of that more individual collection which she had been allowed to inspect on her last visit.

She shuddered at the image of that other Brian, remembering but too vividly how she had last seen him, kneeling to her, claiming her as his own. God! could he so claim her? Was she verily his, to summon at his will?— his by the law of heaven and earth, and only enjoying her liberty by his sufferance?

The thought was horrible. She snatched a book from the shelf—anything to distract her mind. Happily, the book was Shakespeare, and she was soon lost in Lear's woes, wilder, deeper than any sorrow she had ever tasted.

She read for an hour, the soft air fanning her, the sun shining upon her, the scent of roses and lilies breathing gently round her as she sat in the deep oak window-seat. Then the clock struck three, and it was time to think of leaving this enchanted castle, where no prince or princess of fairy tale ever came.

There was no need for haste. She might depart at her leisure, and dawdle as much as she pleased on her homeward way. All she wanted was to be seated neat and trim in a carefully arranged room, ready to pour out Aunt Betsy's afternoon tea, when the cobs returned from Romsey. She put Lear back in his place, and strolled slowly through the rooms, opening one into another, to the hall, where she stopped idly to look at her favourite picture, that portrait of Sir Tristram Wendover which was attributed to Vandyke—a noble portrait, and with much of Vandyke's manner, whoever the painter. It occupied the place of honour in a richly-carved panel above the wide chimney-piece, a trophy of arms arranged on each side.

Ida stood gazing dreamily at that picture—the dark, earnest eyes, under strongly marked brows, the commanding features, somewhat ruggedly modelled, but fine in their general effect—a Rembrandt face—every line telling; a face in which manhood and intellect predominated over physical beauty; and yet to Ida's fancy the face was the finest she had ever seen. It was her ideal of the knightly countenance, the face of the man who has won many a hard fight over all comers, and has beaten that last and worst enemy, his own lower nature, leaving the lofty soul paramount over the world, the flesh, and the devil. So must Lancelot have looked, Ida thought, towards the close of life, when conscience had conquered passion. It was a face that showed the traces of sorrows lived down and temptations overcome—a face which must have been a living reproof to the butterfly sybarites of Charles the Second's Court. Ida knew no more of Sir Tristram's history than that he had been a brave soldier and a faithful servant of the Stuarts in evil and good fortune; that he had married somewhat late in life, to become the father of an only son, from whom the present race of Wendovers were descended. Ida had tried in vain to discover any resemblance to this pictured face in the Colonel or his sister; but it was only to be supposed that the characteristics of the loyal knight had dwindled and vanished from the Wendover countenance with the passage of two centuries.

'No, there is not one of them has that noble look,' murmured Ida, thinking aloud, as she turned to leave the hall.

She found herself face to face with a man, who stood looking at her with friendly eyes, which in their earnest expression and grave dark brows curiously resembled the eyes of the picture. Her heart gave one leap, and then seemed to stand still. There could be only one man in the world with such a face as that, and in that house. Yes, it was a modified copy of the portrait—younger, the features less rugged, the skin paler and less tawny, the expression less intense. Yet even here, despite the friendly smile, there was a gravity, a look of determination which verged upon severity.

This time she was not deceived. This was that very Brian Wendover whom she had thought of in her foolish day-dreams, the first romantic fancy of her girlhood, last year; and now, in the flush and glory of summer, he stood before her, smiling at her with eyes which seemed to invite her friendship.

'I am glad you like my ancestor's portrait,' he said. 'I could not resist watching you for the last five minutes, as you stood in rapt contemplation of the hero of our race; so unlike the manner of most visitors to the Abbey, who give Sir Tristram a casual glance, and go on to the next feature in the housekeeper's catalogue.'

She stood with burning cheeks, looking downward, like a guilty thing, and for a moment or two could hardly speak. Then she said, faltering—

'It is a very interesting portrait,' after which brilliant remark she stood looking helplessly towards the open door, which she could not reach without passing the stranger.

'I think I have the pleasure of speaking to Miss Palliser,' he said. 'Old Mrs. Rowse told me you were here. I am Brian Wendover.'

Ida made him a little curtsey, so fluttering, so uncertain, as to have elicited the most severe reproof from Madame Rigolette could she have seen her pupil at this moment.

'I hope you do not mind,' she said, hesitatingly. 'Bessie and I have roamed about the Abbey often, while you were away, and to-day I came alone, and have been reading in the library for an hour or so.'

'I am delighted that the old house should not be quite abandoned.'

How different his tone in speaking of the Abbey from the false Brian's! There was tenderness and pride of race in every word.

'And I hope that my return will not scare either you or Bessie away; that you will come here as often as you feel inclined. I am something of a recluse when I am at home.'

'You are very kind,' said Ida, moving a little way towards the door. 'Have you been to The Knoll yet?'

'I have only just come from Winchester. I landed at Hull yesterday afternoon, and I have been travelling ever since. But I am very anxious to see my aunts and cousins, especially Aunt Betsy. If you will allow me, I will walk back to Kingthorpe with you.'

Ida looked miserable at the suggestion.

'I—I—don't think Miss Wendover will be at home just yet,' she said. 'She has gone to The Grange, near Romsey, you know, to luncheon.'

'But a luncheon doesn't last for ever. What time do you expect her back?'

'Not till five, at the earliest.'

'And it is nearly half-past three. If you'll allow me to come with you I can lounge in that dear old orchard till Aunt Betsy comes home to give me some tea.'

What could Ida say to this very simple proposition? To object would have been prudish in the last degree. Brian Wendover could not know what manifold and guilty reasons she had for shrinking from any association with him. He could not know that for her there was something akin to terror in his name, that a sense of shame mingled with her every thought of him. For him she must needs be as other women, and it was her business to make him believe that he was to her as other men.

'I shall be very happy,' she said, and then, with a final effort, she added, 'but are you not tired after your journey? Would it not be wiser to rest, and go to the Homestead a little later, at half-past seven, when you are sure of finding Miss Wendover at home?'

'I had rather risk it, and go now. I am only tired of railway travelling, smoke and sulphur, dust and heat. A quiet walk across the common and through the wood will be absolute refreshment and repose.'

After this there was nothing to be said, and they went out into the carriage-way in front of the Abbey, side by side, and across the broad expanse of turf, on which the cedars flung their wide stretching shadows, and so by the Park to the corn-fields, where the corn waved green and tall, and to the open common, above which the skylarks were soaring and singing as if the whole world were wild with joy.

They had not much to talk about, being such utter strangers to each other, and Brian Wendover naturally reserved and inclined to silence; but the little he did say was made agreeable by a voice of singular richness and melody—just such a voice as that deep and thrilling organ which Canon Mozley has described in the famous Provost of Oriel, and which was a marked characteristic of at least one of Bishop Coplestone's nephews—a voice which gives weight and significance to mere commonplace.

Ida, not prone to shyness, was to-day as one stricken dumb. She could not think of this man walking by her side, so unconscious of evil, without unutterable humiliation. If he had been an altogether commonplace man—pompous, underbred, ridiculous in any way—the situation would have been a shade less tragic. But he came too near her ideal. This was the kind of man she had dreamed of, and she had accepted in his stead the first frivolous, foppish youth whom chance had presented to her, under a borrowed name. Her own instinct, her own imagination, had told her the kind of man Brian of the Abbey must needs be, and, in her sordid craving for wealth and social status, she had allowed herself to be fobbed off with so poor a counterfeit. And now her very ideal—the dark-browed knight, with quiet dignity of manner, and that deep, earnest voice—had come upon the scene; and she thought of her folly with a keener shame than had touched her yet.

Brian walked at her side, saying very little, but not unobservant. He knew a good deal about this Miss Palliser from Bessie's letters, which had given him a detailed account of her chosen friend. He knew that the damsel had carried on a clandestine flirtation with his cousin, and had been expelled from Mauleverer Manor in consequence; and these facts, albeit Bessie had pictured her friend as the innocent victim of tyranny and wrong, had not given him a favourable opinion of his cousin's chosen companion. A girl who would meet a lover on the sly, a girl who was ignominiously ejected from a boarding-school, although clever and useful there, could not be a proper person for his cousin to know. He was sorry that Aunt Betsy's good nature had been stronger than her judgment, and that she had brought such a girl to Kingthorpe as a permanent resident. He had imagined her a flashy damsel, underbred, with a vulgar style of beauty, a superficial cleverness, and all those baser arts by which the needy sometimes ingratiate themselves into the favour of the rich. Nothing could be more different from his fancy picture than the girl by whose side he was walking, under that cloudless sky, where the larks were singing high up in the blue.

What did he see, as he gravely contemplated the lady by his side? A perfect profile, in which refinement was as distinctly marked as beauty of line. Darkly fringed lids drooping over lovely eyes, which looked at him shyly, shrinkingly, with unaffected modesty, when compelled to look. A tall and beautifully modelled figure, set off by a simple white gown; glorious dark hair, crowned with the plainest of straw hats. There was nothing flashy or vulgar here, no trace of bad breeding in tone or manner. Was this a girl to carry on illicit flirtations, to be mean or underhand, to do anything meriting expulsion from a genteel boarding-school? A thousand times no! He began to think that Bessie was right, that Aunt Betsy's judgment, face to face with the actual facts, had been wiser than his own view of the case at a distance.

And then, suddenly remembering upon what grounds he was arriving at this more liberal view, he began to feel scornful of himself, after the manner of your thinking man, given to metaphysics.

'Heaven help me! I am as weak as the rest of my sex,' he said to himself. 'Because she is lovely I am ready to think she is good—ready to fall into the old, old trap which has snapped its wicked jaws upon so many victims. However, be she what she may, at the worst she is not vulgar. I am glad of that, for Bessie's sake.'

He tried to make a little conversation during the rest of the way, asking about different members of the Wendover family, and telling Ida some stray facts about his late wanderings. But she did not encourage him to talk. Her answers were faltering, her manner absent-minded. He began to think her stupid; and yet he had been told that she was a wonder of cleverness.

'I daresay her talent all lies in her fingers' ends,' he thought. 'She plays Beethoven and works in crewels. That is a girl's idea of feminine genius. Perhaps she makes her own gowns, which is a higher flight, since it involves usefulness.'

It was only four o'clock when they went in at the little orchard gate, and Miss Wendover could hardly be expected for an hour. What was Ida to do with her guest, unless he kept his word and stayed in the orchard?

'Shall I send you out the newspapers, or any refreshment?' she asked.

There were rustic tables and chairs, a huge Japanese umbrella, every accommodation for lounging, in that prettiest bit of the spacious old orchard which adjoined the garden, and here Ida made this polite offer of refreshment for mind or body.

'No, thank you; I'll stay here and smoke a cigarette. I can get on very well without newspapers, having lived so long beyond easy reach of them.'

She left him, but glancing back at the garden gate she saw him take a book from his pocket and settle himself in one of the basket chairs, with a luxurious air, like a man perfectly content. This was a kind of thing quite new to her in her experience of the Wendovers, who were not a bookish race.

She went into the house, and made all her little preparations for afternoon tea, filling the vases with freshly-cut flowers, drawing up blinds, arranging book-tables, work-baskets, curtains—all the details of the prettiest drawing-room in Kingthorpe, but walking to and fro all the while like a creature in a dream. She had not half recovered from her surprise, her painful wonder at Brian Wendover's appearance, at his strange likeness to her ideal knight—strange to her, but not miraculous, since such hereditary faces are to be found after the lapse of centuries.

When all her small duties had been performed she went up to her room, bathed her face and brushed her hair, and put on a fresher gown, and then sat down to read, trying to lose herself in the thoughts of another mind, trying to forget this embarrassment, this sense of humiliation, which had come upon her. She sat thus for half an hour or so, reading 'The Caxtons,' one of her favourite novels, and felt a little more composed and philosophical, when the rythmical beat of Brimstone and Treacle's eight iron shoes told her that Miss Wendover had returned.

She ran to the gate to welcome that kind friend, looking so fresh and bright in her clean white gown that Aunt Betsy saw no sign of the past struggle.

'Mr. Wendover is here,' she said, shyly, when Aunt Betsy had kissed her and given her some brief account of the day's adventures. The rest of the party had been deposited at The Knoll.

'Whom do you mean by Mr. Wendover, child?'

'Mr. Wendover of the Abbey. He is reading in the orchard.'

'Of course, I never saw him without a book in his hand. So he has come back at last. I am very glad. He is a good fellow, a little too reserved and self-contained, too fond of brooding over some beautiful truism of Plato's when he ought to be thinking of deep drainage and a new school-house; but a good fellow for all that, and always ready with his cheque-book. Let us go and look for him.'

'You will find him in the orchard,' said Ida. 'I will go and hurry on the tea. You must want some tea after your dusty drive.'

'Dusty!' exclaimed Miss Wendover; 'we are positively smothered. Yes. I am dying for my tea; but I must see this nephew of mine first.'

Ida went back to the drawing-room, where everything was perfectly ready, as she knew very well beforehand; but she shrank with a sickly dread from any further acquaintance with the master of Wendover Abbey. She hoped that he and his aunt might say all they had to say to each other in the orchard, and that he would go on to The Knoll to pay his respects to the rest of his relations.

In this she was disappointed. Scarcely had she seated herself before the tea-table when Aunt Betsy and her nephew entered through the open window.

'You two young people have contrived to get acquainted without my aid,' said Miss Wendover, cheerily, 'so there's no necessity for any introduction. Now, Brian, sit down and make yourself comfortable. Give him some tea, Ida. I believe he is just civilized enough to like tea, in spite of his wanderings.'

'On account of them you might as well say, Aunt Betsy. I drank nothing but tea in Scandinavia. It was the easiest thing to get.'

Ida's occupation at the table gave her an excuse for silence. She had only to attend to her cups and saucers, and to listen to Miss Wendover and her nephew, who had plenty to talk about. To hear that deep full voice, with its perfect intonation, was in itself a pleasure—pleasant, also, to discover that Brian Wendover, albeit a famous Balliol man and a Greek scholar after the Porsonian ideal, could still be warmly interested in simple things and lowly folk. She began to feel at ease in his presence; she began to perceive that here was a thoroughly noble nature, a mind so lofty and liberal that even had the man known her pitiful sordid story he would have been more inclined to compassionate than to condemn.

Having recovered her favourite nephew, after so long a severance, Aunt Betsy was in no wise disposed to let him go. She insisted upon his staying to dinner; and before the evening was over Ida found herself quite at home with the dreaded master of the Abbey. At Miss Wendover's request she played for nearly an hour, and Brian listened with evident appreciation, sitting at his ease just outside the open window, among the roses and lilies of June, under a moonlit sky. It was a calm, peaceful, rational kind of evening, and Ida's mind was tranquillized by the time it was over; and when she went to her room, after a friendly parting with Miss Wendover's nephew, she told herself that she was not likely to be often troubled with his society. He was too much a lover of learned solitude to be likely to be interested in the small amusements and occupations of the family at The Knoll—too much in the clouds to concern himself with Aunt Betsy's various endeavours to improve her poorer neighbours in themselves and their surroundings.

She did not long remain under this delusion. She was busy in the garden, with basket and scissors, trimming away fading roses and cankered buds from the luxuriance of bush and standard, arch and trellis, at eleven o'clock next morning, when she heard the garden gate open, and beheld Mr. Wendover, Bessie, and Urania coming across the lawn.

'We are going for a botanical prowl in the woods,' said Bessie, 'and we want you to come with us. You are always anxious to improve your mind, and here is a grand opportunity for you. Brian is a tremendous botanist, and Mr. Jardine is not an ignoramus in that line.'

'Oh, then Mr. Jardine is going to prowl too?' said Ida, smiling at her.

'Yes, he is going to give himself a holiday, for once in a way. Blanche is packing a basket. She and Eva are to have the car, but the rest of us are going to walk. Come along, Ida, just as you are. We are going to grovel and grub after club-mosses and toad-stools. Your oldest gown is too good.'

'Please wear a white gown, as you did yesterday,' said Brian. 'White has such a lovely effect amidst the lights and shadows of a wood.'

'Isn't it rather too violent a contrast?' argued Urania. 'A faint sage-green, or a pale gray—or even that too lovely terra-cotta red—'

'Flower-pot colour!' screamed Bessie. 'Horrid!'

'I should like to go,' faltered Ida, 'but I have so much to do—an afternoon class—no, it is quite impossible. Thank you very much for thinking of me, all the same.

'You utterly disagreeable thing!' exclaimed Bessie; and at this moment Miss Wendover came upon the scene, from an adjacent green-house, where she had been working diligently with sponge and watering-pot. She heard the rights and wrongs of the case, and insisted that Ida should go.

'Never mind the afternoon class—I'll take that. You work hard enough, child; you must have a holiday sometimes.'

'I had a holiday yesterday, Aunt Betsy; and really I had rather not go. The day is so very warm, and I have a slight headache already.'

'Go and lose it in the wood, where Rosalind lost her heart-ache. Nothing like a long ramble when one is a little out of sorts. Go and get rid of your basket, and get your sunshade. Where are you going for your botanising?'

'All over the world,' said Bessie; 'just as fancy leads us. If you will promise to meet us anywhere, we'll be there.'

'So be it,' replied Aunt Betsy. 'Suppose we arrange a tea-meeting. I will be ready for you by the Queen Beech, in Framleigh Wood, as the clock strikes five, and we will all come home together. And now run away, before the day gets old. Glad to see you unbending for once in a way, Urania.'

Miss Rylance had been curiously willing to unbend this morning, when Bessie ran in and surprised her at her morning practice with the wonderful tidings of Brian's return. She appeared delighted at the idea of a botanising expedition, though she cared as little for botany as she did for Hebrew. But when a young lady of large aspirations is compelled to vegetate in a village—even after her presentation at court and introduction into society— she is naturally avid for the society of the one eligible man in the parish.

'Mr. Jardine is coming with us,' Bessie told her, as a further temptation.

Urania gave her hand a little squeeze, and murmured, 'Yes, darling, I'll come: Mr. Jardine is so nice. Will my frock do?'

The frock was of the pre-Raffaelite or Bedford-Parkian order, short-waisted, flowing, and flabby, colour the foliage of a lavender bush, relieved by a broad brick-dust sash. An amber necklace, a large limp Leghorn hat with a sunflower in it, and a pair of long yellow gloves, completed Urania's costume.

'Your frock will be spoilt in the woods,' said Bessie; but Urania did not mean to do much botanical work, and was not afraid of spoiling her frock.

They found Mr. Jardine waiting for them at the churchyard gate, and to him Bessie presented her cousin, somewhat reversing the ceremonial order of things, since Brian Wendover was the patron of the living, and could have made John Jardine vicar on the arising of a vacancy.

Brian and the Curate walked on ahead with Miss Rylance, who seemed bent upon keeping them both in conversation, and Bessie fell back a little way with Ida.

'You dearest darling,' she exclaimed, squeezing her arm rapturously.

'What has happened, Bess? Why such unusual radiance?'

'Do you suppose I am not glad of Brian's return?'

'I thought you liked the other one best?'

'Well, yes; one is more at home with him, don't you see. This one was a double-first—got the Ireland Scholarship. Why Ireland, when it was at Oxford he got it? He is awfully learned; knows Greek plays by heart, just as that sweet Mr. Brandram who came last winter to read for the new school-house knows Shakespeare. But I am very fond of him, all the same; and oh, Ida, what a too heavenly thing it would be if he were to fall in love with you!'

'Bessie!' exclaimed Ida, with an indignant frown.

'Don't look so angry. You should have heard how he spoke of you this morning at breakfast; such praise! Approbation from Sir Hubert What's-his-name is praise indeed, don't you know. There's Shakespeare for you!' added Bessie, whose knowledge of polite literature had its limits.

'Bessie, you contrived once—meaning no harm, of course—to give me great pain, to humiliate me to the very dust,' said Ida, seriously. 'Let us have no more such fooling. Your cousin is—your cousin—quite out of my sphere. However civil he may be to me, however kindly he may speak of me, he can never be any more to me than he is at this moment.'

'Very well,' said Bess, meekly, 'I will be as silent as the grave. I don't think I said anything very offensive, but—I apologize. Do you think you would very much mind kissing me, just as if nothing had happened?'

Ida clasped the lovable damsel in her arms and kissed her warmly. And now Mr. Jardine turned back and joined them at the entrance to a wood supposed to be particularly rich in mosses, flowers, and fungi. Urania still absorbed the attention of Mr. Wendover, who strolled by her side and listened somewhat languidly to her disquisitions upon various phases of modern thought.

'What a beautiful girl Bessie has discovered for her bosom friend,' he said, presently.

'Miss Palliser: yes, she is quite too lovely, is she not?' said Urania, with that air of heartiness which every well-trained young woman assumes when she discusses a rival beauty; 'but she has not the purity of the early Italian manner. It is a Carlo-Dolci face—the beauty of the Florentine decadence. I was at school with her.'

'So I understood. Were you great friends?'

'No,' replied Miss Rylance, decisively; 'if we had been at school for as many years as it took to evolve man from the lowest of the vertebrata we should not have been friends.'

'I understand. The thousandth part of an inch, unbridged, is as metaphysically impassable as the gulf which divides us from the farthest nebula. In your case there was no conveying medium, no sympathy to draw you together,' said Brian, answering the young lady in her own coin.

She glanced at him doubtfully, rather inclined to think he was laughing at her, if any one could laugh at Miss Rylance.

'She was frankly detestable,' said Urania. 'I endure her here for Bessie's sake; just as I would endure the ungraceful curves of a Dachshund if Bess took it into her head to make a pet of one; but at school I could keep her at a distance.'

'What has she done to offend you?'

'Done? nothing. She exists, that is quite enough. Her whole nature— her moral being—is antagonistic to mine. What is your opinion of a young woman who declares in cold blood that she means to marry for money?'

'Not a pleasant avowal from such lips, certainly,' said Brian. 'She may have been only joking.'

'After events showed that she was in earnest.'

'How so? Has she married for money? I thought she was still Miss Palliser?'

'She is; but that is not her fault. She tried her hardest to secure a husband whom she supposed to be rich.'

And then Miss Rylance told how in frolic mood his penniless cousin had been palmed upon Miss Palliser as the owner of the Abbey; how she had fallen readily into the trap, and had carried on a clandestine acquaintance which had resulted in her expulsion from the school where she had filled the subordinate position of pupil-teacher.

'I have heard most of this before, from Bessie, but not the full particulars of the practical joke which put Brian Walford in my shoes,' said Mr. Wendover.

He felt more shocked, more wounded than there was need for him to feel, perhaps; but the girl's beauty had charmed him, and he was prepared to think her a goddess.

'How do you know that Miss Palliser did not like my cousin for his own sake?' he speculated presently. 'Brian Walford is a very nice fellow.'

'She did not like him well enough to marry him when she knew the truth,' replied Urania. 'I believe the poor fellow was passionately in love with her. She encouraged him, fooled him to the top of his bent, and then flung him over directly she found he was not the rich Mr. Wendover. He has never been to Kingthorpe since. That would show how deeply he was wounded.'

'The fooling was not all on her side,' said Mr. Wendover. 'She had a right to resent the trick that had been played upon her. I am surprised that Bessie could lend herself to such a mean attempt to put her friend at a disadvantage.'

'Oh, I am sure Bessie meant only the most innocent fun; her tremendous animal spirits carry her away sometimes, don't you know. And then, again, she thinks her chosen friend perfection. She could not understand that Miss Palliser could really marry a man for the sake of his houses and lands. *I* knew her better.'

'And it was you who hatched the plot, I think,' said Brian.

Miss Rylance had not been prepared to admit as much. She intended Bessie to bear whatever blame there might be attached to the escapade in Mr. Wendover's mind; but it seemed from this remark of his that Bessie had betrayed her.

'I may have thrown out the idea when your cousin suddenly appeared upon the scene. We were all in wild spirits that day. And really Miss Palliser had made herself very absurd by her romantic admiration of the Abbey.'

'Well, I hope this young lady-like conspiracy did no harm,' said Brian; 'but I have a hearty abhorrence of all practical jokes.'

They were in a deep, rutty lane by this time, a lane with banks rich in ferns and floral growth, and here came Blanche and Eva and the youngest boy, released from Latin grammar and Greek delectus at an earlier hour than usual. The car was sent on to the wood, and Bessie and her two sisters produced their fern trowels, and began digging and delving for rare specimens—real or imaginary—assisted by Mr. Jardine, who had more knowledge but less enthusiasm than the girls.

'I can't think what you can want with more ferns,' said Urania, disdainfully; 'every corner at The Knoll has its fernery.'

'Oh, but one can't have too much of a good thing; and then there is the pleasure of looking for them. Aren't you going to hunt for anything?'

'Thanks, no. It is a day for basking rather than work. Shall we go to the end of the lane—there is a lovely view from there—and sit and bask?'

'With all my heart,' replied Mr. Wendover. 'Come, Miss Palliser, of course you'll join the basking detachment.'

Urania would have liked to leave Ida out of the business, but she smiled sweetly at Mr. Wendover's speech, and they all three strolled to the end of the lane, which ascended all the way, till they found themselves upon a fine upland, with a lovely view of woodland and valley stretching away towards Alresford. Here in the warm June sunshine they seated themselves on a ferny bank to wait for the diggers and delvers below. It was verily weather in which to bask was quite the most rapturous employment. The orchestral harmonies of summer insects made a low drowsy music around them. There was just enough air to faintly stir the petals of the dog-roses without blowing them from their frail stems. The dazzling light above, the cool verdure around, made a delicious contrast. Ida looked dreamily across the bold grassy downs, with here and there a patch of white, which shone like a jewel in the sun. It was very pleasant to sit here—very pleasant to listen to Brian Wendover's description of Norway and the Norwegians. A book of travels might have been ever so much better, perhaps; but there was a charm in these vivid pictures of recent experiences which no printed page could have conveyed. And then the talk was delightfully desultory, now touching upon literature, now upon art, now even descending to family reminiscences, stories of the time when Brian had been a Winchester boy, as his cousins were now, and his happy hunting grounds had been among these hills.

Ida talked very little. She was disposed to be silent; but had it been otherwise she would have found slight opportunity for conversation. Miss Rylance, educated up to the standard of good professional society, was ready to give her opinions upon anything between heaven and earth, from the spectrum analysis of the sun's rays to the latest discovery in the habits of ants. She did not mean Ida to shine, and she so usurped the conversation that Miss Palliser's opinions and ideas remained a blank to Mr. Wendover.

Yet a glance at Ida's face now and then told him that she was not unintelligent, and by the time that summer day was over, and they all sat round the gipsy tea-kettle in the wood, with Aunt Betsy presiding over the feast, Mr. Wendover felt as if he knew a good deal about Miss Palliser. They had talked, and walked, and botanized together in the wood, in spite of Miss Rylance; and Urania felt somehow that the day had been a failure. She had made up her mind long ago that Mr. Wendover of the Abbey was just the one person in Hampshire whom she could allow herself to marry. Anyone else in that locality was impossible.

Under these circumstances it was trying to behold Mr. Wendover laying himself, as it were, at the feet of a poor dependent and hanger-on of his family, merely because that young person happened to be handsome. He could have no ulterior views; he was only revealing that innate shallowness and frivolity of the masculine mind which allows even the wisest man to be caught by a pair of fine eyes, a Grecian nose, and a brilliant complexion. Mr. Wendover was no doubt a great deal too wise to have any serious ideas about such a person as Ida Palliser; but he liked to talk to her, he liked to watch the sensitive colour come and go upon the perfect oval of her cheek, while the dark eye brightened or clouded with every change of feeling; and while he was yielding to these vulgar distractions there was no chance of his falling in love with Urania Rylance.

It was a crushing blow to Miss Rylance when a little conversation at tea-time showed that Mr. Wendover was not disposed to think Miss Palliser altogether a nobody, and that a young woman who earned a salary as a useful companion might belong to a better family than Miss Rylance could boast.

'I have heard your name before to-day, Miss Palliser,' said Brian. 'Is your father any relation to Sir Vernon Palliser?'

'Sir Vernon is my father's nephew.'

'Indeed! Then your father is the Captain Palliser of whom I've heard Vernon and Peter Palliser talk sometimes. Your cousins are members of the Alpine Club, and of the Travellers', and we have often met. Capital fellows, both of them.'

'I have never seen them,' said Ida, 'so much of my life has been spent at school. Sir Vernon and his brother went to see my father and step-mother last October, and made a very good impression. But that is all I know of them.'

A baronet for a first cousin! and she had never mentioned the fact at Mauleverer, where it would have scored high. What an unaccountable kind of girl, and quite wanting in human feeling, thought Urania, listening intently, though pretending to be interested in a vehement discussion between Blanche and Bessie as to whether a certain puffy excrescence was or was not a beef-steak fungus, and should or should not be cooked for dinner.

'Do you know your cousin's Sussex property? Have you ever been at Wimperfield?' inquired Brian.

'Never. I have heard my father say it is a lovely place, a little way beyond Petersfield.'

'Yes, I know every inch of the country round. It is charming.'

'It cannot be prettier than this,' said Ida, with conviction.

'I hardly agree with you there. It is a wilder and more varied landscape. Hampshire has nothing so picturesque on this side of the New Forest. If Sir Vernon and his brother are at Wimperfield this summer, we might make up a party and drive over to see the place. I know he would give us a hearty welcome.'

Ida was silent, but Aunt Betsy and her niece declared that it was a splendid idea of Brian's, and must certainly be carried out.

'Fancy Brian introducing Ida to her cousin!' exclaimed Bessie. 'Would it not be quite too deliciously absurd? "Sir Vernon Palliser, permit me to introduce you to your first cousin!"

And then Bessie, who was an incorrigible matchmaker where Ida was concerned, began to think what a happy thing it would be if Sir Vernon Palliser were to fall in love with his cousin, and incontinently propose to make her mistress of this delightful place near Petersfield.

They all walked back to Kingthorpe together, and parted at the Homestead gate.

Miss Rylance, who hated woods, wild-flowers, ferns and toadstools, and all the accompaniments of rustic life, went back to her aesthetic drawing-room in a savage humour, albeit that fine training which comes of advanced civilization enabled her to part from her friends with endearing smiles.

She expected her father that evening, and she was looking forward to the refreshment of hearing of that metropolis which suited her so much better than Hampshire hills and woods; nay, there was even the possibility that he might bring someone down with him, as it was his custom to do now and then. But instead of Dr. Rylance she found an orange-coloured envelope upon the hall table containing an apologetic message.

'Sorry to disappoint you. Have been persuaded to go to first representation of new play at Lyceum with Lady Jinks and the Titmarshes. All London will be there.'

'And I am buried alive in this loathsome hole, where nobody cares a straw about me,' cried Urania, banging her bedroom door, and flinging herself upon her luxurious sofa in as despairing an attitude as if it had been the straw pallet of a condemned cell.

From the very beginning of things she had hated Ida Palliser with the jealous hatred of conscious inferiority. She who had made up her mind to go through life as a superior being, to be always on the top rung of the social ladder, found herself easily distanced by the penniless pupil-teacher. This had been bitter to bear even at Mauleverer, where that snobbish feeling which prevails among schoolgirls had allowed the fashionable physician's daughter a certain superiority over the penniless beauty. But here at Kingthorpe, where rustic ignorance was ready to worship beauty and talent for their own sakes, it was still harder for Urania to assert her superiority; while in the depths of her inner consciousness lurked the uncomfortable conviction that she was in many ways inferior to her rival. And now that she discovered Ida Palliser's near relationship to a baronet of old family, owner of a fine property within thirty miles of Kingthorpe, Urania began to feel that she must needs be distanced in the race. She might have held her own against the shabby half-pay captain's daughter, but Sir Vernon Palliser's first cousin was quite a different person. If Brian Wendover admired Ida, her lack of fortune was hardly likely to influence him, seeing that in family she was his equal. Such a man might have shrunk from allying himself with a woman of obscure parentage and vulgar associations; but to a man of Brian Wendover's liberal mind and ample fortune, Ida Palliser would no doubt seem as suitable a match as a daughter of a duke.

Miss Rylance had grown worldly-wise since her introduction to London society, that particular and agreeable section of upper-middle class life which prides itself upon cleverness rather than wealth, and which spices its conversation with a good deal of smart personality. She had formed a more correct estimate of life in general, and her father's position in particular, and had acquired a keener sense of proportion than she had learnt at Mauleverer Manor. She had learnt that Dr. Rylance, of Cavendish Square, was not quite such a great man as she had supposed in the ignorant faith of her girlhood. She had discovered that his greatness was at best a kind of lap-dog or tame cat distinction; that he was better known as the caressed and petted adviser of patrician dowagers and effeminate old gentlemen, of fashionable beauties and hysterical matrons, than as one of the lights of his profession. He was a clever specialist, who had made his fortune by half-a-dozen prescriptions as harmless as Morrison's pills, and who owed more to the grace of his manner and the excellence of his laundress and his tailor, than to his original discoveries in the grandest science of the age. Other people made discoveries, and Dr. Rylance talked about them; and he was so quick in his absorption of every new idea, so glib in his exposition of every new theory, that his patients swore by him as a man in the front rank of modern thought and scientific development. He was a clever man, and he had a large belief in the great healer Nature, so he rarely did much harm; while his careful consideration of every word his patients said to him, his earnest countenance and thoughtful brow, taken in conjunction with his immaculate shirt-front and shapely white hand, rarely failed to make a favourable impression.

He was a comfortable physician, lenient in the article of diet, exacting only moderate sacrifices from the high liver. His Hygeia was not a severe goddess—rather a friendly matron of the monthly-nurse type, who adapted herself to circumstances.

'We have been taking a pint of Cliquot every day at luncheon, and we don't feel that we could eat any luncheon without it.'

Well, well, suppose we try about half the quantity, very dry, and make an effort to eat a cutlet or a little bit of plain roast mutton, Dr. Rylance would murmur tenderly to a stout middle-aged lady who had confessed that her appetite was inferior to her powers of absorption. Men who were drinking themselves to death in a gentlemanly manner always went to Dr. Rylance. He did not make their lives a burden to them by an impossible regimen: he kept them alive as long as he could, and made departure as gradual and as easy as possible; but his was no kill-or-cure system; he was not a man for heroic remedies. And now Urania had found that her father was not a great man—that he was praised and petted, and had made his nest in the purple and velvet of this world, but that he was not looked up to or pointed at as one of the beacon-lights on the coast-line of the age—and that he being so small a Somebody, she his daughter was very little more than Nobody. Knowing this, she had made up her mind that whenever Brian Wendover of the Abbey should appear upon the scene, she would do her uttermost to make him her captive.

CHAPTER XV
MR. WENDOVER PLANS AN EXCURSION

The happy summer glided by—the season of roses and butterflies, strawberries and cream, haymaking, lawn tennis, picnics, gipsy teas—an idle, joyous life under blue skies. The Knoll family gave themselves up heart and soul to summer pleasures—simple joys which were at once innocent and inexpensive—and Ida Palliser found herself a sharer in all these holiday rambles. Conscience told her that she had no right to be there, that she was an impostor sailing under false colours. Conscience, speaking more loudly, told her that she had no right to accept Brian Wendover's quiet homage, no right to be so happy in his company day after day; for there were few of their summer joys in which he was not among them. Bessie was warm in her praises of him, full of wonder at his having developed into such a companionable being.

'Norway has done him good,' she said. 'He used to be such a reserved creature, dawdling away day after day in his library, poring over Greek and Latin, and now he is almost as companionable as Brian Walford.'

'He'll have to live a good many years before he's up to B. W.,' said Horace, who had walked across the hills for an afternoon at home and the chance of a tip, 'B. W. knows every music-hall in London, and can sing a topical song as well as men who get their sixty pounds a week.'

'I wish you wouldn't put on that knowing air. What do you know of men who get sixty pounds a week?' exclaimed Bessie, contemptuously.

'As much as you do, anyhow,' answered her brother.

Ida made many faint efforts to keep aloof from the summer revelries, but Miss Wendover insisted upon her enjoying herself with the others. She had been such a conscientious and devoted coadjutor in all Aunt Betsy's good works, she had been so thoroughly energetic and industrious, never relaxing her efforts or growing weary of labour, that it seemed only right and fair that she should enjoy the summer holiday-time, the blessed season when every day was full of temptations.

'Enjoy yourself to your heart's content, my dear,' said Aunt Betsy. 'Our English summers are so short that if we do not make the most of the bright warm days while they are with us, we have to endure all the pangs of remorse through a rainy autumn and a cold winter.'

Not only did Miss Wendover give this generous advice, but she herself joined in many of their expeditions, and her presence was always a source of pleasure. She was so genial, so hearty, so thoroughly well-informed, and yet so modest in the use of her knowledge, that the young people loved to have her with them. Her enjoyment of the free, roving life was almost as keen as theirs, while her capacity for planning an agreeable day, and her foresight in the commissariat department, far exceeded that of youth. And so, and so, June and July drifted by, and it was the beginning of August, and Ida felt as if she had known Mr. Wendover of the Abbey all her life.

What did she know of him after two months of almost daily association? She knew that no unworthy thought ever found utterance upon his lips; that no vulgar instinct ever showed itself in his conduct; that he was essentially to the very core of his heart a gentleman; that without any high-flown affectation of chivalry he was as chivalrous as Bayard; that without any languid airs and graces of the modern aesthetic school he was a man of the highest and broadest culture; and that—oh, *rara avis* among modern scholars and young laymen—he was honestly and unaffectedly religious, a staunch Anglican of the school of Pusey, and not ashamed to confess his faith at all times and seasons. In this day, when the majority of young men affect to regard the services of their church as an intolerable bore, only endured as a concession to the weaklings of the inferior sex, it was pleasant to see the master of the Abbey a regular attendant at his parish church, an earnest and frequent worshipper at the altar at which his parents and progenitors had knelt before him.

This much and a great deal more had Ida Palliser discovered of the man whom nearly a year ago her fancy had exalted into an ideal character. It was strange to find her most romantic visions realised; strange, but a strangeness not without pain. He was full of kindness and friendliness for her whenever they met; but she told herself that his manner to her involved no more than kindly feeling and friendliness. To imagine anything beyond this was foolhardiness and vanity. And yet there were times when she felt she had no right to be in his society—that every day she spent at Kingthorpe was an offence against honour and right feeling.

One August afternoon Ida had, for once in a way, succeeded in making her domestic occupations an excuse for absenting herself from what Bessie called a 'barrow-hunt' on the downs. Brian Wendover being a great authority upon this ancient form of sepulture, and discoursing eloquently on those widely different races whose funeral chambers are hidden under the long and the round barrow.

The day, closely as Ida had been occupied, had seemed just a little dreary, certainly much duller than such days had been wont to seem before Brian's return to the Abbey: yet she was glad to be alone; it was a relief even to be a trifle melancholy, rather than to enjoy that happiness which was always blended with a faint consciousness of wrong-doing. And now the slow day was nearly over: she had worked at the village girls'-school in the morning; she had lectured upon domestic economy to a class of incipient house-maids and scullery maids after luncheon; and now at five o'clock she was sitting in a basket chair in the rose-wreathed verandah working at the swallows and bulrushes upon that elaborate design which she had begun before Christmas for the adornment of Miss Wendover's piano.

It was a deliciously drowsy afternoon, but Ida's active brain was not prone to slumber. She sat working diligently and thinking deeply, when a shadow came between her and the sunshine and on looking up she saw Mr. Wendover standing before her.

'How do you do? Have they all come home?' she asked, laying aside her work on the convenient basket table and preparing to welcome Aunt Betsy.

'I have not been with them—at least not since the morning, answered Brian. 'I left Bessie to hunt out her own barrows; she is so lazy-minded that as long as I do all the pointing she will never know the true barrow from the natural lumpiness of the soil. Besides, she has Aunt Betsy, a tower of strength in all things.'

'And Miss Rylance, I suppose?'

'No, Miss Rylance thought there would be too much walking for her or for Pinet. I have been at the Abbey all day, getting up my arrears of correspondence. This fine weather has made me incorrigibly idle. After I had written about a score of letters I thought myself entitled to a little rest and refreshment, so I strolled over here to tell you some news and to ask you for a cup of tea.'

'You shall have some tea directly,' said Ida, going indoors to ring the bell, an act in which she was naturally anticipated by her guest. 'What news can you possibly have that concerns me?' she asked, when they had come back to the verandah. 'I know by your face that it is not bad news.'

'God forbid I should ever have to tell you that. I think it would hurt me more than you,' said Brian, with an earnestness which brought the crimson glow into Ida's cheeks, and made her bend a little lower over the swallows in her crewel-work. 'No, this is pleasant news I hope. I wrote to Vernon Palliser more than a month ago to propose that I should drive you and a lot of people over to luncheon. He was in Switzerland, as usual, and I had no answer to my letter till the second post to-day, when I received a most hearty invitation to bring my party immediately. But you shall hear your cousin's own words.'

Mr. Wendover produced the letter and read as follows: —

'I shall be delighted to make my cousin's acquaintance. She was in England when I last saw her father at his retreat near Dieppe. Bring her as soon as you can, and with as large a party as you like—the larger the better, and the sooner the better—as Peter and I will most likely be on the wing again for Scotland soon after the twelfth. We shall come back for the partridges, which I hear are abundant. The road is rather intricate, so you had better bring your ordnance map, but pretty fair in dry weather like this; and you'll come through some lovely scenery. Telegraph your time, and Peter and I will be in the way to welcome you!'

'What do you say to our going to-morrow? I waited to know what you would like before I telegraphed.'

'You are very good: but there are others to be consulted,' replied Ida, with her head still bent over her work.

Good manners demanded that she should look at him, but at this particular moment she felt it quite impossible to be mannerly. He had said nothing of a thrilling nature, yet his whole tone and expression, his air of deferential regard, stirred a new feeling in her mind—the conviction that he cared for her more than it was well for either of them that he should care.

'You are the first person to be consulted,' he said; 'would you like to go to-morrow?'

'I will go whenever the others like,' answered Ida, still intent upon the shading of her swallow's wing; 'but I really think you had better leave me out of your party—I have wasted so much time roaming about—and there are so many things I want to finish before the summer is over.'

'That elaborate arrangement in swallows and rushes, for instance,' said Brian, laughingly: 'you are working at it as if for a wager. Perhaps it is a wager—so many stitches in so many consecutive days—is that it? No, Miss Palliser, your swallows must wait. The party has been planned on your account, and to leave you at home would be like leaving Hamlet out of the play. Besides, I thought you would like to see your cousins and your ancestral halls.'

'I shall be very glad to see my cousins, for my father likes them very much; but I do not feel any thrilling interest in the ancestral halls.'

'And yet your father was born there.'

'Yes, that is a reason for being interested in Wimperfield. But my father has so seldom talked about his birthplace. He speaks a great deal more of India. That life in a strange far-away land seems to have blotted out the memory of his childhood. He talks of Addiscomb sometimes but hardly ever of Wimperfield.'

She laid aside her work as the youthful butler brought out the tea-table. It was no new thing for her to pour out Mr. Wendover's tea, since it was his custom to drop in at his aunt's very often at this hour, when the day had not been given up to excursionising; but it was new for her to be alone with him at this social meal, and she found herself longing ardently for Aunt Betsy's return.

She who could have found so much to talk about had her mind been at ease, was curiously silent as she handed Mr. Wendover his tea, and offered the cake and fruit, which always accompanied the meal at the Homestead. Her heart was beating much faster than it should have done, and she was considering whether it was worth while to place herself in the way of feeling the pain, the hidden shame, the sense of falsehood which oppressed her at this moment; whether it would not be better to run any risk, even the hazard of offending Betsy Wendover, the kindest friend she had in the world, rather than remain in her present position.

One thing she could have done which would have given her immediate extrication, and that which seemed the most natural thing to do. She could have told the truth—told Betsy Wendover all about her unlucky marriage. But she would rather have killed herself than do this one righteous thing; for she thought that if her marriage were once known to Brian's relations she would be compelled to assume her natural position as his wife. So long as the marriage remained a secret to all the world except those two whom it most concerned they were free to ignore the tie. They could live their lives apart; and to the end of time it might be as if such a marriage had never been. Her husband being consentient to this life-long separation, her lot might be fairly happy. She had never tried to penetrate the future. Perhaps to-day for the first time there had flashed into her mind the thought of what a bright and glorious future might have been hers had she not so forfeited her freedom.

Voices, at least half a dozen, all talking at once, told her that the barrow-hunt was winding homewards; gleams of colour athwart the hedges told her that the hunters were in the lane; and in a minute or two Miss Wendover and her young kins-folk appeared, all more or less sunburnt and towzled by their tramp across the downs.

'Found a splendid long barrow,' said Bessie, 'on a lovely point, one of the finest views in the county. What clever corpses they must have been to pick such glorious spots! Long barrow, long-headed race, dolichocephalic skulls, men of the stone age, eh?' she said, looking at Brian. 'You see I know my lesson; but it was very mean of you not to come with us, all the same.'

'I wanted you to exercise your own acumen, to cultivate the antiquarian *flair*. Besides, I had a heap of letters to write.'

'You only found that out after we had started. You never have letters to write when Ida is with us,' said Bessie; a remark which made two people blush. 'To think that I had known that spot all my life and never suspected a barrow,' she continued. 'I thought it was only a convenient bank which Providence had thrown up ready for picnics.'

Ida had enough to do now in providing for the wants of half a dozen hungry people. Blanche of the short petticoats was at an age when girls are ogres, distinguished for nothing but the rapidity of their digestion and the length of their legs. There was a demand for jam, and the unsophisticated half-gallon loaf instead of the conventional thin bread and butter.

'Eat as much as you like, dears,' said Aunt Betsy, 'but remember that your father will expect you to have some appetite at seven.'

'We won't disappoint him,' said Bessie; 'seven is an hour and half from now. Blanche can do wonders in an hour and a half.'

Blanche's appetite was one of the stock family jokes, like Urania's tight boots; so there was a laugh, and the others went on eating.

Brian Wendover told them about to-morrow's excursion. 'I shall put four horses into the wagonette,' he said. 'I almost wish I had a drag to do honour to the occasion; but we must resign ourselves to a wagonette. You will go, of course, Aunt Betsy? and Bessie must come; and I suppose we ought to invite Miss Rylance. She has joined in most of our excursions, and it would be invidious to leave her out of this. And I dare-say Bessie would think the whole thing flat without Mr. Jardine?'

'It's very kind of you to think of him; but I don't believe he'll be able to spare the day,' said Bessie.

'We'll ask him, at any rate, and then you can't say we've used you badly. That makes a party of six. I'll go and telegraph to Sir Vernon.'

'Will there be lawn-tennis after lunch?' asked Blanche, with a very long face.

'I shouldn't wonder if there were,' answered Brian: 'does that mean that you want to go?'

'I shall not have a creature to speak to at home, and I never go anywhere,' said Blanche, despairingly.

Both statements were obvious untruths, but no doubt the damsel herself believed them.

'Have you a gown that covers your knees?' asked Aunt Betsy, severely.

'My new frock is awfully long. It only came from the dress-maker's last week.'

'Then you have hardly had time to grow out of it,' said Brian.

'Suppose we strain a point, Aunt Betsy, and take her. It will enable us to say, "we are seven."'

'We shall be a tremendous party,' said Miss Wendover. 'I hope Sir Vernon is a hospitable, easy-going man, and that your intimacy with him warrants such an intrusion.'

'I am taking him a cousin,' answered Brian, stealing an admiring glance at Ida; 'surely that ought to secure our welcome.'

'I hope his housekeeper has large ideas about luncheon,' said Bessie, 'or Blanche's appetite will throw her out in her calculations. If she is the sort of person who thinks a pair of ducklings and a dish of rissoles substantial fare for a large party, I pity her.'

'You're vastly witty,' said Blanche, preparing her final slice of bread and jam; 'one would think you lived upon roses and lilies, like the ascetics.'

'The poor child means aesthetes,' explained Bessie.

'Bother the pronunciation! But if people had seen you eating rabbit-pie on the barrow—why a wolf wouldn't have been in it,' concluded Blanche, who acquired her flowers of speech from the Wintonians.

'I'll go and despatch my telegram,' said Brian, taking up his hat.

CHAPTER XVI
THICKER THAN WATER

The weather was altogether favourable for the thirty-mile drive. The wagonette with its scratch team and a couple of smart grooms, was at the Homestead gate at ten o'clock, and after picking up Miss Wendover and her companion, went on to The Knoll for Bessie and Blanche, and then to Dr. Rylance's for Urania, who had accepted the invitation most graciously. Kingthorpe was unwontedly excited by this gorgeous apparition, and the inhabitants remained at garden gates and cottage doors while so much as a horse's tail was visible. Everybody was pleased to see the young squire driving four-in-hand. It had been supposed that as a bookish young man, given over to Greek and Latin, he must needs be a poor hand with horses. But this morning's exhibition gave rise to more hopeful views.

'We shall see the squire setting up his coach, and settling down at the Abbey,' said one.

'Ay, when he gets married,' said another; 'that's what'll settle he. I believes as him is sweet on that young 'ooman at the Homestead. Her be a clipper, her be.'

Over the hills and far away went the scratch team—a little fresh, but behaving beautifully. Aunt Betsy sat beside her nephew, and watched his coachmanship with a jealous eye, conscious that she could have kept the team better in hand herself, but still with moderate approval. The girls and the grooms were in the back of the vehicle—Bessie, Blanche, and Ida full of talk and merriment, Urania thoughtful. This day's entertainment was too much in Ida's honour to be pleasant to Miss Rylance; yet she could not deny herself the painful privilege of being there. She wanted to see what happened—how far Mr. Wendover was disposed to make an idiot of himself. She saw more than enough in the glances of the charioteer, when he turned to talk to the girls behind him—now to point out some feature in the landscape, now to ask some idle question, but always with looks that lingered upon one face, and that face was Ida Palliser's.

It was a long cross country drive, by rustic lanes and dubious roads, but Mr. Wendover took things easily. He had sent forward a second scratch team over night to a village half way, and here they changed horses, while he and his party spent half an hour pleasantly enough exploring an old gray church and humble graveyard, where the tombstones all bore record of unrenowned lives that had slowly rusted away in a pastoral solitude, Blanche, whose schoolroom appetite was wont to damp its keen edge upon bread and butter at this hour, felt it rather a hard thing that no one proposed a light refection at the lowly inn; but she bore her inward gnawings in silence, conscious of the dignity of a frock which almost reached her ankles, and desirous to prove that she was worthy to be the associate of grown-ups.

Half way between this village inn and Wimperfield they met a couple of horsemen. These were no other than Sir Vernon and his brother Peter, who had come to meet their guests, and show them the nearest way, which from this point became especially intricate.

Brian walked his team gently up a gentle hill, while Sir Vernon and his brother walked their horses beside him, and during this ascent all necessary introductions were duly made, everybody being properly presented except Blanche, who felt that she was being treated with contumely.

'I am very glad to see you at last, cousin Ida,' said Sir Vernon, pleasantly. 'I have been hearing of you all my life, but we seemed fated not to meet.'

He was a fine, broad-shouldered young fellow, with a frank, fresh-coloured countenance, auburn whiskers, and curly brown hair. His brother was after the same pattern, hair a little lighter, no whiskers, eyes rather a brighter blue. They were as much alike as brothers can be without being mistaken for each other. There was nothing romantic looking about either of them, Bessie thought, regretfully. She would have liked Sir Vernon to have resembled her favourite hero in fiction (the man she always put in confession books), and to have fallen desperately in love with Ida at first sight. And here he was, a most matter-of-fact looking young man, riding behind the wagonette in a provokingly matter-of-fact way.

Yet perhaps there was a providence in this; for if Brian of the Abbey were in love with Ida, as Bessie shrewdly suspected, it would have been a terrible thing for him to have found a rival in a titled cousin. If Ida were ambitious, the title might have turned the scale.

'And I have so set my heart upon having her for my cousin, thought Bessie. 'The other Brian was a failure, but this Brian may win the prize.'

Mr. Jardine had not been able to leave his parish for a long day; so Bessie had plenty of leisure to speculate upon the possible loves of other people, instead of enjoying the blissfulness of her own love affair.

Wimperfield was a mansion built in the Italian manner which prevailed about a century ago, a style about as uninteresting as any order of domestic architecture, but which makes a house a good feature in a fine landscape. The Corinthian façade of Wimperfield stood boldly out against the verdant slope of a hill, backed and sheltered on either side by woods. Behind that classic portico there was the usual prim range of windows, and there were the usual barrack-like rooms. The furniture was of the same heavy and substantial character, rich dark rosewood, amber satin hangings faded by a quarter of a century; Spanish mahogany in dining-rooms and bedrooms; Gillow's fine workmanship everywhere, but the style dating back to the very infancy of that ancient house.

The large, finely-lighted hall, which looked like the vestibule of some learned institute, was adorned with four Carrara marble statues, placid gods and goddesses smirking at vacancy, on pedestals of verde antico. The only pictures in the reception-rooms were family portraits, and a few of those large Dutch landscapes, battle scenes, sea-pieces and fruit-pieces, which cry aloud that they are furniture pictures, and have been bought to fit the panelling of the rooms.

But for its noble situation this temple of English domestic life would have been utterly without charm; but the situation was superb, the gardens were in beautiful order, and the stables, as Aunt Betsy declared after personal inspection, were perfect.

Sir Vernon did the honours of his house in a frank, friendly manner. He took his guests round the gardens and stables, showed Ida the old nursery in which his father and her father had spent their infancy; the gun-room in which their first guns were carefully preserved; the very rocking-horse on which they had ridden, and which now occupied a recess in an obscure lobby opening into the garden.

'Peter and I didn't care to ride him,' said Sir Vernon. 'We had Shelties when we were three-year-olds; but I know when I began Virgil I used to think the wooden horse that got into Troy was an exaggerated copy of this one.

He showed his cousin the room in which her grandfather and grandmother died—an immense apartment, wherein stood, grim and tall, a gigantic mahogany four-poster, draped with dark green velvet.

'I can't fancy anybody doing anything else in such a room,' said Ida, to whom the spacious chamber looked as gloomy as a charnel-house. 'I beg your pardon. I hope you don't sleep here.'

'No, my diggings are at the other end of the house, looking into the stable-yard. I like to be able to put my head out of window and order my horse—saves time and trouble. We keep the rooms at this end for visitors.'

The gong boomed loud and long, much to the relief of poor Blanche, whose spirits had been slowly sinking, in unison with her inward cravings, and who had begun to think that the promised luncheon was a delusion and a snare, which would end in the fashionable frivolity of afternoon tea.

Sir Vernon offered his arm to Miss Wendover, and asked Brian to take Miss Palliser, while Peter was told off to Miss Rylance, leaving Bessie and the clinging Blanche like twin cherries on one stem. It was curious for Ida to find herself seated presently beside the wealthy cousin of whom she had heard as a far-off and almost mythical personage, of very little account in her life; since it was so improbable that any of his wealth would ever come her way.

The luncheon was of the old-fashioned and ponderous order, excellent of its kind: the orchard-houses had given up their finest peaches and nectarines and their earliest grapes to do honour to the occasion. Miss Rylance contemplated the table decorations with mute scorn, which she hardly cared to disguise. No Venetian wine-flasks, no languorous lilies swooning in Salviati goblets, no pottery of the new green and yellow school, but massive silver, and heavy diamond-cut glass—gaudy Staffordshire china of 'too utterly quite' the worst period of art. Everything essentially Philistine.

Sir Vernon had placed his cousin on his left hand, and he talked to her a good deal during luncheon—asking questions as to her past life, which she answered with perfect candour. It was only when he spoke of her future that the fair brow clouded, and the cheeks reddened with a painful glow.

'I hope, now that the ice has been broken, that we are not going to be strangers any more,' said Vernon, pleasantly. 'To think that you should be such a near neighbour of mine, and that I should know nothing about it! You have been at Kingthorpe since last November, you say? How long are you going to stay there?'

'For a good many Novembers, I hope,' said Aunt Betsy, 'unless she gets tired of rural solitude, or unless a husband steals her away from me.'

'Ah, that is what all young ladies anticipate. They never are but always to be blest,' replied Vernon, laughing. He was one of those open-hearted souls who always appreciate their own mild jokelets.

Brian, who saw Ida's pained expression, made haste to change the conversation, by an inquiry about Sir Vernon's plans for the autumn, which set that gentleman on a sporting tack, and spared Miss Palliser all further trouble.

After luncheon they went to look at the hot-houses, and dawdled away the time very agreeably until afternoon tea, Miss Rylance doing her best to improve the occasion with Peter, who was not educated up to the standard of metropolitan or South Kensingtonian young ladyhood, and who came out very badly under the process of development; for when talked to about Ruskin he was at first altogether vacuous, but, on being pushed har believed there was a biggish swell of some such name among the Oxford dons, about whom he could not fairly be expected to know anything, as he and his brother were Cantabs: while on being languidly asked his opinion of Swinburne's last tragedy, he grew cheerful, and said he had seen him play the King to Irving's Hamlet, and that it was a very fine performance, the actor in question being a good stayer.

The thing was hopeless, and Miss Rylance felt she was wasting herself upon a dolt. After this she hardly took the trouble to suppress her yawns; yet if she had condescended to question Peter about his Alpine adventures, or to talk about his horses, guns, and dogs, she would have found him lively enough as a companion; but an education of musical 'at homes' and afternoon teas had tuned Miss Rylance's slender pipe to one particular strain, which did not suit everybody's dancing. She was heavy at heart, feeling that the whole business of the day had conduced to Ida Palliser's glorification. To be the daughter of a man born in that substantial family mansion—scion of a respectable old county family—was in itself a distinction far beyond anything Miss Rylance could boast, her grandfather having been a chemist and druggist in an obscure market town, and her father the architect of his own fortunes. She had done her best to forget this fact hitherto, but it was brought home to her mind unpleasantly to-day, when she saw the articled pupil, whose three pairs of stockings had moved her to scornful wonder, strolling about her ancestral home by the side of her first cousin, and that first cousin a baronet of Charles II's creation.

Sir Vernon and his brother were full of cordiality for their cousin, full of anticipations of future meetings, and of hopes that Captain Palliser would come to them in October for what they called a 'shy' at the pheasants.

Ida had good cause to remember that parting in front of the classic portico in the warm afternoon sunlight, the two brothers standing side by side, with frank, bright faces, looking up at their departing guests, all smiles and cheerful pleasure in this world's pleasantest things—a Dandie Dinmont and a big black-and-tan colley looking on at their master's knees—the *beau idéal* of young English manhood—frank, generous, outspoken, fearless—the men who can do and die when the need comes. Her eyes lingered affectionately on that picture as the wagonette drove away by the broad gravel sweep towards the avenue; and those two figures in the sunlight haunted her memory in the days to come.

CHAPTER XVII
OUGHT SHE TO STAY?

A week after the drive to Wimperfield Miss Wendover received a very big box of peaches and grapes, enclosing a very brief letter from Vernon Palliser to his cousin Ida.

'My dear Ida,—I venture to send Miss Wendover some of our fruit,' he wrote, 'for I understood her to say she has not much glass, and grows only flowers. Peter and I are just off to Scotland, where I suppose we shall do a little shooting, and I hope a good deal of yachting and fishing. I wish you and that nice plump little friend of yours—Bessie, I think you called her—were coming to us. Such a jolly life, bobbing about between the islands and the mainland, with the chance of an occasional storm. But I shall look forward to seeing you again in October, when I hope Miss Wendover will bring you over to stay for a week or two. What splendid ideas she has about summering hunters!—never met a more sensible woman. Always your affectionate cousin, VERNON PALLISER.'

Aunt Betsy was pleased with the tribute of hothouse fruit, and even more gratified by that remark about summering horses.

'Your cousin is a fine thoroughbred young fellow,' she said. 'If I had not been fully satisfied you came from a good stock, by my knowledge of your own organisation, I should be sure of the fact now I have seen those two young men. They are all that Englishmen ought to be.'

Ida was silent, for to her mind there was one Englishman who more completely realised her ideal of manhood—one who was no less generous and outspoken than her kind young cousins, but whose intellectual gifts, whose highly cultivated mind, and passionate love of all that is most beautiful in life, made him infinitely their superior.

And now came, perhaps, the most bitter trial of a young life which had already seen more cloud than sunshine. The hour had come when Ida told herself that she must no longer dawdle along the flowery path of sin, no longer palter with fate. Stern duty must be obeyed, She must leave Kingthorpe. It was no longer a question of feeling, but a question of conscience—right against wrong, truth against falsehood, honour against dishonour; for she knew in her heart of hearts that Brian loved her, and that she gave him back his love, measure for measure. He had said nothing definite; she had contrived to ward off anything like a declaration; but she had not been able to prevent his absorbing her society on all possible occasions, taking possession of her, as it were, as of one who belonged to him in the present and the future, deferring to her lightest wish as only a lover defers to his mistress, studying her preferences in everything, and hardly taking the trouble to hide his comparative indifference to the society of other people. It had come to this, and she knew that there must be no further delay.

One evening, when she and Aunt Betsy had been dining alone, and had returned to the drawing-room, where it was Ida's custom at this hour to play her kind patroness to sleep with all the dreamiest and most pensive melodies in her extensive *répertoire*, the girl suddenly faltered in her playing, wandered from one air into another, and with a touch so uncertain that Aunt Betsy, who was fast lapsing into dreamland, became broad awake again all at once, and wanted to know the reason why.

'Is anything the matter? Are you ill, child?' she asked, abruptly.

Ida rose from the piano, where her tears had been dropping on the keys, and came out of the shadowy corner to the verandah, where Aunt Betsy sat among her roses, wrapped in a China crape shawl, one of the gifts of that Indian warrior, Colonel Wendover. August was nearly over, but the weather was still warm enough for sitting out of doors in the twilight.

'What is the matter, Ida? What has happened?' repeated Miss Wendover, with her hand on the girl's shoulder, as she bent to listen to her.

Ida was kneeling by Aunt Betsy's side, her head leaning against the arm of her chair, her face hidden.

'Nothing, nothing that you can help or cure, dearest friend,' she answered in a broken voice. 'You must know how good you have been to me. Yes, even you must know that, although it is your nature to make light of your goodness. I think you know I love you and am grateful. Tell me that you believe that before I say another word.'

'I do believe it. Your whole conduct since you have been with me has shown as much,' answered Miss Wendover, calmly. She saw that Ida was powerfully moved, and she wanted to tranquillise her. 'What is the meaning of this preface?'

'Only that I must ask you to let me leave you.'

'Leave me! Oh, you want a holiday, I suppose?—that is natural enough. We needn't be tragic about that. You want to go over to Dieppe to see your people?'

'I want to go away from Kingthorpe for ever.'

'For ever? Ah, now we are really tragic!' said Miss Wendover, lightly, her broad, firm white hand tenderly smoothing the girl's hair and brow. 'My dear child, what has gone amiss with you? Something has, I can see. Have you and Miss Rylance quarrelled? I know she is a viper; but I did not think she would play any of her viperish tricks with my property.'

'Miss Rylance has done nothing. I have quarrelled with nobody. I love and honour you and the whole house of Wendover with all my heart and mind. But there is a reason—a reason which I implore you to refrain from asking—why I ought never to have come into your house, as I did come— why I ought to leave it—must leave it for ever!'

'This is very mysterious,' said Aunt Betsy, thinking deeply. 'I could understand a reason—which might exist in a girl's romantic mind—a mistaken generosity, or a mistaken pride—the outcome of late events— which might urge you to run away—like that always wrong-headed and misguided young person, the heroine of a novel: but what reason there could have been when you came to me last winter against your coming— no—that is more than I can comprehend.'

'You are not to comprehend. It is my secret—my burden—which I must bear. I want you to believe me, that is all,—only to believe me when I say that I love you dearly, and that I have been unspeakably happy in your house—and just quietly let me go and seek my fortune elsewhere—without saying anything to anybody until I am gone.'

'And a nice weeping and wailing there will be from Bessie and her brothers and sisters when you *are* gone!' exclaimed Miss Wendover; 'a pleasant time I shall have of it, with all of them—to say nothing of my own feelings. Do you think it is fair, Ida, to treat me like this; to make yourself pleasant to me, useful, necessary to me—to wind yourself into my heart— and then all at once, with a sudden wrench, to pluck yourself out again, and leave me to do without you? Do you call that fair play?'

'I know that it must seem like base ingratitude,' answered Ida, calm now, with a despairing calmness; 'but I cannot help myself. I am more proud than I can say that you should care for me—that my loving services have not been unwelcome. I know that you took me out of charity; and it is a delight to know that I have not been altogether a bad bargain. But I must go away.'

'I begin to see light,' said Miss Wendover, who had been thinking all this time. 'It's your father's doing. He thinks you are not making a profitable use of your education and talents. He has ordered you to go where you will get a larger salary. But don't let his needs separate us, my dear. I love you better than a few pounds a quarter. I will give you seventy, or even eighty pounds a year, if that will satisfy Captain Palliser.'

'No, no, dear Aunt Betsy. Thank God, my father is not that kind of man. He knows how happy I have been, he is grateful to you for all your goodness to me, and more than content that I should be happy without being a burden to him.'

'Then *why* do you want to leave me?' asked Miss Wendover, with her hands on the girl's shoulders, her eyes reading the white agonised face looking up at her in the thickening twilight. There was just light enough for her to see the look of intense pain in that pallid countenance.

'*Why* do you want to go away?' she repeated. 'What kind of reason can that be which you fear to tell me? It must be an unworthy reason; and yet I cannot believe that you could have such a reason. Is it on account of my nephew Brian? Have you found out what I have suspected for a long time? Have you discovered that he is in love with you, and do you fancy yourself an ineligible match for him, because he is rich and you are poor, and do you think that you ought to run away in order to give him a chance of doing better for himself? If you have any such high-flown idea, abandon it. The Wendovers are not a mercenary tribe. We shall welcome Brian's bride, whoever she be, for her own sake, and not for her dowry.'

'It is no such reason. I *cannot* tell you. You must forgive me, and let me go.'

'Then I forgive you, and you can go,' replied Miss Wendover, coldly. 'I am deeply disappointed in you. If you cared for me as you say you do, you would trust me. Love without faith is an impossibility. However, I don't want to distress you. If you are to leave me I will make your departure as pleasant as I can. When do you want to go?'

'Immediately. As soon as you can spare me.'

'I cannot spare you at all; a few weeks or days more or less will make no difference to me. Do you want to go among strangers, to be a governess? or do you wish to go back to your people?'

'I want to earn my own living. The harder I have to work the better I shall like it. I would not mind even going into a school, though my experience of Mauleverer is hateful.'

'You shall not go into a school. I will send an advertisement to the *Times*.'

'Would it not be better for me to go to Winchester and apply at some agency for servants and governesses? When I advertised in the *Times* there was not a single answer.'

'You may have better luck this time,' replied Miss Wendover, in a business-like tone. She was too proud to show any further indications of sorrow, or even to reveal how deeply she was wounded. 'I will do what I can to help you, though—'

'Though I do not deserve it,' said Ida.

'You know best about that. Yes,' after some moments of silent thought, 'it may not be too late even now. When I lunched with the Trevors, at Romsey, the day of Brian's return, Mrs. Trevor's sister, Lady Micheldever, was in a state of anxiety about governesses. Her old governess was to be married in a few weeks, such an inestimable treasure that Lady Micheldever thought it would be impossible to replace her, so sweet, so ladylike, so accomplished. Now, if the situation is not yet filled, I think it would suit you exactly. They are people who would give you a liberal salary—you would be able to help your father.'

'I should be glad of that. Do the Micheldevers live near here?' faltered Ida. 'I want to go quite away.'

'They have property near here, but their place is close to Savernake Forest, and they spend their winters in Italy. Sir George has a weak chest, and all the children are delicate. If you go to them, nearly half your life will be spent abroad.'

'I should like that very much,' said Ida.

'Nothing so pleasant as variety of scenery and people,' replied Miss Wendover, with a touch of irony in her voice.

She began to think Ida cold-hearted and hypocritical. It was evident to her that this feverish longing for change was mere selfish ambition, a desire to be better placed in the world. She had met with the same kind of feeling too often in her rustic *protégées* of the cook and house-maid class, who, when they had learnt all she could teach them, were eager to spread their wings and soar to the servants' halls of Mayfair, and the society of powdered footmen.

'Nine o'clock,' said Miss Wendover, wrapping her shawl round her, and rising to go into the drawing-room as the church clock chimed silver-sweet across the elm tops and the misty meadows. 'Too late for this evening's post;

but I will write to Lady Micheldever to-night, and my letter will be ready for the midday mail to-morrow. I hope she has not found anybody yet.'

'You are too good,' faltered Ida, as they went into the lamplit room.

'I am only doing my duty,' replied Miss Wendover. '"Welcome the coming, speed the parting guest!"'

'You will not tell Bessie, or anyone, till I am gone?' pleaded Ida, earnestly.

'Certainly not—if that is your wish.'

CHAPTER XVIII
AFTER A STORM COMES A CALM

While Ida Palliser was thus planning her escape from that earthly paradise where she was dangerously happy, Brian Wendover was thinking of her and dreaming of her, and building the whole fabric of his life on a happy future to be shared with her, cherishing the sweet certainty that she loved him, and that he had only to say the word which was to unite them for ever. He had been in no haste to say that fateful word; life was so sweet to him in its present stage—he was so confident of the future. He had closely and carefully studied the character of the woman he loved, in the beginning of their acquaintance, before his judgment had lost its balance, before affection had got the better of the critical faculty. He had been in somewise impressed by what Urania had told him about Ida. The slanderer's malice was obvious; but the slander might have some element of truth. He watched Ida narrowly during the first month of their acquaintance, expecting to find the serpent-trail somewhere; but no trace of the evil one had appeared. She was frank, straightforward, intelligent to a high degree, and with that eager thirst for knowledge which is generally accompanied by a profound humility. He could see in her no base worship of wealth for its own sake, no craving for splendour or fashionable pleasures. She found delight in all the simplest things, in rustic scenery, in hill and down and wood, in dogs and horses, and birds and flowers, music and books. A girl who could be happy in such a life as Ida Palliser lived at Kingthorpe must be in a manner independent of fortune; her pleasures were not those that cost money.

'If she is the kind of girl Miss Rylance describes her she will set her cap at me,' he thought. 'If she wants to be mistress of Wendover Abbey, one mistake and one failure will not daunt her.'

But there was no such setting of caps. For a long time Ida treated Mr. Wendover of the Abbey with the perfect frankness of friendship. Then, as his love grew, showing itself by every delicate and unobtrusive token, there came a change, and a subtle one, in her conduct; and the lover told himself with triumphant heart that he was beloved. Her sweet shyness, her careful avoidance of every possible *tête-à-tête*, her evident embarrassment on those rare occasions when she found herself alone with him—surely these things meant love, and love only! There could be no other meaning. He was no coxcomb, ready to believe every woman in love with him. He had gone through the world very quietly, admiring many women, but never till now having found one who seemed to him worth the infinite anxieties, and fevers, and agues of love. And now he had found that pearl above price, the one woman predestinate to be adored by him.

He was happily placed in life for a lover, since a lover should always be an orphan. Fathers and mothers are sore clogs upon the fiery wheel of love. He was rich; in every way his own master. His kindred were kindly, simple-minded people, who would give gracious welcome to any virtuous woman whom he might choose for his wife. There was no impediment to his happiness, provided always that Ida Palliser loved him; and he believed that she did love him. This sense of security had made him less eager to declare himself. He was content to wait for his opportunity.

And now summer was waning, though it was summer still. The days were no less lovely; not a leaf had fallen in the woods; red roses flushed the gardens with bloom, yellow roses hung in luxuriant clusters on arches and walls; but the days were shortening, the sunsets were earlier, coming inconveniently before dinner was over at The Knoll; and the Wykehamists began to be weighed down by a sense of impending doom, in the direful necessity of going back to school.

Bessie's birthday had come round again—that date so fatal to Ida Palliser—and there was much cheerfulness at The Knoll in honour of the occasion. This year the event was not to be signalised by a picnic. They had been picnicking all the summer, and it was felt that the zest of novelty would be wanting to that form of entertainment; so it was decided in family counsel that a friendly dinner at home, with a little impromptu dancing, and perhaps a charade or two afterwards, would be an agreeable substitute for the usual outdoor feast. Brian, Mr. Jardine Dr. and Miss Rylance, Aunt Betsy, and Ida Palliser were to be the only guests; but these with the family made a good sized party. Blanche undertook to play as many waltzes as might be required of her, and also took upon herself the arrangement and decoration of the dessert, which was to be something gorgeous. More boxes of peaches and grapes had been sent over from Wimperfield in the absence of Sir Vernon and his brother, who were still in Scotland.

Bessie's anniversary was heralded somewhat inauspiciously by a tremendous gale which swept across the Hampshire Downs, after doing no small mischief in the Channel, and wrecking a good many fine old oaks and beeches in the New Forest. It was only the tail of a storm which had been blowing furiously in Scotland and the north of England, and no one as yet knew the extent of its destructive force.

The morning after that night of howling winds was dull and blustery, with frequent gusts of rain.

'How lucky we didn't go in for a picnic!' said Horatio, as the slanting drops lashed the windows at breakfast time. 'It may rain and blow as hard as it likes between now and six o'clock, for all we need care. A wet day will give us time to get up our charades, and for Blanche to thump at her waltzes. Be sure you give us the Blue Danube.'

'The Blue Danube is out,' said Blanche, tossing up her pointed chin.

'Out of what? Out of time?'

'Out of fashion.'

'Hang fashion! What do I care for fashion?' cried the Wykehamist. 'Fashion means other people's whims and fancies. People who are led by fashion have no ideas of their own. Byron is out of fashion, but he's *my* poet,' added Horatio, as who should say, 'and that ought to be a sufficient set-off against any lessening of his European renown.'

'Think of the poor creatures at sea!' murmured kind-hearted Mrs. Wendover, as a sharp gust shook the casement nearest to her.

'Very sad for them, poor beggars!' said Reginald; 'but it would have been sadder for us if we'd been starting for a picnic. Travellers by sea must expect bad weather; it's an important factor in the sum of their risk, and their minds are prepared for the contingency; but when one has planned a picnic party on the downs a wet day throws out all one's calculations.'

The rain came and went in fitful showers, the wind blustered a little, and then died away in sobs, while the young Wendovers spent their morning noisily and excitedly, in laborious industries of the most frivolous kind, the end and aim of which was to make a gorgeous display in the evening.

Before luncheon the wind was at rest, and the gardens were smiling in the sunlight under the hot blue sky of summer, and after luncheon the Wendover girls and boys were rushing all over the garden cutting flowers.

'I only wish Dr. Rylance were not coming,' said Blanche, stopping to pant and wipe her crimson countenance, when her two baskets were nearly full. 'He'll impart his own peculiar starchiness to the whole business.'

'Oh, hang it, he'll give the thing a grown-up flavour, anyhow,' replied Reginald. 'Besides, the man *can* talk—though he's deuced shallow—and that is more than anyone else can in these parts.'

'Brian will be the hero of this evening's festivity, just as Brian Walford was of the last. Don't you remember how nice he looked?' said Blanche, as they went back to the house loaded with roses, heliotrope, geranium, and ferns.

'Poor fellow!' sighed Bessie, who was so sentimental that she could but suppose her favourite cousin a martyr to blighted love.

'If Brian of the Abbey proposes to Ida, as I feel convinced he will, and if she accepts him, as she is sure to do, it will simply break Brian Walford's heart.'

'Not a little bit,' said Reginald. 'If he did spoon her last year, is that any reason, do you think, that he should care for her now? If she be not fair to me, what the deuce care I how fair she be? And do you suppose *I* am going to waste in despair, and all that kind of thing? Not if I know it.'

'Say what you like, I believe Brian Walford was deeply in love with Ida, and that he has never been here since that time, because he can't bear to see her, knowing she doesn't care for him.'

'That's skittles!' exclaimed the youthful sceptic, using a favourite expression of his father's to express incredulity. 'The reason Brian doesn't come to Kingthorpe is, that he has other fish to fry elsewhere. As if anybody would come to Kingthorpe who wasn't obliged!'

'Brian used to come.'

'Yes, when he was young and verdant; and I daresay my father used to tip him. He knows better now: he is enjoying himself in Paris—under the pretence of studying law and modern languages—dancing at the *jardin Bullier*, and going on no end, I daresay. *I* know what Paris is.'

'How can you?' exclaimed Bessie; 'you were never there!'

'I was never in the moon, but I'm pretty well acquainted with the geography of that planet. We have fellows in the Upper Sixth who think no more of going to Paris than you do of going to Winchester; and a nice life they lead there. Why, a man who thoroughly knows Paris can steep himself in dissipation for a five-pound note!'

Loud exclamations of horror concluded the conversation.

CHAPTER XIX
AFTER A CALM A STORM

The dinner-party was a success. Bessie beamed radiantly, with her plump arms and shoulders set off by a white gown, and a good deal of rather incongruous trinketry in the way of birthday presents, every item of which she felt bound to wear, lest the givers should be wounded by her neglect. Thus, dear mother's amber necklace did not exactly accord with Mr. Jardine's neat gold and sapphire locket; while the family subscription gift of pink coral earrings hardly harmonised with either. Yet earrings, locket, and necklace were all displayed, and the round white arms were coiled from wrist to elbow with various monstrosities of the bangle breed.

There was a flavour of happiness in the whole feast which could not be damped by any ceremonious stiffness on the part of Dr. Rylance and his daughter. The physician was all sweetness, all geniality; yet a very close observer might have perceived that his sentiments about Miss Palliser were of no friendly nature. He had tried that young lady, and had found her wanting,—wanting in that first principle of admiration and reverence for himself, the lack of which was an unpardonable fault.

He had been willing to pardon her for her first rejection of him; telling himself that he had spoken too soon; that he had scared her by his unwise suddenness; that she was wild and wilful, and wanted more gentling before she was brought to the lure. But after a prolonged period of gentle treatment, after such courtesies and flatteries as Dr. Rylance had never before lavished upon anybody under a countess, it galled him to find Ida Palliser growing always colder and more distant, and obviously anxious to avoid his distinguished company. Then came the appearance of Brian Wendover on the scene, and Dr. Rylance was keen enough to see that Mr. Wendover of the Abbey had acquired more influence over Miss Palliser in a week than he had been able to obtain in nearly a year's acquaintance. And then Dr. Rylance decided that this girl was incorrigible: she was beyond the pale: she was a kind of monster, a being of imperfect development, a blunder of nature—like the sloth and his fellow tardigrades: a psychological mystery: inasmuch as she did not care for him.

So having made up his mind to have done with her, Dr. Rylance found that the end of love is the beginning of hate.

It happened, rather by lack of arrangement than by any special design, that Brian sat next to Ida. Dr. Rylance had taken Mrs. Wendover in to dinner, but Brian was on his aunt's left hand, and Ida was on Brian's left. He talked to her all dinner time, leaving his aunt, who loved to get hold of a medical man, to expatiate to her heart's content on all the small ailings and accidents which had affected her children during the last six months, down to that plague of warts which had lately afflicted Reginald, and which she would be glad to get charmed away by an old man in the village, who was a renowned wart-charmer, if Dr. Rylance did not think the warts might strike inward.

'Our own medical man is a dear good creature, but so very matter-of-fact,' Mrs. Wendover explained; 'I don't like to ask him these scientific questions.'

Brian and Ida talked to each other all through the dinner, and, although their conversation was of indifferent things, they talked as lovers talk—all unconsciously on Ida's part, who knew not how deeply she was sinning. It was to be in all probability their last meeting. She let herself be happy in spite of fate. What could it matter? In a few days she would have left Kingthorpe for ever—never to see him again. For ever, and never, are very real words to the heart of youth, which has no faith in time and mutability.

After dinner the young people all went straying out into the garden, in the lovely interval between day and darkness. There had been a glorious sunset, and red and golden lights shone over the low western sky, while above them was that tender opalescent green which heralds the mellow splendour of the moon. The atmosphere was exquisitely tranquil after last night's storm, not a breath stirring the shrubberies or the tall elms which divided the garden from adjacent paddocks.

Ida scarcely could have told how it was that Brian and she found themselves alone. The boys and girls had all left the house together. A minute ago Bessie and Urania were close to them, Urania laying down the law about some distinction between the old Oxford high-church party and the modern ritualists, and Bessie very excited and angry, as became the intended wife of an Anglican priest.

They were alone—alone at the end of the long, straight gravel walk— and the garden around them lay wrapped in shadow and mystery; all the flowers that go to sleep had folded their petals for the night, and the harvest moon was rising over church-tower and churchyard yews, trees and tower standing out black against the deep purple of that perfect sky. On this same night last year Ida and the other Brian had been walking about this same garden, talking, laughing, full of fun and good spirits, possibly flirting; but in what a different mood and manner! To-night her heart was overcharged with feeling, her mind weighed down by the consciousness that all this sweet life, which she loved so well, was to come to a sudden end, all this tender love, given her so freely, was to be forfeited by her own act. Already, as she believed, she had forfeited Miss Wendover's affection. Soon all the rest of the family would think of her as Aunt Betsy thought—as a monster of ingratitude; and Urania Rylance would toss up her sharp chin, and straighten her slim waist, and say, 'Did I not tell you so?'

Close to where she was standing with Brian there was an old, old stone sundial, supposed to be almost as ancient as the burial-places of the long-headed men of the stone age; and against this granite pillar Brian planted himself, as if prepared for a long conversation.

The voices of the others were dying away in the distance, and they were evidently all hastening back to the house, which was something less than a quarter of a mile off. Brian and Ida had been silent for some moments— moments which seemed minutes to Ida, who felt silence much more embarrassing than speech. She had nothing to say—she wanted to follow the others, but felt almost without power or motion.

'I think we—I—ought to go back,' she faltered, looking helplessly towards the lighted windows at the end of the long walk. 'There is going to be dancing. They will want us.'

'They can do without us, Ida,' he said, laying his hand upon her arm; 'but I cannot do without telling you my mind any longer. Why have you avoided me so? Why have you made it so difficult for me to speak to you of anything but trivialities—when you must know—you must have known— what I was longing to say?'

The passion in his lowered voice—that voice of deep and thrilling tone—which had a power over her that no other voice had ever possessed, the expression of his face as he looked at her in the moonlight, told her much more than his words. She put up her hands entreatingly to stop him.

'For God's sake, not another word,' she cried,' if—if you are going to say you care for me, ever so little, even. Not one more word. It is a sin. I am the most miserable, most guilty, among women, even to be here, even to have heard so much.'

'What do you mean? What else should I say? What can I say, except that I love you devotedly, with all my heart and mind? that I will have no other woman for my wife? You can't be surprised. Ida, don't pretend that you are surprised. I have never hidden my love, I have let you see that I was your slave all along. My darling, my beloved, why should you shrink from me? What can part us for an instant, when I love you so dearly, and know—yes, dearest, *I know* that you love me? *That* is a question upon which no man ever deceived himself, unless he were a fool or a coxcomb. Am *I* a fool, Ida?'

'No, no, no. For pity's sake, say no more. You ought not to have spoken. I am going away from Kingthorpe to-morrow, perhaps for ever. Yes, for ever. How could I know, how could I think you would care for me? Let me go!' she cried, struggling away from him as he clasped her hand, as he tried to draw her towards him. 'It is hopeless, mad, wicked to talk to me of love: some day you will know why, but not now. Be merciful to me; forget that you have ever known me.'

'Ida, Ida,' shrieked shrill voices in the distance. White figures came flying down the broad gravel-walk, ghost-like in the moonlight.

It was a blessed relief. Ida broke from Brian, and ran to meet Blanche and Bessie.

'Ida, Ida, such fun, such a surprise!' shrieked Blanche, as the flying white figures came nearer, wavered, and stopped.

'Only think of his coming on my birthday again!' exclaimed Bessie, 'and at this late hour—just as if he had dropped from the moon!'

'Who,—who has come?' cried Ida, looking from one to the other, with a scared white face.

It seemed to her as if the moonlit garden was moving away in a thick white cloud, spots of fire floated before her eyes, and then all the world went round like a fiery wheel.

'Brian—the other Brian—Brian Walford! Isn't it sweet of him to come to-night?' said Bessie.

Ida reeled forward, and would have fallen but for the strong arm that caught her as she sank earthwards, the grip which would have held her and sustained her through all life's journey had fate so willed it.

She had not quite lost consciousness, but all was hazy and dim. She felt herself supported in those strong arms, caressed and borne up on the other side by Bessie, and thus upheld she half walked, and was half carried along the smooth gravel-path to the house, whence sounds of music came faintly on her ear. She had almost recovered by the time they came to the threshold of the lighted drawing-room; but she had a curious sensation of having been away somewhere for ages, as if her soul had taken flight to some strange dim world and dwelt there for a space, and were slowly coming back to this work-a-day life.

The drawing-room was cleared ready for dancing. Urania was sitting at the piano playing the Swing Song, with dainty mincing touch, ambling and tripping over the keys with the points of her carefully trained fingers. She had given up Beethoven and all the men of might, and had cultivated the niminy-piminy school, which is to music as sunflowers and blue china are to art.

Brian Walford was standing in the middle of the big empty room, talking to his uncle the Colonel. Mrs. Wendover and her sister-in-law were sitting on a capacious old sofa in conversation with Dr. Rylance.

'Oh, you have come at last,' said Brian Walford, as Ida came slowly through the open window, pale as death, and moving feebly.

He went to meet her, and took her by the hand; then turning to the Colonel he said quietly and seriously,

'Uncle Wendover, it is just a year to-night since this young lady and I met for the first time. From the hour I first saw her I loved her, and I had reason to hope that she returned my love. We were married at a little church near Mauleverer Manor, on the ninth of October last. After our marriage my wife—finding that I was not quite so rich as she supposed me to be—fearful, I suppose, for the chances of our future—refused to live with me—told me that our marriage was to be as if it had never been—and left me, within three hours of our wedding, for ever, as she intended.'

Ida was standing in the midst of them all—alone. She had taken her hand from her husband's—she stood before them, pale as a corpse, but erect, ready to face the worst.

Brian of the Abbey, that Brian who would have given his life to save her this agony of humiliation, stood on the threshold of the window watching her. Could it be that she was false as fair—she whom he had so trusted and honoured?

Urania had left off playing, and was watching the scene with a triumphant smile. She looked at Mr. Wendover of the Abbey with a look that meant, 'Perhaps now you can believe what I told you about this girl?'

Aunt Betsy was the first to speak,

'Ida,' she said, standing up, 'is there any truth in this statement?'

'That question is not very complimentary to your nephew!' said Brian Walford.

'I am not thinking of my nephew—I am thinking of this girl, whom I have loved and trusted.'

'I was unworthy of your love and your trust,' answered Ida, looking at Miss Wendover with wide, despairing eyes. 'It is quite true—I am his wife—but he has no right to claim me. It was agreed between us that we should part—for ever—that our marriage was to be as if it had never been. It was our secret—nobody was ever to know.'

'And pray, after having married him, why did you wish to cancel your marriage?' asked Colonel Wendover, in a freezing voice. 'You married him of your own free will I suppose?'

'Of my own free will—yes.'

'Then why repent all of a sudden?'

She stood for a few moments silent, enduring such an agony of shame as all her sad experiences of life had not yet given her. The bitter, galling truth must be told—and in *his* hearing. *He* must be suffered to know how sordid and vile she had been.

'Because I had been deceived,' she faltered at last, her eyelids drooping over those piteous eyes.

Brian of the Abbey had advanced into the room by this time. He was standing by his uncle's side, his hand upon his uncle's arm. He wanted, if it were possible, to save Ida from further questioning, to restrain his uncle's wrath.

'I married your nephew under a delusion,' she said. 'I believed that I was marrying wealth and station. I had been told that the Brian Wendover I knew—the man who asked me to be his wife—was the owner of Wendover Abbey.'

'I see,' said the Colonel; 'you wanted to marry Wendover Abbey.'

Miss Rylance gave a little silvery laugh—the most highly cultivated thing in laughs—but the scowl she got from Brian of the Abbey checked her vivacity in a breath.

'Oh, I know what a wretch I must seem to you all,' said Ida, looking up at the Colonel with pleading eyes. 'But you have never known what it is to be poor—a genteel pauper—to have your poverty flung into your face like a handful of mud at every hour of your life; to have the instincts, the needs of a lady, but to be poorer and lower in status than any servant; to see your schoolfellows grinning at your shabby boots, making witty speeches about your threadbare gown; to patch, and mend, and struggle, yet never to be decently clad; to have the desire to help others, but nothing to give. If any of you—if you, Miss Rylance, with that exquisite sneer of yours, *you* who invented the plot that wrecked me—if you had ever endured what I have borne, you would have been as ready as I was to thank Providence for having sent me a rich lover, and to accept him gratefully as my husband.'

'Brian Walford,' interrogated the Colonel, looking severely at his nephew, 'am I to understand that you married this girl without undeceiving her as to the children's, or rather Miss Rylance's, most ill-judged practical joke—that you stood before the altar in God's House, the temple of truth and holiness, and won her by a lie?'

'I never lied to her,' answered Brian Walford, sulkily. 'My cousins chose to have their joke, but there was no joke in my love for Ida. I loved her, and was ready to marry her, and take my chance of the future, as another young man in my position would have done. I never bragged about the Abbey, or told her that it belonged to me. She never asked me who I was.'

'Because she had been told a wicked, shameful falsehood, and believed it, poor darling,' cried Bessie, running to her friend and embracing her. 'Oh, forgive me, dear—pray, pray do. It was all my fault. But as you have married him, darling, and it can't be helped, do try and be happy with him, for indeed, dear, he is very nice.'

Ida stood silent, with lowered eyelids.

'My daughter is right, Miss Palliser—Mrs. Brian Walford,' said the Colonel, in a less severe tone than he had employed before. 'It is quite true that you have been hardly used. Any deception is bad, worst of all a cheat that is maintained as far as the steps of the altar. But after all, in spite of your natural disappointment at finding you had married a poor man instead of a rich one, my nephew is the same man after marriage as he was before, the man you were willing to marry. And I cannot think so badly of you as to believe that you would marry a man you did not love, for the sake of his wealth and position. No, I cannot think that of you. I take it, therefore, that you liked my nephew for his own sake; and that it was only pique and natural indignation at having been duped which made you cast him off and agree to cancel your marriage. And I say that there is only one course open to you, as a good and honourable young woman, and that is to take your husband by the hand, as you took him in the house of God, for better for worse, and face the difficulties of life honestly and fearlessly. Heaven is always on the side of true-hearted young couples.'

Ida lifted her drooping eyelids and looked, not at the Colonel, not at her husband, not at her staunch friend Aunt Betsy, but at that other Brian—at him who this night only had declared his love. She looked at him with despair in her eyes, humbly beseeching him to stand between her and this loathed wedlock. But there was no sign in his sad countenance, no indication except of deepest sorrow, no ray of light to guide her on her path. The Colonel had spoken with such perfect common sense and justice, he had so clearly right on his side, that Brian Wendover, as a man of principle, could say nothing. Here was this woman he loved, and she was another man's wife, and that other man claimed her. If the King of Terrors himself had stretched forth his bony hand and clasped her, she could not be more utterly lost to the man who loved her than she was by this pre-existing tie. Brian of the Abbey was not the man to woo his cousin's wife.

'Do, dearest, be happy,' pleaded Bessie. 'I'm sure father is right. And you are our cousin, our own flesh and blood now, as it were. And you know I always wanted you to belong to us. And we shall all be fonder of you than ever. And you and Mr. Jardine will be cousins, later on,' she whispered, as a conclusive argument, as if for the sake of so high a privilege a girl might fairly make some sacrifice of inclination.

'Is it my duty to do as Colonel Wendover tells me?' asked Ida, looking round at them all with piteous appeal. 'Is it really my duty?'

'In the sight of God, yes,' said the Colonel and John Jardine.

'Yes, my dear, yes, there can be no doubt of it,' said the Colonel's wife and Aunt Betsy.

Brian of the Abbey said not a word, and Dr. Rylance looked on in silence, with a diabolical sneer.

What a fate for the girl who had refused a house in Cavendish square, one of the prettiest victorias in London, and a matchless collection of old hawthorn blue!

'Then I will do my duty,' said Ida; and then, before Brian Walford could take her in his arms, or make any demonstration of delight, she threw herself upon Miss Betsy Wendover's broad bosom, sobbing hysterically, and crying, 'Take me away, take me out of this house, for pity's sake!'

'I'll take her home with me. She will be calm, and quiet, and happy to-morrow,' said Aunt Betsy. And then, as Brian Walford was following them, 'Stay where you are, Brian,' she said authoritatively. 'She shall see no one but me till to-morrow. You will drive her crazy among you all, if you are not careful.'

Miss Wendover took the girl away almost in her arms, and Brian Walford disappeared at the same time without further speech.

'And now that the bride and bridegroom are gone, I suppose the wedding party can have their dance,' sneered Urania, playing the first few bars of 'Sweethearts.'

But Brian of the Abbey had vanished immediately after his cousin, and no one was disposed for dancing; so, after a good deal of talk, Bessie's birthday party broke up.

'What a dismal failure it has been, though it began so well!' said Bessie, as she and the other juveniles went upstairs to bed.

'What! still you are not happy,' quoted Horatio. 'Why, I thought you wanted Brian Walford to marry Ida Palliser?'

'So I did once,' sighed Bessie; 'but I would rather she had married Brian of the Abbey; and I know he's over head and ears in love with her.'

'Ah, then he'll have to put his love in his pipe and smoke it! That kind of thing won't do out of a French novel,' said Horatio, whose personal knowledge of French romancers was derived from the *Philosophe sous les toits*, as published with grammatical notes for the use of schools; but he liked to talk large.

CHAPTER XX
WAS THIS THE MOTIVE?

Brian Walford came back to The Knoll after the younger members of the family had gone to their rooms.

'Where have you been all this time?' asked the Colonel, who was strolling on the broad gravel drive in front of the house, soothing his nerves with a cheroot, after the agitations of the last hour. 'You are to have your old room, I believe; I heard it was being got ready.'

'You are very kind. I walked half way to the Abbey with my cousin. We had a smoke and a talk.'

'I should be glad of a little more talk with you. This business of to-night is not at all pleasant, you know, Brian. It does not redound to anybody's credit.'

'I never supposed that it did; but it is not my fault that there should be this fuss. If my wife had been true to me all would have gone well.'

'I don't think you had a right to expect things to go well, when you had so cruelly deceived her. It was a base thing to do, Brian.'

'You ought not to say so much as that, sir, knowing so little of the circumstances. I did not deliberately deceive her.'

'That's skittles,' said the Colonel, flinging away the end of his cigar.

'It is the truth. The business began in sport. Bessie asked me to pretend to be my cousin, just for fun, to see if Ida would fall in love with me. Ida had a romantic idea about my cousin, it appears, that he was an altogether perfect being, and so on. Well, I was introduced to her as Brian of the Abbey, and though she may have been a little disappointed—no doubt she was— she accepted me as the perfect being. As for me—well, sir, you know what she is—how lovely, how winning. I was a gone coon from that moment. We kept up the fun—Bess, and the boys, and I—all that evening. I talked of the Abbey as if it were my property, swaggered a good deal, and so on. Then Bess, knowing that I often stayed up the river for weeks on end, asked me to go and see Ida, to make sure that old Pew was not ill-using her, that she was not going into a decline, and all that kind of thing. So I went, saw Ida, always in the company of the German teacher, and took no pains to conceal my affection for her. But I said not another word about the Abbey. I never swaggered or put on the airs of a rich man; I only told her that I loved her, and that I hoped our lives would be spent together. I did not even suggest our marriage as a fact in the near future. I knew I was in no position to maintain a wife.'

'You should have told her that plainly. As a man of honour you were bound to undeceive her.'

'I meant to do it, but I wanted her to be very fond of me first. Then came the row; old Pew expelled her because she had been carrying on a clandestine flirtation with a young man. Her character was compromised, and as a man of honour I had no course but to propose immediate marriage.'

'Her character was not compromised, because Miss Pew chose to act like a vulgar old tyrant. The German governess, everybody in the school, knew that Miss Palliser was unjustly treated. There was no wound that needed to be salved by an imprudent marriage. But in any case, before proposing such a marriage, it was your bounden duty to tell her the truth about your circumstances, not to marry her to poverty without her full consent to the union.'

'Then I did not do my bounden duty,' Brian Walford answered sullenly. 'I believed in her disinterested affection. Why should she be more mercenary than I, who was willing to marry her without a sixpence in her pocket, without a second gown to her back? How could I suppose she was marrying me for the sake of a fine place and a fine fortune? I thought she was above such sordid considerations.'

'You ought to have been sure of that before you married her; you ought to have trusted her fully,' said the Colonel. 'However, having married her, why did you consent so tamely to let her go? Having let her go, why do you come here to-night to claim her?'

'Why did I let her go? Well she shrewed me so abominably when she found out my lowly position that my pride was roused, and I told her she might go where she pleased. Why did I come here to-night? Well, it was an impulse that brought me. I am passionately fond of her. I have lived without her for nearly a year—angry with her and with fate—but to day was the anniversary of our first meeting. I knew from Bessie that my wife was here, happy. There was even some hint of a flirtation between her and *the real Brian*,'—these last words were spoken with intense bitterness,—'and I thought it was time I should claim my own.'

'I think so too,' said Colonel Wendover, severely; 'you should have claimed her long ago. Your whole conduct is faulty in the extreme. You will be a very lucky man if your married life turns out happy after such a bad beginning.'

'Come, Colonel, we are both young,' remonstrated Brian, with that careless lightness which seemed natural to him, as a man who could hardly take the gravest problems of life seriously; 'there is no reason why we should not shake down into a very happy couple by-and-by.'

'And pray how are you to live?' inquired the Colonel. 'You are taking this girl from a most comfortable home—a position in which she is valued and useful. What do you intend to give her in exchange for the Homestead? A garret and a red herring?'

'Oh, no, sir; I hope it will be a long time before we come to that—though Beranger says that at twenty a man and the girl he loves may be happy in a garret. I think we shall do pretty well. My literary work widened a good deal while I was in Paris. I wrote for some of the London magazines, and the editors are good enough to think that I am rather a smart writer. I can earn something by my pen; I think enough to keep the pot boiling till briefs begin to drop in. My cousin was generous enough to offer me an income just now—four or five hundred a year so long as I should require it—but I told him that I thought I could support my wife with my pen for the next few years.'

'Your cousin is always generous,' said the Colonel.

'Yes, he is an open-handed fellow. I suppose you know that he helped me while I was in Paris.'

'I did not know, but I am not surprised.'

'Very kind of him, wasn't it? The fact is, I was dipped rather deeply, in my small way—tailor, and hosier, and so on—before I left London; and I could not have come back unless Brian had helped me to settle with them, or I should have had to go through the Bankruptcy Court; and I daresay some of you would have thought that a disgrace.'

'Some of us!' exclaimed the Colonel; 'we should all have thought so. Do you suppose the Wendovers are in the habit of cheating their creditors?'

'Oh, but it was not a question of cheating them, only of paying them a rather insignificant dividend. My only assets are my books and furniture, and unluckily some of those are still unpaid for.'

'Assets? You have no assets. You are a spendthrift and a scamp!' protested his uncle, angrily. 'I am deeply sorry for your wife. Good night. If you want any supper after your journey there are plenty of people to wait upon you.'

And with that the Colonel turned upon his heel and went into the house, leaving his nephew to follow at his leisure.

'*Comme il est assommant, le patron,*' muttered Brian, strolling after his kinsman.

Brian Walford was not ordinarily an early riser, but he was up betimes on the morning after Bessie's birthday; breakfasted with the family, and strolled across dewy fields to the Homestead a little after nine o'clock. But although this was a late hour in Miss Wendover's household, his young wife was not prepared to receive him. It was Aunt Betsy who came to him, after he had waited for nearly a quarter of an hour, prowling restlessly about the drawing-room, looking at the books, and china, and water-colours.

'I have come for Ida,' he said abruptly, when he had shaken hands with his aunt. 'There is a train leaves Winchester at twenty minutes past eleven. She will be ready for that I suppose?'

He was half prepared for reproaches from his aunt, and wholly prepared to set her at defiance. But if she were civil he would be civil: he did not court a quarrel.

'I don't know that she can be ready.'

'But she must. I have made up my mind to travel by that train. Why should there be any delay? Everybody is agreed that we are to begin our lives together, and we cannot begin too soon.'

'You need not be in such a hurry. You have contrived to live without her for nearly a year.'

'That is my business. I am not going to live without her any longer. Please tell her she must be ready by half-past ten.'

'I will tell her so. I am heartily sorry for her. But she must submit to fate. What home have you prepared for her?'

'At present none. We can go to an hotel for a day or two, and then I shall take lodgings in South Kensington, or thereabouts.'

'Have you any money?'

'Yes enough to carry on,' answered Brian.

Truthfulness was not his strong point, although he was a Wendover, and that race deemed itself free from the taint of falsehood. There may have been an injurious admixture of races on the maternal side, perhaps; albeit his mother personally was good and loyal. However this was, Brian Walford had, even in trifles, shown himself evasive and shifty.

His aunt looked at him sharply.

'Do not take her to discomfort or want,' she said earnestly. 'She has been very happy with me, poor girl; and although she deceived me, I cannot find it in my heart to be angry with her.'

'There is no fear of want,' replied Brian. 'We shall not be rich, but we shall get on pretty comfortably. Please tell her to make haste. The dog-cart will be round in half an hour. I'll walk about the garden till it comes.'

Miss Wendover sighed, and left him, without another word. He went out into the sunlit garden, and walked up and down smoking his favourite meerschaum, which was a kind of familiar spirit, always carried in his pocket ready for every possible opportunity. He had arranged with one of his uncle's men to drive the dog-cart over to Winchester; his travelling-bag was put in ready; he had taken leave of his kindred—not a very cordial leave-taking upon anybody's part, and on Bessie's despondent even to tears. He was not in a good humour with himself or with fate; and yet he told himself that things had gone well with him, much better than he could reasonably have expected. Yet it was hard for a young man of considerable personal attractions and some talent to be treated like one of the monsters of classical legend, a damsel-devouring Minotaur, when he came to claim his young wife.

The dog-cart was at the gate for at least ten minutes, and Brian had looked at his watch at least ten times before Ida appeared at the glass door. He was pale with anxiety. There were reasons why it might be ruin to him to lose this morning train; and yet he did not want to betray too much eagerness, lest that should spoil his chances.

Here she was at last, white as a corpse, and with red swollen eyelids which indicated a night of weeping. Her appearance was far from flattering to her husband, yet she gave him a wan little smile and a civil good morning.

'Here, Pluto, take your Proserpine,' said Miss Wendover, trying to make light of the situation, though sore at heart. 'I wish you would be content to keep her six months of the year, and let me have her for the other six.'

'It needn't be an eternal parting, Aunt Betsy,' answered Brian, with assumed cheeriness; 'Ida can come to see you whenever you like, and Ida's husband too, if you will have him. We are not starting for the Antipodes.'

'Be kind to her,' said Miss Wendover, gravely, 'for my sake, if not for her own. It shall be the better for you when I am dead and gone if you make her a happy woman.'

This promise from a lady who owned a snug little landed estate, and money in the funds, meant a good deal. Brian grasped his aunt's hand.

'You know that I adore her,' he said. 'I shall be her slave.'

'Be a good husband, honest and true. She doesn't want a slave,' replied Miss Wendover, in her incisive way.

Ida flung her arms round that generous friend's neck, and kissed her with passionate fervour.

'God bless you for your goodness to me! God bless you for forgiving me,' she said.

'He is a Being of infinite love and pity, and He will not bless those who cannot pardon,' answered Miss Wendover. 'There, my dear, go and be happy with your young husband. He may not be such a very bad bargain, after all.'

This was, as it were, the old shoe thrown after the bride and bridegroom. In another minute the dog-cart was rattling along the lane, Brian driving, and the groom sitting behind with Ida's luggage, which was more important by one neat black trunk than it had been a year ago.

Bessie and the younger children were standing on the patch of grass outside The Knoll gates, in garden hats, and no gloves, waving affectionate adieux. Brian gave them no chance of any further leave-taking driving towards the downs at a smart pace. 'Do you remember my driving you to catch the earlier train, a year ago this day?' he asked his pale companion, by way of conversation.

'Yes, perfectly.'

'Odd, isn't it?—exactly one year to-day.'

'Very odd.'

And this was about all their discourse till they were at Winchester Station.

'London papers in yet?' asked Brian.

'No, sir. You'll get them at Basingstoke.'

He took his wife into a first-class carriage—an extravagance which surprised her, knowing his precarious means.

'I hope you are not travelling first-class on my account,' she said; 'I am not accustomed to such luxury.'

'Oh, we can afford it to-day. I am not quite such a pauper as I was when I offered you those two sovereigns. If you would like to buy yourself a silk gown or a new bonnet, or anything in that line to-day, I can manage it.'

'No, thank you; I have everything I want,' she answered with a faint shiver.

The memory of that bygone day was too bitter.

'What a wonderful wife! I thought that to be in want of a new bonnet was a woman's normal condition,' said Brian, trying to be lively.

He had bought *Punch* and other comic journals at the station, and spread them out before his wife—as an intellectual feast. The breezy drive over the downs had revived her beauty a little. The eyelids had lost their red swollen look, but she was still very pale, and there was a nervous quiver of the lips now and then which betokened a tendency to hysteria. She sat at the open window, looking away towards those vanishing hills. A moment, and the tufted crest of St. Catherine's had gone—the low-lying meadows—the winding stream—the cathedral's stunted tower—it was all gone, like a dream.

'Dreadful hole of a place,' said Brian, contemptuously; 'a comfortably feathered old nest for rooks and parsons and ancient spinsters, but a dungeon for anybody else.'

'I think it is the dearest old city in the world.'

'Old enough, and dear enough, in all conscience,' answered Brian. 'My uncle's tailor had the audacity to charge me thirty shillings for a waistcoat. But it's the most deadly-lively place I know. All country towns are deadly-lively; in fact, there are only two places fit for young people to live in—London and Paris!'

'I suppose you mean to live in London?' said Ida, listlessly. She did not feel as if she were personally interested in the matter. If she were forced to live with a man she despised, the place of her habitation would matter very little.

'I mean to oscillate between the two,' answered Brian. 'Were you ever in Paris?'

'Never.'

'I envy you. You have something left to live for—a new sensation—a new birth. We will go there in November.'

He looked for a smile, an expression of pleasure, but there was none. His wife's face was still turned towards the landscape, her sad eyes still fixed on the vanishing hills—no longer those familiar hill-tops around the cathedral city, but like them in character. Soon the last of those chalky ridges would vanish, and then would come the heathy tracts about Woking, and the fertile meads in the Thames valley.

The train stopped for five minutes at Basingstoke, and Brian offered his wife tea, lemonade, anything which the refreshment-room could produce, but she declined everything.

'We two have not broken bread together since we were one,' he said, still struggling after liveliness; 'let us eat something together, if it be only a Bath bun.'

'I am not hungry, thanks,' she answered listlessly.

'Papers! papers!' shouted the small imp attached to the bookstall. 'Morning paper—*Times, Standard, Telegraph, Daily News, Morning Post!*'

Brian drew up the window abruptly, as if he had seen a scorpion.

An elderly gentleman trotted up to the carriage, opened the door, and came in, his arms full of newspapers. He settled himself in his corner, and looked about him with a benevolent air, as if courting friendly intercourse. Brian seated himself opposite his wife, looking black as thunder. Ida was indifferent to such petty details of life as unknown elderly gentlemen. Her mind was full of troubled thoughts about the friends she had left—most of all that one friend whose thrilling voice still sounded in her ears—that one voice which had power to move her deepest feeling.

'And come what may, I *have been* bless'd.' That is a woman's first thought in any desperate case of this kind. The poet struck a note of universal truth in that immortal line. There is endless consolation in the knowledge that heart has answered to heart; that the fond futile love to which Fate forbids a happy issue has not been lavished on a dumb, irresponsive idol. If there has been madness, folly, it has not been one-sided foolishness. He too has loved; he too must suffer. Bind Eloisa with what vows, surround her with what walls you will, even in her despair there is one golden thought: her Abelard has loved her—will love on till the end of life—since such a flame should be eternal as the stars.

He had loved her! Pride and rapture were in the thought. She told herself that such pride, such delight was sinful, and that she must fight against and conquer this sin. She must shut Brian of the Abbey out of her mind for evermore; she must school herself to believe that he and she had never met; so train and subjugate herself that a few months hence she might be able to read the announcement of his marriage—should such a thing occur—without one guilty pang.

And then she looked back and tried to recall her life before she had known him. What was it like? A blank? She felt like one who has received some injury to the brain, or endured severe illness which has blotted out all memory of the life which went before. She sat with her pale fixed face turned towards the open window, her eyes gazing on the landscape with a vacant, far-away look—her husband watching her every now and then, furtively, anxiously.

The elderly gentleman in the corner beamed at her occasionally through his spectacles. She was young, handsome, and looked unhappy. He was interested in her; in a benevolent, paternal spirit. He thought it likely that the young man was her brother, though there was no likeness between them; and that she was being parted by family authority from some other young man who was less, and yet more, than a brother. He made up his little story about her, and then, by way of consolation, offered her his *Times*, which he had done with by this time.

Brian turned quickly, and stretched out his hand, as if to intercept the paper; but he was too late. Ida had taken it, and was staring absently at the leading articles. She read on listlessly, vaguely, for a little while, going over the words mechanically, reading how Sir Somebody Something, a leading light of the Opposition, had been holding forth at an agricultural meeting, arguing that never since the date of Magna Charta had the national freedom been in such peril as it was at this hour; never had any Ministry so wantonly trifled with the rights of a great people, or so supinely submitted to the degradation of a once glorious country; never, within the memory of man, or, he would go further and say, within the records of history, was our agricultural interest so wantonly neglected, our commercial predominance so supinely surrendered, our army so unprepared for action, and our influence in the affairs of Europe so audaciously set at naught. The right honourable gentleman gave the Ministry another year to complete the ruin of their country. They might do it in six months; yes, he would venture to say, or even in three months; but he gave them at most a year. Favourable accidents, against which even the blind fatuity and garrulous pig-headedness of septuagenarian senility could not prevail might prolong the struggle; but the day of doom was inevitable, unless—and so on, and so on, with a running commentary by the leader writer.

Ida read without knowing what she was reading, till presently her eyes glanced idly to another part of the page, and there were arrested by a short paragraph headed, FATAL STORM IN THE HEBRIDES.

Was it not in the Hebrides she had last heard of Sir Vernon's yacht the *Seamew*?

'Among other accidents in the terrible gale on Tuesday night and Wednesday morning, we regret to number the loss of the schooner yacht *Seamew*, which was capsized in a squall off the Isle of Skye, with the loss of the owner, Sir Vernon Palliser, his brother, Mr. P. Palliser, Captain Greenway, and seven of the crew. Three men and the cabin-boy were saved by a fishing boat, the crew of which witnessed the sad catastrophe, but were too far off to be of much help.' And then followed a description of the accident, which had been caused by the violence of the storm, rather than by bad seamanship or carelessness on the part of the captain, who, with Sir Vernon and his brother, both skilled seamen, had the vessel well in hand a few minutes before she went down.

Ida let the paper fall from her hand with a cry of horror.

'Vernon, poor Vernon, and Peter too—those good, kind-hearted young men—dead—both—dead!'

She burst into tears, remembering the two frank, kind faces looking at her from the marble portico, in the afternoon sunlight, the warm welcome, the feeling of kindred which had shown itself so thoroughly in their words and looks. And they were gone—they who a month ago were full of life and gladness. The cruel inexorable sea had devoured their youth and strength and all the promises and hopes of their being.

The elderly gentleman moved to the seat next hers full of compassion.

'Look at that,' she said, as Brian picked up the paper; 'my cousins, both of them.'

'I am sorry you have found bad news in the paper,' said the elderly stranger, looking at her sympathetically through his spectacles.

'My two cousins, sir,' she said, 'they have both been drowned. Such fine, honest young fellows. It is too dreadful.'

'That wreck in the Hebrides? Yes, it is a sad thing; and Sir Vernon Palliser and his brother were your cousins?' I am so sorry I showed you the paper. But I wonder you had not heard of this sooner; it was in the evening papers yesterday.'

'Then you must have known that my cousins were dead when you came to Kingthorpe last night?' said Ida, looking up at her husband.

Suddenly, in a flash of memory, came back those thoughtless words of hers spoke at Les Fontaines, when her father talked of the possibility of inheriting a fortune and a baronetcy. She remembered how she had said, in bitterness of spirit, 'Of course they will live to the age of Methuselah. Whoever heard of luck coming our way?' And now this kind of luck, which meant sudden death for two amiable, open-handed young men, had come her way. How lightly she had spoken of those two young lives! how bitter had been her thoughts about the rich and happy!

This thing had been known in London yesterday afternoon. It was this knowledge which had sent Brian Walford to Kingthorpe to claim his wife. She had suddenly become a wife worth claiming—the daughter of Sir Reginald Palliser of Wimperfield.

'You knew this,' she repeated, looking at her husband, with infinite scorn expressed in eye and lip.

'No, upon my soul,' he answered; 'I left town early. It flashed upon me that it was Bessie's birthday—you would be all assembled at The Knoll— there was just time for me to get there before the fun was over—don't you know—'

'And you had not seen the papers? you did *not* know this?' added Ida, fixing him with her eyes.

'No, upon my word. I had no idea!'

She knew that he was lying.

'Then it was a very curious coincidence,' she said freezingly.

'How a coincidence?'

'That after so long an absence you should happen to come to Kingthorpe on the day that made such a change in my father's fortunes.'

'I came because of Bessie's birthday—as I told you before. Does this sad event make any difference to your father?' he asked innocently. 'Are there not——nearer relatives?'

'None that I know of.'

The elderly gentleman, a little hard of hearing, as he called it, looked on and wondered at this somewhat eccentric young couple, who seemed, from those snatches of speech which reached him, to be on the verge of a quarrel. He felt very sorry for the lady, who was so handsome, and so interesting. The young man was gentlemanlike and good looking, but had not that frank bright outlook which is the glory of a young Englishman. He was dressed a little too foppishly for the elder man's liking, and had the air of being over-careful of his own person.

And now the train had passed Sandown, was rushing on to Wimbledon and the London smoke. All the blue had gone out of the sky, all the beauty had gone from the earth, Ida thought, as small suburban villas followed each other in a monotonous sequence, some old and shabby, others new and smart; and then all that is ugliest in the great city surrounded them as they steamed slowly into Waterloo station.

A four-wheel cab took them to an hotel in the purlieus of Fleet Street, a big new hotel, but so shut in and surrounded by other buildings that Ida felt as if she could hardly breathe in it—she who had lived among gardens and green fields, and with all the winds of heaven blowing on her across the rolling downs, from the forest and the sea.

'What a hateful place London is!' she exclaimed. 'Can any one like to live in it?'

'All sensible people like it better than any other bit of the world, bar Paris,' answered Brian. 'But it is not particularly pretty to look at. City life is an acquired taste.'

This was on the stairs, while they were following the waiter to the private sitting-room for which Mr. Walford had asked. It was a neat little room on the first floor, looking into a stony city square, surrounded by business premises.

The waiter, after the manner of his kind, was loth to leave without an order. Ida declined anything in the way of luncheon; so Brian ordered tea and toast, and the man departed with an air of resignation rather than alacrity, considering the order a poor one.

When they were quite alone Ida went up to her husband, laid her hand upon his arm, and looked up at him with earnest, imploring eyes.

'Brian,' she said, 'I have come with you because I was told it was my duty to come—told so by people who are wiser than I.'

'Of course it was your duty,' Brian answered impatiently. 'Nobody could doubt that. We have been fools to live asunder so long.'

'Do you think we may not be more foolish for trying our lives together—if we do not love each other—or trust each other.'

'I love you—that's all I know about it. As for trusting—well, I think I have been too easy, have trusted you too far.'

'But I do not either love you—or trust you,' she said, lifting up her head, and looking at him with kindling eyes and burning cheeks—ashamed for him and for herself. 'I thought once that I could love you. I know now that I never can; and what is still worse that I never can trust you. No, Brian, never. You told me a lie to-day.'

'How dare you say that?'

'I dare say what I know to be the truth—the bitter, shameful truth. You lied to me to-day in the railway-carriage, when you told me that you did not know of my cousins' death last night—that you did not know of the change in my father's position.'

'You are a nice young lady to accuse your husband of lying,' he answered, scowling at her. 'I tell you I saw no evening papers: I left London at half-past five o'clock. But even if I had known, what does that matter? It makes no difference to my right over your life. You are my wife and you belong to me. I was fool enough to let you go last October: you were in such a fury that you took me off my guard; I had no time to assert my rights: and then *vogue la galère* has always been my motto. But the time came when I felt that I had been an ass to allow myself to be so treated; and I made up my mind to claim you, and to stand no denial of my rights. This determination was some time ripening in my mind; and then came Bessie's birthday, the anniversary of our first meeting, the birthday of my love, and I said to myself that I would claim you on that day, and no other.'

'And that day and no other made my father a rich man. Poor Vernon! poor Peter! so brave, so frank, so true! to think that *you* should profit by their death!' this she said with ineffable contempt, looking at him from head to foot, as if he were a creature of inferior mould. 'But perhaps you mistook the case. I am not an heiress, remember, even now. I have a little brother who will inherit everything.'

'I have not forgotten your brother. I don't want you to be an heiress. I want you—and your love.'

'That you never will have,' she cried passionately; and then she fell on her knees at his feet—she to whom he had knelt on their wedding-day—and lifted her clasped hands with piteous entreaty, 'Brian Walford, be merciful to me. I do not love you, I never loved you, can never love you. In an evil hour I took the fatal step which gives you power over me. But, for God's sake, be generous, and forbear to use that power. No good can ever come of our union—no good, but unspeakable evil; nothing but misery for me—nothing but bitterness for you. We shall quarrel—we shall hate each other.'

'I'll risk that,' he said; 'you are mine, and nothing shall make me give you up.'

'Nothing?' she cried, rising suddenly, and flaming out at him like a sibyl—'nothing? Not even the knowledge that I love another man?'

'Not even that. Let the other man beware, whoever he is. And you beware how you keep to your duty as my wife. No, Ida, I will not let you go. I was a fool last year—and I was taken unawares. I am a wiser man now, and my decision is irrevocable. You are my wife, my goods, my chattels—God help you if you deny my claim.'

CHAPTER XXI
TAKING LIFE QUIETLY

It was the second week in October, and the woods were changing their green liveries of summer for tawny and amber tints, so various and so harmonious in their delicate gradations that the eye of the artist was gladdened by their decay. The hawthorns in Wimperfield Park glowed in the distance like patches of crimson flame, and the undulating sweeps of bracken showed golden-brown against the green-sward; while the oaks—symbolic of all that is solid, ponderous, and constant in woodland nature, slow to bloom and slow to die—had hardly a faded leaf to mark the coming of winter.

A fine domain, this Wimperfield Park, with its hill and vale, its oaks and beeches, and avenue of immemorial elms, to be owned by the man who six weeks ago had no better shelter than a lath and plaster villa in a French village, and who had found it a hard thing to pay the rent of that trumpery tenement; and yet Sir Reginald Palliser accepted the change in his circumstances as tranquilly as if it had been but a migration from the red room to the blue. He took good fortune with the same easy indolent air with which he had endured evil fortune. He had the Horatian temperament, uneager to anticipate the future, content if the present were fairly comfortable, sighing for no palatial halls over-arched with gold and ivory, no porphyry columns, or marble terraces encroaching upon the sea. He was a man to whom it had been but a slight affliction to live in a small house, and to be deprived of all pomp and state, nay, even of the normal surroundings of gentle birth, so long as he had those things which were absolutely necessary to his own personal comfort. He was honestly sorry for the untimely fate of his young kinsmen; but he slipped into his nephew's vacant place with an ease which filled his wife and daughter with wonder.

To poor little Fanny Palliser, who had never known the sensation of a spare five-pound note, nay, of even a sovereign which she might squander on the whim of the moment, this sudden possession of ample means was strange even to bewilderment. Not to have to cut and contrive any more, not to have to cook her husband's dinners, or to run about from morning till twilight, supplementing the labours of an incompetent maid-of-all-work, was to enter upon a new phase of life almost as surprising as if she, Fanny Palliser, had died and been buried, and been resolved back into the elements, to be born again as a princess of the blood royal. She kept on repeating feebly that it was all like a dream—she had not been able to realise the change yet.

To Reginald Palliser the inheritance of Wimperfield was only a return to the home of his childhood. To his lowly-born little helpmeet it was the beginning of a new life. It was a new sensation to Fanny Palliser to live in large rooms, to walk about a house in which the long corridors, the wide staircase, the echoing stone hall, the plenitude of light and space, seemed to her to belong to a public institution rather than to a domestic dwelling—a new sensation, and not altogether a pleasant one. She was awe-stricken by the grandeur—the largeness and airiness of her new surroundings.

There was not one of the sitting-rooms at Wimperfield in which, even after a month's residence, she could feel thoroughly at home. She envied Mrs. Moggs, the housekeeper, her parlour looking into the stable-yard, which seemed to Sir Reginald's wife the only really snug room within the four walls of that respectable mansion. Mrs. Moggs' old-fashioned grate and brass fender, little round table, tea-tray, and kettle singing on the hob, reminded Fanny Palliser of her own girlhood, when her mother's sitting room had worn just such an air of humble comfort. Those white and gold drawing-rooms, with their amber satin curtains and Georgian furniture, had a scenic and altogether artificial appearance to the unaccustomed eyes of one born and reared amidst the narrow surroundings of poverty.

And then, again, how terrible was that highly respectable old butler, who knew the ways of gentle folks so much better than his new mistress did; and who put her to shame, in a quiet unconscious way, a hundred times a day by his superior knowledge and experience. How often she asked for things that were altogether wrong; how continually she exposed her ignorance, both to Rogers the butler, and to Moggs, the housekeeper; and what a feeble creature she felt herself in the presence of Jane Dyson, her own maid, who had come to her fresh from the sainted presence of an archbishop's wife, and who was inclined to be slightly dictatorial in consequence, always quoting and referring to that paragon of women, her late mistress, whose only error in life had been the leaving it before Jane Dyson had saved enough to justify her retirement from service. Those highly-educated retainers were a terror to poor little Fanny Palliser. There were times when she would have been glad to be impecunious again, and running after her faithful Lizette, who had every possible failing except that of being superior to her mistress. These Wimperfield servants were models;

but they did not disguise their quiet contempt for a lady who was evidently a stranger in that sphere where powdered footmen and elaborate dinners are among the indispensables of existence.

Only six weeks, and Sir Reginald and his family were established in the place that had been Sir Vernon's, and the old servants waited on their new lord, and all the mechanical routine of life went on as smoothly as if there had been no change of masters. Ida found herself wondering which was the reality and which the dream—the past or the present. There had been a few days of excitement, hurry, and confusion at Les Fontaines after the awful news of the wreck: and then Sir Reginald had come to London with his wife and boy, and had put up at the Grosvenor Hotel while the lawyers settled the details of his inheritance. Sir Vernon had left no will. Everything went to the heir-at-law—pictures, plate, horses and carriages, and those wonderful cellars of old wine which had been slowly accumulated by Sir Reginald's father and grandfather.

Reginald Palliser passed from the pittance of a half-pay captain, eked out by the desultory donations of his open-handed nephew, to the possession of a fine income and a perfectly-appointed establishment. There was nothing for him to do, no trouble of furnishing, or finding servants. He came into his kingdom, and everything was ready for him. Yet in this house where he was born, in which every stone was familiar to him, how little that was mortal was left of those vanished days of his youth! Among all these old servants there was only one who remembered the new master's boyhood; and that was a deaf old helper in the garden, a man who seemed past all labour except the sweeping up of dead leaves, being himself little better than a withered leaf. This man remembered wheeling the present baronet about the gardens in his barrow, forty years ago—his function even then being to collect the fallen leaves—and was a little offended with Sir Reginald for having forgotten the man and the fact.

At the Grosvenor Hotel, calm even in the dawn of his altered fortunes, Brian Walford found his father-in-law, and told, with the pleasantest, most plausible air, the story of Ida's clandestine marriage, slurring over every detail that reflected on himself, and making very light of Ida's revulsion of feeling, which he represented as a girlish whim, rather than a woman's bitter anger against the husband who had allowed her to marry him under a delusion as to his social status.

Sir Reginald was at first inclined to be angry. The whole thing was a mystification—absurd, discreditable. His daughter had grossly deceived him. It needed all the stepmother's gentle influence to soften the outraged father's feelings. But Lady Palliser said all that was kindly about Ida's youth and inexperience, her impulsive nature; and a man who has just dropped into £7,000 a year is hardly disposed to be inflexible. Sir Reginald was too generous even to question Brian closely as to his capability of supporting a wife. The man was a gentleman—young, good-looking, with winning manners, and a member of a family in which his daughter had found warm and generous friends. Ida's father could not be uncivil to a Wendover.

'Well, my good fellow, it is altogether a foolish business,' he said; 'but what's done cannot be undone. I am sorry my daughter did not ask my leave before she plunged into matrimony; but I suppose I must forgive her, and her husband into the bargain. You have both acted like a pair of children, falling in love and marrying, and quarrelling, and making friends again, without rhyme or reason; but the best thing you can do is to bring your wife—your wife? my little Ida a wife?—Good God, how old I am getting!— yes, you had better bring her to Wimperfield next week, and then we can get better acquainted with you, and I shall see what I can do for you both.'

This no doubt meant a handsome allowance. Brian Walford felt, for the first time in his life, that he had fallen on his feet. He hated the country, and Wimperfield would be only a shade better than Kingthorpe; but it was essential that he should please his easy-tempered father-in-law.

'If he wanted me to live in the moon I should have to go there!' he said to himself. And then Lady Palliser went into an adjoining chamber and brought forth little Vernon, to exhibit him, as a particular favour and privilege, to Ida's husband; and Brian, who detested children, had to appear grateful, and to address himself to the irksome task of making friends with the little man. This was not easy, for the boy, though frank and bright enough in a general way, did not take to his new connexion: and it was only when Brian spoke of Ida that his young brother-in-law became friendly. 'Where is she? why haven't you brought her? Take me to her directly-minute,' said the child, whose English savoured rather of the lower than the upper strata of society.

Brian snapped at the opportunity, and carried the boy off instanter in a Hansom cab to that hotel near Fleet Street where his young wife was pining in her second-floor sitting-room, like a wild woodland bird behind the bars of a cage. The young man thought the little fellow might be a harbinger of peace—nor was he mistaken, for Ida melted at sight of him, and seemed quite happy when they three sat down to a dainty little luncheon, she waiting upon and petting her young brother all the while.

'This is partridge, isn't it?' asked Vernie. 'I like partridge. We always have nice dinners now—jellies, and creams, and wine that goes fizz; and we all have the same as pa. We didn't in France, you know,' explained the boy, unconscious of any reason for suppressing facts in the presence of the waiter.

'Mamma and I used to have any little bits—it didn't matter for us, you know—we could pinch. Mamma was used to it, and it was good for me, you know, because I'm often bilious—and it's better to go without rich things than to take Gregory's powder, isn't it?'

'Decidedly,' said Brian, who was not too old to remember that bugbear of the Edinburgh pharmacopæia.

'And now we have dessert every day,' continued Vernie; 'lovely dessert—almonds and raisins, and pears, and nuts, and things, just like Christmas Day. I thought that kind of dessert was only meant for Christmas Day. And we have men to wait upon us, dressed like clergymen, just like him,' added the child, pointing to the waiter.

'Oh, Vernie, it's so rude to point,' murmured Ida.

'Not for me; I can't be rude,' replied the boy, with conviction. 'I'm a baronet's son. I shall be a baronet myself some day. Mamma told me. I may do what I like.'

'No, pet, you must be a gentleman. If you were a king's son you would have to be that.'

'Then I wouldn't. What's the use of being rich if you can't do what you like?' demanded Vernie, who already began to have ideas, and who was as sharp for his age as the chicken which begins to catch flies directly its head is out of the shell.

'What's the good of being somebody if you have to behave just as well as if you were nobody?' said Brian. 'Little Vernon has the feudal idea strongly developed; no doubt an evolution from some long-departed ancestor, who lived in the days when there were different laws for the knight and the villain. Now, how are we going to amuse this young gentleman? I have leave to keep him till half-past seven, when we are all three to dine with Sir Reginald and Lady Palliser at the Grosvenor.'

Vernie, who was half way through his second glass of sparkling moselle, burst out laughing.

'Lady Palliser!' he exclaimed, 'it's so funny to hear mamma called Lady: because she isn't a lady, you know. She used to run about the house all day with her sleeves tucked up, and she used to cook; and Jane, our English servant, said no lady ever did that. Jane and mamma used to quarrel,' explained the infant, calmly.

'Jane knew very little about what makes a lady or not a lady,' said Ida, grieved to find a want of elevation in the little man's ideas. 'Some of the truest and noblest ladies have worked hard all their lives.'

'But not with their sleeves tucked up,' argued the boy; 'no lady would do that. Papa told mamma so one day, and *he* must know. He told her she was cook, slush, and bottle-washer. Wasn't that funny? You worked hard too, didn't you, Ida?' interrogated Vernon. 'Papa said you were a regular drudge at Miss Pew's. He said it was a hard thing that such a handsome girl as you should be a drudge, but his poverty and not his will consented.'

'Vernie quotes Shakespeare,' exclaimed Brian, trying to take the thing lightly, but painfully conscious of the head waiter, who was deliberately removing crumbs with a silver scraper. It could not matter to any one what the waiter—a waif from Whitechapel or the Dials most likely—knew or did not know of Mr. and Mrs. Wendover's family affairs; but there is an instinctive feeling that any humiliating details of life should be kept from these menials. They should be maintained in the delusion that the superior class which employs them has never known want or difficulty. Perhaps the maintenance of this great sham is not without its evil, as it is apt to make the waiter class rapacious and exacting, and ready to impute meanness to that superior order which has wallowed in wealth from the cradle.

'Suppose we go to the Tower?' inquired Brian. 'Perhaps Vernie has never seen the Tower?'

Neither Vernon nor Ida had seen that stony page of feudal history, and Vernon had to be informed what manner of building it was, his sole idea of a tower being Babel, which he had often tried to reproduce with his wooden bricks, with no happier result than was obtained in the original attempt. So another Hansom was chartered, and they all went off to the Tower, Vernon sitting between them, perky and loquacious, and intensely curious about every object they passed on their way.

Interested in the associations of the grim old citadel, amused and pleased by little Vernon's prattle as he trotted about holding his sister's hand, Ida forgot to be unhappy upon that particular afternoon. The whole history of her marriage was a misery to her; the marriage itself was a mistake; but there are hours of respite in the saddest life, and she was brave enough to try and make the best of hers. Above all, she was too generous to wish her husband to be painfully conscious of the change in their relative positions, that he was now in a manner dependent upon her father. Her own proud nature, which would have profoundly felt the humiliation of such a position as that which Brian Walford now occupied, was moved to pity for those feelings of shame and degradation which he might or might not experience, and she was kinder to him on this account than she would have been otherwise.

The dinner at the Grosvenor went off with as much appearance of goodwill and proper family feeling as if there had been no flaw in Ida's matrimonial bliss. Sir Reginald was full of kindness for his new son-in-law: as he would have been for any other human creature whom he had asked to dinner. Hospitality was a natural instinct of his being, and he invited Brian Wendover to take up his abode at Wimperfield as easily as he would have offered him a cigar.

'There are no end of rooms. It is a regular barrack,' he said. 'You and Ida can be very comfortable without putting my little woman or me out of the way.'

This had happened just six weeks ago, and now Ida and her half-brother were wandering about among the ferny hollows and breezy heights of the park, or roving off to adjacent heaths and hills, and it seemed almost as if they had lived there all their lives. Vernon had been quick to make himself at home in the stately old house, rummaging and foraging in every room, routing out all manner of forgotten treasures, riding his father's old rocking-horse, exploring stables and lofts, saddle-rooms, and long-disused holes and corners, going up ladders, climbing walls, and endangering life and limbs in every possible way which infantine ingenuity could suggest.

'Mamma, however could we live so long in that horrid little house in France?' he demanded one day, as he prowled about his mother's spacious morning-room in the autumn dusk, dragging fine old folios out of a book shelf in his search for picture-books, while Lady Palliser and her stepdaughter sat at tea by the fire.

The lady of the house gave a faint sigh.

'I don't know, Vernie,' she said. 'I almost think I was happier there than I am here. It was a poor little place, but I felt it was my own house, and I never feel that here.'

'It will be my house when papa's dead,' replied Vernon, cheerfully, seating himself on the ground in front of the broad bay window and turning over Gell's 'Pompeiiana'; 'everything will be mine. Is that why you don't feel as if it was yours now?'

'No, Vernie, that's not it. I hope it will be a great many years before your father is taken away.'

'But you don't think so,' argued Vernon. 'You told him the other day that if he did not walk more, and take less champagne, he would soon kill himself.'

'But I didn't mean it, darling. I only spoke for his good. The doctor says he must take no champagne, or only the dryest of the dry.'

'What a silly that doctor must be!' interrupted Vernon; 'all wine is wet.'

'The doctor meant wine that is not sweet, dear.'

'Then he should have said so,' remarked Vernon, sententiously. He had lived all his little life in grown-up society, and had been allowed to hear everything, and to talk about everything, whereby he had come to consider himself an oracle.

'The doctor thinks your poor papa has a lym—lym—'

'Lymphatic temperament?' suggested Ida.

'Yes, dear, that's the name of his complaint,' replied Lady Palliser, who was not scientific. 'He has a—well, that particular disease,' continued the little woman, breaking down again, 'and he ought to diet himself and take regular exercise; and he won't diet himself, and he won't walk or ride; and I lay awake at nights thinking of it,' she concluded, piteously.

'You can't lay awake,' said the boy; 'Ida says you can't. You can lay down your hat or your umbrella, but *you* can't lay. It's impossible.

'But I tell you I do, Vernie; I lay awake night after night,' protested Lady Palliser, not seeing the grammatical side of the question. 'Oh, Vernie!' as the folio plates gave an alarming crackle, 'you are tearing that beautiful big book which cost your grandfather so much money.'

'It's a nasty book,' said Vernon, 'all houses and posts and things. Show me some nice books, Ida; please, do.'

Ida was sitting on the carpet beside him in the next minute and together they went through a bulky quarto Shakespeare with awe-inspiring illustrations by Fuseli. She told him what the pictures meant, and this naturally compelled her to tell the stories of the plays, and in this manner she kept him amused till it was time to dress for dinner, and almost bedtime for the little man. The happiest hours of her life were those in which she devoted herself mentally and bodily to her young brother. If he had loved her in adversity a year ago, he loved her still better in prosperity, when she was able to do so much more for his comfort and amusement. He was rarely out of her sight, the companion of all her rides and rambles, the exacting charge of her life. Brian Walford was not slow to perceive that the boy took precedence of him in all his wife's thoughts, that the boy's society was more agreeable to her than that of her husband, and his health and happiness of more importance. As a wife she was amiable, submissive, dutiful; but it needed no hypersensitiveness on the husband's part to warn him that she gave him duty without love, submission without reverence or esteem. The consciousness of his wife's indifference made Mr. Wendover less agreeable than he had been during that brief courtship among the willows and rushes by the river. He was inclined to be captious, and did not conceal his jealousy of the boy from Ida, although he set a watch upon his tongue in the presence of Vernon's father and mother.

After all it was a rather pleasant thing to have free quarters at Wimperfield, to have hunters to ride, and covers to shoot over which were almost as much his own as if they had belonged to him. Sir Reginald Palliser had a large way of conferring benefits, which was instinctive in a man of his open and careless temper. Having given Brian Wendover what he called the run of his teeth at Wimperfield, he had no idea of limiting the privileges of residence there. Even when the stud-groom grumbled at the laming of a fine horse by injudicious bucketting up hill and down hill in a lively run with the Petersfield Harriers. Sir Reginald made light of the injury, and sent Pepperbox into the straw-yard to recover at his leisure. His own use of the stable was restricted to an occasional ride on an elderly brown cob, of aristocratic lineage and manners that would have been perfect but for the old-gentleman-like habit of dropping asleep over his work. The new baronet was too lazy to hunt, too liberal to put down the hunting stable established by his predecessor. The horses were there—let Ida and Brian ride them. Of those good things which the blind goddess had flung into his lap nothing was too good for his daughter or his daughter's husband in Sir Reginald's opinion.

Happily for the domestic peace, Lady Palliser was able to get on harmoniously with her stepdaughter's husband, and was not disposed to grudge him the luxuries of Wimperfield.

Brian Walford had been quick to take that good-hearted little woman's intellectual measure. He flattered her small vanities, and made her so pleased with herself that she was naturally pleased with him. His shallow and frivolous nature made him livelier company than a man of profounder thought and deeper feeling. He sang light and lively music from the comic operas of the day, nay, would even stoop to some popular strain from the music-halls. He was clever at all round games and drawing-room amusements. He enlivened conversation with puns, which ranged from the utterly execrable to the tolerably smart. He quoted all the plays and burlesques that had been acted in London during the last five years; he could imitate all the famous actors; and he was a past master of modern slang. There was not much society within an easy drive of Wimperfield, but the few jog-trot county people who dined, or lunched, or afternoon-tea'd with the Pallisers were enlivened by Mr. Wendover's social gifts, and talked of him afterwards as a talented young man.

So far Mr. Wendover had taken the goods the gods provided with a placid acceptance, and had shown no avidity for independence. He was silent as to his professional prospects, although Sir Reginald had told him in the beginning of things that if he wanted to make his way at the Bar any money required for the smoothing of his path should be provided.

'You are too good,' Brian answered lightly; 'but it isn't a question of money—it's a question of time. The Bar is a horribly slow profession. A man has to eat his heart out waiting for briefs.'

'Yes, I have always heard as much,' said Sir Reginald; 'but will it do as well for you to eat your heart out down here as in the Temple? Will the briefs follow you to Wimperfield when the propitious time comes?'

'I believe they are about as likely to find me here as anywhere else,' answered Brian, moodily,—he was apt to turn somewhat sullen at any suggestion of hard work—'and in the meanwhile I am not wasting my time. I can go on writing for the magazines.'

That writing for the magazines was an unknown quantity. The young man occasionally shut himself in a little upstairs study on a wet day, smoked excessively, and was supposed to be writing laboriously, his intellect being fed and sustained by tobacco. Sometimes the result of the day was a fat package of manuscript despatched to the post-office; sometimes there was no result except a few torn sheets of foolscap in the waste-paper basket Sometimes the manuscript came back to the writer after a considerable interval; and at other times Mr. Wendover informed his wife vaguely that 'those fellows' had accepted his contribution. Whatever honorarium he received for his work was expended upon his *menus plaisirs*—or may be said rather to have dribbled from his waistcoat pocket in a series of trivial extravagances which won him a reputation for generosity among grooms and such small deer. To his wife he gave nothing: she was amply provided with money by her father, who would have lavished his newly-acquired wealth upon her if she had been disposed to spend it; but she was not. Her desires were no more extravagant now than when she was receiving ten pounds a quarter from Miss Wendover. Sooth to say, the temptations to extravagance at Wimperfield were not manifold. Ida's only need for money was that she might give it to the poor, and that, according to Jeremy Taylor, is to send one's cash straight to heaven.

The few old-established inhabitants of the neighbourhood, mostly sons of the soil, who attended the village church, were very plain in their raiment, knowing that they occupied a position in the general regard which no finery of velvets or satins could modify. Did not everybody about Wimperfield know everybody else's income, how much or how little the various estates were encumbered, the poverty or richness of the soil, and the rent of every farm upon it? It was only when Lady Pontifex of Heron Court came down from town, bringing gowns and cloaks and bonnets from Regent Street or the Rue de la Paix, that a transitory flash of splendour lighted up the shadowy old nave with the glow of newly-invented hues and the sheen of newly-woven fabrics. But the natives only gazed and admired. There was nobody adventurous enough to imitate the audacities of a lady of fashion. Miss Emery, of Petersfield, was quite good enough for the landed gentry of this quiet region. She had the fashions direct from Paris in the gaily-coloured engravings of *Le Follet*, and what could anyone want more fashionable than Paris fashions? True that Miss Emery's conscientious cutting and excellent workmanship imparted a certain heaviness to Parisian designs; but who would care to have a gown blown together, as it were, by girls who were not allowed to sit down at their work?

The life at Wimperfield was a pleasant life, albeit exceedingly quiet. There were times when Brian Walford felt the dulness of this rustic existence somewhat oppressive; but if life indoors was monotonous and uneventful, he had a good deal of amusement out of doors—hunting, shooting, football, and an occasional steeple-chase within a day's drive. And a grand point was that nobody asked him to work hard. He could make a great show of industry with books and foolscap, and nobody pryed too closely into the result.

CHAPTER XXII
LADY PALLISER STUDIES THE UPPER TEN

Ida was not left long in ignorance as to the friendly feelings of those she had left behind at Kingthorpe. Bessie's first letter reached her within a few days of her arrival at Wimperfield—a loving little letter, full of sorrowful expressions about the two good young fellows who were gone, yet not concealing the writer's pleasure at her friend's elevation.

'When are we to meet again, dearest?' asked Bessie, after she had given full expression to her feelings; 'are you to come to us, or are we to go to you? What is the etiquette of the situation? Father and mother know nothing about outside points of etiquette. Beyond the common rules of dinners and calls, calls and dinners, I believe they are in benighted ignorance. Shall we tell John Coachman to put four horses to the landau—with himself and the under-gardener as postilions—and post over to Wimperfield—just as they pay visits in Miss Austin's novels? Perhaps now we have gone back to Chippendale furniture, we shall return to muslin frocks and the manners of Miss Austin's time. I'm sure I wish we could. Life seems to have been so much simpler in her day, and so much cheaper. Darling, I am longing to see you. Remember you are my cousin now—my very own near relation. It was Fate, you see, that made me so fond of you, from that first evening when you helped me so kindly with my German exercise.'

There was also a letter from Aunt Betsy, quite as affectionate, but in much fewer words, and more to the purpose.

'We shall drive over to see your father and mother as soon as we hear that they are disposed to receive visitors,' said Miss Wendover in conclusion.

'I wonder Miss Wendover did not say Sir Reginald and Lady Palliser,' observed Ida's stepmother, when she had read this letter.

The little woman had been devoting herself very earnestly to the perusal of books of etiquette—'The Upper Circles,' 'What is What,' 'The Crème de la Crème,' and works of a corresponding order, and was now much more learned in the infinitesimals of polite life than was Sir Reginald or his daughter. She had a profound belief in the mysterious authors of these interesting volumes.

'The "Crême de la Crême" must be right, you know, Ida,' she said, when some dictum was disputed, 'for the book was written by a Countess.'

'A Countess who wears a shoddy tourist suit, and smokes shag, and sleeps in a two pair back in Camden Town, most likely,' said Sir Reginald, laughing.

The new baronet utterly refused to be governed by the hard and fast rules of the 'Crême de la Crême.' He daily did things which were absolute and awful heresies in the sight of that authority, and Lady Palliser was sorely exercised at her very first dinner-party by seeing the county people of Wimperfield setting at naught the precepts of the anonymous Countess at every stage of the evening. They did those things which they ought not to have done, and they left undone those things which they ought to have done, and, from the Countess's point of view were utterly without manners.

But although Lady Palliser thought Miss Wendover's letter deficient in ceremony, she was not the less ready to welcome Ida's Kingthorpe friends; so a hearty invitation to dine and stay the night was sent to the Colonel and his wife, to Aunt Betsy, and as many of the junior members of the family as the biggest available carriage would hold.

It was the beginning of November when this visit occurred, but the foliage was still green on the elm tree tops, while many a lovely tint of yellow and brown still glowed on the woodland. The weather was balmy, sunshiny, the sky as blue as at midsummer; and Ida, with her face as radiant as the sunlight, stood in the porch ready to welcome her friends when the wagonette drove up.

'Oh! but where are Blanche and Eva? and why did not the boys come?' she inquired, when she had shaken hands with the Colonel, and had been kissed and embraced by Mrs. Wendover, Aunt Betsy, and Bessie: 'surely they are coming too?'

'No, dear; I think we are quite a strong enough party as it is,' answered Mrs. Wendover.

'Not half strong enough! you have no idea what a barrack Wimperfield is—but Bessie knows, and ought to have told you. There are two-and-twenty bedrooms. It would have been a charity to have filled some of them. I am dreadfully disappointed!'

'Never mind, dear, you will see enough of them, depend upon it. But where is Brian?'

'Oh! it is one of his harrier days. He left all sorts of apologies for not being at home to receive you. He will be home before dinner. Here is mamma,' as

Lady Palliser came sailing out, in a forty-guinea gown from Jay, all glitter of bugles, and sheen of satin, putting Mrs. Wendover's homespun travelling dress to shame. There was a dinner-gown with the luggage, but a gown which, in comparison with Lady Palliser's satin and jet, would be like the cloudy countenance of Luna on a November night, as compared with the glory of Sol on a midsummer morning. But then, happily, Mrs. Wendover was not the kind of person to suffer at being worse dressed than her hostess. Lady Palliser sank in a low curtsey when Ida murmured a rather vague presentation, and again beheld the Countess's eternal laws violated by her guests, for the Colonel and his wife shook hands with a vigour which in the 'Crème de la Crème' was stigmatised as a barbarous vulgarity; while Aunt Betsy was so taken up with Ida that, after a smile and a nod, she actually turned her back upon the lady of the house.

'My poor child, how horridly ill you are looking,' Miss Wendover exclaimed, holding Ida by both hands and looking searchingly into her face. 'Prosperity has not agreed with you. I can see the traces of sleepless nights under your eyes.'

'It was such a shock,' murmured Ida.

'Yes, it was a terrible shock. Those fine frank young fellows! It was ever so long before I could get the images of them out of my mind. And I could not help feeling very sorry for them, in spite of your good fortune—'

'Don't call it my good fortune,' said Ida; 'I am glad my father is better off; but I was happier when I was poor.'

'And yet you used to say such bitter things about poverty?'

'Yes, I was a worshipper of Mammon in those days; but now I have got inside the temple and have found out that he is a false god.'

'He is not a god, but a devil. "The least erected spirit that fell from heaven." My poor Ida! And so you have found out that there are dust and ashes inside golden apples! Never mind; you will learn to enjoy the privileges and comforts of wealth better when you are better used to being rich. And in the meantime tell me that you are happy in your married life, that you and Brian are getting on pleasantly together.'

'We never quarrel,' said Ida, looking downward.

'Oh, that is a bad sign. Tell me something better than that.'

'You all told me that it was my duty to live with my husband. I am trying to do my duty,' Ida answered gravely.

There was no radiance upon her face now. All the happiness—the unselfish delight of welcoming her friends—had faded, and left her pale and despondent.

She threw off all gloomy thoughts presently, and was running about the house, showing her friends their rooms, giving directions to servants, making a good deal more fuss, and making more use of her own hands, than the author of 'La Crême de la Crême' would have tolerated.

'A lady's hands,' said that exalted personage, 'are not for use, but for ornament. Her first object should be to preserve their delicacy of form and colour; her second to be always *bien gantée*. She should never lift anything heavier than her teacup; and she should rather endure some inconvenience from cold while waiting the attendance of her footman than she should so far derogate from feminine dignity as to put on a shovel of coals. The rule of her life should be to do nothing which her domestics or her *dame de compagnie* can do for her.'

'My dearest Ida,' remonstrated Lady Palliser, remembering this classic passage, 'what do you mean by carrying that bag?' Are there no servants in the house?'

'Half-a-dozen too many, mamma; but I like to do something with my own hands for those I love.'

Lady Palliser sighed, recalling the days when she had cooked her husband's breakfasts and dinners, and had been happier—so it seemed to her now—in performing that domestic duty than in giving orders to a housekeeper of whom she stood in awe. But Fanny Palliser had made up her mind that she ought to become a fine lady, in order to do credit to her husband's altered fortunes, and she was working assiduously with that intent.

The guests had arrived in time for luncheon, and after luncheon Lady Palliser and the three elders went for a long drive in the landau, to explore the best points in the surrounding scenery, while Ida and Bessie, with Vernon in their company, started for a long ramble in the Park and woods. The boy ran about hither and thither, flitting from bank to bank, in quest of flowers or insects, curious about everything in nature, vivid as a flash in all his movements. Thus the two girls were left very much to themselves, and were able to talk as they liked, only occasionally giving their attention to some newly-discovered wonder of Vernon's, a tadpole in the act of shedding his horny beak, or some gigantic development of the genus toadstool, which species was just then in full season.

At first there was a shadow of constraint upon Bessie's manner; and in one whose nature was so frank, the faintest touch of reserve was painfully obvious. For a little while all her talk was of Wimperfield and its beauties.

'And to think that my dear old pet should be a leading member of our county families!' she exclaimed; 'it is too delightful.'

'Indeed, Bess, I am nothing of the kind. I am a very insignificant person—nothing but my father's daughter. Brian and I are only here on sufferance.'

'Oh, that's nonsense, dear. I heard Sir Reginald tell my father that Wimperfield was to be your home and Brian's as long as ever you both like—as long as your father lives, in fact. Brian can have his chambers in town, and work at his profession, but you are to live at Wimperfield.'

'That can hardly be,' answered Ida, gloomily; 'when Brian goes to London, I must go with him. It will be my duty, you know,' with a shade of bitterness.

'Well, then, this will be your country house—and that will be ever so much better; for after all, you know, however delightful the country may be, it is rather like being buried alive to live in it all the year round. I suppose Brian will soon begin to work at his profession—to read law books, and wait for briefs, don't you know.'

'I hope so,' answered Ida, coldly; 'but I do not think your cousin is very fond of hard work.'

'Oh, but he must work—manhood demands it. He cannot possibly go on sponging upon your father for ever.'

'There is no question of sponging. Brian is welcome here, as you have heard. Lady Palliser likes him very much, and we all get on very well together.'

'But you would like your husband to work, wouldn't you, Ida?'

'I should like him to be a man,' answered Ida, curtly.

In all this time there had been no mention of that other Brian—the owner of Wendover Abbey. No word of congratulation had come to Ida from him upon the change in her fortunes; nor had her husband told her of any communication from his cousin. She concluded, therefore, that Brian the elder had made no sign. It might be that he had dismissed her from his mind as unworthy of further thought or care. He had discovered her falsehood, her worthlessness, and she was no longer the woman he had once loved and honoured. She had passed out of his life, like an evil dream which he had dreamed and forgotten.

His voice had been silent when those other voices—the Colonel's and the Curate's—had told her that it was her duty to fulfil the vow she had vowed before God's altar: to share her husband's fate for good or ill. Brian, her lover of a few minutes before, had held his peace. What had he thought of her in those bitter moments? Had there been one touch of pity mingled with his scorn? She could not tell. He had made no sign.

From the moment of her friend's arrival she had tremulously expected some mention of Mr. Wendover's name; but that name had not been spoken. The silence was a relief: and yet she yearned to know something more: whether he had spoken of her with friendly feeling, whether he thought of her with compassion.

Not for worlds would she have questioned Bessie upon this subject: not even Bessie, whose childish love so invited confidence, before whose tender eyes she could never feel ashamed.

After that little talk about Brian Walford there followed a good deal of talk about Mr. Jardine. He was promised a living, not a big benefice by any means, but still an actual living and an actual Vicarage, in the vicinity of Salisbury Plain; and he and Bessie were to be married early in the following year, as soon as there were enough spring flowers to decorate Kingthorpe Church, the Colonel had said.

'It is to be in the time of daffodils, just before Lent,' said Bess; 'Easter comes late next year, you know.'

'I don't know; but no doubt you have found out all about it,' Ida answered, laughing. 'God bless you, dear, and make your wedded life one long honeymoon!'

'I have seen marriages like that,' said Bess. 'Father and mother, for instance. They are always spooning. Oh, Ida! doesn't it seem dreadfully soon to be married?'

'There is plenty of time for reflection,' answered Ida, with a sigh.

Bessie remembered how sudden a thing matrimony had been in her friend's case.

'Ah, darling, I know what you are thinking about,' she said tenderly. 'You married on the spur of the moment, and were just a little sorry afterwards; but I have been so fenced and guarded by parental wisdom that I could not do anything foolish—if I tried ever so. And then John is far too wise to propose anything wild or romantic—yet I think if he had come to me and said, "There is a dog-cart at the gate, let us drive over to Romsey Church and be married," I should hardly have known how to say no. But, Ida, dear, tell me that your hasty marriage has turned out a happy one after all. Brian is so very nice. Confess now that you are happy with him!'

Bessie had intended scrupulously to avoid any such home question; but her feelings carried her away directly she began to talk of John Jardine.

'I cannot tell you a lie. Bessie; no, my life is not a happy one. All colour and brightness, all youthfulness and fervour, went out of me when I left Kingthorpe; but it is an endurable life, and I make the best of it.'

'Brian is not unkind to you, I hope?' cried Bessie, prepared to be indignant.

'No, he is not unkind. I have no complaint to make against him.'

'But surely he is nice,' argued Bessie; 'I have always thought him one of the nicest young men I know. He has very good manners, he knows a good deal, can talk of almost any subject, and he is full of life and spirits, when he wants to be amusing.'

'I have no doubt he is a very agreeable person,' answered Ida, gloomily. 'I have never disputed that. And yet our marriage was a mistake, all the same.'

'But when you married him, surely then you must have cared for him, just a little?'

'I thought I did. It was the glamour of his imaginary wealth. It was the worship of the golden calf, exemplified in one of its vilest phases, a mercenary marriage.'

'Do not lower yourself too much, dearest,' pleaded Bessie hugging her friend's arm affectionately, as they tramped across the withered bracken.' You are too good to have been governed by any sordid feeling. The delusion must have gone deeper?'

'It did. I married in a rhapsody of gratitude, thinking that I had found a modern Cophetua. Say no more about it, Bess, if you love me!'

'I will never say another word, dear,' sighed Bess; 'but I do wish you had been single when you met the other Brian, for I know he was more than half in love with you. And now he is going off to the other end of the world again, and goodness knows if he will ever come back.'

The upper tracts of heaven were beginning to grow gray, the sun was sinking in a bed of red and gold behind a clump of oaks on the edge of the horizon—the dark and delicate outline of leafless branches distinctly marked against that yellow light. Wimperfield Park was almost at its best upon such an afternoon as this, the turf soft and springy after autumnal rains, the atmosphere tranquil and balmy, and all animal creation—deer, oxen, rabbits, feathered game, and an innumerable army of rooks—full of life and motion. Ida was slow to reply to Bessie's news about her cousin. The two girls walked on in silence for a little way, Vernon running ever so far ahead of them to look for fallen nuts in a grove of fine old Spanish chestnuts, which stood boldly out on the top of a hill.

'Don't you feel sorry that he is going away?' asked Bessie at last; 'just as he had established himself among us, and begun all kinds of improvement at the Abbey farm, and was even thinking of building new schools.'

'It is a pity,' said Ida.

'It is simply horrid. He is quite as bad as those Irish Absentees who are continually getting murdered; or he would be as bad, if he had not arranged with my father for the carrying on of all his plans while he is away.'

'That is very good of him.'

'Good, yes; but it will be a dreadful responsibility for poor father, and I daresay we shall all be worried about it. He will have builders on the brain till the work is finished. My poor John has promised to look after the schools; and he is so conscientious that he will wear himself to a shadow rather than neglect the smallest detail.'

'But are you not pleased that he can be of so much use?'

'I am obliged to be pleased. I am going to be a clergyman's wife; and I must teach myself to look at everything from the parochial point of view. John and I will not belong to ourselves, but to our parish. Our own pleasure, our own health, our own interests, must be as nothing to us. We must only exist as machines for the maintenance of the proper church services and for the relief of the sick and poor.'

'If you think it too hard a life, dear, there is time for you to draw back!'

'Oh, Ida, do you think I am like Lot's wife, regretting the false frivolous world I am going to renounce? What life could be too hard shared with *him?*'

'God bless you, dear. I believe your life will be a very happy one,' said Ida, earnestly, and with a touch of melancholy. There was so much that was enviable in Bessie's fate. Then, after a pause, she said hesitatingly, 'Do you know why your cousin is going to leave England?'

'No; I know no reason except his natural restlessness. He is a member of the Geographical, you know, and attends all their meetings. The other day he went up to hear some old fellow prose about the regions north of Afghanistan, and he was so interested that he made arrangements at once for an exploration on his own account. And I daresay he will get killed by some savage tribe, or die of fever.'

'He is not going alone, I hope?'

'No, he has a friend almost as mad as himself, and they are going together. That will mean two for the savages to kill instead of one; and I suppose they will have an interpreter and two or three servants, which will be a few more for the savages.'

'Let us hope they will not go into really dangerous places. There must be so much for a traveller to see in India, without running any great risks,' said Ida, affecting a cheerful tone.

'But you know English travellers love to run risks. It is their only idea of enjoyment. A man like Brian is told of some mountain or some settlement where no Englishman has ever set his foot before, and he says, "That is the very place for me," and the experiment naturally results in his getting murdered.' They had finished their ramble, and were in front of the portico by this time.

'Oh, Bessie!' said Ida, with a stifled sob, 'life is full of sad changes. Do you remember that summer afternoon, three mouths ago, when Vernon and Peter stood on those steps bidding us good-bye, as we drove away with your cousin? and now those two are lying at the bottom of the sea, and he is going to the other end of the world.'

The Wendover visit was altogether a success. There was something so conciliating, so sympathetic, so entirely comfortable in Mrs. Wendover's nature and outward characteristics, that Lady Palliser felt almost immediately at her ease with her, and forgot her newly-acquired manners, becoming a good deal more ladylike in consequence; since the strict and stern system of etiquette, formulated in the 'Crême de la Crême,' did not lie conformably to the original formation of the little woman's disposition. To be free and easy, loquacious, fussy, and kind was Fanny Palliser's nature, and she became odious when she tried to restrain those simple impulses by the armour of formal manners.

'I never had a lady friend I liked better than Mrs. Wendover,' she told Ida, in confidence, on the second day of the visit.

Fanny Palliser was not quite so much at ease with Aunt Betsy. She had an idea that the spinster was satirical, and was inwardly critical of her shortcomings. She was impressed by the wide extent of Aunt Betsy's information, most especially when that lady talked politics with Sir Reginald, and contrived to hem him into corners whence there was no logical thoroughfare. Aunt Betsy was Liberal to the verge of Radicalism; Sir Reginald a Tory of the good old pig-headed type, who looked upon all advance movements as revolutionary, and thought that his own party had gone mad.

'I don't like strong-minded women,' Lady Palliser told Ida when the guests had left. 'I have no doubt Miss Wendover is very kind-hearted and generous—I'm sure her kindness to you was wonderful—but she is not *my* idea of a lady. That brocade dinner-gown was lovely, and fitted her like a glove; but the way she put her elbows on the table when she talked to Sir Reginald at dessert—well, I never did!'

Brian Walford had made himself particularly agreeable during the brief visit of his kindred—agreeable to both sides of the house. It was his desire to stand well with both. He wanted his uncle and aunts to see that he was thought much of at Wimperfield—that he was a valued member of the household, respected and liked by his wife's family, that he had done well for himself by his marriage, and that whatever cloud had overshadowed the opening of his wedded life had vanished altogether from his horizon. People so soon forgive and forget a little wrong-doing if the sinner comes comfortably out of his difficulties, and becomes a prosperous member of society. The Colonel and his wife, who had always liked Ida, liked her all the better now that they saw her established in a stately home—the only daughter of a man of fortune and position.

On the morning of her departure, Miss Wendover contrived to have a *tête-à-tête* with Sir Reginald; in the course of which she informed him that she meant to leave half her money to her niece Bessie, and the other half to her nephew—Brian Walford.

'The land, of course, will go to Brian of the Abbey,' she said. 'We Wendovers can't afford to divide the soil. Our chances of doing good in the land depend upon our having a large interest in the neighbourhood.'

'Why, Miss Wendover, I thought you were a Radical!' exclaimed Sir Reginald.

'So I am in many of my ideas, but not for cutting up the land into little bits, to pass from hand to hand like a ten-pound note, until there should not be an estate left in England with a long family history, nor a rich man left in the rural districts to take care of the poor. England would be badly off without her squirearchy.'

Sir Reginald and Miss Wendover were thoroughly agreed upon this point. He thanked her for her generous intentions towards her nephew; and he told her that he meant to provide fairly for his daughter. 'The entail expires in my person,' he said; 'I can do what I like for my girl. Of course the whole of the estate will go to Vernon. He is the last of his race, and I hope I may live to see him married, and the father of sons to inherit his name. It is a hard thing to think that a good old name must perish off the face of the land. However, I am free to make my will as I like, and I shall leave Ida six or seven hundred a year. She and Brian ought to get on very well with that, and his profession. I should like to see him a little more energetic—a little fonder of hard work,' pursued Sir Reginald, with a sigh, conscious of having never felt a strong inclination that way on his own part; 'but I suppose all young men are idle.'

'No, they are not,' retorted Aunt Betsy, sharply. 'There are workers and idlers in all families—men born to honour or to dishonour—races apart—like the drones and the working bees. Look at my other nephew, for example—a man who has seven thousand a year, and not a creature to gainsay him if he chose to dissipate his days and nights on worldly pleasures. He is your true type of worker—a fine Greek scholar—a naturalist, a traveller, a thorough sportsman, where sport means courage, adventure, intelligence, endurance. Fortune made him a rich man, but he has made himself a man of mark in every circle in which he has ever lived, and I am proud to own him for my own flesh and blood. Nature gave Brian Walford many gifts, and what has he done for himself? Learnt to dress as foplings dress, and to think as foplings think!'

'He is a very nice young fellow!' said Sir Reginald kindly; 'we are all fond of him; only we think—for his own sake—it would be better if he took life more seriously.'

'He must be made to take life seriously,' replied the spinster sternly. 'Yes, he is very nice—that is the worst of it; if he were nasty no one would tolerate him. I'm afraid his good qualities will be his ruin.' And thus, promising good things, yet prophesying evil, Miss Wendover left Wimperfield. Ida was to go and stay with her later on at the Homestead, when Brian Walford should be reading law in those new Chambers which he often talked about. There were times when to hear him talk people thought him a youth gnawed and consumed by ambition, only panting for the opportunity to work.

Two days after the Wendovers had gone back, Brian showed his wife a letter from his cousin, Brian of the Abbey.

'I am leaving England for a longer period than usual, and going farther afield,' wrote the master of Wendover Abbey; 'so before starting I feel myself bound to do something definite for you.'

'He has helped me with odd sums now and then, I suppose you know?' said Brian, as Ida read this passage.

'I did not know,' she answered coldly; 'but I am not surprised to hear that he has been generous to you.'

'No, he is your paragon—your preux chevalier—is he not?' sneered Brian. 'Bessie told me as much.'

'She told you only the truth. No one who lives at Kingthorpe can help knowing that your cousin is a good man.'

She went on with the letter.

'Now you are married the claims upon you will be larger than they have been, and I know you will not care to be a pensioner upon your father-in-law's bounty. I have, therefore, arranged with my bankers that you should draw on me quarterly for a hundred and fifty pounds while I am away. This will help you to keep the wolf from the door while you are reading for the Bar. I hope to find you a successful junior, in the first stage of a prosperous journey to the Bench, when I come back.'

'Six hundred a year. Not half bad, is it, Ida?'

'It is very good of him. I hope you will do as he suggests.'

'How do you mean?'

'Work hard at your profession.'

'I shall work hard enough,' answered Brian, turning sullen, 'unless you all badger me. I hate being badgered.'

CHAPTER XXIII
'ALL OUR LIFE IS MIXED WITH DEATH'

Four years and more had gone, and there were changes at Wimperfield—changes at Kingthorpe. Death had come to the Georgian mansion among the wood-crowned hills. The easy-going master of that good old house had taken life a little too easily, had disregarded the warnings of wife and doctor, had dined and slept, and drunk his favourite wines—not immoderately, but with utter disregard of medical regimen—had neither walked, nor ridden, but had let life slip by him in a placid, plethoric self-indulgence—shunning all exertion, all pleasure even, if it were allied with activity of any kind. So, in an existence almost as sleepy as the spell-bound slumber in Beauty's enchanted palace, Ida's father had left the door of his mansion ajar to the fell visitor Death, and the fatal day had come suddenly, with no more warning than Sir Reginald heard Sunday after Sunday in church, or read any evening in his favourite Horace, as he turned the carmine-bordered leaves of one of Firmin Didot's exquisite duodecimos, and mused pleasantly over the poet's perpetual variations upon the old theme—

'Brother, we must all die.'

The guest came like a thief in the night, and snatched his prey, in the midst of the family circle, in the leisurely lamplit hour after dinner, with the sound of gay voices and light laughter in the air. The senseless body breathed and throbbed for another day and another light: and then all was over—and Ida and her stepmother knelt side by side, clasped in each other's arms, by the clay which both had fondly loved.

They were alone in their sorrow. Brian was in London. Vernon was with Mr. and Mrs. Jardine, at their parsonage on Salisbury Plain, being prepared for Eton. The two women grieved together in a mournful solitude for the first day on which the house was darkened, and the presence of death was palpable in their midst.

Brian hurried down to Wimperfield directly the news reached him. He was agitated by the event, which had happened without any note of warning. He was not given to forecasting the future, and it had seemed to him that life at Wimperfield was to go on for ever in the same groove—immutable as the course of the planets; that he was always to have a luxurious home there—a fine stable—an indulgent father-in-law. He had been really fond of Sir Reginald, after his manner, and his sudden death shocked and grieved him. And then it gave a shade of uncertainty to his own future. He did not know how the estate might be left—how tied up and hedged round by executors and trustees, shutting him out of his present almost proprietorial enjoyment of the place. Some smug London lawyer, perhaps, would put his sleek paw upon everything during the boy's minority. Sir Reginald had never talked to Brian of his will.

The smug town lawyer came down, but not to impound Wimperfield— only to read the late baronet's will, which was entirely in harmony with the dead man's easy and generous temper.

He left his widow an annuity of fifteen hundred pounds, and the privilege of occupying Wimperfield until his son should come of age, and on leaving Wimperfield she was to receive the sum of two thousand pounds, to enable her to furnish any house she might choose to rent for herself. To his daughter he left any two horses she might select from the existing stud, and seven hundred a year in the Three per Cents, the principal to be divided among her children, if of age at the date of her death, or to be held in trust for them if under age. In the event of Vernon dying unmarried, Ida was to inherit everything; in the event of his marrying but having no children, his widow was to take the same annuity as that bequeathed to Lady Palliser, and the estate was to go to Ida, with reversion to her eldest son, or, in the event of no son, to her eldest daughter, whose husband was to take the name of Palliser. In this manner had short-lived man endeavoured to make his name live after him.

Ida and her stepmother were left joint guardians of the boy, Vernon.

To Brian Walford Wendover, Sir Reginald bequeathed only his favourite hunter, a leash of chumber spaniels, and fifty pounds for a memorial ring. Mr. Wendover could not find fault with a will which left his wife seven hundred a year; but he felt that his position was diminished by his father-in-law's death, and he was morbidly jealous of the boy, who had absorbed so much of his wife's care and affection from the first hour of their coming to Wimperfield.

'I suppose we are to turn out now,' he said to Ida the night after the funeral, when they two were slowly and sadly pacing the terrace, in front of the drawing-room windows. It was the beginning of December—bleak, cheerless weather—and the woods looked black against a dull gray sky. There was only one feeble streak of pale yellow light in the west yonder, behind gaunt patriarchal oaks.

'Your father's will is a very handsome will,' continued Brian, 'but it leaves no provision for our living on here, and I suppose we shall have to clear out.'

'Leave Wimperfield! Oh, no, I'm sure Lady Palliser has no idea of such a thing. Leave Wimperfield, and Vernon? He has a double claim upon me now, my fatherless darling.'

'Of course, Vernon is your first thought,' sneered Brian. 'But wouldn't it be just as well to think of ways and means! Who is to keep up Wimperfield? Lady Palliser, on her fifteen hundred a year; or you, on your seven hundred?'

'I can help mamma. She can have all my income, except just enough to buy my clothes; and my father gave me gowns enough to last for the next five years. But I heard the lawyer say that the place would be kept up for Vernie. Lady Palliser would hardly have any occasion to spend her income, except in paying for actual personal expenses, her own servants, and so on.'

'Good for Lady Palliser; but that doesn't make our position any more secure, if she should want to get rid of us?'

'I'm sure she will want us to stay. You ought to know her better than to suggest such a thing. You must know her affectionate nature, and how fond she is of us both.'

'I never presume to *know* anything of any woman. She seems to like us; but who can tell what may lurk under that seeming. She may marry again, and want to make a clean sweep of old associations.'

'Mamma! How can you think of such a horrid thing? No, she is as true as steel; she has been a good and loyal wife to my father.'

'That doesn't prevent her being good and loyal to a second husband; nay, her very virtues—affectionateness, a soft clinging nature—point to the probability of a second marriage. It is just such women who fall into the adventurer's trap. However, we won't quarrel about her, and so long as she is cordial, and likes to have us here, Wimperfield can be our country house.'

This was a somewhat loose way of speaking, for Wimperfield had been Ida's only house during her married life. Brian had his chambers in the Temple at a rent of a hundred and twenty-five pounds a year, his sitting-room furnished with none of that Spartan ruggedness which so well became George Warrington, of Pump Court, but in the willow-pattern and peacock-feather style of art; the dingy old walls glorified by fine photographs of Gerôme's Roman Gladiators, Phryne before her judges, Socrates searching for Alcibiades at the house of Aspasia, and enlarged carbonized portraits of the reigning beauties in London society. But these chambers, though supposed to be devoted to days of patient work and much consumption of midnight oil, had served chiefly as a basis for late breakfasts, club-dinners, and theatre-going, while the midnight oil had been mostly associated with lobster salad at snug little suppers after the play. Ida had never been at these chambers, although she had been invited there frequently during the first few months of her husband's tenancy. As time went by Mr. Wendover found it was more convenient that his town and country residences should be completely distinct; and it had gradually become an accepted fact at Wimperfield that Temple Chambers were a kind of habitation which a man's wife could hardly visit without violating the first principles of legal etiquette.

Brian Walford was speedily reassured as to his position at Wimperfield. Lady Palliser clung to her stepdaughter in her widowhood with a still warmer affection than she had shown during her husband's lifetime. Ida was her adviser, her strong rock, her resource in all difficulties and perplexities, social or domestic. Nor would she allow her stepdaughter or her stepdaughter's husband to share the expenses of housekeeping at Wimperfield. The allowance for the young baronet's maintenance during his minority was large enough to cover all expenses of the very quiet household, likely to be even more quiet now that Sir Reginald Palliser, a man of particularly social habits, was gone.

Lady Palliser had never been able to feel thoroughly at home among the county people. Their language was not her language, nor their habits her habits. She could have got on ever so much better with them had they been less homely and free and easy in their ways. She had schooled herself in a politeness of line and rule, had learnt good manners by rote; and to find all her theories continually ignored or traversed was a perplexity and a trouble to her. If the county people had only treated her with the rigid stiffness enjoined in a three-and-sixpenny manual, she could have met them upon equal ground. She could have remembered the social laws made and provided for her guidance as guest or hostess—how to enter and leave a room, in what attitude to stand or sit, with the fitting use of every item of table furniture, from the fish knife and fork to the salver of rose water. But when she beheld the county people doing outrageous things with their legs, and altogether heterodox in their way of eating and drinking, when she heard them talk very much as the 'lady friends' of her girlhood had talked over their washtubs, or kitchen ranges, yet with an indescribable difference, and never by any chance realising her own innate ideas of company manners, Lady Palliser felt herself more and more at sea in this new world of hers. Thus it was that she fell into the way of letting Ida manage everything for her, and of meekly accepting such friends as Ida brought round her, and making much of those mothers whose boys were of an age to be play-fellows for her own beloved son.

And now the master of the house, the central figure in the family picture, was gone, and the two women had to face life for the most part alone. Brian had grown fonder of London lately. He had held a few briefs during the last twelve months and could plead business in the metropolitan law-courts as a reason for being very little at Wimperfield out of the hunting season. The boy was with the Jardines at Hopsley Vicarage, except during the happy interval of holidays. He was always glad to come home, but he was generally tired of home before the holiday was over, and went back to the Jardines with a keen delight which made his mother's heart ache.

Ida's character had ripened and strengthened in the years which were gone, years of quiet, submissive performance of duty. She had been a fond and obedient daughter, an almost adoring sister, a good and faithful wife. If she had not given her husband the love he had hoped to inspire, she had been more considerate, more sympathetic than many a wife who has married for love. She had never wounded him by hard words, had never exacted sacrifices from him, never pursued her own pleasure when it was at variance with his. She had long ago gauged his shallow nature—she knew but too well that he was a reed, and not a rock, and that in all the trials of life she would have to stand alone; but if she sometimes inwardly scorned him, she never betrayed her scorn, either to him or to the world after she had once made up her mind as to the nature of the bond between them, and the duties attached to that bond. With ripening years and growing wisdom she had atoned nobly for the errors of impulse and reckless anger.

Brian knew that she was good and loyal; but although he admired and respected her, he could not forgive her for that innate superiority which made him all the more conscious of his own shortcomings, for that growing strength of character which accentuated his own weakness. When the charm of novelty had departed, when the triumph of having won her in spite of herself was over, Brian Walford's love for his beautiful wife wore to a very thin thread. The tie was not broken, but it was sorely attenuated. He had never ceased to be jealous of the brother whom she loved so much more fondly than she had ever loved, or even pretended to love, her husband; but he had left off expressing that jealousy in open unbraiding. Once he had been in the habit of saying, 'You will have a boy of your own some day, and then Master Vernie will be nowhere;' but that hoped-for son had never come, and Vernon was still all in all to his sister. Brian knew that it was so, and submitted to his lot in sullen acquiescence. After all, his marriage had brought him much that was good—had smoothed his pathway in life;

and if—if, by-and-by, some such fatality as that which had cleared the way for Reginald Palliser, should clear the way for Ida, his wife would be the owner of one of the finest estates in Sussex. He wished no evil to the young baronet, he bore no grudge against him for Ida's idiotic fondness; but the fact remained that the boy's death would make Brian Walford Wendover's wife a rich woman. It is not in the nature of a man living among sharp-witted lawyers and men about town to ignore a fact of this kind. His friends had talked to him about it after the publication of Sir Reginald Palliser's will.

'A fine thing for you if that young gentleman were to go off the hooks,' said they; but Brian protested that he had no desire for such promotion. He was fond of the boy, and was very well satisfied with his own position.

'I daresay you do like the little beggar,' answered his particular friend, who was loafing away the earlier half of the afternoon in Mr. Wendover's chambers, smoking Mr. Wendover's cigarette, and sipping Mr. Wendover's Apollinaris slightly coloured with brandy—a very modest form of entertainment surely, and yet the cigarettes and the superfine cognac, which were always on tap in Elm Court, made no small appearance in the accounts of tobacconist and wine merchant. 'You would be sorry if anything were to happen to him, no doubt; just as I shall be sorry when the governor bursts up—poor old fellow! But I know I want his money very badly; and I think you could spend a good deal more than your present income.'

Brian admitted with a light laugh that his capacity for expenditure was considerably in excess of his resources.

'You know how quietly I live,' he began.

'Comme çi, comme ça,' muttered his friend.

'And yet even now I am in debt.'

'And have been ever since I first knew you, and would be if you had fifty thousand a year!'

'Oh, that's inevitable,' said Brian. 'A man with an income of that kind must always be in debt. He never can know when he comes to the boundary line. When a man starts in life by believing he is enormously rich, and can have everything he wants, he is pretty sure to go to the dogs. That's the way the sons of millionaires so often drift towards the gutter.'

CHAPTER XXIV
'FRUITS FAIL AND LOVE DIES
AND TIME RANGES'

Brian found Wimperfield duller as a place of residence after Sir Reginald's death; or it may be that he found London gayer, and his professional duties more absorbing. It was not often that his wife and mother-in-law were gratified by any public notification of his engagements; but now and then the name of Mr. Wendover appeared as junior counsel in some insignificant case, and Lady Palliser, who read the *Times* and *Post*, diligently apprised Ida of the fact.

'You see Brian is getting on quite nicely,' she said approvingly, 'and by-and-by when he has plenty of work, you will have a small house in town, I suppose—somewhere about Belgravia—and only come to Wimperfield for your holidays.'

Fanny Palliser had never left off compassionating Ida for her frequent separation from her husband. She had never divined that Ida was happier in Brian's absence than when he was with her. The wife had so borne herself that her husband should not be put to shame by her indifference. She lived the larger half of her life apart from him; but Lady Palliser and her gossips believed that in so doing the young couple sacrificed inclination to prudence. So soon as they could afford to maintain a town house they would have one.

It was midsummer weather, and the rose garden at Wimperfield, that garden which had been Ida's own peculiar care for the last four years, the garden which she had improved and beautified with every art learned from that ardent rose-worshipper Aunt Betsy, was glorious with its first blooms. Sir Reginald Palliser had been dead a year and a half, but Ida still wore black gowns, and the widow had in no wise mitigated the severity of her weeds. The two women had lived peaceably and affectionately together ever since the baronet's death, leading a quiet but not unhappy life, the placid monotony of their existence agreeably varied by frequent intercourse with the family at Kingthorpe.

The only changes at The Knoll were of a gentle domestic character. No cloud of trouble had darkened that happy household. Bessie had become a brisk, business-like little matron, dividing her cares between her yearling baby and her husband's parish; troubled, like Martha, about many things, but only in such a manner as women of her temperament like to be troubled. Reginald had begun his University career as an undergraduate of Balliol, and talked largely about Professor Jowett, and Greek. Horatio was still a Wintonian. The Colonel had grown a little stouter, and his wife was too polite to cultivate a slimness which might have seemed a reproach to her husband's comfortable figure. Blanche was 'out,' a development of her being which meant that she was occasionally invited to a friendly dinner-party with her father and mother, that her clothes cost three times as much as they had cost while she was 'in,' that she had ideas about blue china and sunflowers, lamented the shabbiness of The Knoll drawing-room and the general untidiness of the household, and that she abandoned herself to despondency whenever there was a long interval between one garden party and another. The child Eva had become exactly what Blanche had been four years ago. Urania was still Urania Rylance, just a shade more self-opinionated, and more conscious of the inferiority of her fellow-creatures. These innate instincts had been ripened and developed by several London seasons, and were now accompanied by a flavour of sourness which was meant for wit. She had not been without offers, but there had been no offer tempting enough to induce her to abandon her privileges as Dr. Rylance's daughter. She had an idea that her marriage would be the signal for Dr. Rylance to take unto himself a second wife; and she was disinclined to give that signal. The more anxious her father seemed to dispose of her in the marriage market, the more tenaciously she clung to the privileges of spinsterhood.

'I hope you are not in a hurry to get rid of me, father,' she said at breakfast one morning, when Dr. Rylance urged the claims of a cultured youth in the War Office.

'No, my dear; I don't think I have shown any undue haste. This is your fifth London season.'

I hope you do not call my intermittent glimpses of town a season,' sneered Urania.

'I have you here as often and as long as I can,' answered her father, becoming suddenly stony of countenance, 'and I take you out as much as I can. Mr. Fitz Wilson has seven hundred a year. I could give you—say three; and surely with a thousand a year two young people might live in very good style—even in these pretentious days.'

'No doubt. But I don't care for Mr. Fitz Wilson, and I care still less for the kind of style which can be maintained upon a thousand a year,' replied Urania, with the air of a duchess. 'That would mean a small house on the skirts of Regent's Park, or a flat in the Marylebone Road, I suppose—and no carriage.'

'Marry whom you please, my love, and when you please,' said her father; 'but remember that time is not standing still with any of us.'

There had been no change at the Abbey in the years which were gone since Brian Walford claimed his bride, except that the new schools had been built under Colonel Wendover's superintendence. The old house still resembled the palace of the sleeping beauty; except that trustworthy servants took care of it, and kept moths, spiders, mice, and all such small deer at a distance. The owner of the mansion was still absent, roaming about somewhere in Northern India, as it was supposed; but his letters were few and far between. His kindred at Kingthorpe were accustomed to think of him as a wanderer in far-away places, and gave themselves very little anxiety about him. To have been anxious once would be to be anxious always, since a traveller's risks are manifold, and there is never a year when the eager spirit of some valiant explorer is not quenched in sudden death. Brian Wendover had been away so long that people had left off talking about him; and it seemed a natural condition for the Abbey to be tenantless—a capital place for picnics and afternoon teas. The Wendovers of The Knoll took all their visitors there as a matter of course—played tennis on the lawn between the goodly old cedars; and Blanche, who was of a much more enterprising disposition than her sister Bessie, had tried her hardest to induce Mrs. Wendover to give a ball in the old refectory.

Ida and her husband were strolling about the rose-garden in the quiet hour after luncheon, while Lady Palliser dozed over her knitting-needles in her favourite chair by the long French window. Brian had come to Wimperfield somewhat unexpectedly, while the London season was still at its height, and all the law courts in full swing. He came home invalided, and wanting rest and care: but he refused to consult the family doctor, a general practitioner born and bred in the adjacent village,—clever, sagacious, homely in dress and manners, and, in the opinion of Lady Palliser, a tower of strength. She liked a fatherly doctor.

'What is the use of seeing old Fosbroke when I have had the best advice in London?' Brian said, peevishly, when urged by his mother-in-law to take advice from the family doctor. 'I know exactly what ails me—nervous exhaustion, an over-worked brain, and that kind of thing. I suppose it is a natural consequence of modern civilisation: men's brains have to go at express speed in order to keep pace with the average intelligence of the time.'

'If you had only a better appetite!' sighed Lady Palliser, who had been distressed at seeing her son-in-law send away plate after plate, with its contents hardly touched.

'I wouldn't mind having a bad appetite if I could sleep, said he; 'it's insomnia that tells upon a fellow.'

Brian did not enter into the causes of this dire malady, which had begun with long nights given to dissipation—not to gross pleasures or vulgar companions, but to a semi-intellectual dissipation: wit, fun, copious talk about all things between heaven and earth, in the society of artists, actors, journalists, Bohemians of all the arts. To the man who begins by doing without sleep there sometimes comes a day when sleep will refuse to answer to his bidding. He has acquired the habit of perpetual wakefulness. The sleep-mechanism of the brain is out of gear. It will go for half-an-hour, perhaps, or for a few minutes, in spasmodic jerks: and then it stops all at once, as if the machinery had gone wrong.

So it was with Brian. Those festive nights given over to the feast of reason and the flow of soul—not to riot or drunkenness, but to the half-unconscious consumption of much brandy and soda—nights in which the atmosphere seemed charged with wit and wisdom as with mental electricity—nights in which a young man, able to talk smartly upon any given topic, was carried away by the consciousness of his power, and thought himself a god.

Brian was a member of all those joyous clubs—the night flowers of the club world, which unfold their petals in the small hours, when the playhouses are shut, and the lights have been extinguished in all sober households. There was no offence in any of these institutions, and they offered a fine intellectual arena, afforded a splendid training for literary youth: but to a man who loved them too well they meant a shattered constitution.

Brian had come to Wimperfield in the hope that quiet and country air would bring back sleep to his eyelids and steadiness to his nerves; but he had been there a week, and his hand was no steadier, his nights were no less wakeful. He fancied himself growing weaker day by day, and although the great authority in Harley Street had strictly forbidden any stimulant except one glass of stout with his mutton chop at luncheon, Brian, who was quite unable to eat the chop, found it impossible to lunch without plenty of dry sherry, or to dine without champagne, and after dinner drank a good deal of that fine old port which had been laid down by old Sir Vernon Palliser in forty-seven.

Ida was very kind and gentle to her husband at this time, seeing that he was really in need of her tenderness. She devoted herself to his amusement, walked with him, rode with him, drove with him; but although he was grateful, he was not happy. A terrible depression of mind, broken by flashes of hilarity, had taken possession of him. The London physician had told him frankly that his nerves were shattered, but that all would be well with him if he left off all stimulants, ate chops and steaks, and lived in the open air; but as yet he had been unable to cope with the most diminutive chop, or to exist for three hours without stimulants. Even those rides and drives with Ida seemed a weariness to him, and he would have escaped them if he could.

This afternoon he paced the rose-garden listlessly by Ida's side, smoking a cigarette—that cigarette which was rarely absent from his lips.

'Are you sure your London doctor does not object to your smoking so much?' Ida asked presently, noting the languid uncertainty of the fingers which held the cigarette.

'I am not sure about anything. I told him I could not live without tobacco, and he said I might smoke two or three cigarettes in the course of the day—'

'Oh, Brian, and you smoke—'

'Two or three dozen! Not quite so bad as that, eh? But no doubt I do go considerably outside the medico's mark. I could no more exist by line and rule in that way than I could fly. No, if I am to die of tobacco and late hours, I am doomed.'

'But there is no such thing as being doomed; every man is his own master—he can mould his life as he likes.'

'Can he? That depends upon the man. I am not going into the mystery of fate and free will. There is the question of temperament—hereditary instinct. If I cannot have intellectual society—new ideas—variety—I must die. I could not lead the life you live here—not life, but stagnation.'

'I have the books I love, this dear park, and all the lovely country round us—horses—dogs—and some very pleasant neighbours: and I try to do a little good in my generation.'

'All very well; but you are as much out of the world as if you were in the centre of Africa. I could not exist under such conditions. Better fifty years of

Europe than a cycle of Cathay. This to me would be as bad as Cathay. But now I suppose you are going to be perfectly happy, now that your brother is coming home.'

'Yes. I am always happy, when I have him—he is more and more companionable every day of his life.'

Vernon was expected that afternoon. He was coming home for a summer holiday, just when summer was at her loveliest. He was not bound by public school rules, or obliged to wait for the stereotyped watering-place season. The Jardines were to bring him over this afternoon, and were to stay at Wimperfield for a couple of days. Ida glanced towards the avenue every now and then, expecting to catch a glimpse of the approaching carriage between the leafy elms.

Brian strolled by her side with a listless air, smoking, and murmuring a few words now and then for courtesy's sake. He had very little to say to his wife. She did not care for the things he cared for, or understand the kind of life he lived. She loved books, the books which are for all time; he was a mere skimmer of books and reviews—mostly reviews; and he cared only for new books, new ideas, new theories, new paradoxes. His cleverness was the cleverness of the daily press—the floating froth upon the sea of knowledge. He liked to talk to a man of his own stamp, with whom he could argue upon equal terms; but not to a woman who had steeped her mind in the wisdom and poetry of the past.

He stifled a yawn every now and then, in that half-hour of waiting, longing to go back to the dining-room and refresh his parched lips with the contents of a syphon dashed with brandy. He had given his own orders to the butler, and the spirit stand was always on the sideboard ready for his use. The butler had made a note of the brandy which was dribbled away in this desultory form of refreshment, and had made up his own mind as to Mr. Wendover's habits; but it is a servant's duty to hold his peace upon such matters.

At last there came the sound of wheels, and Ida flew round to the portico to receive her guests, Brian following at his leisure. The slender figure in the black gown reminded Brian of those old days by the river—the tranquil October afternoons—the clear light—the placid water—a gray river under a gray sky, with a lovely line of yellow light behind the tufted willows. How happy he had been in those days!—caring nothing for the future—bent on winning this girl at any price—laughing within himself at her delusion—

trusting to his own merits as an ample set-off against his empty purse when he should stand revealed as the wrong Brian.

Things had gone fairly enough with him since then. He had had plenty of pleasure; a good deal of money, though not half enough; and very little work. And yet he felt that his life was a failure—and he was languid and old before his time. An idle life had exhausted him sooner than other men are exhausted by a hard-working career. He knew of men at the Bar who had lived hard and worked like galley slaves, and who yet retained all the fire and freshness of youth.

The guests had alighted by the time Brian reached the portico, and Vernon was in his sister's arms. She held him away from her, to show him to her husband—a thin fair-haired boy of eleven, in a gray highland kilt and jacket, like a gillie—fresh rosy cheeks, bright blue eyes.

'Hasn't he grown, Brian? and isn't he a darling?' she asked, hugging him again.

'He is a jolly little fellow, and he shall go out shooting with me as soon as there is anything to shoot.'

'We can fish,' said Vernon; 'there's plenty of trout; but you don't look strong enough to throw a fly. My rod's ever so heavy,' he added, with a flourish of his arm.

That weakness and languor which was obvious even to the boy, was still more apparent to Mr. and Mrs. Jardine. Bessie had not seen her cousin since Christmas, when he and Ida had spent a couple of days at Kingthorpe.

'Oh, Brian,' she exclaimed, 'have you been ill? Nobody told me anything.'

'I have had no illness worth telling about; but I have not been in vigorous health. London life takes too much out of a man.'

'Then you should not live in London. You ought to be out all day, roaming about on those pine-clad hills yonder—"hangers," I think you call them in these parts.'

'Yes,' answered Ida, 'we are very proud of our hangers; but Brian is not able to walk much just yet.'

Bessie was full of concern for Brian after this. She devoted herself to him in the interval before dinner, and left Ida free to roam about the garden with Vernie. She remembered how he had always been her favourite cousin. She had been angry with him for allowing that foolish practical joke of hers to take so fixed and fatal a form; but now she saw him wan and broken-looking she was prepared to forgive him everything.

'You must take care of yourself, Brian,' she said, when they were sitting side by side in one of the drawing-room windows, while Lady Palliser dispensed afternoon tea.

'I am taking care of myself; I am here for that purpose; but it is dreary work.'

'What! dreary work to live in this lovely place, and with such a sweet wife! But I know you never liked the country.'

'I frankly detest it.'

'And you miss the intellectual society to which you are accustomed in London—literary men—poets—playwrights. How delightful it must be to know the men who write books!'

'They are not always the pleasantest people in the world. I never cared much for your deep-thinker—the man who believes he is sent into the world to promulgate his own particular gospel. But the men who write for newspapers—critics, humourists—they are jolly fellows enough.'

'And you have glorious nights at your clubs, don't you? We had a friend of John's with us the other day who had met you at some literary club near the Strand. Do you ever sing comic songs now?'

'Sometimes, after midnight. One does not feel moved to that kind of thing till the small hours.'

'Ah!' sighed Bessie, 'our only idea of the small hours is getting up at four, to be ready for a five o'clock service. But I don't think the small hours agree with you, Brian. You are looking ten years older than when you were at Kingthorpe last summer.'

'Better wear out than rust out,' said Brian.

After dinner Vernie was eager for an exploration of the village, and Blackman's Hanger, the wild, pine-clad hill which sheltered the village from north-east winds and the salt breath of a distant sea.

Ida was ready to go with him, and the Jardines, always tremendous walkers, were equally anxious for a ramble; but Brian was much too languid for evening walks.

'I'll stay and smoke my smoke and talk to the Mater,' he said, always contriving to keep on pleasant terms with Lady Palliser; 'I hate bats, owls, twilight, and all the Gray's Elegy business.'

'But you stop such a time over your cigar,' said the widow. 'Last night I sat for an hour waiting tea for you. I like company over my cup of tea.'

'To-night you shall have the advantage of intellectual society,' said Brian. 'I will come and dribble out my impressions of the last *Contemporary Review*, which I dozed over between breakfast and luncheon.'

Brian stayed in the dining-room, dimly lighted by two hanging moderator lamps, while the soft shades of evening were just beginning to steal over the landscape outside. He had his favourite pointer for company—the last Sir Vernon's favourite, a magnificent beast, and of almost human intelligence, and he had plenty of wine in the decanters before him—choice port and claret, which had been set on the table in honour of the Jardines, who had hardly touched it. He had his cigarette case and his own thoughts, which were idle as the smoke-wreaths which went curling up to the ceiling, light as the ashes of his tobacco.

Out of doors the evening was divine. Vernon was delighted to be frisking about upon his patrimonial soil. The five years he had lived at Wimperfield seemed the greater half of his life—seemed, indeed, almost to have absorbed and blotted out his former history. He remembered very little of the shabbier circumstances of his babyhood, and had all the feelings of a boy born in the purple, to whom it was natural to be proprietor of the landscape, and to patronise the humbler dwellers on the soil.

Blackman's Hanger was a rugged ridge of hill above the village of Wimperfield. They lingered here to listen to the nightingales, and to admire the sunset; and then, when the glow above the western horizon was changing from golden to deepest crimson, they all went down into the village, where lights were beginning to glimmer faintly in some of the cottages.

Wimperfield was a snug primitive settlement, consisting of about five-and-twenty habitations, not one of which had been built within the last century, a general shop, a bakery, and three public-houses, a fact which shows that the brewing interests were well protected in this part of the world. One of these village taverns, a dingy old low-browed cottage, with a pile of out-buildings which served for stable, piggery, or anything else, and about half an acre of garden, stood a little way aloof from the village, and on the skirt of the copse that clothed the sloping steep below Blackman's Hanger. There was a piece of waste land in front of this inn which served as the theatre for such itinerary exhibitors, Cheap Jacks, and Bohemians of all kinds who took quiet little Wimperfield in the course of their perambulations.

Here to-night in the dusk, there stood a covered cart of the peddler order and Vernon, who had been walking on in front with Mr. Jardine, rushed back to his sister to say that there was a Cheap Jack in front of the 'Royal Oak.'

'Oh, he has been there for a long time—ever since the beginning of the year,' said Ida; 'he is quite an institution.'

'What's an institution?' asked Vernon.

'Something fixed and lasting, don't you know. I believe he does no end of good among the villagers—doctoring them, and advising them, and helping them when they are ill or out of work; but he has a very churlish way with the gentry. Mr. Mason, our curate, says the man always reminds him of the Black Dwarf, except that he is not so ugly, nor deformed in any way.'

'Then he can't be like the Black Dwarf,' said Vernon, who knew almost all Sir Walter's novels, his sister having read Shakespeare, Scott, and Dickens to him for hours on end, during the long winter evenings at Wimperfield.

'Does he live in that cart always?' asked Bessie.

'Not always; he has taken possession of that dilapidated cottage upon the Hanger, which used to be occupied by Lord Pontifex's gamekeeper, and I believe he oscillates between the cart and the cottage. I have hardly seen him, for he is such a morose personage that he always hides when any of the gentry approach his hut.'

'Sulks in his tent, like Achilles,' said Mr. Jardine.

They were on the edge of the little patch of green by this time. The cart—painted a lively yellow, and with a little window on each side—stood in the middle of the green, backed by a clump of tall elms. There was a little crowd in front of the cart, and a man with a black beard and a red fez cap was discoursing in a deep, sonorous voice to the assembly—descanting, with seeming fluency, upon a picture which he held in his hand, his tawny, gipsy-like face only half shown by the flame of a flaring naphtha lamp, and his features rendered grotesque by the play of lights and shadows. The party from the park, however, had very little opportunity for seeing what manner of man he was; for no sooner did he catch sight of Mr. Jardine's tall hat over the circle of rustic heads, than he flung the engraving he had been exhibiting inside the cart, extinguished his lamp, wished his audience an abrupt good night, and shut the door of his dwelling upon the outside world.

The rustics gave him a round of applause before they dispersed. The women and children moved towards the village; the men and lads lingered a little on the green, irresolute, and then slowly gravitated to the 'Royal Oak,' touching their hats as they passed the gentlefolks. Mr. Jardine stopped one of the men midway.

'A curious customer that,' he said, looking towards the cart.

'Yes, sir, so he be; but rale right down clever.'

'Was he trying to sell you that picture?'

'No, sir; him don't often sell things to we; sometimes him do—knives, and comforters, and corderoy waistcoats, and flannel shirts, and such like, and oncommon good they be, too, and oncommon cheap. He wor givin' we a bit of a lecture loike, on lions and tigers, and ryenosed-horses, and such-loike beasts, and on they queer creatures wot lived before the flood. Lord! there was one beast with a long neck, and paddles for swimmin' with, as made we all ready to bust with laughin' when him showed us the pictur' of his skeleton.'

'Does he often give you a lecture of that kind?'

'Yes, sir; him do lecture we about all manner o' things—flowers, and ferns, and insects—kindness to hanimals—hinstinct in dogs—Lord knows what; but he have a way of makin' it all go down—much better nor parson; and ha allus gets a good laugh out o' we. And when there's any on us ill, or out o' work, then Cheap Jack be a real good friend, and very ready with the brass.'

'But can he afford to help you? is he so much better off than you are?'

'Well, sir, you see him haven't got no missus nor young 'uns, and I fancy him's got a few pounds saved in a old stocking. Him don't drink, nayther—not so much as a mug o' beer.'

'Is he a native of these parts?'

'Lor no, sir, him's a furriner; why, his skin's as brown as a berry!'

'Is he a gipsy, do you think?'

'I ain't sure o' that, but him can talk their patter; and when the gipsies come this way him and them is as thick as thaves.'

'I see—half a gipsy and half a foreigner, and altogether a rover, I suppose. Well, I'm glad he gives you a little instruction and amusement now and then, and I hope he'll find the way to keep you out of the public-house,' said Mr. Jardine.

'Why, you see, parson, a man must have his mug o' beer; but it's summot to the good if he don't sit down over it and make it three or four mugs o' beer. There ain't been so much sitting down since Cheap Jack comed among us.'

'Isn't that a desolate hovel up on the hill where he lives sometimes?'

'It was oncommon deserlate till Cheap Jack took it in hand; there ain't a owl in the wood that would have liked to live in it; but Jack hammers a bit of wood here, and a plank there, and a bit o' matting up agen the walls, and puts in a stove from Petersfield, and makes it as snug as a burd's nest. I've smoked many a pipe with him alongside that stove, and drank many a cup o' coffee. That's Jack's drink—not a drain o' beer or sperrits ever goes inside o' he.'

'That accounts for the money in the stocking,' said Bessie.

The rustic shook his head dubiously.

'Him ain't got no childer,' he said. 'It's them as makes the coin go.'

'I wish he'd come out again and go on lecturing,' exclaimed Vernon, with an aggrieved air. 'I do so want to hear him.'

'Oh, but him won't show the end of his nose now you're here, Sir Vernon,' answered the rustic. 'Him can't abide gentlefolks. Parson ha' tried his hardest to get round he, but Jack shuts the door in parson's face. Him don't want nothing of 'em, and don't want their company.'

'A natural corollary,' said Mr. Jardine, laughing. 'But I'm afraid your friend is a desperate radical.'

'Well, I don't know, sir. Him don't speak hard agen the Queen; him don't want to do away with soldiers and sailors, like grocer down street; and though Jack don't go to church, Jack reads his Bible, and holds by his Bible. I fancy as some rich gentleman must ha' done he a great injury once upon a time, and that it turned he agen the breed.'

'Very like the Black Dwarf,' said Mr. Jardine to Ida. 'I daresay I shall hear of your playing the part of Isabella Vere, and interviewing this half-savage, half-Christian recluse. But do you mean to tell me that he has lived here six months, within a mile and a half of your house, and you have never seen him?'

'It is a fact. You had a specimen of his manners just now. Whenever I have passed his cottage he has shut the door or the window in my face, if he happened to be standing at either. To Mr. Mason he has been absolutely rude.'

'It isn't every man who appreciates the privilege of being interviewed by a parson,' said John Jardine.

'Oh, Jack,' cried Bessie! 'all your people love to see you at their doors.'

'Yes, they are a sociable lot. That comes from living on Salisbury Plain, far from the madding crowd.'

After this they went home, watching the golden summer moon rise above the pine-clad Hanger as they went. They found Lady Palliser nodding in her arm-chair in front of the low tea table, the teapot still intact. It was ten o'clock, but Brian had not come in to talk to her after her tea. John Jardine went in quest of him, and found him in the dining-room, mooning over his wine. He murmured a vague excuse about feeling too tired to talk to anybody, and then bade Mr. Jardine good night, and went up to his room; not to sleep, but to fling the window wide open, and lean his elbows on the sill, and stare out into the exquisite summer night, the leafy wood, the moon-kissed crest of the hill, in a half-dreamy, half-hysterical state of mind.

'I begin to think I am like Swift, and shall go first at top,' he said to himself; 'this quiet life is killing; and yet if I was to go back I should be worse. The nights in Elm Court, when I went home alone after a glorious evening, were devilish.

CHAPTER XXV
'MY SEED WAS YOUTH, MY CROP WAS ENDLESS CAKE'

Mr. and Mrs. Jardine went back to their Wiltshire parsonage after a two days' visit, and Ida had her boy all to herself. His education, from a classical and mathematical point of view, had only begun when he went to John Jardine; but the foundations of education, the development of thought and imagination had begun long ago at Les Fontaines, when Ida and he took their long wintry rambles together, and the girl talked to the child of all things in heaven and earth, imparting in the easiest way much of that information which she had acquired as pupil and teacher in the educational mill at Mauleverer. Beyond learning to read and to write, and the most elementary forms of arithmetic, this oral instruction was all the education which Vernie had received up to the time of his leaving home; but then what a large range of information can be imparted by an intelligent woman who reads a great deal, and who reads with the student's deep love of knowledge. Vernon, without being a prodigy, like the infant Goethe, or that wondrous product of paternal scholarship, John Stuart Mill, knew more about things in general, from the course of the planets to the constitution of the glowworms in the hedges, than many full-grown undergraduates. Flowers and ferns, shells and minerals, had been his playthings. His sister had taught him the nature and attributes of all the animals and birds he loved, or slaughtered; and then his imagination had been fed upon Shakespeare and Scott, Dickens and Goldsmith. He had derived his first vivid impressions of history from Shakespeare and Scott, his knowledge of a wide range of life outside his own home from Dickens; and with that knowledge a quickened sympathy with the joys and sorrows of the humbler classes. All that Vernon knew of the struggles of the lower middle classes was derived from that great panorama of life which Charles Dickens painted for us. His own small experiences of village life had taught the boy very little; for he had only seen the rustic from that outside and smoothly varnished aspect which the tiller of the soil presents to the squire.

And now the boy had come home, after an absence of some months, and he wanted to absorb Ida from morning till night. She must walk and drive with him, read to him, play with him, be interested in his dogs, his guns, his fishing-tackle, every detail of his busy young life.

Ida was never happier than when thus occupied. The boy seemed to her the incarnate spirit of youth, and joy, and hope, and all those bright impulses which wear out in ourselves at so early a stage of life's journey that we are very glad to taste them vicariously in the unspoiled ardour of childhood. To be with Vernon was to escape from the narrowness of her own fettered life, to forget its disappointments, its disillusions, its one deep incurable regret—regret for her own mad folly, which had bartered freedom for a sordid hope—folly as mad as Esau's when he sold his birthright—regret for him who loved her too late.

Unhappily, even her unselfish delight in her brother's society was not unalloyed with pain. She never forgot her duty as a wife, nor failed in any act of attention to her husband. And yet Brian's morbid jealousy of the boy was but too evident. He rarely spoke of Vernon without a sneer, when he and his wife were alone; although he was careful not to say anything uncivil before Lady Palliser. He scoffed at the little lad's position, as if it had been an offence in the child himself—called him the microscopic baronet, the baby thane, laughed with bitterest laughter at any little touch of arrogance which clouded the natural sweetness of the boy's character.

Ida endured this morbid jealousy with a patience that was almost heroic. She saw that her husband was ill, and that this mysterious malady of his, which had at first seemed to her sheer hypochondriasis, was only too real. It was a malady which affected the mind more than the body. Brian's character had undergone a complete change since his illness. He who had been of old so easy-tempered, so lively, was now melancholy and irritable, at times garrulous to a degree that was painful to his hearers, keenly resentful of trifles, always fancying himself neglected or slighted.

In vain did Lady Palliser and Ida urge the necessity of medical advice. Brian obstinately refused to see the local apothecary; and, as there was nothing tangible in his illness and he was able to be about all day, to go out of doors, and do pretty much as he pleased, there was no excuse for calling in the doctor without his permission.

'If I felt that I wanted advice, I would go up to town and see Mallison,' he said; 'but there is nothing amiss with me, except a disappointed life. I begin to feel that I am a failure. Other fellows of my age have passed me in the race; and it is hard at nine-and-twenty to feel oneself beaten.'

'But, Brian,' his wife answered gently, 'don't you think if your contemporaries have outstripped you, it is because they have tried harder than you? Remember what St. Paul says about the one who obtaineth the prize.'

'For Heaven's sake, don't preach!' cried Brian, irritably. I tell you I tried hard enough; tried—yes, slaved night after night; scribbling articles for those infernal magazines, to get my manuscript returned with thanks after nearly a twelve-month's detention; spelling over dry-as-dust briefs for a guinea fee, in order to post up some bloated Queen's Counsel, who treated me as if I were dirt, and pretended not to know my name. I tell you, Ida, the Bar is a sickening profession; literature is worse; all the professions are played out, Europe is overcrowded with educated men; they swarm like aphides in a hot summer—your single fly the progenitor of a quintillion of living creatures. When I see the men in their wigs and gowns, hurrying up and down the Temple courts, swarming on all the staircases, choking up the doors of the law-courts, they remind me of the busy, hungry creatures on an ant-heap.

"Every door is barred with gold, and opens but to golden keys, Every gate is thronged with suitors, all the markets overflow."

He was walking up and down the room in an agitated way, angry, excited beyond the occasion.

'But in your case, Brian, it seems to me that the path has been made so smooth. With such an independence as ours, it must be so easy to get on.'

'I thank you for reminding me how much I owe your father,' sneered her husband.

'I was not thinking especially of my father. You owe as much to your cousin.'

'Yes, my cousin has been vastly generous—damnably generous; but if I had married any other woman, do you suppose he would have done as much? Of course, I know it was for your sake he gave me that income. Was he ever so liberal before, do you think? No, he dribbled out an occasional hundred or two when I was up a tree, but nothing more. It was for your sake his purse-strings relaxed.'

'You have no right to say that,' Ida answered indignantly. 'I have a right to say what I think to my wife. I have not forgotten what you said to me at the hotel that day. You told me to my face that you loved another man. Do you think I was such a dullard as not to guess that man's name? You fell in love with Wendover of the Abbey, before you saw him; and your innocent love for the shadow grew into guilty love for the man, after you were my wife. I knew all about it; but I was not going to let you give me the slip. I have known all along that I am nothing to you, that you despise me, detest me, perhaps; and that knowledge has made me what I am—a broken, blighted man, a wreck, at nine-and-twenty.'

'Oh, Brian, this is too cruel! Have I ever failed in my duty to you?'

'Damn duty!' cried Brian, savagely. 'I wanted your love, not your duty—love such as I thought you gave me in those autumn days by the river. Great God, how happy I was in those days! I hadn't a sixpence; I was up to my eyes in debt; but I thought you loved me, and that we were going to be happy in our garret till good fortune tumbled down the chimney.'

'I don't think a garret would have suited you long, Brian, had I been ever so devoted. You are too much of a sybarite.'

'I should have been happy with you. I should have thought myself in Eden. Well, fate never meant me to be happy. I am a wretch, judged before I was born, foredoomed to misery in this world and the next. Yes, I begin to think Calvin was right—there are some creatures predestined to damnation. Before ever the stars spun into their places, when all the suns and moons and planets were rings of fiery gas revolving in space, my doom was already written in the book of fate.'

It had been a common thing of late for Brian to ramble on in such despondent strains as these, half angry, half despairing. Ida was supremely patient with him, sometimes soothing him, sometimes arguing with him; yet hardly knowing how much of his talk arose from real gloom of mind, or how much was sheer rhodomontade. The hours which she spent with him were intensely painful, and as the days went by he became more and more exacting, more and more resentful of her absence, and grudgingly jealous of Vernon.

Another cause for pain was Ida's growing conviction that her husband's frequent doses of soda and brandy, and the champagne which he drank at dinner, and the port or Burgundy which he took after dinner, had a great deal to do with his altered mental condition. Painful as it was to speak of such a thing, she took courage one morning, and told him plainly that she believed he was suffering from, the effect of habitual—almost unconscious— intemperance.

'You are taking soda and brandy all day long. You have brandy in your bedroom at night, Brian,' she said. 'I am sure you can have no idea how much you take in the course of the twenty-four hours.'

'I have no idea that I am a drunkard, if that's what you mean,' he answered, white with rage; and then he burst into a torrent of abuse—such language as she had never heard from mortal lips until that hour, and his wife fled, shuddering and terror-stricken, from the room.

When next they met he cowed before her with a craven air, and made no allusion to this scene. But after this she observed that he pretended to drink less, and had a crafty way of getting his glass refilled at dinner. He no longer kept a brandy bottle on the table beside his bed, as he had done heretofore, on the pretence that a little weak brandy and water helped him to sleep, nor did the soda-water bottles and spirit decanter adorn one of the tables in his study; but more than once his wife met him creeping to the dining-room with a stealthy air to supply himself at the sideboard, and when she went into his room at night to see if he slept, his fevered breath reeked of brandy. It seemed to her later, as time went on, that even his garments exhaled spirituous odours.

It was not long after this that he began to talk mysteriously of some trouble which menaced him, which gradually took the shape of a criminal prosecution overhanging him. He had been falsely accused of some awful crime—some nameless, unspeakable offence—hateful as the gates of hell. He was innocent, but his enemies were legion; and at any moment a detective might be sent to Wimperfield to arrest him. One evening, in the summer twilight after dinner, he took it into his head that one of the footmen—a man whose face ought to have been thoroughly familiar to him—was a detective in disguise. He flew at the worthy young fellow in a furious rage, and the butler had hard work to prevent his doing poor John Thomas a mischief. But when the lamps were brought in, Brian perceived his mistake, and apologised to the footman for his violence.

'You don't know what devils those detectives are,' he said, deprecatingly; 'they can make themselves look like anybody. And if they once get hold of me, the case will be tried at Westminster Hall. It will take weeks to try, and all the Bar will be engaged; and then it will have to go to the House of Lords. There has not been such a case within the last century. All Europe will ring with it.'

'Dear Brian, I am sure this is a delusion of yours,' said Ida, trying to soothe him; 'you cannot have done anything so wicked.'

'Done! no, I am as innocent as a baby; but the whole Bar—the Bench too—is in league against me. They'll make out their case, depend upon it. "It's a case for a jury;" that's what the Lord Chancellor said when I told him about it.'

After this there could be no doubt that there was actual mental disturbance. Lady Palliser sent for the local medical man, who had very little difficulty in diagnosing the case. Sleeplessness, restless nights, tossing from side to side, an utter inability to keep still, horrible dreams, impaired vision, clouds floating before the eyes,—these symptoms Mr. Fosbroke heard from the wife. The patient himself was obstinately silent about his sensations, declared that there was nothing the matter with him, and let the doctor know he considered his visit an impertinent intrusion.

'I had a touch of brain fever early in the year,' he said. 'I had the best advice in London during my illness, and afterwards. I know exactly how to treat myself. The symptoms which alarm my wife are nothing but the natural reaction after a severe shock to the nervous system. The tonics I am taking will soon pull me up again; but as I am now under a special treatment by Dr. Mallison, of Harley Street, you will under, stand that I don't care about further advice.'

'Undoubtedly,' replied the medical man, meekly. 'But I believe it would be a satisfaction to Lady Palliser and to Mrs. Wendover both if you would do me the honour to consult me, and allow me to look after you while you are here, I could place myself under Dr. Mallison's instructions, if you like.'

'No, there is no necessity. I tell you I know exactly what is amiss, and how to manage my own health.'

Mr. Fosbroke argued the point, but in vain. Brian would not even allow him to feel his pulse. But the doctor knew very well what was amiss, and told Mrs. Wendover, with delicate circumlocution, that her husband was suffering from an imprudent use of stimulants for some time past.

'That is what I feared,' said Ida; but it is too dreadful. It is the very last thing I expected. I thought nobody drank nowadays.'

'Very few people get drunk, my dear Mrs. Wendover,' replied the doctor; 'but, unhappily, though there is very little drunkenness, there is a great deal of what is called "pegging"—an intermittent kind of tippling which goes on all day long, beginning very early and ending very late. A man, whose occupation in life is headwork, begins to think he wants a stimulant—begins by having his brandy and soda at twelve o'clock perhaps; then finds he can't get on without it after eleven; then takes it before breakfast—in lieu of breakfast; and goes on with brandy and soda at intervals till dinner-time. At dinner he has no appetite, tries to create one with a bottle of dry champagne, eats very little, but dines on the champagne, feels an unaccountable depression of spirits later on in the evening, and takes more brandy, without soda this time; and so on, and so on; till, after a period of sleeplessness, he begins to have ugly dreams, then to see waking visions, hear imaginary voices, stumble upon the edge of an imaginary precipice. If he is an elderly man he gets shaky in the lower limbs, then his hands become habitually tremulous, especially in the early morning, when he is like a figure hung on wires—and so on, and so on; and unless he pulls himself up by a great moral effort, the chances are that he will have a sharp attack of *delirium tremens*.'

'You do not fear such an attack for my husband?

'Mr. Wendover is a young man, but he has evidently abused his constitution; there is no knowing what may happen if you don't take care of him. Alcohol is a cumulative poison, and that "pegging" I have told you of is diabolical. Nature throws off an over-dose of alcohol, but the daily, hourly dose eats into the system.'

'How am I to take care of him?' asked Ida, despairingly.

'You must keep wine and spirits away from him, except in extreme moderation.'

'What! speak to the butler? Tell him that my husband is a drunkard?'

'You need not go quite so far as that, but it will be necessary to cut off the supplies somehow, and to substitute a nourishing diet for stimulants.'

'Yes, if he could eat: but he has no appetite—he eats hardly anything.'

'Unhappily, that is one of the symptoms of his disease, and the most difficult to overcome. But you must do your utmost to make him eat, and to prevent his getting brandy. A little light claret or Rhine wine may be allowed; nothing more. I will send you a sedative which you can give him at bedtime.'

'I do not think he will take anything of that kind. He has set his face against accepting your advice.'

'I believe if you were to take a decided tone, he would succumb; if not, you had better ask Dr. Mallison to come down and see him. It will be a costly visit, and money thrown away, as the case is perfectly simple; but I dare say you will not mind that.'

'I should mind nothing if he could be cured. It is horrible to see such ruin of body and mind in one so young,' Ida answered sadly.

'Well, you must see what influence you can exercise over him for his own good. I will call every other day, and hear how you are getting on with him; and if you fail, we must summon Dr. Mallison.'

Ida spoke to the butler. It was a hard thing to do, and it seemed to her a kind of treachery against her husband—as if she were inflicting everlasting disgrace upon him in secret, like a midnight assassin, who stabs his victim in the back. Her voice trembled, and her face was deadly pale as she spoke to the butler, an old servant who had been in the household from his boyhood.

'Rogers, I want you to be a little more careful in your arrangements about wine and spirits,' she began, falteringly. 'Mr. Wendover is in a low state of health—suffering from a nervous complaint, in fact; and we fear that he is taking too much brandy. Will you kindly try to prevent it?'

'It will be very difficult, ma'am. Mr. Wendover gives his orders, and he expects to be obeyed.'

'But upon this one point you must not obey him. You can say that you have Lady Palliser's orders that no more brandy is to be brought up from the cellar. I shall tell her that I have told you this.'

'Yes, ma'am. I was afraid too much brandy was being drunk, but it was not my place to mention it,' said Rogers, politely.

He would have said the same, perhaps, had the house been on fire.

Neither sherry nor champagne was served at dinner that day, and the claret which was offered Mr. Wendover was of a very thin quality.

'I'll take champagne,' he said to the butler.

'There is not any upstairs, sir.'

Brian turned angrily upon the man, and Ida, pale but resolute, came to the rescue.

'We do not drink champagne at dinner when we are alone, Brian,' she said; 'and I don't think it is quite fair to Vernie's cellars that Moët should be served every day because you are here.

'Vernon's cellars! Ah, I forgot that we are all here on sufferance, and, that I am drinking Vernon's wine.'

'You may have as much of my champagne as you like,' said Vernie, getting very red; 'but I don't think it does you any good, for you are always so cross afterwards.'

Brian looked at the boy with a savage gleam in his eyes, and muttered something, but made no audible reply.

'I'll go back to my chambers to-morrow,' he said: 'I can have a bottle of Moët there without being under an obligation to anybody. Give me some brandy and soda,' he said to the butler; 'I can't drink this verjuice.'

'There is no brandy, sir.'

'Oh! Sir Vernon's cognac is to be kept sacred, too. I congratulate you, Vernon, upon having two such economical guardians. Your minority will be a period of considerable saving.'

He made no further remonstrance, drank neither claret nor hock, ate hardly anything, but sat through the dinner in sullen silence, and went off to his room directly Lady Palliser had said grace, leaving the others to take their strawberries and cream alone. Vernon was what Rogers the butler called 'a mark on' strawberries and cream.

When Vernie had finished his strawberries, Ida went to her husband's study; but the door was locked, and when she asked to be admitted Brian refused.

'I'd rather be alone, thank you,' he answered, curtly. 'I have an article to write for one of the legal papers. You can amuse yourself with the baronet. I know you are always glad to be free.'

'Come for a stroll in the park, Brian,' she pleaded gently, pitying him with all her heart, more tenderly inclined to him in his decay and degradation than she had been in his prime of manhood, before these fatal habits began. 'Do come with us, dear. We won't walk further than you like; it's a lovely evening.'

'I hate a summer twilight,' returned Brian; 'it always gives me the horrors—a creepy time, when all sorts of loathsome creatures are abroad— bats, and owls, and stag-beetles, cockchafers, and other abominations. Can't you let me alone?' he went on, angrily. 'I tell you I have work to do.'

Ida left him upon this, without a word. What was she to do? This was her first experience of a mind diseased, and it seemed to her worse than any trouble that had ever touched her before. She had stood beside her father's death-bed, and the hair of her flesh had stood up at the awful moment of dissolution, when it was as if verily a spirit had passed before her face, calling her beloved from the known to the unknown. Yet in the awe and horror of death there had been holiness and comfort, a whisper of hope leading her thoughts to higher regions, a promise that this pitiful, inexplicable parting was not the end. This dissolution in the living man, this palpable progress of degradation, visible day by day and hour by hour, was worse than death. It meant the decay and ruin of a mind, the wreck of an immortal soul. What place could there be in heaven for the drunkard, who had dribbled away his reason, his power to discriminate between right and wrong, by perpetual doses of brandy? what could be pleaded in extenuation of this gradual and deliberate suicide?

Ida went slowly downstairs, her soul steeped in gloom, seeing no ray of light on the horizon; for with the most earnest desire to save her erring husband, she felt herself powerless to help him against himself. If he were denied the things he cared for at Wimperfield, there was little doubt that he would go back to his solitary chambers, where he was his own master. He was not so ill either in mind or body as to justify her in using actual restraint.

At the moment she thought of telegraphing for Aunt Betsy, whose firm manly mind might offer valuable aid in such a crisis; but she shrank from the idea of exposing her husband's degradation even to his aunt. She did not want the family at Kingthorpe to know how low he had fallen. Mr. and Mrs. Jardine had been impressed by the change in him, and Bessie had harped upon his lost good looks, habitual irritability, and deteriorated manners; but neither had hinted at an inkling of the cause; and Ida hoped the hideous truth had been unsuspected by either. She decided, therefore, during those few minutes of meditation which she spent in the portico waiting for Vernon, that she would rely on her own intelligence, and upon professional aid rather than upon any family intervention. If she could, by her own strong hand, with the help of the London physician, lead her husband's footsteps out of this Tophet into which he had sunk himself, she would spare no trouble, withhold no sacrifice, to effect his rescue, and she and her stepmother, the kindliest of women, would keep the secret between them.

Vernon came bounding out of the hall, eager for the accustomed evening ramble. This evening walk with the boy had been Ida's happiest time of late, perhaps the only portion of her day in which she had enjoyed the sense of freedom from ever present anxiety, in which she had put away troubled thought. She had gone back to her duty meekly and resignedly when this time of respite was over, but with a sense of unspeakable woe. Wimperfield with its lighted windows, stone walls, and classic portico, had seemed to her only as a prison-house, a whited sepulchre, fair without and loathsome within.

Vernie was full of curiosity about that little scene at the dinner table. The boy had that quick perception of the minds and acts of others which is generally developed in a child who spends the greater part of his life with grown-up people; and he had been quite as conscious as his elders of the unpleasantness of the scene.

'I hope Brian doesn't think I'm stingy about the wine,' he said; 'he might drink it all for anything I should care. I don't want it.'

'I know, darling; but you were quite right in what you said at dinner. The wine does Brian harm, and that's why mamma and I don't want him to take any.'

'Has it always done him harm?' asked Vernon.

'Always; that is, lately.'

'Then why did you let him take so much—a whole bottle, sometimes two bottles—all to himself at dinner? I heard Rogers tell Mrs. Moggs about it.'

'Rogers ought not to have given him so much.'

'Oh! but Rogers said it wasn't his place to make remarks, only he was very sorry for poor Mrs. Wendover—that's you, you know—not Mrs. Wendover at Kingthorpe.'

'Oh, Vernie, you were not listening?'

'Of course not. I wasn't listening on purpose; but I was in the lobby outside the housekeeper's room, waiting for some grease for my shooting boots. I always grease them myself, you know, for nobody else does it properly; and Rogers said the brandy Mr. Wendover had drunk in three weeks would make Mrs. Moggs' hair stand on end; but it couldn't,—could it?—when she wears a front. A front couldn't stand on end,' said Vernon, exploding at his own small joke, which, like most of the witticisms of childhood, was founded on the physical deficiencies of age.

'Look, Vernie! there is going to be a lovely sunset,' said Ida, anxious to change the conversation.

But Vernon's inquiring mind was not satisfied.

'Is it wicked to drink champagne and brandy?' he asked.

'Yes, dear, it is wicked to take anything which we know will do us harm. It would be wicked to take poison; and brandy is a kind of poison.'

'Except for poor people, when they are ill; they always come to the vicarage for brandy when they are ill, and Mrs. Jardine gives them a little.'

'Brandy is a medicine sometimes, but it is a poison if anyone takes too much of it—a poison that ruins body and soul. I hope Brian will not take any more; but we mustn't talk about it, darling, above all to strangers.'

'No, I shouldn't talk of it to anybody but you, because I like Brian. He used to go fishing with me, and to be so good-natured, and to tell me funny stories, and do imitations of actors for me; but now he's so cross. Is that the brandy?'

'I'm afraid it is.'

'Then I hate brandy.'

They were in the park by this time, wandering in the wildest part of the ground, where the bracken grew breast high in great sweeps of feathery green. They came to a spot on the edge of a hill where three or four noble old elms had been felled, and where a couple of men in smock frocks were sawing coffin boards.

'What are those broad planks wanted for?' the boy asked; 'and why do you make them so short?'

'They're not uncommon short, Sir Vernon,' the man answered, touching his hat; 'the shortest on 'em is six foot. Them be for coffins, Sir Vernon.'

'How horrid! I hope they won't be wanted for ages,' said the boy.

'Not much chance o' that, sir; there's allus summun a wantin' a weskit o' this make,' answered the man, with a grin, as Vernon and Ida went on, uncomfortably impressed by the idea of those two men sawing their coffin-boards in the calm, bright evening, with every articulation of the branching fern standing sharply out against the yellow light, as on the margin of a golden sea.

They rambled on, and presently Ida was repeating passages from those Shakespearian plays which had formed Vernon's first introduction to English history, and of which he had never tired. Ida knew all the great speeches, and indeed a good many of the more famous scenes, by heart, and Vernon liked to hear them over and over again, alternately detesting the Lancastrians and pitying the Yorkists, or hating York and compassionating Lancaster, as the fortunes of war wavered. And then there was Richard the Second, more tenderly touched by Shakespeare than by Hume or Hallam; and Richard the Third, whose iniquities were made respectable by a kind of diabolical thoroughness; and that feebler villain John. Vernon was as familiar with them as if they had been flesh and blood acquaintances.

'Cheap Jack knows Shakespeare as well as you do,' said Vernon presently, when they had left the park by a wooden gate that opened into a patch of common land, which lay between the Wimperfield fence and Blackman's Hanger.

'Who is Cheap Jack?' asked Ida absently.

'The man you saw the night I came home, when Mr. Jardine was with us. Don't you remember?'

'The man in the cart—the showman? Yes, I know; but I did not see him.'

'No; he hates the gentry, and women, too, I think. But he likes Shakespeare.'

'I shouldn't have thought he would have known anything about Shakespeare.'

'Oh, but he does—better than you even. When he was mending my fishing-rod—you remember, don't you?—I told you how clever he was at fishing-rods.'

'Yes, I remember—it was the day you were out so long quite alone; and I was dreadfully frightened about you.'

'Oh, but that was silly. Besides, I wasn't alone—I was with Jack all day. And if I had been alone, I can take care of myself—I shall be twelve next birthday. Nobody would try to steal me now,' said Vernon, drawing himself up and swaggering a little.

'What, not even good Mrs. Brown? Well, no; I think you are too clever to be stolen. Still you must not go out again without Robert.' (Robert was a youth of two-and-twenty, Sir Vernon's body-guard and particular attendant, to whom the little baronet occasionally gave the go-by.) 'Besides, I don't think you ought to associate with such a person as this Cheap Jack—a vagabond stroller, whose past life nobody knows.'

'Oh, but you don't know what kind of man Jack is—he's the cleverest man I ever knew—cleverer than Mr. Jardine; he knows everything. Let's go up on the hanger.'

'No, dear, it's getting late; we must go home.'

'No, we needn't go home till we like—nobody wants us. Mamma will be asleep over her knitting,—how she does sleep!—and she'll wake up surprised when we go home, and say, "Gracious, is it ten o'clock? These summer evenings are so short!"'

'But you ought to be in bed, Vernie.'

'No, I oughtn't. The thrushes haven't gone to bed yet. Hark at that one singing his evening hymn! Do come just a wee bit further.'

They were at the foot of the hanger by this time, and now began to climb the slope. The atmosphere was balmy with the breath of the pines, and there was an almost tropical warmth in the wood—languorous, inviting to repose. The crescent moon hung pale above the tops of the trees, pale above that rosy flush of evening which filled the western sky.

'What makes you think Jack so clever?' inquired Ida, more for the sake of sustaining the conversation than from any personal interest in the subject.

'Oh, because he knows everything. He told me all about Macbeth, the witches, don't you know, and the ghost, and Mrs.—no, Lady Macbeth— walking in her sleep, and then he made my flesh creep—worse than you do when you talk about ghosts. And then he told me about Agamemnon, the same that's in Homer. I haven't begun Greek yet, but Mr. Jardine told me about him and Cly—Cly—what's her name?—his wife. And then he told me about Africa and the black men, and about India, and tiger-hunts, and snakes, and the great mountains where there are tribes of wild monkeys;—I should so like to have a monkey, Ida! Can I have a monkey? And he told me about South America, just as if he had been there and seen it all.'

'He must be a genius,' said Ida, smiling.

'Can I have a monkey?'

'If your mother doesn't object, and if we can get a nice one that won't bite you.'

'Oh, he wouldn't bite me; I should be friends with him directly. When I am grown up I shall shoot tigers.'

'I shall not like Mr. Cheap Jack if he puts such ideas into your head.'

'Oh, but you must like him, Ida, for I mean to have him always for my friend; and when I come of age I shall go to the Rockies with him, and shoot moose and things.'

'Oh, you unkind boy! is that all the happiness I am to have when you are grown up.'

'You can come too.'

'What, go about America with a Cheap Jack! What a dreadful fate for me!'

'He is not dreadful—he is a splendid fellow.'

'But if he hates women he would make himself disagreeable.'

'Not to you. He would like you. I talked to him about you once, and he listened, and seemed so pleased, and made me tell him a lot more.'

'Impertinent curiosity!' said Ida, with a vexed air. 'You are a very silly boy to talk about your relations to a man of that class.'

'He is not a man of that class,' retorted Vernon angrily; 'besides I didn't talk about my relations, as you call it. I only talked about you. When I told him about mamma he didn't seem to listen. I could see that by his eyes, you know; but he made me go on talking about you, and asked me all kinds of questions.'

'He is a very impertinent person.'

'Hush, there he is, smoking outside his cottage,' cried the boy, pointing to a figure sitting on a rude bench in front of that hovel which had once sheltered Lord Pontifex's under-keeper.

Ida saw a tall, broad-shouldered figure with a tawny face and a long brown beard. The face was half hidden under a slouched felt hat, the figure was clad in clumsy corduroy. Ida was just near enough to see that the outline of the face was good, when the man rose and went into his hut, shutting the door behind him.

'Discourteous, to say the least of it,' she exclaimed, laughing at Vernon's disconcerted look.

'I'll make him open his door,' said the boy, running towards the cottage; but Ida ran after him and stopped him midway.

'Don't, my pet,' she said; 'every man's house is his castle, even Cheap Jack's. Besides I have really no wish to make your friend's acquaintance. Oh, Vernie,' looking at her watch, 'it's a quarter-past nine! We must go home as fast as ever we can.'

'He is a nasty disagreeable thing,' said Vernon. 'I did so want you to see the inside of his cottage. He has no end of books, and the handsomest fox terrier you ever saw—and such a lot of pipes, and black bear skins to put over his bed at night—such a jolly comfortable little den! I shall have one just like it in the park when I come of age.'

'You talk of doing so many things when you come of age.'

'Yes; and I mean to do them, every one; unless you and mother let me do them sooner. It's a dreadful long time to wait till I'm twenty-one!'

'I don't think we are tyrants, or that we shall refuse you anything reasonable.'

'Not a cottage in the park?'

'No, not even a cottage in the park.'

They walked back at a brisk pace, by common and park, not loitering to look at anything, though the glades and hills and hollows were lovely in that dim half-light which is the darkness of summer. The new moon hung like a silver lamp in mid-heaven, and all the multitude of stars were shining around and above her, while far away in unfathomable space, shone the mysterious light which started on its earthward journey in the years that are gone for ever.

Lady Palliser was not calmly slumbering in front of the tea-table, in the mellow light of a duplex lamp, after her wont. She was standing at the open window, watching for Ida's return.

'Oh, my dear, I have been so frightened,' she exclaimed, as Ida and Vernon appeared.

'About what, dear mamma?'

'About Brian. He has been going on so. Rogers came to tell me, and I went up to the corridor, and asked him to unlock his door and let me in, but he wouldn't. Perhaps it was providential that he didn't unlock the door, for he might have killed me.'

'Oh, mamma, what nonsense!' exclaimed Ida. She hurried Vernon off to bed before his mother could say another word, and then went back to the widow, who was walking about the drawing-room in much perturbation.

'Now tell me everything,' said Ida; 'I did not want Vernon to be frightened.'

'No, indeed, poor pet. But oh! Ida, if he should try to kill Vernon!'

'Dear mother, he has no idea of killing anyone. What can have put such dreadful notions in your head?'

'The way he went on, Ida. I stopped outside his door ever so long listening to him. He walked up and down like a mad-man, throwing things about, talking and muttering to himself all the time. I think he was packing his portmanteau.'

'There is nothing so dreadful in that—nothing to alarm you.'

'Oh! Ida, when a person is once out of their mind, there is no knowing what they may do.'

Ida did all in her power to soothe and reassure the frightened little woman, and, having done this, she went straight to her husband's room.

She knocked two or three times without receiving any answer; then came a sullen refusal: 'I don't want to be worried by anyone. You can go to your own room, and leave me alone.'

But, upon her assuming a tone of authority, he opened the door, grumbling all the while.

The room was in frightful confusion—a couple of portmanteaux lay open on the floor; books, papers, clothes, were scattered in every direction. There was nothing packed. Brian was in shirt-sleeves and slippers, and had been smoking furiously, for the room was full of tobacco.

'Why don't you open your windows, Brian?' said his wife; 'the atmosphere is horrible.'

She went over to one of the windows, and flung open the sash. 'That's a comfortable thing to do,' he said, coming over to her, 'to open my window on a snowy night.'

'Snowy, Brian! Why, it's summer—a lovely night!'

'Summer! nonsense. Don't you see the snow? Why, it's falling thickly. Look at the flakes—like feathers. Look, look!' He pointed out of the window into the clear moonlit air, and tried to catch imaginary snowflakes with his long, nervous fingers.

'Brian, you must know that it is summer-time,' Ida said, firmly. 'Look at the woods—those deep masses of shadow from the oaks and beeches—in all the beauty of their summer foliage.

'Yes; it's odd, isn't it?—midsummer, and a snow-storm!'

'What have you been doing with all those things?'

'Packing. I must go to London early to-morrow. I have an appointment with the architect.'

'What architect?'

'The man who is to plan the alterations for this house. I shall make great alterations, you know, now that the place is yours. I am going to build an underground riding school, like that at Welbeck.'

'The place mine? What are you dreaming of?'

'Of course it is yours, now Vernon is dead. You were to inherit everything at his death. You cannot have forgotten that.'

'Vernon dead! Why, Brian, he is snug and safe in his room a little way off. I have seen him within this half-hour.'

'You are a fool,' he said; 'he died nearly three months ago. You are the sole owner of this place, and I am going to make it the finest mansion in the county.'

He rambled on, talking rapidly, wildly, of all the improvements and alterations he intended making, with an assumption of a business-like air amidst all this lunacy, which made his distracted state so much the more painful to contemplate. He talked of builders, specifications, estimates, and quantities—was full of self-importance—described picture galleries, music rooms, high-art decorations which would have cost a hundred thousand pounds, and all with absolute belief in his own power to realise these splendid visions. Yet every now and then in the very rush of his projects there came a sudden cloud of fear—his jaw fell—he looked apprehensively behind him—became darkly brooding—muttered something about that hideous charge hanging over him—a conspiracy hatched by men who should have been his friends—the probability of a great trial in Westminster Hall; and then he ran on again about builders and architects—Whistler, Burne Jones—and the marvellous mansion he was going to erect on the site of this present Wimperfield.

He rambled on with this horrible garrulity for a time that seemed almost an eternity to his agonised wife, and only ceased at last from positive exhaustion. But when Ida talked to him with gentle firmness, reminding him that Vernon was still the owner of Wimperfield, and that she was never likely to be its mistress, he changed his tone, and appeared to be in some measure recalled to his right senses.

'What, have I been talking rot again?' he muttered, with a sheepish look. 'Yes, of course, the boy is still owner of the place. The alterations must stand over. Get me some brandy and soda, Ida, my mouth is parched.'

Ida rose as if to obey him, and rang the bell; but when the servant came she ordered soda-water only.

'Brandy and soda,' Brian said; 'do you hear? Bring a bottle of brandy. I can't get through the night without a little now and then.'

Ida gave the man a look which he understood. He left the room in silence.

'Brian,' she said, when he was gone, 'you must not have any more brandy. It is brandy which has done you harm, which has filled your brain with these horrible delusions. Mr. Fosbroke told me so. You affect to despise him; but he is a sensible man who has had large experience.'

'Large experience! in an agricultural village—physicking a handful of rustics!' cried Brian, scornfully.

'I know that he is clever, and I believe him,' answered Ida; 'my own common sense tells me that he is right. I see you the wreck and ruin of what you have been; and I know there is only one reason for this dreadful change.

'It is your fault,' he said sullenly. 'I should be a different man if you had cared for me. I had nothing worth living for.'

Ida soothed him, and argued with him, with inexhaustible patience, full of pity for his fallen state. She was firm in her refusal to order brandy for him, in spite of his angry protest that he was being treated like a child, in spite of his assertion that the London physician had ordered him to take brandy. She stayed with him for hours, during which he alternated between rambling garrulity and sullen despondency; till at last, worn out with the endeavour to control or to soothe him, she withdrew to her own room, adjoining his, and left him, in the hope that, if left to himself, he would go to bed and sleep.

Rest of any kind for herself was impossible, weighed down with anxiety about her husband's condition, and stricken with remorse at the thought that it was perhaps his ill-starred marriage which had in some wise tended to bring about this ruin of a life. And yet things had gone well with him, existence had been made very easy for him, since his marriage; and only moral perversity would have so blighted a career which had lain open to all the possibilities of good fortune. The initial difficulty—poverty, which so many men have to overcome, had been conquered for Brian within the first year of his marriage. And now six years were gone, and he had done nothing except waste and ruin his mind and body.

Ida left the door ajar between the two rooms, and lay down in her clothes, ready to go to her husband's assistance if he should need help of any kind. She had taken the key out of the door opening from his room into the corridor, so that he would have to pass through her own room in going out. She had done this from a vague fear that he might go roaming about the house in the dead of the night, scaring her stepmother or the boy by some mad violence. She made up her mind to telegraph for the London physician early next morning, and to obtain some skilled attendant to watch and protect her husband. She had heard of a man in such a condition throwing himself out of a window, or cutting his throat: and she felt that every moment was a moment of fear, until proper means had been taken to protect Brian from his own madness.

She listened while he paced the adjoining room, muttering to himself; once she looked in, and saw him sitting on the floor, hunting for some imaginary objects which he saw scattered around him.

'How did I come to drop such a lot of silver?' he muttered; 'what a devil of a nuisance not to be able to pick it up properly?'

She watched him groping about the carpet, pursuing imaginary objects, with eager sensitive fingers, and muttering to himself angrily when they evaded him.

By-and-by he flung himself upon his bed, but not to sleep, only to turn restlessly from side to side, over and over again, with a weary monotony which was even more wearisome to the watcher than to himself.

Two or three times he got up and hunted behind the bed curtains, evidently with the idea of some lurking foe, and then lay down again, apparently but half convinced that he was alone. Once he started up suddenly, just as he was dropping off to sleep, and complained of a flash of light which had almost blinded him.

'Lightning,' he muttered; 'I believe I am struck blind. Come here, Ida.'

She went to him and soothed him, and told him there had been no lightning; it was only his fancy.

'Everything is my fancy,' he said, 'the world is built out of fancies, the universe is only an extension of the individual mind;' and then he began to ramble on upon every metaphysical theory he had ever read about, from Plato and Aristotle to Leibnitz and Kant, from Hegel to Bain—talking, talking, talking, through the slow hours of that terrible night.

At last, when the sun was high, he fell into what seemed a sound sleep; and then Ida, utterly worn with care and watching, changed her gown for a cashmere *peignoir*, and lay down on her bed.

She slept soundly for a blessed hour or more of respite and forgetfulness, then woke suddenly with an acute consciousness of trouble, yet vaguely remembering the nature of that trouble Memory came back only too soon. She rose hurriedly, and went to look at her patient.

His room was empty. He had passed through her room and gone out into the corridor, without awakening her. She rang her bell, and was answered by Lady Palliser's own maid, Jane Dyson, who came in a leisurely way with the morning cups of tea. It was now seven o'clock.

'Is Mr. Wendover downstairs—in the dining-room or library?' Ida asked, trying not to look too anxious.

'I have not seen him, ma'am.'

'Inquire, please. I want to know where he is, and why he left his room so much earlier than usual.'

She had a dismal feeling that all the household must know what was amiss, that the shame and degradation of the case could hardly be deepened.

'Yes, ma'am; I'll go and see.'

'Do, please, while I take my bath,' said Ida. 'You can come back to me in ten minutes.'

The cold bath refreshed her, and she was dressing hurriedly when Jane Dyson returned to announce that Mr. Wendover and Sir Vernon had gone out fishing at half-past six—the under-housemaid had seen them go, and had heard Mr. Wendover say that they would have a long day.

'Go and ask her if she heard where they were going,' said Ida, going on with her dressing, eager to be out of doors on her brother's track.

That wild talk of Brian's last night—that horrible delusion about the boy's death—coupled with this early expedition, filled her with unspeakable fear. It was no new thing for Brian and the boy to go out fishing together. They had spent many a long day whipping distant trout streams in the summer that was gone, but this year Vernon had vainly endeavoured to tempt his old companion to join him in his wanderings with rod and line. Brian had refused all such invitations peevishly or sullenly; as if it were an offence to remind him how poor a creature he had become. And now, after a night of wakefulness and delirium, Brian, with his brain still wild and disordered, perhaps, had taken the boy out with him on some indefinite excursion—alone—the helpless child in the power of a maniac!

Ida did not wait for the return of the maid, but ran downstairs as soon as she was dressed, and questioned Rogers the butler. Rogers, as an old and valuable servant, took his ease of a morning, and only appeared upon the scene when underlings had made all things comfortable and ready to his hand. He therefore knew nothing of the mode and manner of Mr. Wendover and the boy's departure.

Robert, Sir Vernon's body-guard, groom, and general out-door retainer, was fetched from his breakfast; and he was able to inform Mrs. Wendover how Sir Vernon had gone out to the stables at twenty minutes past six, with his fishing basket slung over his shoulder, to ask for some artificial flies which Robert had been making for him, and to say that he should not want the pony or Robert all the morning, as he was going out with Mr. Wendover. He had not mentioned his destination, but Robert knew that the water meadows on the other side of Blackman's Hanger were his favourite ground for such sport. He had been there with Robert many a day.

His remotest point in this direction was five or six miles from home. The boy was able to walk twelve miles in a day without undue fatigue, resting a good deal, and taking his own time; but in a general way he rode his pony when he went on any long excursion, and dismounted from time to time as the fancy took him.

'I'm afraid he may overtire himself with Mr. Wendover, said Ida, anxious to give a good reason for her anxiety. 'Get Cleopatra ready for me, and get a horse for yourself, and we'll ride after them. Mr. Wendover is an invalid, and ought not to have the trouble of a child upon his hands all day. If I can overtake them, I shall persuade them both to come back.'

'If they don't, they'll be likely to get caught,' said Robert, exploring the clouds with the sagacious eyes of a rustic observer schooled by long experience to read signs and tokens in the heavens. 'There'll be a storm, I'm afeard, before dinner-time.'

Dinner-time with Robert meant the hour of the sun's meridian, which he took to be the universal and legitimate dinner-hour for all mankind, designed so to be from the creation.

'How soon can you have the horses ready?'

'In a quarter of an hour, ma'am.'

Ida flew upstairs, meeting her step-mother on the way. Lady Palliser had gone to her son's room as soon as she left her own—her custom always; and on missing the boy, had made instant inquiries as to his whereabouts, and had already taken fright.

'Oh, Ida, if that dreadful husband of yours should lure him into some lonely place, and kill him! My boy, my beloved, my lovely boy!'

'Dear mother, be reasonable. Brian would not hurt a hair of his head. Brian loves him,' urged Ida soothingly, yet with a torturing pain at her heart, remembering Brian's delirious raving last night.

'What will not a madman do? Who can tell what he will do?' cried Lady Palliser, wringing her hands.

'Trust in God, mother; no harm will come to our boy. No harm shall come to him—except perhaps a wetting. Get warm clothes ready for him against I bring him home. I am going to ride after him,' said Ida, hurrying off to her room.

In less than ten minutes she had put on her habit, and was in the stable yard; and three minutes afterwards Fanny Palliser, roaming up and down and round about her son's room like a perturbed spirit, heard the clatter of hoofs, and saw her stepdaughter ride out of the yard attended by Robert, the best and kindest of grooms, and devoted to his young master.

Lady Palliser went downstairs, and again interrogated the housemaid who had witnessed Sir Vernou's departure. 'How had Mr. Wendover seemed?' she asked—'good-tempered, and pleasant, and quiet?'

Very good-tempered, and very pleasant, the girl told her, but not quiet; he talked and laughed a great deal, and seemed full of fun, but in a great hurry.

The mother remembered how many a time her boy and Brian Wendover had been out together, and tried to put away fear. After all, Brian was a nice fellow—he had always made himself agreeable to her. It was only of late that he had become fitful and strange in his ways. She had seen such a case before in her own family, her own flesh and blood, her mother's only brother. That victim to his own vice had been elderly at the time she knew him—a chronic sufferer. She but too well remembered his tottering knees, and restless, tremulous feet: those painful morning hours when he shook like an aspen leaf: those dreadful nights, when he sat cowering over the fire, glancing askant over his shoulder every now and then, haunted by phantoms, hearing and replying to imaginary voices, striving with restless, shivering hands to rid himself of imaginary vermin. He had been mad enough at times in all conscience, as mad as any lunatic in Bedlam; but he had never tried to injure any one but himself. Once they found him with an open razor, possibly contemplating suicide; but he abandoned the idea meekly enough when surprised by his friends, and explained himself with one of those lies with which his tremulous tongue was every so ready.

Arguing with herself by the light of past experience, that after all this drink-madness was a disease apart, seldom culminating in actual violence,

Lady Palliser sat down before her silver urn, and made believe to breakfast, in solitary state, thinking as she poured out her tea how very little all these grand things upon the table could help or comfort one in the hour of trouble. Nay, in such times of misfortune, the little sitting-room of her childhood, the round table and shabby old chairs, the kettle on the hob, and the cat upon the hearth, had seemed to possess an element of sympathy and comfort entirely wanting in this spacious formal dining-room, with its perpetual repetition of straight lines, and its chilling distances.

Ida rode through the park, and across the common, and round the base of Blackman's Hanger, as fast as her clever mare could carry her with any degree of comfort to either. The clever mare was somewhat skittish from want of work, and inclined to show her cleverness by shying at every stray rabbit, or crocodile-shaped excrescence in the way of fallen timber, lying within her range of vision; but Ida was too anxious to be disconcerted by any such small surprises, and rode on without drawing rein to the banks of the trout-stream which wound its silvery way through the valley on the other side of Blackman's Hanger. If they could have crossed the hill, the distance would have been lessened by at least two-thirds, but the steep was much too sheer for any horse to mount, and Ida had to circumnavigate the wooded promontory, which narrowed and dwindled to a furzy ridge at the edge of the river. Once in the valley her way was easy, with only here and there a low hedge for the mare to jump, just enough to put her in good spirits. But after riding for about seven miles along the bank of the stream, Ida pulled up in despair, to ask Robert where next she must look for his master. It was evident this was the wrong scent.

'They'd hardly have come further nor this within the time,' Robert admitted, with a rueful look at the lather on Cleopatra's dark brown neck and shoulder; 'and this is further nor ever I come with Sir Vernon. We must try somewheres else, ma'am.

And so they turned, and at Robert's direction Ida rode off, this time at a walking pace, for another of Vernon's happy hunting grounds.

A sudden ray of hope occurred to her as they returned by the base of Blackman's Hanger. What if Vernon should have taken Brian to Cheap Jack's cottage, to have introduced him to that gifted misanthrope, who, among his other accomplishments, had a talent for repairing fishing tackle?

Moved by this hope, Ida dismounted, and gave Cleopatra's bridle to Robert, who was on his feet almost as soon as his mistress.

'Let the mare rest for a little while, Robert,' she said;' I am going up to the top of the hill to see the pedlar—Sir Vernon may have been with him this morning.'

'Not unlikely, ma'am—he be a rare favourite with Sir Vernon.'

'I hope he's a respectable person.'

'Oh, I think the chap's honest enough,' answered the groom, with a patronising air; 'but he's a queer customer—a reg'lar Peter the wild boy, he is.'

Ida, who had never heard of this gentleman, was not particularly enlightened by the comparison. She went lightly and quickly up the steep ascent, and along a furzy ridge which rose imperceptibly skywards, until she came to the fir plantation which sheltered the gamekeeper's cottage. The lattice stood wide open, and a man was leaning with folded arms on the sill as she came in sight, but in a flash the man had gone, and the lattice was closed.

She ran on, nothing deterred by this discourtesy, and knocked at the door with the handle of her whip.

'Is my brother, Sir Vernon Palliser, here?' she asked.

'No,' a gruff voice answered from within.

'Please open the door, 'I want to ask your advice. The boy has wandered off on a fishing expedition. Have you seen anything of him this morning?'

'No.'

'Are you sure?'

'Do you think I should tell you a lie?' growled the sulky voice from within.

'What a surly brute!' thought Ida. 'How can Vernon like to make a companion of such a man?'

She lingered, only half convinced, and nervously repeated her story— how Sir Vernon had gone out with Mr. Wendover that morning before seven, and how she had been looking for them, and was afraid they would be caught in the storm which was evidently coming.

'You'd better go home before you're half drowned yourself,' growled the surly voice. 'I'll look for the boy and send him home to you, if he's above ground.'

'Will you! will you really look for him?' faltered Ida, in a rapture of gratitude. 'You know his ways, and he is so fond of you. Pray find him, and bring him home. You shall be liberally rewarded. We shall be deeply grateful,' she added hastily, fearing she had offended by this suggestion of sordid recompense.

'I'll do my best,' grumbled the woman-hater, 'when you've cleared off. I shan't stir till you're gone.'

'I am going this instant, my horse is at the bottom of the Hanger. God bless you for your goodness to my brother.'

'God bless you,' replied the voice in a deeper and less strident tone.

Big drops were falling slowly and far apart from the lowering sky as Ida went down the hill, a steep and even dangerous descent for feet less accustomed to that kind of ground.

'You'd better ride home as fast as you can, ma'am,' said Robert, as he mounted Cleopatra's light burden. 'The mare's had a good blow, and you can canter her all the way back.'

'I don't care about the storm for myself. Sir Vernon must be out in it.'

A low muttering peal of thunder rolled slowly along the valley as she settled herself in her saddle.

'Sir Vernon won't hurt, ma'am. Besides, who knows if he ain't at home by this time?'

There was comfort in this suggestion; but after a smart ride home, under a drenching shower diversified by thunder and lightning, Ida found Lady Palliser waiting for her in the portico. There had been no tidings of the boy. Two of the gardeners had been despatched in quest of him—each provided with a mackintosh and an umbrella; and now the mother, no longer apprehensive of homicidal mania on the part of Brian, was tortured by her fear of the fury of the elements, the pitiless rain which might give her boy rheumatic fever, lightnings which might strike him with blindness or death, rivers which might heave themselves above their banks to drown him, trees which might wrench themselves up from their roots on purpose to tumble on him. Lady Palliser always took the catastrophic view of nature when she thought of her boy.

Luncheon was out of the question for either Ida or her stepmother. They went into the dining-room when the gong sounded, and each was affectionately anxious that the other should take some refreshment; but they could do nothing except watch the storm, the fine old trees bending to the tempest, the darkly lurid sky brooding over the earth, thick sheets of rain, driven across the foregound, and almost shutting out the distant woods and hills. The two women stood silently watching that unfriendly sky, and listened for every footstep in the hall, in the fond hope of the boy's return. And then they tried to comfort, each other with the idea that he was under cover somewhere, at some village inn, eating a homely meal of bread and cheese, happy and cheery as a bird, perhaps, while they were so miserable about him.

'I have an idea that Cheap Jack will find them,' said Ida by-and-by. 'Vernon says he is such a clever fellow; and a rover like that would know every inch of the country.'

The day wore on; the storm rolled away towards other hills and woods; and a rent in the dun-coloured clouds showed the bright blue above them. Soon all the heaven was clear, and the wet grass was shining in the afternoon sunlight.

One of the messengers now returned with the useless mackintosh. He had been able to hear nothing of Sir Vernon and his companion. He had been at Wimperfield village, and through two other villages, and had taken a circuitous way back by another meadow-stream, where there might be a hope of trout; but he had seen no trace of the missing boy. The field labourers he had met had been able to give him no information.

There was nothing to be done but to wait, and wait, and wait. Robert had mounted a fresh horse and had gone off to scour the country, wondering not a little that there should be such a fuss about a day's fishing.

Five o'clock came, and afternoon tea, usually the pleasantest hour of the day; for in this summer-time the five o'clock tea-table was prepared in the rose garden in front of the drawing-room, under a Japanese umbrella, and in the shade of a screen of magnolia and Portugal laurel, mock orange and guelder rose, that had been growing for half a century. To-day Lady Palliser and her step-daughter took their tea in silent dejection. They had grown weary of comforting each other—weary of all hopeful speculations.

It was on the stroke of six—the boy and his companion had been away nearly twelve hours. They could do nothing but wait.

Suddenly they heard voices—two or three voices talking excitedly and all together—and then a shrill sweet cry in a voice they both knew so well.

'He is alive!' cried Fanny Palliser, starting up and rushing towards the house.

She had scarcely gone half-a-dozen steps when Rogers came out, crimson, puffing with excitement, leading Vernon by the arm.

'Here he is, my lady, safe and sound!' said Rogers; 'but he has had a rare drenching—the sooner we put him to bed the better.'

'Yes, yes, he must go to bed this instant. Oh, thank God, my darling, my darling! Oh, you naughty boy, how could you give me such a fright! You have almost broken your poor mother's heart, and Ida's too.'

'Dear mother, dear Ida, I am so sorry. But I didn't go alone. I went with Brian. That wasn't naughty, was it?' the boy asked, innocently.

'Naughty to stay away so long—to go so far. Where have you been?'

'Bird's-nesting in the woods, and I have got a honey-buzzard's nest—two lovely eggs, worth ten shillings apiece—the nest is built on the top of a crow's nest, don't you know. First we went fishing, but there were no fish; and then I asked Brian to let me do some bird's-nesting, and we went into the woods—oh, a long, long way, and I got very tired—and we had no lunch. Brian had something in a bottle; he bought it at an inn on the road; I think it was brandy. He swore because it was so bad, but he didn't give me any; and when the storm came on we were on Headborough Hanger, and Brian and I lost each other, and I suppose he came straight home.'

'No, Brian has not come home.'

'Oh, dear,' said the boy; 'I hope he's not looking for me all this time.'

'Come, darling, you must go to bed; we must get off these wet clothes,' said Ida, and Vernon's mother and sister carried him off to his room, where a fire was lighted, and blankets heated, and hot-water bottles brought for the comfort of the young wanderer.

The boy prattled on unweariedly all the time he was being undressed, telling his day's adventures,—how Brian had been frightened because he thought there were some men following them, who wanted to take Brian to prison. He did not see the men, but Brian saw them hiding behind trees, and watching and following them secretly.

'I was very tired,' said the boy, with a piteous look, 'and my feet ached, for Brian would go so fast. And I wanted to come home badly; but Brian said the men were after us, and we must double upon them; and we went round and round and round till we lost ourselves; and then Brian told me to rest on the trunk of a tree while he went a little way further to see if the men were really gone; and I sat and waited till I got very cold, but he did not come back; and then I went to look for him, and couldn't find him; and then I began to cry. I was not frightened, mother, but I was so tired.'

'My poor darling! how could Brian be so cruel?' sobbed the mother, hugging her boy, while Ida was preparing warm negus and chicken sandwiches for his refreshment.

'He wasn't cruel,' explained Vernon; 'he was frightened about those men, ever so much more afraid than I was. But I never saw any men, Ida. How was it Brian could see them, when I couldn't?'

'How did you find your way home at last, dearest?' asked Ida.

'I didn't find it. I should be in the wood still if it was not for Jack—Jack found me, and carried me across the Hanger on his back, and took me up to his cottage, and took off my clothes and dried them, and gave me some brandy in a teaspoon, and then wrapped me in a bear-skin, and carried me all the way here.'

'How good of him!' said Ida; 'and how I should like to thank him for his kindness!'

'He doesn't want to be thanked. He hates girls,' said Vernon, with perfect frankness. 'He just gave me into Rogers' arms and walked off. But I shall go and thank him to-morrow morning, and I shall take him my onyx breast-pin,—the one you gave me last Christmas, mother. You don't mind, do you?'

'No, dear; you may give him anything you like. But I think he would rather have a sovereign—or a nice warm overcoat for the winter. What would be the good of an onyx pin to him?'

'What would be the good of it! Why, he would keep it for my sake, of course!' answered Vernie, with a grand air.

Vernon had no appetite for the chicken sandwiches, or inclination for *Madeira negus*. He took a few sips of the latter to please his womankind, but he could eat nothing. He had fasted all day, and now, in his over excited state, he had no power to eat. Lady Palliser took fright at this, and sent off for the family doctor, that fatherly counsellor in whose wisdom she had such confidence. The boy was evidently feverish, his eyes were too bright, his cheeks flushed. He was restless, and unable to sleep off his fatigue in that placid slumber of childhood which brings healing with its rythmical ebb and flow.

The dinner-gong sounded, and Brian was still missing, but at half-past eight he came in, and walked straight to the drawing-room, where Ida was sitting alone. Neither she nor her stepmother had sat down to dinner. Lady Palliser was in her boy's room, waiting for the doctor.

'Oh, Brian, thank God you are safe!' said his wife, as he came slowly into the room, and sank into a chair. 'What a scare you have given us all!'

'Did you think I was drowned, or that I had cut my throat?' he asked, sneeringly. 'I don't think either event would have mattered much to anyone in this house.'

His manner was entirely different from what it had been last night. His words were cool and deliberate, his expression moody, but in nowise irrational.

'You have no right to say that; but people who say such things seldom mean what they say,' replied Ida, quietly. 'Had you not better go to your room at once and change your clothes, or take a warm bath. It is a kind of suicide to wander about all day in wet clothes as you have done.'

'Who told you I was wandering about all day?'

'Vernon told us.'

'Vernon!' He started, as if suddenly remembering the boy's existence; and then in an agitated manner asked, 'Did he come home? Is he all right?'

'He came home, thank God; at least, he was brought home. I doubt if he could have found his way back alone. I am afraid he is going to be ill.'

'Nonsense! a little cold, perhaps; nothing more. It was a diabolical day. I never saw such rain—a regular tropical down-pour. But what is a shower of rain for a healthy boy?'

'Not much, perhaps, if he is able to change his clothes directly afterwards. But to be wandering about for hours in wet clothes, without food,—that is enough to kill a stronger boy than my brother.'

'It won't kill him, you may depend,' said Brian, with a cynical laugh; 'I should profit too much by his death: and I'm not one of fortune's favourites. He's tough enough.'

'Brian, you have no more heart than a stone.'

'Perhaps not. All the heart I had I gave to you, and you made a football of it; but "Why should a heart have been there, in the way of a fair woman's foot?" as the poet asks.'

'Had you not better go to your room and take off your wet clothes?' repeated Ida.

She had no inclination to argue or remonstrate with a man whose mind was so evidently askew, who had long ago passed the boundary line of principle and noble thought, and had become a mere creature of impulse, blown this way or that way by every gust of passion,—so weak a sinner that her scornful anger was tempered by pity.

'If you are anxious I should escape a severe cold, perhaps you will be liberal enough to allow me a little brandy,' said Brian.

Ida was doubtful how to reply. She had been told to withhold all stimulants, and yet this was an exceptional case. Happily at this very moment the door was opened, and Mr. Fosbroke, the family doctor, was announced.

She ran to meet him. 'Vernon has had a severe wetting, and we are afraid he is going to be ill,' she said. 'I'll take you upstairs at once. Mamma is with him.'

As soon as they were outside in the hall she told him about Brian's request, and asked his advice.

'I think I would give him a small tumbler of grog after his wetting. To refuse would seem too severe. But take care he hasn't the control of the bottle.'

She ran back to her husband, told him she would take some brandy and water to his room for him by the time he had hanged his clothes, and then she went with Mr. Fosbroke to Vernon's room, that bright airy room overlooking the rose garden, which maternal and sisterly love had decorated with all possible prettinesses, and furnished with every appliance of comfort.

Mr. Fosbroke examined the boy carefully, and seemed hardly to like the aspect of the case, though he maintained the customary professional cheeriness.

The boy was feverish, very feverish, he admitted;—pulse a good deal too rapid; temperature high. One could never tell how these cases were going to turn. The boy had suffered unusual fatigue and deprivation, and for a child so reared the strain was severe; but in all probability a gentle febrifuge, which would throw him into a perspiration, and a good night's rest, would be all that was needed, and he would be as well as ever to-morrow morning.

'These small things get out of order so easily,' said Mr. Fosbroke, smiling down at the flushed cheek on the pillow. 'They are like those foolish little Geneva watches ladies are so fond of wearing. My old turnip never goes wrong. You must make haste and grow big, Vernon, and then mamma will not be so easily frightened about you.'

Vernon smiled faintly, without opening his eyes.

'You see, you have contrived between you to make him an exotic,' said the doctor; 'and you mustn't be surprised if he gives you a little trouble now and then. Orchids are beautiful flowers, but they are difficult to rear.'

'Oh, Mr. Fosbroke,' said Lady Palliser, 'how can you say so! Vernie is so hardy—riding his pony in all weathers.'

'Yes, but always provided with a mackintosh—always told to hurry home at the first drop of rain. Well, I dare say he will be ready for his pony to-morrow, if he takes my draught.'

To-morrow came, but Vernon was not in a condition to ride his pony. The fever and prostration were worse than they had been over night, and while Brian seemed to have taken no harm from his exposure to the storm, the boy had evidently suffered a shock to the system, from which he would be slow to recover.

Tortured with anxiety about this idolised brother, Ida did not forget her duty to her husband. She did what she had resolved to do during the long watches of that agonising night, in which she had seen Brian the victim of his own weak self-indulgence, to all intents and purposes a madman, yet unworthy of the compassion which lunacy inspires, since this madness was self-induced,—she telegraphed to the London physician whose advice her husband affected to value; and at five o'clock in the afternoon she had the satisfaction of seeing a soberly-clad gray-haired gentleman alight from a Petersfield fly in front of the portico. This was Dr. Mallison, of Harley Street, a great authority in all nervous disorders—as thorough and as real a man as Dr. Rylance was artificial and shallow, yet a man whom some of Dr. Rylance's most profitable patients denounced as a brute.

Dr. Mallison's plain and straightforward manner invited confidence, and Ida confided her fears and anxieties to him without scruple, telling him faithfully all that she had observed in her husband's conduct before and after that one dreadful night, which she described shudderingly.

'Yes, I remember his case. This seems to have been rather a sharp attack. He had one early in the spring, just before he came to me.'

'An attack—like this one—an attack of—'

'Delirium tremens. Not quite so bad as this last, from his own account; but then one can never quite trust a patient's account. And you say he is better now?'

'Yes; he has been in his room all to-day, writing or reading. He seems dull and low-spirited, that is all.'

'No delusions to-day?'

'Not that I have discovered; but I have only seen him now and then. My little brother is ill, and I have been in his room most of my time.'

'Poor soul! that is a bad job,' said Dr. Mallison, kindly. 'Well, you must have an attendant for your husband. Can you get anybody here, do you think? Or shall I send you a man from town?'

'I shall be very grateful if you will send some one. It would be difficult to get any one here.'

'I dare say it would. I'll get a person despatched to you by the mail train, if I am back in time. Your husband must not be left to himself. That is a vital point. Still so long as he is reasonable, and shows no sign of violence, it will not do to let him suppose that he is watched. That would aggravate matters. You must be diplomatic. Let the man pass as an extra servant, not a professional nurse. All invalids detest professional nurses.'

'Is this dreadful malady likely to pass away?' asked Ida, falteringly.

It was unspeakably painful to her to discuss her husband's failing; and yet she wanted to learn all that could be known about it.

'Undoubtedly. Remove the cause, and the effect will cease. But you have to do more than that. You have to restore the constitution to its normal state—to renew the tissues which intemperance has destroyed—in a word, to eliminate the poison and then the craving for drink will cease, and your husband may begin life again, like Naaman after his seventh dip in Jordan. At Mr. Wendover's age, such a habit ought not to be fatal. There is ample time for reform; but I give you fair warning that it is not an easy disease to cure. I'm not talking of delirium tremens, which is a symptom rather than a disease, but of alcoholic poisoning. The craving for alcohol once established is an ugly weed to root out.'

'If patience and care can cure him, he shall be cured,' said Ida, with a steadfast look, which gave new nobility to her beautiful face in the observant eyes of the physician—a man keen to appreciate every gradation of the physical and the mental, and to tell to the nicest shade where sense left off and soul began. Here was a woman assuredly in whom soul predominated over sense.

'I believe that, madam,' he said, kindly; 'and you shall have my best assistance, depend upon it.'

'Why should a young man bring upon himself such an affliction as this?' Ida asked, wonderingly. 'Ours is counted a sober era.'

'Why, indeed? After-dinner boozing and three-bottle men are a tradition of the dark ages; and yet there are dozens of young men in London—gifted young men some of them—who are doing this thing every year. Half the untimely deaths you hear of might be traced home to the brandy bottle, if a man had only the curiosity to look into first causes. One man dies of congestion of the lungs. Yes, but he had burnt up his lungs first with perpetual alcohol. Another is a victim to liver. Why, madam, a temperate man may work thirty years under an Indian sun, and hardly know that he has a liver. Another is said to have died of too much brain work. Yes, work done by a brain steeped in alcohol—not a brain, but a preparation in spirits. They all do the same thing—pegging—pegging—pegging—from breakfast to bed-time; and most of them would deny that they are drunkards.'

'Do you think that if my husband drank it was because he was not happy—because he had something on his mind?'

'Much more likely that it was because he had nothing on his mind, my dear madam. These briefless barristers in the Temple—men with private means, not obliged to hunt for work, with a little fancy for literature, and a little taste for the drama—these idle youths, whose only idea of social intercourse is to be gossiping and drinking in one another's rooms all day long, living an undomestic life in chambers, without the public interests or athletic sports of a university—these are the chosen victims of alcohol. Of course, I don't pretend for a moment that they all drink; but where the tendency to drink exists this is the kind of life to foster it.'

'My husband was not obliged to live in chambers—he had a home here.'

'Yes; but young men, unless they are sportsmen, hate the country; and then, once in the London vortex, a man can't easily escape. And now, I suppose, I had better go and see the patient. Does he know I have been sent for?'

'No.'

'Then perhaps we shall have a scene. He may be angry.'

'I must risk that,' said Ida, firmly. 'He refused to be treated by our family doctor, and I felt that things could not go on any longer as they were going on.'

She led the way to Brian's room. He was lounging by the open window, smoking; his books and papers were scattered about the tables in reckless disorder.

'Dr. Mallison has come to see you, Brian,' said Ida, quietly, as the physician followed her into the room.

'You sent for him, then!' exclaimed Brian, starting up angrily.

'There was no alternative; you refused to be attended by Mr. Fosbroke.'

'Fosbroke—a village apothecary, the parish doctor, who would have poisoned me. Yes, I should think so. How dare you send for anyone? How dare you treat me like a child?'

'I dare do anything which I believe to be for your good,' Ida answered, unflinchingly.

He quailed before her, and changed his tone in a moment. 'Well, if it gratifies you to spend your money upon physicians—How do you do, Dr. Mallison? Of course, I am very glad to see you, as a friend; but I want no doctoring.'

'I'm afraid you do,' said the physician. 'You have not done what I told you when I saw you in London.'

'What was that?'

'To give up all stimulants.'

'Oh, that was impossible! It's just like asking a man to shut his mouth, and breathe only through his nostrils, when he has lived all his life with his mouth open. No man can change his habits all at once, at the fiat of a physician. But I have been very moderate ever since I saw you.'

'And yet you have had another attack?'

'Who told you that?' asked Brian, with an angry glance at his wife.

'Your own appearance tells me—yes, and your pulse. You have been indulging in the old habits—nipping all day long; and you have been sleeping badly.'

'Sleeping badly!' muttered Brian moodily; 'I wish to Heaven I could sleep anyhow. I have forgotten the sensation of being asleep—I don't know what it means. Just as I fancy myself dropping off there comes a flash of light in my eyes, and I am broad awake again. The other night I thought it lightened perpetually, but my wife said there was no lightning.'

'A case of shattered nerves, and all your own doing,' said Dr. Mallison. 'You must leave off brandy.'

'Brandy has left me off,' retorted Brian. 'My wife and her step-mother have gone in for strict economy. I am not allowed a spoonful of cognac, although I tell them it is the only thing that staves off racking neuralgic pains.

'You must endure neuralgia rather than go on poisoning yourself with brandy. For you alcohol is rank poison—you are suffering now from the cumulative effect of all you have taken within the last twelve months. There are men who can drink with impunity—go on drinking hard through a long life; but you are not one of those. Drink for you means death.'

'A man can die but once,' grumbled Brian; 'and an early death is better than an aimless life.'

'For shame!' said the physician. 'If I had such a wife as you have, the aim of my life would be to make myself worthy of her, and to win distinction for her sake.'

'Ah, there was a time when I thought the same,' answered Brian; 'but that's over and done with.'

Ida left the doctor and his patient together, and walked up and down the corridor outside her husband's room, waiting to hear Dr. Mallison's final directions. He remained closeted with Brian for about a quarter of an hour.

'I have said all I could, and I have written a prescription which may do some good,' he told Ida. 'This is a case for moral suasion rather than medical treatment. If you can exercise a good influence over your husband, and keep all stimulants away from him, he will recover. But his constitution has been undermined by bad habits—an indolent unhealthy life—a life spent in hot rooms, by artificial light. Get him out of doors as much as you can, without exposing him to bad weather or undue fatigue. He is very weak, and altogether out of gear; and you mustn't expect much improvement until he recovers tone and appetite; but if you can ward off any return of the delirium, that will be something gained.'

'Indeed it will. The delirium was too terrible.'

'Well, keep all drink away from him.'

'Even if he seems to suffer for want of it?'

'Yes. The old-fashioned idea was that stopping a man's drink suddenly would bring on an attack of delirium tremens; but we know better than that now. We know that the delirium is only a consequence of alcoholic poisoning, and inevitable where that goes on.'

Ida went back to the drawing-room with the doctor. The tea-table was ready, and there were decanters and sandwiches on another table. Dr. Mallison took a cup of tea and a sandwich, while he gave Ida minute directions as to the treatment of the patient. And then he accepted the handsome cheque which had been written for him, with Mr. Fosbroke's advice as to amount, and took his departure, promising to send a skilled attendant within the next twelve hours.

Ida felt happier after she had seen Dr. Mallison. There was very little that could be done for her husband. He had sown his wild oats, and that light scattering of the seeds of folly had been pleasant enough, no doubt, in the time of sowing; and this was the unanticipated result—a bitter harvest of care and pain which had to be endured somehow.

And now came for that household at Wimperfield a period of agonising trouble and fear. The boy's illness developed into an acute attack of rheumatic fever, and for three dreadful days and nights his life trembled in the balance. Not once did Ida enter her husband's room during that awful period of fear. She could not steel herself to look upon the man whose sin, or whose folly, had brought this evil on her beloved one. 'My murdered boy,' she kept repeating to herself. Even on her knees, when she tried to pray, humbly and meekly appealing to the Fountain of mercy and grace—even then, while she knelt with bowed head and folded hands, those awful words flashed into her mind. Her murdered boy.

If he were to die, who could doubt that his death would lie at Brian's door? who could put away the dark suspicion that Brian had wantonly, and with murderous intent, exposed the delicate child to bad weather and long hours of fasting and fatigue?

CHAPTER XXVI
'AND, IF I DIE, NO SOUL WILL PITY ME'

At last their long watchings, their tender care, directed by one of the most famous men in London—who was summoned to Wimperfield at Mr. Fosbroke's suggestion within a week of Dr. Mallison's visit—and attended twice or thrice a day by the clever apothecary, were rewarded by the assurance that the time of immediate danger was over, and that now a slow and gradual recovery might fairly be anticipated. It was only then that Ida could bring herself to face Brian again, and even then she met him with an icy look, as if the life within her were frozen by grief and care, and those rigid lips of hers could never again melt into smiles.

Brian had been leading a fitful and wandering life during the boy's illness, watched and waited upon by Towler, the man from London, with whom he quarrelled twenty times a day, and who needed his long experience of the "ways" of alcoholic victims to enable him to endure the fitfulness and freakishness of his present charge.

Warned by Dr. Mallison that he must spend as much of his life in the open air as possible, Brian had taken to going in and out of the house fifty times a day, now wandering for five or ten minutes in the garden, anon rambling as far as the edge of the park, then running into the stable yard, and ordering a horse to be saddled instantly, but never mounting the horse. After seeing the animal led up and down the yard once or twice, he would always find some excuse for not riding; the fact being that he had no longer courage enough to get into the saddle. His riding days were over. Even the stable mastiff, an old favourite with Brian, gave him a painful shock when the great tawny brute leapt out of his kennel, straining at his chain, and baying deep-mouthed thunder by way of friendly greeting.

Towler had a hard time of it, following his charge here and there, waiting upon him, bearing his abuse; but Towler had a peculiar gift, a faculty for getting on with patients of this kind. He knew how to dodge, and follow, and circumvent them; how to take liberties with them, and scold them, without too deeply wounding their *amour-propre*; how to humour and manage them; and although Mr. Wendover quarrelled with his attendant fifty times a day, he yet liked the man, and tolerated his presence; and had already come to lean upon him, and to be angry when Towler absented himself.

'Well,' said Brian, looking up as Ida entered his room on that happy morning on which she had been told that her brother was out of danger— 'the boy is better, I hear?'

These things are quickly known in a household, when there has been general anxiety about the issue of an illness.

'Yes, he is better. By God's grace, he will live; but his life has trembled in the balance. Brian, it would have been your fault if he had died.'

'Would it? Yes, I suppose indirectly I should have been the cause. I was a fool to take him out that morning; but,' shrugging his shoulders, 'I wanted a ramble, and I wanted company. Who could tell there would be such a diabolical storm, or that we should lose our way? Thank God he is out of danger. Poor little beggar! Did you think I wanted to put him out of the way?' he asked, suddenly, looking at her with a keen flash of interrogation.

'To think that would be to think you a murderer,' she answered, coldly. 'I have thought that you had little affection for him or for me when you exposed him to that danger; and then I schooled myself to think better of you—to remember that, perhaps, on that day you were hardly responsible for your actions.'

'In fact, that I was a lunatic,' said Brian.

'I would rather think you mad than wicked.'

'Perhaps I am neither. Why have you put that man as a spy upon me?'

The discreet Towler had retired into the adjacent bedroom during this conversation.

'He is not a spy. Dr. Mallison said you ought to have a servant specially to wait upon you, that in your sleepless nights you might not be left alone.'

'No, they are a trial, those long nights. Towler is not a bad fellow, but he irritates me sometimes. Last night he let a black-muzzled gipsy brute hide behind my curtains, and then told me it was my "delusions." Delusions! when I saw the fellow as plain as I see you now.'

Ida was silent. She had hoped that the patient had passed this stage, and was on the road to recovery of health and reason. She interrogated Towler by-and-by, and he assured her that Mr. Wendover had taken no stimulants since he had been attending upon him.

'Are you sure he cannot get any without your knowledge?' Ida asked. 'Dr. Mallison told me that in this malady a patient is terribly artful—that he will contrive to evade the closest watchfulness, if it is any way possible to get drink.'

'Ah, that's true enough, ma'am,' sighed the man; 'there's no getting to the bottom of their artfulness: but I'm an old hand, and I know all the ins and outs of the complaint. It isn't possible for Mr. Wendover to get any drink in this house, and he never goes out of it without me. Every drop of wine and spirits is under lock and key, and all the servants are warned against giving him anything.'

Ida sighed, full of shame at the thought that her husband, the man whom it was her duty to honour and obey, should be degraded by such humiliating precautions; and yet there was no help for it. He had brought himself to this pass. This is the end of ambrosial nights, the feast of reason, the flow of soul, wit drowned in whisky, satire stimulated by brandy and soda.

Ida went back to her brother's room. It was there her love, her fears, her cares were all concentrated. Duty might make her careful and thoughtful for her husband, but here love was paramount. To sit by his pillow, to talk to him, or read to him, or pray for him, to minister to him, jealous of the skilled nurse who had been hired to perform these offices,—these things were her delight. Lady Palliser, worn out with watching and anxiety, had now broken down altogether, and had consented to take a long day's rest; but Ida's more energetic nature could do with much less rest—half an hour's delicious sleep now and then, with her head on her darling's pillow, was all-sufficient to restore her.

And so the blessed days of hope went on, and every morning and every afternoon Mr. Fosbroke's report was more favourable. It was a tedious recovery from a cruel disease, happily shortened by at least two-thirds of its old-fashioned length by modern treatment; but all was going well, and the hearts of the watchers were at ease. The boy lay swathed in cotton wool, very helpless, very languid, fed and petted from morning till night, like a young bird brought up by hand: and Ida and her stepmother had to be patient and thankful.

Ida had often thought during the boy's illness of the man who had found him, and brought him safely home to them on that anxious day; and she wished much to testify her gratitude to the misanthropic dweller in the gamekeeper's cottage; but she hesitated as to her manner of approaching him. To go herself would be futile, when he had so obdurately shut his door against her. Then she had Vernon's assurance that this Bohemian hated women. She might have sent a servant with a message; but she had reason to know, from Vernon's description of the man, that he was altogether above the servant class, and would be likely to resent such a form of approach. She might have written to him; but her pride recoiled from that course, remembering his cavalier treatment of her. And so she let the days slip by, until Vernon began to recover strength and good spirits, and to inquire about his friend.

'I want Jack to come and see me, and sit with me,' said the boy; 'he could come to tea couldn't he, mother? You wouldn't mind, would you?'

'My dear, he is not a proper person for you to associate with,' replied Lady Palliser. 'You oughtn't to bemean yourself by associating with your inferiors.'

'Bemean fiddlesticks!' cried Vernie; 'I don't believe there is such a word. Jack is the cleverest man I know—cleverer than Mr. Jardine, and that's saying a great deal.'

Vainly did the widow endeavour to awaken her son's mind to the great gulf which divides a baronet from a hawker—a gulf not to be bridged over by the genius of a Dalton or a Whewell—and to those nice distinctions which obtain between a casual out-of-door intercourse with a man of this class, and a deliberate invitation to tea.

'When I'm well enough to go out I can go to him,' answered Vernon, doggedly; 'but now I'm ill he must come to me; and it's very unkind of you not to let him come. Blow his station in life! If he was a duke I shouldn't want him.'

'I can't think what you can want with this low person, when Ida and I are always doing everything to amuse you,' moaned Lady Palliser.

'Ida's a darling, and you too, mother,' said the boy, putting his thin little arms round his mother's neck. He was now just able to move those poor arms, which had been so racked with pain a little while ago. 'But I get tired of everything—Shakespeare, Dickens, even. It's so long to stay in bed; and I think Jack would amuse me more than anyone, if you'd let him come.'

'He shall come, darling. Is there anything I could refuse you?' said the mother, eagerly, moved by the sight of tears in Vernon's innocent blue eyes.

'Ask him to come to tea this afternoon.'

'Yes, love; I'll go and see about it this minute.'

Lady Palliser went in quest of Ida, who was sitting in Brian's study reading, while her husband wrote, or made believe to write, at a table in the window piled with books of reference, which he consulted every now and then, lolling back in his chair and reading listlessly—altogether a mere show and pretence of study, never likely to result in anything—a weary dawdling away of the long summer morning.

To Ida, Lady Palliser explained her difficulty. A note of some kind must be written to this Cheap Jack; and the little woman did not know how to word that note.

'If I say, "Lady Palliser presents her compliments to Mr. Cheap Jack, and requests the pleasure of his company," it seems like patting myself on a level with him, don't you know. I wish you'd write for me, Ida.'

'Willingly, dear mother; but I'm afraid the man won't come. He is such a very rough diamond.'

'Oh! but surely he will be gratified at an invitation to tea!'

'I'm afraid not. But I'll write at once. Anything to please Vernon.' Ida wrote as follows:—

'Sir Vernon Palliser, who is slowly recovering from a serious illness, will be very pleased if his friend Jack will spend an hour or two with him this afternoon. Any hour convenient to Jack will be agreeable to Sir Vernon, but he would much like Jack to drink tea with him between four and five. The other members of the family will not intrude upon the sick room while Jack is there.'

'I think that will do,' said Ida; and Lady Palliser carried off the note, wondering at her stepdaughter's cleverness, yet inclined to fear that the hermit of Blackman's Hanger might be offended at being addressed as Jack, *tout court*; and yet how could one deal ceremoniously with a man who acknowledged no surname, and was known to all the neighbourhood only as 'Cheap Jack'?

Mr. Fosbroke came for his noontide visit just after this business of the letter, and found Ida and her stepmother both with the invalid. He was told what they had done.

'Do you think he'll come?' Vernon asked, eagerly.

'I should think he would. Sir Vernon,' answered the doctor; 'for I know he takes a keen interest in your recovery. All the time you were really bad he used to hang about the Park gate every day as I went out, and stopped me to ask how you were. And he asked after you, too, Mrs. Wendover,—seemed to be afraid your anxiety about this little man would be too much for you.'

'Remarkably polite of him,' said Ida, laughing; 'yet he treated me in the most bearish manner when I went to his cottage.'

'If he is a bear, he is a bear with gentlemanly instincts,' replied the doctor. 'Nothing could be more respectful, more delicate, than his inquiries about you; and I could see by the expression of his eyes that he really felt for you. He has very fine eyes.'

'One of the tokens of his gipsy blood, I suppose,' said Ida.

'Yes; I believe he is a gipsy. They are a keen-witted race.'

'A gipsy!—and with so much plate as there is in this house!' exclaimed Lady Palliser. 'Oh, Vernie, you ought not to have asked me to ask him!'

'Don't be afraid, mother,' said Ida; 'he shall be sharply looked after, if he does come.'

'Looked after, indeed! Why, you might give him the run of a silver mine. What does he care for your trumpery silver spoons?' cried Vernon, contemptuously.

The invalid was doomed to disappointment. About two hours after Ida's letter had been despatched, a small boy brought Cheap Jack's reply, to the following effect:—'Jack is very sorry he cannot drink tea with his little friend—'

'Little friend, indeed! What vulgar familiarity!' exclaimed Lady Palliser.

'But he belongs to the dwellers in tents, and would be out of place in a fine house—'

'Then he *is* a gipsy,' said Lady Palliser. 'What a luck; escape!'

'He looks forward to the pleasure of seeing Sir Vernon on the Hanger before long. Meanwhile he can only send his duty and best wishes for Sir Vernon's speedy recovery.'

'The end is a little better than the commencement,' said Lady Palliser; 'but I call it a great liberty for a Cheap Jack to talk of my son as his little friend.'

'He might have left out "little," considering that I shall be twelve next birthday,' said Vernon, with dignity. 'But I am his friend, mother; and I mean to be his friend always. And when I am grown up I shall take him to the Rocky Mountains, and we will hunt moose and things.'

Lady Palliser sighed, and hoped that this passion for low company would pass with the other follies of childhood.

Now that all danger was past, and that Vernon was on the high-road to health, Ida spent the greater part of her time in attendance upon her husband. It was her duty, she told herself; and she who had so failed in love must needs fulfil every duty. But the performance of this simple, wifely duty of attendance on an invalid husband was fraught with pain: his temper was so irritable, his mind was so weak, his whole being so degraded and sunk by his infirmity, that the progress of his decay was, of all forms of dissolution, the most painful for the looker-on. That he was sinking into a lower depth of degradation, rather than recovering, was sadly obvious to Ida, in spite of occasional intervals of better feeling and rare flashes of his old brightness.

The case was altogether perplexing. Towler admitted that he was more puzzled than he had ever been about any patient whom he had enjoyed the honour of attending. Mr. Wendover, under his present conditions of absolute sobriety, and with youth on his side, ought to have shown a decided improvement by this time; and yet there was no substantial amelioration of his state, and his latest fit of the horrors, which occurred only a night ago, had been quite as bad as the first which Towler had witnessed.

'You do not think that he gets brandy without your knowledge?' inquired Ida, blushing at the question.

'No, ma'am; I'm too careful for that. I've searched his trunks even, and every cupboard in his rooms; and I've looked behind the registers of the stoves, which are very handy places for patients hiding bottles in summer time; but there's not so much as an ounce phial. And Mr. Wendover's hardly out of my sight, except when he takes his bath, or just going in and out of his bath-room, where he keeps his pipes, as you know, ma'am. Besides, even if he had any hiding-place for the drink, who is likely to supply him with it?'

'No; I hope there is no one,' said Ida, thoughtfully. 'I hope no one in this house would so betray my confidence.'

'I've taken stock of all the servants, ma'am, and I don't think there's one that would do it.'

Ida was of the same opinion. The servants were old servants, as loyal to the heads of the house as a highland clan to their chief.

Sunday came—a peaceful summer Sabbath—a day of sunshine and azure sky, and Ida, whose anxiety about Vernon had kept her away from her parish church for the last three Sundays, was able to set out upon her walk to the village with a heart quite at rest on the boy's account. Even the mother could find no excuse for staying at home with her boy, and felt that conscience and society alike required that she should assist at the service of her parish church. Vernie was convalescent, able to sit up in his bed, propped with pillows, and eat hot-house grapes, and turn over the leaves of endless volumes of *Punch*, laughing with his hearty childish laugh at Leech's jokes and the curious garments of a departed era.

'How could men wear such trousers? and how could women wear such bonnets?' he asked his mother, wonderingly contemplating fashionable youth as represented by the great pen-and-ink humourist.

'I don't know why we shouldn't wear them, Vernie,' said his mother, with rather an offended air; 'those spoon bonnets were very becoming. I wore one the day your pa first saw me.'

'And hoops under your gown like that?' said Vernie, pointing; 'and those funny little boots? What a guy you must have looked!'

When a boy has come to this pass he may fairly be left with servants for a couple of hours; so Lady Palliser put on her stateliest mourning—her thick corded silk, flounced with crape and her Mary Stuart bonnet, and went across the park, and up hill and down hill, for it was a country of hills and hollows—to the parish church of Wimperfield, a very ancient edifice, with massive columnar piers, Norman groined roof, and walls enriched by a grand array of memorial tablets, setting forth the honours and virtues of those dead and gone landowners whose bones were mouldering in the vaults below the square oaken pews in which the living worshipped. In the chancel there was the usual stately monument to some magnate of the middle ages, who was represented kneeling by his wife's side, with a graduated row of sons and daughters kneeling behind them, as if the whole family had died and petrified simultaneously, in the act of pious worship.

Ida did not invite her husband to join her in her Sabbath devotions, assured that he would claim an invalid's privilege to stay at home. He had very rarely attended the parish church with his wife, affecting to despise such humdrum and conventional worship. He had just that thin smattering of modern science which enables shallow youth to make a merit of disbelief in all things beyond the limit of mathematical demonstration. He had skimmed Darwin, and spoke lightly of mankind as the latest development of time and matter, and no higher a being, from a spiritual point of view, than the first worm that wriggled in its primeval slime. He had dipped into Herbert Spencer, and talked largely of God as the Unknowable; and how could the Unknowable be supposed to take pleasure in the automatic prayers of a handful of bumpkins and clodhoppers met together in a mouldy old church, time out of mind the temple of superstitions and ceremonies. The vast temple of the universe was Brian Walford's idea of a church; and a very fine church it is, if a man will only worship faithfully therein; but the man who abandons formal prayers and set seasons of devotion with a vague idea of worshipping in the woodland or on the hill top, very rarely troubles himself to realise his ideal.

Brian's broadly-declared agnosticism had long been a cause of pain and grief to his wife. She had felt that this alone would have made sympathy impossible between them, had there been no other ground for difference. She thought with a bitter sense of contrast of his cousin, who was a student and a thinker, and who yet was not ashamed to believe and to worship as a little child. Surely it was not a sign of a weak intelligence for a man to believe in something better and higher than himself, when Socrates, Plato, Aristotle, Homer, and Virgil could so believe. Brian Walford's idea of cleverness was to consider himself the ultimate product of incalculable antecedent time, the full-stop of creation.

Here were all the pious parishioners, the county families, and the country bumpkins, meekly kneeling on their knees, and uplifting their voices in perfect faithfulness—not thinking very deeply of any element in the service perhaps, but honest in their reverence and their love. The old church was a pretty sight on such a summer morning—the white robes of the choristers touched with supernal radiance, the light tempered by the deep rubies and purples and ambers in windows old and new—the very irregularities and architectural anomalies of the building producing a quaintness which was more pleasing than absolute beauty.

The litany was nearly over when Ida heard a familiar step on the stone pavement of the nave. It was Brian's step; and presently he stopped at the door of the high oaken pew, opened it, and came in and seated himself-on the bench, opposite to the spot where she knelt by her step-mother's side. It was a capacious old pew, and would have held ten people. Brian kicked about the hassocks, and made himself comfortable; but he did not kneel, or take any part in the service. He sat with his elbows on his knees, and his chin in his hands, staring at the floor. His presence filled Ida with anxiety. He had not risen from his bed when she left home, and Towler had given her to understand that he would not get up for some time, as he had had a very bad night. He must have risen and dressed hurriedly in order to follow her to church. His eyes had the wild look in them which she had noticed on the night when he saw visions.

It was in vain that Ida tried after this to fix her mind upon the service—every movement, every look of Brian's, alarmed her. She was thankful for the high pew which sheltered him from the gaze of the congregation; and presently when they stood up to sing a hymn, she was glad that Brian remained seated, albeit there was irreverence in the attitude.

But when the last verse was being sung, he rose suddenly and looked all round the church with those wild eyes of his, took up a book and turned the leaves abstractedly, and remained standing like a sleep-walker for a minute or so, after the congregation had gone down on their knees for the communion service.

When the gospel was read he rose again, and lolled with his back against the plastered wall, his head just under a winged cherub head in marble, which adorned the base of a memorial tablet. This time he stood till all the service was over, so obviously apart from all the rest of the congregation, so evidently uninterested in anything that was going on, that Ida felt as if every eye must be watching him, every creature in the church conscious of his infirmity. He was carelessly dressed, his collar awry, his necktie loose, his hair unbrushed. His very appearance was a disgrace, which Lady Palliser, whose great object in life was to maintain her dignity before the eyes of the county families, felt could hardly be lived down in the future.

That pale haggard countenance, those bloodshot, wandering eyes, — surely every creature in the church must know that they meant brandy!

The sermon began—one of those orthodox, old-fashioned, dry-as-dust sermons often heard in village churches, a discourse which sets out with a small point in Bible history, not having any obvious bearing upon modern thought or modern life, and discusses, and explains, and enlarges upon it with deliberate scholarship for about half-an-hour, and then, in a brisk five minutes, endeavours to show how the conduct of Ahab, or Jehoram, or Ahaziah, in this little matter, was an exact counter-part or paradigm of our conduct, my dear brethren, when we, etc., etc.

The Vicar had not arrived at this point, but was still expatiating upon the unbridled wickedness of Jehoram, when Brian, who after a period of alarming restlessness had been sitting like a statue for the last few minutes, suddenly started up, and exclaimed wildly, 'I can't endure it a moment longer—the stench of corruption—the dead rotting in their graves—the horrid, nauseous odour of grave-clothes—the foul stink of earth-worms! How can you bear it! You must have no feeling! you must be made of stone!'

Ida and her stepmother had both risen, each in her way was trying to soothe, to quiet him, to induce him to sit down again. The Vicar had stopped in his discourse, scared by that other voice, but as Brian's loud accents sank into mutterings he took up the thread of his argument, and went on denouncing Jehoram.

'Brian, indeed there is nothing—no bad odour here.'

'Yes, there is the stench of death,' he protested, staring at the ground, and then pointing with a convulsive movement of his wasted hand he cried, 'Don't you see, under that seat there, the worms crawling up through the rotten flooring, there? there!—fifty—a hundred—legion. For God's sake get me out of this charnel house! I can hear the dry bones rattle as the worms swarm out of the mouldering coffins.'

His deadly pallor, his countenance convulsed with disgust, showed how real this horror was to him. Ida put her hand through his arm, and led him quietly away, out of the stony church into the glow of the summer noontide.

He sank exhausted upon a grassy mound in the churchyard—a village child's grave, with the rose wreath which loving hands had woven fading above the sod.

'How can you sit in such a vault?' he asked; 'how can you live in such foul air?'

'Indeed, dear Brian, it is only fancy. There is nothing amiss.'

'There is everything amiss. Death is everywhere—we begin to die directly we are born—life is a descending scale of decay—we rot and rot and rot as we walk about the world, pretending to be alive. First a man loses his teeth, and then his hair, and then he looks in the glass and sees himself withered, and haggard, and wrinkled, and knows that the skeleton's clutch is upon him. I tell you we are always dying. Why go to that vault yonder,' pointing to the church, 'to breathe the concentrated essence of mortality?'

'It is good for us to remember the dead when we worship God, Brian. He is the God of the dead as well as the living. There is nothing terrible in death, if we believe.'

'If we believe! If! The whole future is an "if!" The future! What future can there be for us? We came from nothing, we go back to nothing—we are resolved into the elements which renew the earth for new comers. The wheel of progress is always revolving—for the mass there is eternity, infinity—no beginning, no end; but for the individual, his little span of life begins and ends in corruption.'

The sound of the organ and the fresh rustic voices singing a familiar hymn told Ida that the sermon was over. Lady Palliser was in an agony of anxiety to get Brian away before the congregation came out. She and Ida contrived to beguile him out of the churchyard and away towards Wimperfield Park by a meadow path which was but little frequented. He grew more rational as they walked home, but talked and argued all the way with that semi-hysterical garrulity which was so painful to his hearers.

They found Vernon sitting up in bed, reading 'Grimm's Goblins,' and in very high spirits. A most wonderful event had happened. Cheap Jack had been to see him. He came with Mr. Fosbroke at twelve o'clock. He had overtaken Mr. Fosbroke in the park, and had asked leave to go up to the house with him, just for a peep at his patient.

'He only stayed a quarter of an hour,' said Vernie, 'for old Fos was in a hurry; but it was such fun! He made me laugh all the time, and Fos laughed, too,—he couldn't help it; and he said Jack's funny talk was better for me now than all the medicine in his surgery; and I am to get up for an hour or two this afternoon; and I am to have some chicken, and as much asparagus as ever I can eat—and in less than a week I shall be able to go up to the hanger and see Jack.'

'My darling, you will have to be much stronger first,' said Ida.

'Oh, but I am very strong now, Ah, there's Brian,' as his brother-in-law looked in at the door. 'What a time since you're been to see me! You've been ill, too, mother said. Come in, Brian. Don't mind about giving me a bad cold that day. It wasn't your fault.'

Brian came into the room with a hang-dog look, and sat by the boy's bed.

'Yes, it was my fault, Vernie. I am a wretched creature. Everything that I do ends badly. I didn't mean to do you any harm.'

'Of course not. You thought it was fun, and so did I, till I got tired and hungry. But those men who were chasing you! There were no men, were there? *I* didn't see any,' said the boy, with his clear blue eyes on Brian's haggard face.

'Yes, they were there, dodging behind the trees. I saw them plain enough,' answered Brian, moodily. 'It was about that business I told you of. No, I couldn't tell you; it was not a thing to tell a child—a shameful accusation; but I have given them the slip.'

'Brian,' said Ida, laying her hand on his shoulder, 'why do you say these things? You know you are talking nonsense.'

'Am I?' he muttered, cowering as he looked up at her. 'Well, it's as likely as not. Ta, ta, Vernie! You're as well as ever you were. It is I who am booked for a coffin!'

He went away with his feeble shuffling steps, so unlike the step of youth; Ida following him, thinking sadly of the autumn afternoons when he used to come leaping out of his boat—young, bright, and seemingly full of life and energy, and when she half believed she loved him.

CHAPTER XXVII
JOHN JARDINE SOLVES THE MYSTERY

The Jardines came the next day, self-invited guests. Ida had tried to prevent any such visit, in her desire to keep her husband's degradation from the knowledge of his kindred; but Bessie was not to be so put off. She had heard that Brian was ill, and that Vernon had been dangerously ill; and her heart overflowed with love and compassion for her friend. It was not easy for Mr. Jardine to leave his parish, but he would have done a more difficult thing rather than see his wife unhappy; so on the Monday morning after that scene in the church, Ida received a telegram to say that Mr. and Mrs. Jardine were going to drive over to see her, and that they would claim her hospitality for a couple of days.

It was a drive of over thirty miles, only to be done by a merciful man between sunrise and sunset. Mr. and Mrs. Jardine started at five o'clock, breakfasted and lunched on the road, and brought their faithful steed, Drummer Boy, up to the Wimperfield portico at seven in the evening, with not a hair turned. Ida was waiting for them in the portico.

'You darling, how pale and worried you look!' exclaimed Bessie, as she hugged her friend; 'and why didn't you let me come before?'

'You could have done me no good, dear, when my troubles were at the worst. Thank God the worst is over now—Vernie is getting on splendidly. He was downstairs to-day, and ate such a dinner. We were quite afraid he would bring on a relapse from over-eating. He is delighted at the idea of seeing you and Mr. Jardine.'

'Has he gone to bed? I'll go up to see him at once, if I may,' said John Jardine.

'He is in his own room. He asked to stop up till seven on purpose to see you.'

'Then I'll go to him this instant.'

The luggage had been brought out of the light T cart, and the Drummer Boy had been led round to the stables. Ida took Bessie to a room at the end of the house, remote from Brian's apartments.

'Why, this isn't our usual room!' said Bessie, astonished.

'No, I thought this would be a pleasanter room in such warm weather. It looks east,' Ida answered, rather feebly.

'It's a very nice room; only I felt more at home in the other. I have occupied it so often, you know, I felt almost as if it were my own. Oh, you cruel girl! why didn't you let me come sooner? I wanted so to be with you in your trouble; and I offered to come directly I heard Vernie was ill!'

'I know, dear; but you could have done no good. We were in God's hands. We could only pray and wait.'

'Love can always do good. I could have comforted you!

'Nothing could have comforted me if he had died.'

'And Brian—poor Brian has been ill, too. I thought him very much changed when we were here—so thin, so nervous, so depressed.'

'Yes, he was ill then—he is very ill now. We take all the care we can of him, but he doesn't get any better.'

'Poor dear Brian! and he was once the soul of fun and gaiety—used to sing comic songs so capitally. I suppose it is a poor thing for a man to do, but it was very nice, especially at Christmas time. There are so few people who can do anything to help one over Christmas Eve and Christmas Day. Brian was good at everything—charades, clumps, consequences, dumb crambo. And to think that he should be ill so long! What is his complaint, Ida?' asked Bessie, suddenly becoming earnest, after a lapse into childishness.

'It is a nervous complaint,' faltered Ida; 'he will soon get over it, I hope and believe, if we take proper care of him. He is very excitable, very unlike his old self; and you must not be astonished at anything he may say or do.'

'You don't mean that he is out of his mind?' said Bessie, with an awe-stricken look.

'No, no; nothing of the kind—at least, nothing that is likely to be lasting; but he has delusions sometimes—a kind of hysterical affection. Oh, Bessie, I did not want you to know anything; I tried to keep you away.'

Bessie had her arms round her old friend, and Ida, quite broken down by the fears and agitations of the last six weeks, hid her face upon Mrs. Jardine's shoulder and sobbed aloud. It was a complete collapse of heroic resolutions, of that unflinching courage and strength of mind which had sustained her so long; but it was also a blessed relief to the overcharged heart and brain.

'It is very selfish of me to plague you with my troubles,' she said, when Bessie had kissed and comforted her with every expression of sympathy and tenderness in the gamut of womanly love, 'but I wanted you to be prepared for the worst. And now, let me help you to change your gown, if you are going to make any change for dinner. The gong will sound in less than half-an-hour.'

'Oh, those gongs, they always fill me with despair!' cried Bess. 'I am never ready when ours begins to buzz through the house, like a gigantic, melancholy-mad bumble bee. Of course I must change, dear; firstly, because I am smothered with dust, and sixthly, as Dogberry says, because I have brought a pretty gown to do honour to Wimperfield.'

And Bessie, rushing to her portmanteau, and tearing out its contents in a frantic way, shook out the laces and ribbons of a gracious Watteau-like arrangement in Madras muslin, while she chattered to her hostess.

'Shall I send for Jane Dyson?' the immaculate maid, who had lived with an archbishop's wife. 'She can unpack your things.'

'Not for worlds. I have oceans to tell you, and I should hate that prim personage looking on and listening. Such news, Ida: Urania is engaged.'

'At last!'

'That was what everybody said. This was her sixth season, and it was rapidly becoming a case of real distress, and she was getting blue, oh, to a frightful extent—a perambulatory epitome of Huxley-cum-Darwin,—that's what our boys call her. And now, after refusing ever so many nice young men in the Government offices because they were not rich enough for her, she is going to make a great match, and marry a nasty old man.'

'Oh, Bessie! nasty and old!'

'Strong language, isn't it? but the gentleman has been to Kingthorpe, and there is no doubt about the fact. One wouldn't mind his being elderly if he were only a gentleman; but he is not.'

'Then why in mercy's name does Miss Rylance marry him?'

'Because he is Sir Tobias Vandilk, one of the richest men on the Stock Exchange. He is of Dutch extraction, they say; and this is supposed to account for his utter destitution with regard to English aspirates. He has a palace in Park Lane, and a park in Yorkshire; gives dinners of a most *recherché* description every Thursday in the season; and immense shooting parties, at which I am told he and his friends slaughter quintillions of pheasants, and flood the London market every autumn; and it is whispered that he has lent money to royal personages.'

'Is Urania happy?'

'If she is not, I know who is. Dr. Rylance looks twenty years younger since the engagement. He was beginning to get weighed down by Urania. You remember with what a firm hand he managed her in days gone by! Well, after she took to Huxley and Darwin, and the rest of them, that was all over. She was always tripping him up with some little shred of scientific knowledge, fresh from Tyndall; always attacking his old-fashioned notions with some new light. He was as merry as a boy let loose from school when he came down to Kingthorpe the other day. He went to one of our picnics, and made himself tremendously agreeable. We took Sir Tobias to see the Abbey, and had afternoon tea there. He pretended to admire everything, but in a patronising way that made me savage; affected to think Wendover Abbey a little bit of a place, as compared with his modern barrack in Yorkshire, with its riding-school, tan gallop, range of orchard-houses, picture-gallery, and so on. And Urania's grandeur is something too large for words. "You and Mr. Jardine must come and stay with us at Hanborough some day," she said, as if she were promising me a treat; so I told her plainly that my husband's parish work made such a visit impossible. "Oh, but some day," she said sweetly. "Never," said I; "we are rooted in the chalk of Salisbury Plain." "Poor things!" she sighed, "what a destiny!"'

'And you all drank tea at the Abbey,' said Ida, musingly; 'dear old Abbey! I can fancy you there, in the long low library, with the afternoon sunlight shining in at the open windows, and Mary Stuart smiling at you from the panelling over one fire-place, and crafty Elizabeth looking sideways at you from over the other, and the Dijon roses clambering and twining round every lattice.'

'How well you remember the old place. Isn't it horrid of Brian to stay away all these years?'

'It is—rather eccentric.'

'Eccentric! It is positively wicked, when we know how agreeable he can make himself. Why, in that happy summer we spent at the Abbey he brightened all our lives. Didn't he, now, Ida?'

'He was very kind,' faltered Ida, like a slave giving evidence under torture. 'Have you heard from him lately?'

'Not for more than a year, but father hears of him through his London agent, and we know he is well. He sent us all lovely presents last Christmas—Indian shawls, prayer-rugs, ivories, carved sandalwood boxes. The Vicarage is glorified by his gifts.'

The gong began booming and buzzing as Bessie pinned a big yellow rose among the folds of her Madras fichu, and Mrs. Jardine and her hostess went down to the drawing-room lovingly arms entwined, as in that long-ago holiday, when Ida was a guest at Kingthorpe.

Lady Palliser and Mr. Jardine were in the drawing-room talking to each other, while Brian paced up and down the room, pale and wan, as he had looked yesterday in the church. He offered his arm to Bessie at his wife's bidding, without a word. Mr. Jardine followed, with Lady Palliser and Ida; and the little party of five sat down to dinner with a blight upon them, the awful shadow of domestic misery. There are many such dinners eaten every day in England—than which the Barmecide's was a more cheerful feast, a red herring and bread and butter in a garret a banquet of sweeter savour.

For the first two courses Brian preserved a sullen silence. He ate nothing—did not even pretend to eat—and drank the sherry and soda-water which were offered to him without comment. With the third course the butler, who had supplied him with the prescribed amount of sherry, gave him plain soda-water. He looked at his tumbler for a moment or so, and burst out laughing.

'Byron used to drink soda-water at dinners when he was the rage in London society,' he said. 'It was *chic*, and Byron was like Sara Bernhardt— he would have done anything to get himself talked about.'

'I should have thought the fame he won by "Childe Harold" would have satisfied him, without any outside notoriety as a total abstainer,' said Mr. Jardine.

'Oh, if you think that, you don't know Byron,' exclaimed Brian. 'He wanted people always to be talking of him. A man may write the greatest book that was ever written, and the world will accept it, and put him on a pinnacle; but they soon leave off talking about him unless he does something. He must keep a bear in his rooms—quarrel with his wife—wear a pea-green overcoat—cross the Channel in a balloon—and go on doing queer things— if he wants to be famous. Byron was an adept in the art of *réclame*—just as Whistler is on his smaller scale. It wasn't enough for Byron to be the greatest poet of modern Europe, he wanted to be the most notorious rake and *roué* into the bargain.'

'It was a curious nature,' said Mr. Jardine—'half gold and half tinsel.'

'Ah, but the tinsel caught the public. I really don't think, for a man who wants to make a stir in his generation, a fellow could have played his cards better than Byron did.'

'It is a life that one can only contemplate with infinite pity and regret—a great nature, wrecked by small vices and smaller follies,' said Mr. Jardine; and then Brian took up the strain, and talked with loud assertiveness of the right of genius to do what it likes in the world, launching out into a broad declaration of infidelity and rank materialism, which shocked and scared the three women who heard him.

Ida gave an imploring look at her stepmother, and they all three rose simultaneously, and hastily retired, driven away by that blatant blasphemy. John Jardine closed the door upon the ladies, and then went quietly back to his seat. He heard all that Brian had to say—he listened to his wild ramblings as to the voice of an oracle; and then, when Brian had poured out his little stock of argument in favour of materialism, had quoted Aristotle, and Holbach, and Hume, and Comte, and Darwin, and had perverted their arguments against a personal God into the divine right of man to ruin his soul and body, John Jardine, who had read more of Aristotle than Brian knew of all the metaphysicians put together, and who had Plato, Kant, and Dugald Stewart in his heart of hearts, gravely took up the strain, and made mincemeat of Mr. Wendover's philosophy.

Brian listened meekly, and did not appear to take offence when the Vicar went on to warn him against the peril here and hereafter of a life misspent, a constitution ruined by self-indulgence, talents unused, opportunities neglected. The pale and haggard wretch sat cowering, as the voice of reproof and warning went on, solemnly, earnestly, with the warm sympathy which springs from perfect pity, from the Christian's wide love of his fellow-men.

'For your wife's—for your own sake—for the love of Him in whose image you were made—wrestle with the devil that possesses you,' said John Jardine, when they had risen to leave the room, laying his hand affectionately upon Brian's shoulder. 'Believe me, victory is possible.'

'Not now,' Brian answered, with a semi-hysterical laugh. 'It is too late. There comes an hour, you know, even in your all-merciful creed, when the door is shut. "Too late, ye cannot enter now." The door is shut upon me. I fooled my life away in London. It was pleasant enough while it lasted, but it's over now. I can say with Cleopatra—"O my life in Egypt, O, the dalliance and the wit."'

They were in the hall by this time. The broad marble-paved hall, with its marble figures of gods and goddesses, of which nobody ever took any more notice than if they had been umbrella stands. They were crossing the hall on their way to the drawing-room, when Brian suddenly clutched John Jardine's arm and reeled heavily against him, with an appalling cry.

'Hold me!' he screamed; 'hold me! I am going down!'

It was one of the dreadful symptoms of his dreadful disease. All at once, with the solid black and white marble beneath his feet, he felt himself upon the edge of a precipice, felt himself falling, falling, falling, into a bottomless pit.

It was an awful feeling, a waking nightmare. He sank exhausted into John Jardine's arms, panting for breath.

'You are safe, it is only a momentary delusion,' said Mr. Jardine. 'Have you had that feeling often before?'

'Yes—sometimes—pretty often,' gasped Brian.

Mr. Jardine's wide reading and large experience as a parish priest had made him half a doctor. He knew that this was one of the symptoms of delirium tremens, and a symptom seen mostly in cases of a dangerous type. He had suspected the nature of Mr. Wendover's disease before now; but now he was certain of it.

He went with Brian to his room, advising him to lie down and rest. Brian appearing consentient, Mr. Jardine left him, with Towler in attendance.

In the drawing-room the Vicar contrived to get a little quiet talk with Ida, while at the other end of the room Lady Palliser was expatiating to Bessie upon the minutest details of her boy's illness. He invited Ida's confidence, and frankly told her that he had fathomed the nature of Brian's disease.

'I have seen too many cases in the course of my parochial experience not to recognise the painful symptoms. I am so sorry for you and for him. It is a bright young life thrown away.'

'Do you think he will not recover?'

'I think it is a very bad case. He is wasted to a shadow, and has a worn, haggard look that I don't like. And then he has those painful hallucinations— that idea of falling down a precipice, for instance, which are oftenest seen in fatal cases.'

Ida told him of the scene in the church yesterday—she confided in him fully—telling him all that Dr. Mallison had said of the case.

'What can I do?' she asked, piteously.

'I don't think you can do more than you are doing. That man who waits upon your husband is a nurse, I suppose?'

'Yes. Dr. Mallison sent him.'

'And care is taken that the patient gets no stimulants supplied to him?'

'Every care—and yet—'

'And yet what?'

'I have a suspicion—and I think Towler suspects too—that Brian does get brandy—somehow.'

'But how can that be, if your servants are honest, and this attendant is to be depended upon?'

'I can't tell you. I believe the servants are incapable of deceiving me. Towler, the attendant, comes to us with the highest character.'

'Well, I will be on the alert while I am with you,' said Mr. Jardine; and Ida felt as if he were a tower of strength. 'I have seen these sad cases, and had to do with them, only too often. On some occasions I have been happy enough to be the means of saving a man from his own folly.'

'Pray stop as long as you can with us, and do all you can,' entreated Ida. 'I wish I had asked you to come sooner, only I was so ashamed for him, poor creature. I thought it would be a wrong to him to let anyone know how low he had fallen.'

'It is part of my office to know how low humanity can fall and yet be raised up again,' said Mr. Jardine.

'You won't tell Bessie—she would be so grieved for her cousin.'

'I will tell her nothing more than she can find out for herself. But you know she is very quick-witted.'

There was a change for the worse in Towler's charge next morning, when Ida, who still occupied the room adjoining her husband's bedchamber, went in at eight o'clock to inquire how he had passed the night. Brian was up, half dressed, pacing up and down the room, and talking incoherently. He had been up ever since five o'clock, Towler said; but it was impossible to get him to dress himself, or suffer himself to be dressed. A frightful restlessness had taken possession of him, more intense than any previous restlessness, and it was impossible to do anything for him. His hallucinations since daybreak had taken a frightful form; he had seen poisonous snakes gliding in and out of the folds of the bedclothes; he had fancied every kind of hideous monster—the winged reptiles of the jura formation—the armour-plated fish of the old red sandstone—everything that is grotesque, revolting, terrible—

skeletons, poison-spitting toads, vampires, were-wolves, flying cats—they had all lurked amidst the draperies of bed or windows, or grinned at him through the panes of glass.

'Look!' he shrieked, as Ida approached him, soothing, pleading in gentlest accents; 'look! don't you see them?' he cried, pointing to the shapes that seemed to people the room, and trying to push them aside with a restless motion of his hands; 'don't you see them, the lares and lemures? Look, there is Cleopatra with the asp at her breast! That bosom was once beautiful, and see now what a loathsome spectacle death has made it—the very worms recoil from that corruption. See, there is Canidia, the sorceress, who buried the boy alive! Look at her hair flying loose about her head! hair, no, those locks are living vipers! and Sagana, with hair erect, like the bristles of a wild boar! See, Ida, how she rushes about, sprinkling the room with water from the rivers of hell! And Veia, whose cruel heart never felt remorse! Yes, he knew them well, Horace. These furies were the women he had loved and wooed!'

Fancies, memories flitted across his disordered brain, swift as lightning flashes. In a moment Canidia was forgotten, and he was Pentheus, struggling with Agave and her demented crew. They were tearing him to pieces, their fingers were at his throat. Then he was in the East, a defenceless traveller in the tropical desert, surrounded by Thugs. He pointed to one particular spot where he saw his insidious foe—he described the dusky supple figure, the sinuous limbs, gliding serpent-like towards him, the oiled body, the dagger in the uplifted hand. An illustration in Sir Charles Bell's classic treatise had flashed into his brain. So, from memory to memory, with a frightful fertility of fancy, his unresting brain hurried on; while his wife could only watch and listen, tortured by an agony greater than his own. To look on, and to be powerless to afford the slightest help was dreadful. Up and down, and round about the room he wandered, talking perpetually, perpetually waving aside the horrid images which pursued and appalled him, his eyeballs in constant motion, the pupils dilated, his hollow cheeks deadly pale, his face bathed in perspiration.

'Send for Mr. Fosbroke,' said Ida, speaking on the threshold of the adjoining room, to the maid who brought her letters; and, in the midst of his distraction, Brian's quick ear caught the name.

'Fosbroke me no Fosbrokes!' he said. 'I will have no village apothecaries diagnosing my disease, no ignorant quack telling me how to treat myself.'

'I will telegraph for Dr. Mallison, if you like, Brian,' Ida answered, gently; 'but I know Mr. Fosbroke is a clever man, and he perfectly understands—'

'Yes, he will have the audacity to tell you he knows what is the matter with me. He will say this is *delirium tremens*—a lie, and you must know it is a lie!'

To her infinite relief, Mr. Jardine appeared at this moment. He questioned Towler as to the possibility of tranquillising his patient; and he found that the sedatives prescribed by Dr. Mallison had ceased to exercise any beneficial effect. Nights of insomnia and restlessness had been the rule with the patient ever since Towler had been in attendance upon him.

'I never knew such a brain, or such invention!' exclaimed Towler; 'the people and the places, and the things he talks about is enough to make a man's hair stand on end.'

'The natural result of a vivid memory, and a good deal of desultory reading.'

'Most patients takes an idea and harps upon it,' said Towler. 'It's the multiplication table—or the day of judgment—or the volcanoes and hot-springs, and what-you-may-call-ems, in the centre of the earth; and they'll go on over and over again—always coming back to the same point, like a merry-go-round; but this one is quite different. There's no bounds to his delusions. We're at the North Pole one minute, and digging up diamonds in Africa the next.'

Brian had flung himself upon his bed, rolled in the damask curtain, like Henry Plantagenet, what time he went off into one of his fury-fits about Thomas Becket; and Mr. Jardine and Towler were able to talk confidentially at a respectful distance.

'Are you sure that he does not get brandy without your knowledge?'

'No, sir,' said Towler; 'that is what I am not sure about. It's a puzzling case. He didn't ought to be so bad as he is after my care of him. There ought to be some improvement by this time; instead of which it's all the other way.'

'What precautions have you taken?'

'I've searched his rooms, and not a thing have I found stowed away anywhere. It isn't often that he's left to himself, for when I get my midday sleep Mrs. Wendover sits with him; or, if he's cranky, and wants to be alone, she stays in the next room, with the door ajar between them; and Robert, the groom, is on duty in the passage, in case the patient should get unmanageable.'

'I see—you have been very careful; but practically your patient has been often alone—the half-open door signifies nothing—he was unobserved, and free to do what he pleased all the same.'

'But he couldn't drink if there was no liquor within reach.'

'Was there none? that is the question!' answered Mr. Jardine.

'Look about the rooms yourself, sir, and see if he could hide anything, except in such places as I've overhauled every morning,' said Towler, with an offended air; and then, swelling with outraged dignity, he flung open doors of wardrobes and closets, pulled out drawers, and otherwise demonstrated the impossibility of anything remaining secret from his eagle eye.

'What about the next room?' asked Mr. Jardine, going into the adjoining room, which was Brian's study.

The room was littered with books and papers heaped untidily upon tables and chairs, and even strewn upon the carpet. Brian had objected to any attempt at setting this apartment in order—the servants were to leave all books and papers untouched, on pain of his severe displeasure. Thus everything in the shape of litter had been allowed to accumulate, with its natural accompaniment, dust. Everyone knows the hideous confusion which the daily and weekly newspapers alone can make in a room if left unsorted and unarranged for a month or so; and mixed with these there were pamphlets, magazines, manuscripts, and piles of more solid literature in the shape of books brought up from the library for reference and consultation.

In one corner there were a pile of empty boxes, and on one of these Mr. Jardine's eye lighted instantly, on account of its resemblance to a wine merchant's case.

He pulled this box out from the others—a plain deal box, roughly finished, just the size of a two-dozen case. One label had been pulled off, but there was a railway label which gave the date of delivery, just three weeks back.

'Have you any idea what this box contained?' inquired Mr. Jardine.

'No, sir. It was here when I came, just as you see it now.'

'It looks very like a wine merchant's box.'

'Well, it might be a wine-case, sir, as far as the look of it goes; but it might have held anything. It was empty when I came here, and there's no stowage for wine bottles in these rooms, as you have seen with your own eyes.'

'Don't be too sure of that; and now go back to your patient, and get him to eat some breakfast, if you can, while I go downstairs.'

'He can't eat, sir. It's pitiful; he don't eat enough, for a robin. We try to keep up his strength with strong soups, and such like; but it's hard work to get him to swallow anything.'

Mr. Jardine went down to the family breakfast room, where his wife, Ida, and her stepmother were sitting at table, with pale perturbed faces, and very little inclination for that excellent fare which the Wimperfield housekeeper provided with a kind of automatic regularity, and would have continued to provide on the eve of a deluge or an earthquake. He told Ida that all was going on quietly upstairs, and that he would share Towler's task as nurse all that day, so that she might be quite easy in her mind as to the patient. And then the servants came trooping in, as the clock struck nine, and they all knelt down, and John Jardine read the daily portion of prayer and praise.

It had been decreed by medical authority that on this day, provided the sky were propitious and the wind in a warm quarter, Vernon was to go out for his first drive. Mr. Jardine accordingly entreated that the three ladies would accompany him, and that Ida would have no fear as to her husband's welfare during her absence.

'I don't like to leave him,' she said, in confidence, to Mr. Jardine; 'he seems so much worse this morning—wilder than I have ever seen him yet—and so white and haggard.'

'He is very bad, but your remaining indoors will do him no good. I will not leave him while you are away.'

Ida yielded. It was a relief to her to submit to authority—to have some one able to tell her to do this or that. She felt utterly worn out in body and mind—all the energy, the calm strength of purpose, which had sustained her up to a certain point, was now exhausted. Despair had taken possession of her, and with despair came that dull apathy which is like death in life.

John Jardine took his wife aside before he went back to Brian's rooms.

'I want you to take care of Ida, to keep with her all day. She has been sorely tried, poor soul, and needs all your love.'

'She shall have it in full measure,' answered Bessie. 'How grave and anxious you look! Is Brian very ill?'

'Very ill.'

'Dangerously?'

'I am afraid so. I shall hear what Mr. Fosbroke says presently, and if his report be bad, I shall telegraph for the physician.'

'Poor Brian! How strangely he talked at dinner last night! Oh, John, I hardly dare say it—but—is he out of his mind?'

'Temporarily—but it is the delirium of a kind of brain fever, not madness.'

'And he will recover?'

'Please God; but he is very low. I am seriously alarmed about him.'

'Poor dear Brian!' sighed Bess. 'He was once my favourite cousin. But I must go back to Ida. You need not be afraid of my neglecting her. I shan't leave her all day.'

Mr. Jardine went to the housekeeper's room to make an inquiry. He wanted to know what that box from London had contained, a box delivered upon such and such a date.

The housekeeper's mind was dark, or worse than dark upon the subject— an obscurity enlightened by flashes of delusive light. Two housemaids, and an odd man who looked after the coal scuttles, were produced, and gave their evidence in a manner which would have laid them open to the charge of rank prevarication and perjury, as to the receipt of a certain wooden box, which at some stages of the inquiry became hopelessly entangled with a hamper from the Petersfield fishmonger, and a band-box from Lady Palliser's Brighton milliner.

'The carriage must have been paid,' said the housekeeper, 'that's the difficulty. If there'd been anything to pay, it would have been entered in my book; but when the carriage is paid, don't you see, sir, it's out of my jurisdiction, as you may say,' with conscious pride in a free use of the English language, 'and I may hear nothing about it.'

But now the odd man, after much thoughtful scratching of his head, was suddenly enlightened by a flash of memory from the paleozoic darkness of three weeks ago. He remembered a heavy wooden box that had come in his dinner-time—the fact of its coming at that eventful hour had evidently impressed him—and he had carried it up to Mr. Wendover's own sitting-room.

It was very heavy, and Mr. Wendover had told him that it contained books.

'Did you open it for Mr. Wendover?'

'No, sir; I offered to open it, but Mr. Wendover says he'd got the tools himself, and would open it at his leisure. He had no call for the books yet awhile, he says, and didn't want it opened.

'I see, the box contained books. Thank you, that's all I wanted to know.'

John Jardine had very little doubt in his mind now as to the actual contents of the box. He had no doubt that Brian, finding himself refused drink, for which he suffered the drunkard's incessant craving, had contrived to get himself supplied from London; and that if the fire of his disease had known no abatement it was because the fuel that fed the flame had not been wanting.

The only question that remained to be answered was how Brian, carefully attended as he had been, had managed to dispose of his secret store of drink, under the very eyes, as it were, of his keeper. But Mr. Jardine knew that the sufferer from alcoholic poison is no less cunning than the absolute lunatic, and that falsehood, meanness, and fraud seem to be symptoms of the disease.

When he went back to Brian's rooms, he found the patient lying on his bed, exhausted by the agitation and restlessness of the last few hours. He was not asleep, but was quieter than usual, in a semi-conscious state, muttering to himself now and then. Towler was sitting at a little table by the open window, breakfasting comfortably; his enjoyment of the coffee-pot, and a dish of ham and eggs, being in no manner lessened by the neighbourhood of the patient.

'Haven't been able to get him to take any nourishment,' whispered Towler, as Mr. Jardine came quietly into the room. 'He's uncommon bad.'

'Mr. Fosbroke will be here presently, I hope.'

'I don't think he'll be able to do much good when he does come,' said Towler; 'doctors ain't in it with a case of this kind. If he don't go off into a good sleep by-and-by, I'm afraid this will be a fatal case.'

Mr. Jardine made no reply to this discouraging observation. There are times when speech is worse than useless. He stood by the window, looking over at that shrunken figure on the great old-fashioned four-post bed, with its voluminous drab damask curtains, its cords, fringes, tassels, and useless decorations—the nerveless, helpless figure of wasted youth, the wreckage of an ill-spent life. The haggard countenance, damp with the dews of mental agony, and of a livid pallor, looked like the face of death. What could medicine do for this man beyond diagnosing his case, and giving an opinion about it, for the satisfaction—God save the mark!—of his friends? John Jardine knew in his heart that not all the doctors in Christendom could pick this shattered figure up again, and replace it in its former position among mankind.

Still intent upon solving that mystery about the contents of the wine-case, Mr. Jardine's eyes wandered about the room, trying to discover some hiding-place which the careful had overlooked. But so far he could see no such thing There was the tall four-poster, with its square cornice, a ponderous mahogany frame with fluted damask stretched across it. Could Brian have hidden his brandy up yonder, behind the mahogany cornice? Surely not. First the damask would have bulged with the weight of the bottles, and, secondly, the place was not accessible enough. He must have hidden his poison in some spot where he could apply himself to it furtively, hurriedly twenty, fifty, a hundred times in the day or night.

Presently Mr. Jardine's glance fell on the half-open door of the bath-room. It was a slip of a room cut off the study, a room that had been created within the last twenty years. It was the only room which Mr. Jardine had not inspected before he went down to breakfast.

He pushed open the door, and went in, followed by Towler, wiping the egginess and haminess from his mouth as he went.

'You kept your eye upon this room as well as the others, I suppose,' said Mr. Jardine, looking about him.

'Yes, sir, I have kept an eye upon everything.'

The apartment was not extensive. A large copper bath with a ponderous mahogany case, panelled, moulded, bevelled, the elaborate workmanship of local cabinet-makers; a row of brass hooks hung with bath towels, which looked like surplices pendent in a vestry; a washstand in a corner, a dressing-table and glass, with its belongings, in the window, and a wicker arm-chair, comprised the whole extent of furniture. No hiding-place here, one would suppose.

Mr. Jardine looked about the room thoughtfully. It was the one apartment in which the patient could hardly be intruded upon by his attendant. Here he could be sure of privacy.

'Did you examine the case of the bath,' he inquired presently, his mathematical eye quick to take in the difference between the inner shell of copper and the outer husk of mahogany.

'No, sir,' answered Towler, briskly. 'Is it 'oller?'

'Of course it's hollow. Surely your eye tells you that.'

'Yes, sir; but there's the hot-water pipes inside—and there's no getting at it, except for a plumber.'

'Nonsense,' said Mr. Jardine, kneeling down at one end of the bath, where there was a convenient mahogany door for the accommodation of the plumber, a door which lay somewhat in shadow, and had escaped Towler's observation.

'Bring me a candle,' said Mr. Jardine, unconsciously imitating the brotherhood of plumbers, whose consumption of candles is a household terror.

Towler returned to fetch a candle, while Mr. Jardine with cautious hand explored the cavern-like recesses between the bath and its outer shell, recesses in which lurked serpent-like convolutions of hot-water pipes and cold-water pipes, waste and overflow.

Yes, before Towler could arrive with the candle, he had fathomed the mystery. Three or four full bottles, and a large number of empties, were stowed away in this dusty receptacle. He drew one of the full bottles out into the light. 'Hennessy's Fine Old Cognac,' said the label. This had been the secret source of fever and delirium—here had lurked the evil which had made all remedial measures vain.

Mr. Fosbroke was announced while John Jardine was washing the dust and the stains of rusty iron from his hands. Brian was in too low a condition to be rude to the country practitioner, much as he had protested against his interference. He suffered the apothecary to sit by his bed and feel his pulse, without a word of remonstrance.

'How do you find him?' asked Mr. Jardine, when Mr. Fosbroke had left the bedside.

'Very bad; pulse small and thready—a hundred and forty in the minute; violent throbbing in the temporal and carotid arteries; profuse perspiration—all bad signs. What medicines has he been taking?'

He was shown the prescriptions.

'Hum—hum—digitalis—bromide of potassium. I should like to inject chloral; but as the case is in Dr. Mallison's hands—'

'If you think there is danger I will telegraph for Mallison.'

'There is always danger in this stage of the malady, especially in the case of a patient of Mr. Wendover's age. The season, too, is unfavourable—

the mortality in this complaint is nearly double in summer. If we can get him into a sound sleep of some hours he may wake with a decided turn for the better—the delirium subjugated; but in his low state, even sleep may be fatal—there is so little vital power. Yes, I should certainly telegraph for Dr. Mallison; and in the meantime I'll try what can be done with chloral.'

'You must do the utmost you can. Mrs. Wendover has implicit faith in you.'

'I'll drive back and get the chloral.'

When the apothecary was gone, Mr. Jardine's first act was to telegraph to the London physician, his next, to put the unused bottles of cognac under lock and key, and, with Towler's help, to clear away the empty bottles without the knowledge of the servants. No doubt every member of the household knew the nature of Mr. Wendover's illness; but it was well to spare him the exposure of these degrading details.

CHAPTER XXVIII
AN ENGLISHMAN'S HOUSE IS HIS CASTLE

Ida felt a strange relief to her spirits, despite the absolute blackness of her domestic horizon, when the carriage drove away from Wimperfield. She had left the house very seldom of late, feeling that duty chained her to the joyless scene of home; and there was an infinite relief in turning her back upon that stately white building in which was embodied all the misery of her blighted life. No charnel-house could be fuller of ghastly, unspeakable horrors than Wimperfield had become to her since that long, never-to-be-forgotten night when she had listened to her husband's ravings, and when all the loathsome objects his distracted fancy had conjured into being, and his never-resting tongue had described, had been only a little less real to her mind than they had been to his. Could she ever again know peace and rest in those rooms; ever tread those corridors without shuddering and dread, ever know happiness again in all the days of her life? She leaned back in the carriage as they drove along the avenue, and rested with half-closed eyes, her soul heavy within her, her body weighed down by the soreness and weariness of her mind. If life could but end now! She felt that she could be of no more use in the world. She could do nothing to help her wretched husband. He had chosen to go his own way to destruction, and he was too near the edge of the pit now to be snatched back by any friendly hand. She felt that his fate had passed beyond the regions of hope. God might pity the self-destroyer, and deal lightly with him at the great audit; but on this earth there was no hope of cure. Brian Wendover was going down to the pit.

Bessie sat by Ida's side tenderly watching her worn white face, while Lady Palliser was entirely absorbed by the delight of administering fussily to her boy, who was well enough to laugh her shawls and comforters and motherly precautions to scorn, and to jump about in the carriage, as at each break in the wood some new object of interest caught his eye—a rabbit, a squirrel, a hawk high up in the blue, invisible to any gaze less eager than his own. He was in wild spirits at being out of doors again, a restless eager soul, not to be restrained by any medical ordinances or maternal anxieties.

They went for a long drive, the horses, very fresh after the little exercise of the last month, devouring the ground under them—the summer breeze brisk and inspiring—the country beautiful beyond measure—an ever-varying landscape of hill and wood and valley, green pastures and golden grain.

Bessie chatted gaily in her desire to distract Ida's mind, and the boy's vivacity never flagged; but Ida sat silent, feeling the blessedness of this brief respite from the horror of home, but quite unable to talk of indifferent subjects. She was haunted by the image of her husband as she had seen him that morning—his ashen countenance, the perpetual movement of his eyes, those nervous attenuated hands, almost transparent in their bloodlessness, for ever pushing aside the formless horrors that crowded round him—pictures painted on the empty air, pictures for ever changing, yet hideously real to that disorganised brain, pictures that spoke and gibbered at him, shadows with which he carried on conversations.

With this awful image fresh in her mind, Ida could not even pretend to be cheerful, or interested in common things.

'Don't be unhappy about me, dear,' she said once when Bessie squeezed her hand, and looked at her with tender anxiety; 'I must bear my burden. Nobody can help me.'

'Except God,' whispered the Vicar's faithful wife. 'He lightens all burdens, in His good time.'

On the homeward road they wound near the base of Blackman's Hanger, and at this point Vernon got up and ordered the coachman to drive as near as he could to the old gamekeeper's cottage.

'We can walk the rest of the way,' said the boy.

'Walk!' shrieked Lady Palliser. 'Oh, Vernie, what are you dreaming about? Mr. Fosbroke never said you might walk.'

'Very likely not,' retorted the boy; 'but you don't suppose I'm going to ask old Fosbroke's leave before I use my legs. Look here, mother dear, I'm as well as ever I was, and I'm not going to be mollicoddled any more.'

'But Vernie—'

'I am not going to be mollicoddled any more, and I'm going to see old Jack.'

'Nonsense, Vernie.'

'He came to see me, and I'm going to see him,' said Vernon, resolutely. 'Remember what your favourite author, the Countess of Seven Stars, says about the necessity of returning a call—"and if the person calling happen to be your inferior in social status, the obligation to return the visit within a reasonable time will be so much the stronger." There, mother; there are the very words of your "Crême de la Crême" for you.'

'But, Vernon, the countess would never have imagined such a person as a Cheap Jack calling upon anyone for whom her book was intended.'

'The book was intended for a parcel of stuck-up cads,' said Vernon. 'Get on, Jackson.'

This to the coachman, who was driving slowly, perfectly conscious of the squabble going on behind him, and anticipating the reversal of Sir Vernon's order. But Lady Palliser said nothing, so Jackson quickened his pace a little, and drove along the rough winding road which skirted the base of the hill.

Directly he drew up his horses Vernon leapt out, and the three women followed him. After all, the mother inwardly argued, it were a pity to thwart her darling. He was in such high spirits, and seemed so thoroughly himself again. His very wilfulness was delightful, for it told of renewed vigour.

They all climbed the hill together, by a cork-screw track which was not too distressing. The atmosphere was cool and fresh at this altitude, the odour of the pines ambrosial.

'I suppose we had better wait a little way off, Vernie,' said Ida, when they were within a dozen yards of the hut. 'Your friend is so very uncivil to ladies.'

'Yes, you'd better rest yourselves on that fir tree,' answered Vernon, pointing to a prostrate giant of the grove which had been lately felled, 'while I run on and see him.'

They obeyed, but in less than five minutes Vernon came back.

'Jack is out, but his house is open,' he said, eagerly, 'and I want you all to come and see it. I want you to see the house that my Jack built.'

'But would it be right to go into his cottage when he is away?' asked Ida.

'Of course it would,' cried her brother, dancing along before them. 'You must come—there's nothing to be ashamed of, I can tell you. Mother will see that my Jack isn't a vulgar person, that he can read and write, and has the ways of a gentleman.'

'I should certainly like to see what kind of person my son associates with,' said Lady Palliser, who, in common with the non-studious class of mankind, was a keen inquirer into the details of daily life.

She liked to know where her acquaintance had their gowns made, and what wages they gave their cooks, and to be the first to hear of matrimonial engagements and dangerous illnesses.

The cottage door stood wide open, and as there was neither hall nor passage, the moment the three Fatimas had crossed the threshold they were standing in the innermost sanctuary of Mr. Cheap Jack's private life, and the character of the man stood revealed to them, so far as surroundings can reveal a man's character.

He was a smoker, for the room, albeit the lattice stood wide open, smelt strongly of tobacco, and over the narrow wooden mantelpiece were slung three pipes, one a long cherry-wood tube of decidedly Oriental appearance.

'Quite gentlemanly looking pipes,' said Lady Palliser.

The room was in perfect order, everything arranged with an exquisite neatness. The floor was covered with a coarse, substantial matting, spotlessly clean. The furniture consisted of a clumsy old walnut-wood table, evidently picked up at some farmhouse or cottage in the neighbourhood, a heavy piece of cabinet work of the same order, half secretaire half bookcase, a couple of substantial arm-chairs, and a ponderous old oak chest—also the relic of some dismantled homestead. There was a brass clock on the chimney-piece, and there were a number of rather dingy-looking volumes in the bookcase, while the floor under the table was piled with quartos and thick octavos, which looked like books of reference. An old leathern despatch box, much the worse for wear, stood on the table. Ornaments, pictures, or photographs there were none.

'It really looks like a gentleman's room,' said Lady Palliser, after her eyes had devoured every detail.

'It *is* a gentleman's room,' answered Vernon, decisively. 'Didn't I tell you my friend Jack is a gentleman?'

'Vernie dear, a man who goes about the country in a cart selling things can't be a gentleman!' said his mother.

'I don't quite see that, Lady Palliser,' exclaimed Bessie, who was inspecting the book-shelves. 'A gentleman may fall upon evil days, and have to earn his living somehow, don't you know; and why shouldn't he have a cart, and go about selling things? There's nothing disreputable in it, though he could hardly go into society, perhaps, while he was driving the cart, because the mass of mankind are such fools. Why shouldn't Vernie's instinct be right, and this Cheap Jack be a reduced gentleman? Froude says that in the colonies Oxford men may be seen mending the roads. Why shouldn't one man in the world have the courage to do humble work in his own country? This Jack is a University man.'

'How do you know that?' asked Lady Palliser, eagerly. She was ready to bow down before a University man as a necessarily superior being. There had never been such a person of her own blood.

'Here is a volume of Æschylus—the Clarendon Press—with his college arms. He is a Balliol man, the same college as my cousin Brian's.'

'That proves nothing,' said Lady Palliser, contemptuously. 'He may have bought the book at a stall. All his furniture is second-hand, why not his books?'

'Oh, but here are more books with the Balliol arms—Pindar, Theocritus, Catullus, Horace, Virgil.'

'Can't you find his name in any of them?'

'No; that has been erased in some of the books, and has never been written in the others. Poor fellow! I daresay he would not like his real name to be known.'

'Didn't I tell you he was a gentleman, mother?' exclaimed Vernon, triumphantly.

Lady Palliser was almost convinced. The neat, substantially furnished room—so free from frippery or foppishness—the queer Oriental pipes—the well-used books in sober calf bindings, which had once been splendid—the college arms on almost every volume—these details impressed her in spite of herself.

'Poor young man! I should like to send him some money,' she said.

'He would not take it; he would scorn your money,' said Vernon. 'What does he want with pounds, shillings, and pence? He told me that so long as he has his books to read, his pipe to smoke, and a fine country to roam about, he cares for nothing else. Your money wouldn't buy him anything.'

'You don't understand, Vernie dear. We might do something substantial for him—set him up in a nice little shop at Petersfield, perhaps a stationer's, or,' with a glance at the rack of pipes, 'a tobacconist's.'

'My Jack keeping a shop! my Jack behind a counter!' cried Vernon: 'if you knew anything about him you would never talk of such a thing. Why he likes to be as free as the birds of the air—to roam about all day—and sit up reading half the night.'

They were all clustered in front of the bookcase, Bessie and Ida looking at the books, Lady Palliser and her boy intent on their own talk, when the door was flung open, and the master of the house suddenly appeared amidst them—a tall, broad-shouldered figure, roughly clad in shooting jacket, corduroy, and leather, like a gamekeeper—a dark bearded face under a slouched hat. But the intruders had only the briefest time in which to observe his appearance. At sight of the group by the bookcase, Jack tilted his felt hat further over his brows, and strode across the room to that corner whence a cork-screw stair led to the upper story. He went up these stairs in three or four bounds, banged and bolted the door of the upper chamber; and his unbidden guests were left looking at each other in bewildered silence.

Lady Palliser, after a gasp or two, was the first to speak.

'Did you ever see such manner?' she exclaimed; 'such a perfect brute? Vernie, you must never speak to that horrid creature again. I never want to have anything more to do with University men if this is a specimen of their manners! Never so much as to take off his hat to us!'

'We had no right to come crowding into his room,' said Bessie, who could seldom find it in her heart to be angry with anyone. 'I daresay the poor thing feels the change in his position. When Brian, of the Abbey, comes home—if ever he does come home—I'll ask him to hunt this poor fellow out, and help him in some way. One Balliol man ought to help another.'

'Let us go back to the carriage instantly,' said Lady Palliser, almost shouting the substantive, in order that Jack might be reminded what kind of people he had insulted by his ruffianly bearing. 'I feel that I am bemeaning myself every moment I stay in this house.'

They hurried down the sandy hill path to the road where they had left the carriage, and Lady Palliser hustled them into it, breathless, with the combined effect of the rapid descent and her indignation.

'Why, Ida, how deadly pale you are!' exclaimed Bessie. 'I hope you are not ill. Have we walked too fast for you?'

'No, dear—only—that man's face reminded me—'

'Of Brian's when he first came home from Norway, and was so dreadfully sunburnt?' said Bessie; 'so it did me. The idea flashed upon me, as the rude wretch rushed past us, that he had a sort of look of Brian. Just the way he carried his head, you know, and something in the shape of his shoulders—not a real resemblance.'

'Of course not.'

CHAPTER XXIX
'AS ONE DEAD IN THE BOTTOM OF A TOMB'

Dr. Mallison came to Wimperfield at the same hour as on the occasion of his first visit. He was with the patient for nearly half-an-hour, and he confabulated with Mr. Fosbroke for at least another half hour, so it could not be said that he performed the physician's duty in a careless or perfunctory manner. But his opinion was not hopeful; and there was a gravity in his manner when he talked to Ida and her stepmother which was evidently intended to prepare them for the worst. He gave a peremptory order for a second nurse, an able-bodied experienced woman, who could relieve Towler in his now most onerous duties—duties growing hourly more painful, since the last development of the patient's delirium was a violent hatred of his attendant, who, as he believed, was always lying in wait to do him some injury. Dr. Mallison also advised that Mrs. Wendover should no longer occupy the bedroom adjoining her husband's. Upon this point he was very firm, when Ida urged her anxiety to forego no duty which she owed to her husband.

'I am so sorry for him,' she said. 'I would do anything in the world to help or to comfort him.'

'Unhappily, dear madam, you can do neither. 'When these paroxysms are upon him he will mistake his best friend for his worst enemy—he was quite violent to Towler just now. You can do absolutely nothing, and your presence is even likely to irritate him. He must be given over entirely to his nurses. Towler will obey my directions implicitly, and the female attendant— Mr. Fosbroke tells me he can find a thoroughly competent person—will assist him in carrying them out. If we can stimulate the patient's vital power, which is just now at the lowest ebb, and if we can induce natural sleep, why, there may still be a favourable result. But I do not conceal from you that Mr. Wendover's condition is critical—very critical. Lady Palliser, you will insist, I hope, that your daughter removes to an apartment at some distance from her husband's for the present. A few days hence, when the delirium is subjugated, as I trust it may be, by—ahem—the removal of the exciting cause, Mrs. Wendover may resume her attendance upon her husband. Just at present the less she sees of him the better for both.'

Ida could not disobey this injunction, especially as Lady Palliser and Mrs. Jardine took the matter into their own hands. Jane Dyson was ordered to convey all Mrs. Wendover's belongings to a room on the second and topmost floor of the mansion, exactly over that she now occupied—a fine airy apartment, with a magnificent view, but less lofty, and less ponderously furnished than the apartments of the first floor. Bessie vowed that this upper chamber, with its French bedstead, and light chintz draperies, and maple furniture, was a much prettier room than the one below. She ran up and down stairs carrying flowers, Japanese fans, tea-tables, and other frivolities, until she made the new room a perfect bower, and then carried Ida off triumphantly to inspect her new quarters.

'Isn't it lovely,' she said, 'such a nice change? Do let us have our tea up here, if that good Dyson won't mind bringing it. Nearly six o'clock, and we haven't had a cup of tea! I do so enjoy thoroughly new surroundings. We'll have the table just in front of this window. What a sweet architect to give this room windows down to the ground, and a lovely balcony! You must have some large Japanese vases in the balcony, Ida. That lovely deep red, or orange tawny. Oh, you poor pet, how wretched you look!'

'I have just been talking to the new nurse, Bessie. She seems a good, honest creature. She has nursed other people in the same complaint, and—and—she thinks Brian is desperately ill.'

'Oh, but he may get over it dear! The London doctor did not give him up; and there is no good in your making yourself ill with worry and fear. If you do, you won't be able to wait upon Brian when he begins to get better; and convalescents want so much attention, don't you know.'

The tea came, and Bessie persuaded her friend to take some, prattling on all the time in the hope of diverting Ida from the silent contemplation of her trouble. But the horror of the case had taken too stern a hold upon Ida's brain. It was the dominant idea; as with the somnambulist whose perceptions are dead to every other subject save the one absorbing thought, and all subsidiary ideas linked with it by the subtle chain of association. Ida smiled a wan smile, and pretended to be interested in Bessie's parochial anecdotes—the idiosyncrasies of the new curate, the fatuity of every young woman in the parish in running after him.

'He is such a perfect stick; but then certainly there is no other single man in the parish under forty. He is like Robinson Crusoe. It is an awfully deceptive position for a young man to occupy. I know he is beginning to think himself quite handsome, while as for pimples—well, his face is like a Wiltshire meadow before it has been bush-harrowed.'

Ida did not go down to dinner that evening. She felt utterly unequal to the effort of pretended cheerfulness, and she did not want to inflict a countenance of stony gloom upon Mr. and Mrs. Jardine, or on Vernie, who was going to dine late for the first time since his illness. So she sat by the open window overlooking the woods, gray in the universal twilight grayness, and she read Victor Cousin's 'History of Philosophy,' which was a great deal more comforting than fiction or poetry would have been, as it carried her into regions of abstract thought where human troubles entered not.

For the next three days things went on quietly enough. Brian never left his own apartments, now an ample range, since Ida's bedroom had been thrown into the suite, so as to give him space and verge enough for his roaming when the restless fit was on him: and, alas! how seldom did he cease from his restlessness. He now saw scarcely anyone but his nurses and Mr. Fosbroke, who called three times a day, and was altogether devoted in his watchfulness of the case.

Ida had not ceased from visiting the invalid until it became too obvious that her presence was irritating to him. He recalled the most painful scenes of their past experience, raved about his marriage, and accused his wife of cruelty and greed of wealth, wept, stormed, blasphemed, until Ida rushed shuddering from the room. To the nurses this wild talk was only part and parcel of the patient's hallucinations; to Ida it was too real.

Mr. Jardine and his wife stayed till the end of the week, but on Saturday the Vicar was compelled to go back to his parishioners; and although Bessie wanted to remain at Wimperfield, separating herself from her husband for the first time in her wedded life, Ida would not consent to such a sacrifice. Vernon, who was pronounced thoroughly convalescent, was to go back to Salisbury Plain with the Jardines, everybody being agreed that Wimperfield Park was no place for him under existing circumstances. If Brian's malady were doomed to end fatally, it was well that the boy should be gone before the dreaded guest crossed the threshold.

Ida saw her friends depart with a sense of despair too deep for words. She hugged Vernie with the passionate fervour of one who never hoped to see him more. She felt as if it were she whose hours were numbered, she for whom the thin thread of life was gradually dwindling to nothingness. The very atmosphere was charged with the odour of death. The light was shadowed by the gloom of the grave. Again and again in troubled dreams she had recalled that dreadful scene in the church with Brian; and she had seen the worms crawling out through the mouldering timbers of the church-floor—she had smelt the sickening taint of corruption.

She stood in the portico in the early summer morning, watching Mr. Jardine's phaeton dwindle to a speck in the distance of the avenue, and then she went slowly back to the house, feeling as if she were quite alone in her misery. It was not that Fanny Palliser was wanting in kindness or sympathy, but she was wanting in comprehension of Ida's feelings, and the stronger nature could not lean upon the weaker; and then the mother would be absorbed in her grief at the loss of her boy, who had become doubly precious since his illness. No, Ida felt that now John Jardine was gone she must bear her burden alone. Help for her, strength outside her own courageous nature, there was none.

She longed on this exquisite morning to be roaming about the park and woods, or riding far afield; but she had made up her mind that, so long as her husband remained in his present critical condition, it was her duty to stay close at hand, within call, lest at any moment there might be a return to reason, and she might again have power to soothe and support him, as she had done many a time in the long down-hill progress of his malady.

With this idea she spent the greater part of her day in the bedroom which Bessie had made so bright and so comfortable. Here she was within easy reach of the nurse in the rooms below, and could be summoned to her husband without a minute's delay. Here she had her favourite books, and the view of park and woods in all their summer glory. She could sit out in her balcony, reading, or looking idly at the wide expanse of hill and valley, brooding sadly over days that were gone, full of fear for the immediate present, and not daring to face the dreaded future.

'Don't think me unsociable,' she said to Lady Palliser, before going back to her room after a hasty breakfast; 'but I am too completely miserable to put on the faintest show of cheerfulness, and I should only make you wretched if I were with you. Go out for a drive, and pay a few visits, mamma. You have had a trying time, and you must want a little change of scene.'

'I believe I do, Ida,' replied Lady Palliser, gravely. 'I feel that I am below par, and that I really want sea air. What should you think of our going to Bournemouth directly after the funeral?'

'The funeral!' murmured Ida, pale as death.

'Yes, dear. Mr. Fosbroke has quite given up all hope, I know; and after the funeral you will want a change as badly as I do. I thought it would be as well to write to the Bournemouth agent to secure nice apartments, for I shouldn't care about staying at an hotel.'

'Oh, mamma, don't make your plans so much beforehand! Wait till he is dead,' said Ida, bitterly.

There seemed to her something ghoulish and stony-hearted in this prevision of coming doom, this arrangement for making the best of life and being comfortable when the sufferer upstairs should have ceased from the struggle with man's last foe.

Lady Palliser contrived to get on without her step-daughter's society. She had Jane Dyson, who was a person of considerable conversational powers, and who had an inexhaustible well-spring of interesting discourse in her recollections of the Archbishop's wife's lingering illness. The mistress and maid spent the morning not unpleasantly in conversation of the charnel house order, and in looking over Lady Palliser's wardrobe, with a view to discovering what new mourning she would require in the event of Brian's death. She had liked him, and had been kind to him in life, and she was not going to stint him in death by any false economy in crape or bugles.

CHAPTER XXX
A FIERY DAWN

The Jardines had been gone three days, and there was no change either for good or evil in Brian's condition. Mr. Fosbroke admitted that he was as ill as he could possibly be—the malady must either take a turn for the better, or end fatally within a day or two. The servants all talked of the impending funeral as complacently as Lady Palliser. The event must happen; and it would be as well to make the best of it. They had not yet gone out of mourning for Sir Reginald; and here was another death at hand to start them again with new suits of black. This was one of the advantages of service in a really good family, where the King of Terrors was treated with proper distinction.

It was eleven o'clock at night, and the house was hushed in silence—save in that suite of rooms where the invalid and his nurses were hardly ever at rest. One of the men servants slept in his clothes on a truckle bed in the corridor, ready for service in any emergency. Every one else had gone to bed, except Ida, who sat at her window, looking out at the wild windy sky and the forest trees swaying in the gale.

The day had been rainy and tempestuous, and the wind was still raging—just such a wind as Ida remembered upon Bessie's birthday, the day of that terrible storm which had cost so many lives, and had made Reginald Palliser master of Wimperfield.

She sat gazing idly at the sky, in sheer despondency and weariness. Her devotional books, which had been her chief comfort in these dark days and nights, lay unopened on her table. The effort to read any other kind of literature had been abandoned for the last day or two. Her mind refused to understand the words which her eyes mechanically perused. She could only read such books as spoke of comfort to a weary soul, of hope beyond a sinful world.

She had eaten hardly anything for the last few days, living on cups of tea, and semi-transparent slices of bread and butter. Her nights had been almost sleepless, her brief snatches of slumber disturbed by hideous dreams. She was thoroughly worn out in body and mind, and as she sat by the open window loosely dressed in a tea gown, with a china-crape shawl wrapped round her shoulders, the monotonous moaning of the wind in the elms had a soothing sound like a lullaby, and hushed her to sleep. She lay back in her low luxurious chair, with her head half buried in the comfortable down pillow, and slept as she had not slept for a month. It was the slumber of sheer exhaustion, deep and sweet, and long—very long; for when she opened her eyes and looked about her, awakened by a strange oppression of the chest, there was the livid light of earliest dawn in the room—a light that changed all at once to a bright red glow, vivid as the sky at sundown.

The oppression of her breath increased, she felt suffocated. The livid dawn, the crimson sunset, changed to gray; the atmosphere around her grew thick; there was a smarting sensation in her eyes, a stifling sensation in her throat. Mechanically, not knowing what she did, she began to grope her way to the door. But in that thickening atmosphere she did not know which was the door—her outspread arms clasped some heavy piece of furniture— the wardrobe. She leaned against it exhausted, helpless stupified by that horrible smoke; and as she leaned there a wild shrill shriek pealed out from below—the cry of 'Fire!' Again and again that dreadful cry resounded, in a woman's piercing treble. Then came a hubbub of other voices—without, within—she could not tell where, or how near, or how far—but all the sounds seemed distant.

She could just see the open window by which she had been sleeping a few minutes ago—she could distinguish it by the red light outside, which was just visible through the dense smoke within, momently thickening.

She made for the window—anything to escape from that suffocating atmosphere; but just as she was approaching that red patch of light shining amidst the blackness, a sudden tongue of flame shot up from below, caught the light chintz drapery, and in an instant the window was framed in fire, The flame ran from one curtain to another; fanned by the wind which was still blowing—valence, draperies, all the ornamentation of the three windows were in a blaze. Ida stood helpless, motionless as Lot's wife, confronting the flames. To rush through them, to leap through the open window although it were to certain death, was her first impulse. Any death must be better than to fall down suffocated on the floor, and to be burned alive.

Then came the thought of her husband—so weak, and mad, and helpless—of her stepmother. Were they, too, in danger of instant death? Or was she on this upper floor the only victim?

The thin chintz curtains flamed and blazed into nothingness while she was looking at them. The wood-work round the windows crackled and blistered, but the flame died out into ashes. Only the intolerable smoke remained, and the ever-increasing glow of the fire below, more vivid with every moment. She made one mad rush for the balcony. Great Heaven, what a scene greeted her eyes as she looked downwards! Masses of flame, mingled with black smoke clouds, were being vomited out of the lower-windows. There was a little crowd of men below—gardeners, stablemen, who lived close at hand. Some of these were making feeble efforts with garden engines, sending out little jets of water which seemed only to feed the flames as if the water had been oil, while others were trying to adjust a fire escape, deposited in the stables years ago, in the reign of Sir Reginald's father, and out of working order from long disuse. Three or four grooms were rushing to and fro with buckets, and splashing water against the stone walls, with an utter absence of any effect whatever.

Ida stood in the balcony, leaning against the iron-work, waiting for rescue or death. The atmosphere was a little less stifling here, but every now and then a dense cloud of smoke rolled over her and almost suffocated her before the wind drove it upward. The sky was alight with reflected fire. The burning pyre of Dido or Sardanapalus could hardly have made a grander effect—and far away in the east, against the dark undulations of wooded hills there was another light—the tender roseate flush of summer dawn, full of promise and peace.

Ida stood with clasped hands, and lips moving dumbly in prayer. She gave her soul back to her Creator; she prayed for pardon for her sins; she closed her eyes waiting meekly for death.

Suddenly, as she prayed, full of resignation, the balcony creaked under a footstep—a strong arm was wound round her waist—she was lifted bodily over the iron rail and carried carefully, firmly, easily down a ladder, amidst a shout of rapture from the little crowd below.

Every Englishman is not heroic, but every Englishman knows how to admire heroism in his fellow-man.

Before the bearer of his burden reached the lowest rung of the ladder, Ida was unconscious. She lay lifeless and helpless in her preserver's arms. When they were on the solid ground, he bent his bare head over hers, which rested on his shoulder, and kissed her on the forehead.

The crowd saw and did not condemn the action.

'It might be a liberty,' said the head gardener, 'but he'd earned the right to do it. None of us could have done what he did.'

When Ida awakened to consciousness she was lying in the lodge-keeper's little bedroom at the Park gates, and her stepmother was seated at the bedside ready to offer her the usual remedy for all feminine woes—a cup of tea.

'Thank God, you are safe!' said Ida, the memory of that terrible dawn quickly recurring to her mind, a little bewildered at the first moment by her strange surroundings. 'Where is Brian?'

Fanny Palliser burst into tears.

'Oh, Ida, it was Brian set the house on fire, in one of his mad fits—hunting for some horrible thing behind his bed-curtains; and poor Towler and the nurse were both asleep when it happened—at least, Towler, who was sitting up with him had fallen into a doze, and heard Brian talk about looking for serpents in the curtains, and then about flames and fire—but didn't take any notice, or so much as open his eyes—for his talk had been so often of fire and flames—poor creature!—and when he woke the whole room was in a blaze, and the fire had spread through the open door to the window curtains in the next room. Towler and the nurse, and Rogers, all did their uttermost, and risked their lives trying to get Brian away; but he wouldn't leave the burning rooms. He got wilder and wilder; and then, just as they were calling a couple of the stablemen to help them, meaning to get him away by main force, he rushed to the window and threw himself out.'

'And he was killed!' cried Ida.

'Yes; the shock killed him. But you know, dear, there's no use in fretting. Mr. Fosbroke says that he could not have lived till the end of the week. His constitution was quite gone. It was a happy release.'

'Not such a death,' murmured Ida, tears streaming down her wan cheeks; 'such a death could not be a happy release.'

Lady Palliser shook her head, and sighed plaintively. Perhaps she had been inclined to take the survivor's view of the question. Euthanasia to Fanny Palliser's mind meant a death which relieves the family of the deceased from the burden of a long illness.

'He did not suffer at all, dearest,' she said, soothingly.

'Mr. Fosbroke said the shock killed him. There were no bones broken. He fell on the grass in front of the library windows. And oh, Ida, what a blessing that everything at Wimperfield is fully insured! The house is completely gutted!'

Ida could not feel sorry about Wimperfield. The place had been to her of late the abode of horror. If she could be glad of anything in her present frame of mind, it would have been to know that Wimperfield House was razed to the ground.

'The portico and the walls are standing,' pursued Lady Palliser; 'and no doubt a clever architect will be able to build the house up again in the old style.'

'But, mamma, it was an ugly, uninteresting house—not a hundred years old.'

'Exactly so. If it had been really an old house, one would be glad to get rid of it; but it was all as good as new, and so thoroughly substantial! and how you can call it ugly, with such a portico, I can't imagine. I wonder you have not more classical taste. I love anything Grecian. The only thing I ever felt proud of at Les Fontaines was the plaster urns with scarlet geraniums in them!'

'Mamma, how was I saved? Who was it saved me?' asked Ida, presently, when she had taken her cup of tea, and the Swiss clock over the chimney-piece had struck nine.

The sun was shining through the open lattice and upon the roses and the lilies in the little lodge garden. Everything wore a glad and cheerful aspect in the summer morning.

'Ah, my dear, that *is* a story!' exclaimed Lady Palliser, nodding her head with intense significance, and pleased at being able to divert Ida's thoughts from her husband's miserable end; 'I never did! You will be surprised! Oh, my dear, I thought it was all over with you! All the gardeners and stablemen were there—and Rogers—and John and William—and Henry—half dressed and in slippers, poor creatures; and I begged and implored of them to save you—to get to your room somehow—inside or out. But the staircase to the second floor was choked with smoke and flame, and falling timbers; one of the men tried to go up, but he came back and said he must wait for the firemen—nobody but a fireman could do it. And then they got ladders, but the first ladder wasn't long enough, and nobody seemed to be in their proper senses. Thomas rode off to Petersfield for the engine directly the fire broke out, but that's eight miles off, as you know, and it all seemed hopeless. I was running about among them all like a mad woman, in my dressing-gown and slippers; and as for Jane Dyson, she sat on the lowest step of the portico, and went out of one fit of hysterics into another, just as she did when the Archbishop's wife died; and I thought all hope was over, when a man rushed in among us, snatched the longest ladder from the men who were bringing it from the walled garden, and put it up against the balcony. He went up it just like a sailor, and before I could hardly breathe he was coming down again with you in his arms, safe and sound. And who do you think the man was?'

'The fire-brigade man, I suppose.'

'Not a bit of it. The man who saved you was Vernie's friend, Cheap Jack.'

CHAPTER XXXI
'SOLE PARTNER AND SOLE PART OF ALL THESE JOYS'

More than a year had gone by since that awful night, and a new Wimperfield House was slowly rising from the ashes of the Bath stone mansion with the Grecian portico. Only the walls and the portico had remained intact after the fire, and these had been pulled down to make room for a spacious edifice in the Early English manner, the heavy insurances on the old building providing for the cost of this newer and more beautiful Wimperfield. But Ida was not near to watch the new Wimperfield in the progress of erection. She had spent the greater part of the last year at the Homestead with Miss Wendover, and the residue with her stepmother at Bournemouth, where Lady Palliser had taken and furnished for herself one of the pretty villas on the Boscomb estate, a pleasant home for the placid joys of widowhood, and a nice place for Vernon's holidays, were he contented to spend them there, which he was not, greatly preferring the more rustic life of Kingthorpe. Here he was a welcome guest both at the Knoll and at the Homestead; while there was a third house open to him within a walk of the village, for Mr. Wendover had returned from his distant wanderings, and he and Vernie were on very friendly terms.

Ida had as yet seen but little of the master of the Abbey, albeit she heard of him almost daily from some of The Knoll family. He had returned at Easter, unexpectedly, as usual, and much to the surprise of a neighbourhood which had grown accustomed to the idea of his never coming back at all. But although he had settled himself at the Abbey, declaring that he had made an end of his wanderings, seen all he wanted to see, and never meant to go far afield any more, he had taken no share in the picnics and rustic festivities with which the Knoll family celebrated their worship of the great god Pan; whereupon Blanche informed her cousin frankly that he was not half so nice as he had been seven years ago, when he had joined in their fungus hunts and barrow hunts and blackberry gatherings, just as if he had been one of themselves.

'Seven years ago I was seven years younger, Blanche. We were all children then.'

Blanche sighed, and shook her head despondently.

'As for me, I feel centuries old,' she said; 'but that is only natural in such a dead-and-alive hole as Kingthorpe.'

Which speech being interpreted meant that Miss Wendover had not had a new frock or an invitation to a garden party for the last fortnight.

'Still,' she argued,' one ought to make the best of one's life even at Kingthorpe, and picnics and rambles help one to endure existence. You used to be such a delightful companion, and now no one but little Vernie ever seems to get any fun out of you. He is always talking of the larks he has at the Abbey.'

'Sir Vernon is good enough to call the mildest form of diversion a lark!' said Brian Wendover, smiling at her.

'Come now, I will make a bargain with you,' said Blanche. 'John Jardine and Bess are coming over next week to spend Bessie's birthday with us, which, as you know, is a family festival that we never allow to be celebrated anywhere else. Bess and John and the babies are coming to us, and Vernon Palliser is going to the Homestead, and his mother is coming over from Bournemouth to stay a few days with Aunt Betsy; so you see it will be a grand family gathering of Wendovers and Pallisers. Now, if you are anything like the man you were seven years ago, prove it by joining us on this occasion.'

'I cannot refuse; and I will try my uttermost to forget that I have lived seven lonely years since that happy summer.'

'Ah, it was a happy summer!' sighed Blanche, who affected to be weighed down by the burden of mature years. 'I wasn't *out* in those days, and I hadn't a care.'

'What form does your festival take this year? and where do you mean to celebrate it?'

'Oh, a picnic, of course, if this lovely weather only holds out. We have not had one really proper picnic this year.'

'But don't you think the seventh of September is just a little late for an *al fresco* feast? Suppose we were to make it luncheon and afternoon tea at the Abbey, with unlimited tennis in the afternoon.'

'That would be simply delicious,' said Blanche, concluding that Mr. Wendover intended to invite all the eligible young men of his acquaintance to be found within twenty miles.

'Then it is agreed. You need give yourself no further trouble. You have only to bring your people—the Knoll party, and the Homestead party.'

'Precisely. Of course *you* can ask as many as you like.'

The year which was gone had been one of perfect peace for Ida, peace overshadowed by the memories of pain and horror; but those memories had been lightened, and her mind had been comforted, and soothed, and fortified by Aunt Betsy's loving companionship, by that common-sense and broad way of thinking which was as a tower of strength in the day of trouble. Yet for months after that awful time at Wimperfield her nights had been broken by dreadful dreams or too vivid reminiscences of her husband's evil fate, that terrible decay of mind and body, that gradual annihilation of the energies and powers of manhood which it had been her painful lot to witness.

Aunt Betsy took care that the young widow's days should be too busy for much thought. She found constant occupation for her. She sent her about to the remotest corners of the parish to minister to the sorrows of others; she gave her the sick to nurse, and the old and feeble to care for, and the young to teach; so that there should be no leisure left from dawn to sunset for futile lamenting over the irrevocable past. But in the silence of night those dreaded memories crept out of their hiding-places, as other vermin creep out of their holes under cover of darkness, and it was long before they began to grow less vivid and less terrible.

From the moment Miss Wendover appeared at Wimperfield on the afternoon after the fire, coming as quickly after the receipt of the news as horses could convey her, Ida had been sheltered and protected by her love. No sooner was Brian laid at rest in his grave in Wimperfield churchyard than Aunt Betsy carried off the hopeless, broken-down widow to the Homestead, where Ida resumed all her old duties; so that there were times when it seemed as if all the years of her married life were but a dream from which she had awakened, a dream which had subdued and saddened her whole nature, and had made her feel old and weary.

But there was much of happiness in her life, so much that she was fain to put aside all signs and tokens of grief except her dense black gowns and crape bonnets, and to rejoice with those who rejoiced; for here was Aunt Betsy, the most cheery and unselfish of women, whose life ought to be all sunshine, inasmuch as she spent so large a portion of it in brightening the lives of others; and here were the boys and girls from the Knoll, always in uproarious spirits, and wanting Ida's sympathy in all their delights; and here was Vernon coming over from the Vicarage on Salisbury Plain, at all times and seasons, for a few days' holiday, rosier and stronger and more sporting every time she saw him, great upon hawking and hunting, and full of grand schemes for his future life at the new Wimperfield. He had forgotten Brian's melancholy doom, as easily as youth is apt to forget everything, in the hurry and ardour of life's morning; but his love for his sister knew no abatement. He wanted her to share in all his future joys.

'You are not going to stay at the Homestead all your life, are you?' he asked one day. 'Of course you are going back to Wimperfield directly the new house is finished?'

'No, dear, I could never live at Wimperfield again,—it would recall too many sad scenes. When Aunt Betsy is tired of me I shall go abroad. I have seen so little of the world, you know.'

'Oh, if you want to travel, you can go with me when I come of age; but in the meantime you must help mother to keep house at Wimperfield. It will be quite a new place—everything new—nothing to remind you of father or Brian. And then in a few years I shall be of age, and then we can go off to the Rockies together.'

'With Cheap Jack for our guide, philosopher and friend.' said Ida.

'Well, no; I'm afraid Cheap Jack won't go with us!' answered Vernon, laughing.

'I have such a reason to be grateful to him that I could hardly object to his company,' said Ida; 'and I am quite unhappy at never having been able to thank him or reward him for saving my life.'

'He didn't want to be thanked or rewarded. Didn't I tell you that he was not that kind of man?'

'But why should any man go through life doing good to others, and never getting thanks or praise for his goodness,' said Ida. 'It is a most unpleasant form of misanthropy. I feel quite uncomfortable under the burden of my obligations to Mr. Jack; and though I have made every effort to put myself in communication with him, through Mr. Mason and others, I have not been able to find out where he is or anything about him.'

'Odd, isn't it?' said Vernon. 'He left the cottage on the day after the fire, didn't he? shut it up, and took the key to Lord Pontifex's steward, and drove off with his books and things packed in his cart, goodness knows where, after having made a free gift of his stock to the villagers.'

'Not a very profitable way of carrying on business,' said Ida. 'He must have had means independent of his trade.'

'Well, I don't suppose we shall ever see him again,' returned Vernon, cheerfully, somewhat to Ida's disgust; for this indifference to the sudden close of a once enthusiastic friendship argued a lightness and fickleness of disposition in Sir Vernon Palliser.

And now it was again the eve of Bessie's birthday, that day which had twice been fraught with fatal influences for Bessie's friend; and Ida could not put away the feeling that this seventh of September, finding her once again on the scene of past fatalities, must needs bring her some new evil, some undreamed of crisis in her life. Yet what would happen to her now? she asked herself. The play was played out. She had lived her life. For her tragedy and comedy were alike over and done with.

The morning of the seventh dawned fair and bright. If there were any omen in those pinky clouds which flecked the tender gray of early morning, surely it must be a portent of good and not of evil; although Lady Palliser, who was not given to over-cheerful views, declared at breakfast that such roseate hues in early morning meant bad weather before noon.

'Let the weather be never so unkind, we'll find a way of enjoying ourselves at the Abbey,' said Aunt Betsy, who was in tremendous spirits, 'won't we, Vernie?'

'Of course,' answered Vernon. 'Mother has a new bonnet, and is afraid of getting it spoiled. The weather won't interfere with us. We can play hide-and-seek in the Abbey cellars.'

'Oh, Vernie! and get shut behind a secret panel or in a chest, like that poor girl in the poem Ida used to read to us.'

'Don't be afraid, mother. If I get into a chest, you may depend I shall know how to get out of it. That girl in the poem was a duffer for not having made more row; and her lover was a beastly sneak for not ferreting out her hiding-place.'

'They ought to have had a detective down from London,' remarked Lady Palliser, ignoring both the scene and the date of the story.

Her reading had lain much among novels in which the private detective was omnipotent, the unraveller of all mysteries, the avenger of every wrong.

Miss Wendover drove Lady Palliser to the Abbey in her phaeton, and the party from the Knoll went in the roomy family waggonette; but Vernon and his sister walked across the fields and the common, by that path which Ida had trodden on the day she first saw the master of the Abbey. How vividly she recalled her feelings on that day—the pain and embarrassment she felt in Brian Wendover's presence, the agony of humiliation! And then had followed the too happy, too perilous days in which he had been her familiar friend, the fatal night on which he had declared himself her lover.

Well, she was free now. She could meet him and think of him without sin; but since his return she had met him at most half a dozen times, and then always in the company of other people. He had greeted her cordially, as friend should greet friend, but he had not sought her society. He knew that she was living in his aunt's house, but he had only been to that house once since his return.

'Time was, time is, time's past,' said the brazen oracle. Ida began to tell herself that for her time was verily past. Life, and youth, and love had been hers; but fate had been adverse, and she had wasted them, and they were over and gone.

She had some time for pensive reverie, as she walked to the Abbey, Vernon being as usual more occupied hy the inhabitants of the hedges and ditches than by his companion; but once arrived at the Abbey, there was no time for sadness. Bessie was on the threshold to welcome her, and the whole Knoll family were swarming in the great hall, where Brian, standing under the picture of the famous Sir Tristram, was giving cordial welcome to everyone.

How handsome he looked under the likeness of his ancestor! and how vividly the modern face recalled the ancestral lineaments! Time had only deepened the noble lines of his countenance, and added dignity to his figure and bearing. He looked happy, too, like a man upon whom the future smiles assuringly. The fancy flashed across Ida's mind that he was engaged to be married, and that he meant to announce the fact to his family to-day, perhaps, and to introduce the lady. She looked hastily round the hall, almost expecting to see some new face, young, lovely, beaming with smiles — the face of the chosen one. But there was no one except Lady Palliser and the house of Wendover.

'I have not asked any strangers, Blanche,' said Brian. 'I thought we should all have more fun if we had the old place to ourselves.'

'How good of you!' replied the matronly Bess. 'I'm sure we shall all enjoy ourselves ever so much more.'

Blanche was disappointed. Lawn-tennis among relations was all very well, but she had plenty of that at the Knoll. She felt sorry she had put on her best hat and Indian silk frock, elaborately frilled with twine-coloured lace. A cotton gown, and the oldest thing in garden hats, would have been good enough for such an assembly.

The Colonel and Mrs. Wendover had driven over with their children. It was quite a family party — Bessie's babies, a girl able to toddle, and a boy in the nurse's arms, were the great features of the entertainment, the grandmother openly worshipping them, the grandfather condescending to occasional patronage of this third generation, but evidently anxious to dissemble his pride.

'Bessie makes such a preposterous fuss about her babies,' said Blanche, after declining lawn-tennis with Eva and her two brothers. 'I hope if ever I am deluded into marrying, I shall not degenerate into an upper nurse.'

The Abbey had been swept and garnished in honour of the occasion, every room brightened with flowers—even that sacred apartment, Brian's study, thrown open to the public. After luncheon it happened somehow—Ida could hardly have explained how—that she and Brian were alone together in this very room, the afternoon sunlight shining on them—for in spite of Lady Palliser's prophecy the day had been lovely—the scent of stocks and mignonette and sweet-peas blowing in upon them from the old-fashioned garden at the back of the Abbey. They had strayed to this spot with the others; and the others had strayed off and left them, Ida looking absently at the backs of the Greek dramatists, Brian looking intently at her.

'I don't think you have been in this house since the day we first met in the hall below?' he said, interrogatively.

'No, I have never been here since.'

'And yet you were once fond of the Abbey. You used to like wandering about the old house and gardens. You would sit reading in the library. The housekeeper has often talked to me about you.'

She stood before him with lowered eyelids, pale and dumb, shrinking from him almost as she had shrunk from him seven years ago by the old sundial in the moonlit garden, when it was a sin to listen to his ardent avowal.

'Ida, why are you silent? Why will you not speak of the past?'

'The past is past!' she said, falteringly. 'It was full of grief and shame for me. I want to forget it if I can.'

'Forget all that is bitter, remember all that is sweet!' he pleaded, drawing nearer to her. 'There is much of that old time which is unspeakably dear to me—the happy time in which I first loved you, deeming you were free to be loved and won. You are free now, Ida, sole mistress of your fate and mine; and I love you as dearly now as I loved you seven years ago. More I could not love you, for I loved you then with all my heart and mind. Ida, you once talked of being mistress of Wendover Abbey. Its master is at your feet, your faithful slave to the end of his life. Will you have this old house for your own, Ida, and thus, and thus only, make it home for me?

His arm was round her, gently, experimentally, the answer not being quite certain, even yet.

She slowly lifted the dark-fringed lids, looked at him with adoring eyes—eyes which never before had looked thus upon the face of man.

'Can you be in earnest?' she asked, in a low sweet voice. 'Can you lift me so high—I, that had fallen so low?'

He clasped her to his heart, and sealed the promise of their unclouded future with a passionate kiss.

'At last, at last, I hold you in my arms!' he said, fondly; 'but not for the first time, my angel!'

'What do you mean?'

'Who was it carried you out of the burning house last year?' he asked, smiling at her.

'Cheap Jack.'

'I was Cheap Jack.'

'You!'

'Yes. I lived far from the sight of this dear face, as long as I could bear my life, and then after five years of exile in far lands, where my soul sickened for the sight of you, I came back to England, heard in London that your husband was an idler and a drunkard, and foresaw evil days for my darling. I could be nothing to her; but at least I could watch over her, near at hand, yet unknown. So I took up my abode on the Hanger within a mile or so of her dwelling. Don't pity me, dearest. It was not a hard life after all. I had my books and Nature for my companions, all the joy I could have, not having you.'

'However shall I repay you?'

'Only look up to me as you looked just now, and let me feel you are my own for ever.'